ALSO BY DREW CHAPMAN

The Ascendant

THE KING OF FEAR

A GARRETT REILLY THRILLER

DREW CHAPMAN

SIMON & SCHUSTER PAPERBACKS

NEW YORK LONDON TORONTO SYDNEY NEW DELHI

Simon & Schuster Paperbacks
An Imprint of Simon & Schuster, Inc.
1230 Avenue of the Americas
New York, NY 10020

First Simon & Schuster trade paperback edition February 2016

SIMON & SCHUSTER PAPERBACKS and colophon are registered trademarks of Simon & Schuster, Inc.

For information about special discounts for bulk purchases, please contact Simon & Schuster Special Sales at 1-866-506-1949 or business@simonandschuster.com.

The Simon & Schuster Speakers Bureau can bring authors to your live event. For more information or to book an event, contact the Simon & Schuster Speakers Bureau at 1-866-248-3049 or visit our website at www.simonspeakers.com.

Manufactured in the United States of America

10 9 8 7 6 5 4 3 2 1

Library of Congress Cataloging-in-Publication Data
   Chapman, Drew, author.
   The king of fear : a Garrett Reilly thriller / Drew Chapman.—First Simon & Schuster trade paperback edition
      pages cm
   Sequel to: The Ascendant.
   ISBN 978-1-4767-2591-8 (paperback)—ISBN 978-1-5011-3105-9 (ebook part 1)—ISBN 978-1-5011-3106-6 (ebook part 2)—ISBN 978-1-5011-3107-3 (ebook Part 3)
   1. Savants (Savant syndrome)—Fiction. 2. Brokers—Fiction. I. Title.
   PS3603.H3635K56 2016
   813'.6—dc23
                                                                            2015032690

ISBN 978-1-4767-2591-8
ISBN 978-1-4767-2593-2 (ebook)

TO LISA
FOR ALL THE LOVE AND SUPPORT

PART 1

Alan Daniels knocked twice on the door to his boss's West Wing office, waited a moment for a response—but didn't get one—then pushed the door open. "You got two minutes?"

The national security adviser already had her purse slung over her shoulder. She let out a long, overly dramatic sigh, then smiled brightly and nodded yes. Julie Fiore liked Daniels. He was her deputy adviser and was loyal and smart. She wanted to get home—her husband was cooking grilled salmon with a honey-mustard glaze, her favorite—but she had two minutes for Daniels. She motioned him across the room.

He laid a thin file folder on her desk. "Elections. Belarus. Early results just came in."

"They have elections in Belarus?" She grinned mischievously.

"Apparently they do. And as of this morning"—Daniels checked the world clock on his smartphone—"one fifty-three a.m., GMT, they seem to matter."

Fiore pulled her reading glasses out of her purse, opened the file folder, scanned the single sheet of paper inside, and frowned. "Not possible."

"And yet"—Daniels thrust two open hands in the air as if to signify that this was something only God could fathom—"there you have it."

"He's been reelected four times. They believe in democracy like I believe in unicorns." She pulled the glasses from the bridge of her nose and rubbed briefly at her eyes with her other hand. She was *so* tired. "How could this happen?"

"Fairy dust?"

Fiore shot Daniels a grim look.

He straightened up immediately, wiping the smile from his face. "I checked with the CIA five minutes ago. They were blindsided as well. Analysis is going to work on it overnight, lay out scenarios."

"Good Lord. After Ukraine, this is . . . this is a disaster. . . ." Her voice trailed off as she turned away from her deputy and looked out her window to the darkened North Lawn. She tried to imagine a faraway place, halfway around the world, a building larger than the White House but just as well guarded, bathed in morning sunlight, full of ministers and generals and their counselors, all simultaneously spitting out their coffee in horror. "Over there. You know where." She pointed up and into the darkness, as if picking a spot on an invisible map that only she and Daniels could see. "They're having heart attacks right now. Emergency staff meetings and collective heart attacks."

"Yes, they are. And when they recover from their heart attacks . . ." Daniels paused to consider his words. He might have couched the idea in a diplomatic euphemism, something vague and less threatening, but alone, with his boss, at the end of the day, weary and ever so slightly jumpy from monitoring the globe's seemingly endless crises, that just didn't seem appropriate. "They're going to start killing people. A lot of people."

G arrett Reilly was good with numbers. He was good at seeing crests in interest rates, downward trends in commodity prices, and convergences in muni bond yields. But he was equally adept at counting the percentage of men wearing Birkenstocks versus Nikes on a summer's day on West Broadway, or the ratio of car-to-beer commercials in an hour's worth of prime-time television. Seeing patterns came naturally to him; he felt them as much as he saw them. If asked, he'd say patterns started on the outer layer of his skin, a tingling that began at his fingertips—as the descending sine wave of jets on final approach to LaGuardia began to match phase with the frequency of helicopters over the Hudson River—then ran up through his central nervous system, to finally burst into glorious view in a cascade of numbers in his head.

Patterns were the air Garrett breathed. They were how he made his money trading bonds on Wall Street, and they were how he organized his life. He was a natural processor of data, and he was comfortable in that role.

What he was less comfortable with, lately, was distinguishing the real from the unreal.

For instance, a middle-aged man was sitting across from Garrett in the living room of his fourth-floor walk-up on Manhattan's Lower East Side. Garrett knew the man well—balding, avuncular, mild mannered. Garrett loved the man and knew that the man loved him back; the man thought of Garrett as the son he'd never had and had looked after him through much of Garrett's short, tumultuous life. It brought Garrett intense joy to have the man sitting with him, at two in the morning, sharing beers, the only family he had left in the world, talking about this and that, life and love, and nothing at all. Garrett Reilly could not have been happier.

The problem was, the man was dead. Twelve months dead, and Garrett knew it.

Garrett Reilly, twenty-seven years old, a half-Mexican, half-Irish bond trader from Long Beach, California, had been taking a lot of prescription medication lately. Tramadol, Vicodin, meperidine, Percocet, to name a few. If he could convince a doctor to prescribe it, Garrett would swallow it. He'd fractured his skull in a bar fight a year ago, and while the crack in his head had healed, the lightning bolts of pain from the injury never quite seemed to go away. In fact, the trend line of the ache was upward, and accelerating. If his brain injury were a stock, Garrett would have taken out a long position on it and watched the bountiful returns pour in.

He used to carefully track the dosages he took, but the pain had morphed into something so persistent, so insidious, that lately he just downed whatever was at hand and tried not to think about the consequences. Of course, one of the consequences was the very deceased middle-aged man sitting in a La-Z-Boy in Garrett's living room.

"You need to take care of yourself, Garrett," Avery Bernstein said, garish green-and-gold sweater vest open over a pressed white shirt. Avery had been Garrett's boss before he died, a math professor turned brokerage house CEO, one of the few people in the world who saw life much as Garrett saw it—as a series of beautiful equations, waiting to be solved. Avery shifted slightly in his chair, eyes scanning the room. "You need to get out more. Get some exercise. See people."

Garrett knew that the thing across the room from him was a hallucination, brought on by a combination of too many meds, too much alcohol, and not enough sleep. But he also understood that whatever the hallucination was saying was some projection of his own unconscious. A message that he was sending himself. He did need to take better care of himself, and he should get out more. As for exercise . . .

"I hate exercise," Garrett said to his empty living room. "I'm not going to join some stupid gym and run around in fucking yoga pants. I have some pride left."

"That's my boy." Avery smiled. "Never change. Why should you? You're perfect just the way you are."

Garrett laughed, and it occurred to him that he was laughing at his own joke. He was going to have to watch that. "You are not here, Avery. I am imagining you."

"Of course I'm not here. I died in a hit-and-run accident more than a year ago. An accident that you've never really gotten to the bottom of, by the way, the thing that might or might not be," Avery said. "But you have a serious problem, Garrett, and you need to deal with it."

"I know, I know, too many prescription drugs. Don't nag. You're not my mother, not that she would give a shit. I'm gonna cut down. It's just that—"

He let his jaw hang open, not bothering to finish the sentence. The truth was, his hallucinations had been, in general, benign: a dog leashed to a parking meter had quoted stock prices to him when he had walked past it on Broome Street; an old Carpenters song—"Close to You"—had played, nonstop, from his wing-tip shoes last week at work; and now Avery Bernstein was visiting him in his apartment. He missed Avery horribly. Just seeing him there, overweight and kindly, made Garrett's heart sing. A thought came to his mind: perhaps he wasn't taking all that medication to deal with his head pain.

Perhaps he took it to deal with his grief.

"No," Avery said, a hint of stern menace rising in his voice. "You know what the problem is, and you are ignoring it."

Garrett's breath seemed to catch in his throat. He did know what the problem was. He'd felt the pattern growing over the last few weeks. He'd seen it hinted at on the Web and had begun to spot its earliest incarnations on the global equity markets. It was a tangle, complicated and dense, hiding something dark and terrifying. He had tried to ignore it because he didn't want to get involved. He wanted to stay apart from the wider world and its endless, myriad problems; he'd experienced enough of the globe's crises lately to last a lifetime. But if Avery Bernstein's ghost was a projection of Garrett's unconscious, then his deepest instinct was bubbling to the surface, trying to warn him.

"They're coming," Garrett's beloved ex-mentor said, the edges of his lips curling down in a sudden, nightmarish scowl. "They're coming for you."

Garrett's heart thudded alarmingly in his chest.

"They're coming to destroy everything."

The June weather was perfect: a cloudless blue sky, a light morning breeze blowing off the Hudson River. Because it was so nice, Phillip Steinkamp decided to get off the 4 train one stop early, at the Brooklyn Bridge station in lower Manhattan, and walk the last eight blocks to his office. Steinkamp did this as often as he could, to get a bit of exercise before his busy day, to clear his head, but mostly to grab a cup of coffee and say hello to the shopkeepers on Nassau Street.

He knew that he shouldn't. He knew that he should instead ride the 4 train one more stop, to Fulton Street, and quickly walk the two blocks to his office—two blocks that were lined with policemen and barricades, plainclothes detectives and private security guards—but Steinkamp sometimes felt as if he lived in a bubble, and on a beautiful June morning, a bubble was the last place he wanted to be. He was still an American, after all, free to do as he pleased, even if he was president of the Federal Reserve Bank of New York, the largest and most important of the twelve district Fed banks.

Yes, nearly a trillion dollars in gold, deposits, and promissory notes were sitting underneath his office at 33 Liberty Street, and yes, he was the second-most influential banker on the planet, but if he wanted to wave hello to Chanji at the electronics store and buy a coffee from Sal at the Greek diner, goddamn it, he would. Jeffries, his head of security, could yell all he wanted—Steinkamp would not let his job define him. He refused to shut out the real world.

Steinkamp breathed deep of the morning. He was a slight man, just under five foot eight, with a former accountant's permanent stoop and a ring of thinning brown hair around his mostly bald head. He could smell a hint of salt water in the air, a taste of the New York harbor, as he turned left onto Nassau Street. He walked fast, but not too fast, waved to Chanji chattering on his cell in front of Value Village Electronics—or was it Ranjee, Steinkamp could never remember—and smiled at the other bankers and brokers striding their way to their myriad offices in lower Manhattan. They all looked so stern and preoccupied. Money on their minds, nothing but money.

Well, that was always on his mind too. Money and interest rates, and politics as well. His job produced a never-ending litany of worries. Head of the New York Fed was second-in-command to the chairman of the Federal Reserve, and if the chairman had been at her current job longer—and not been appointed a mere three months ago—then Steinkamp could have breathed easier. But the truth was, the current Fed chair was something of an unknown entity, a former Cal-Berkeley professor, reclusive, and a bit of an egghead. Steinkamp had for a moment thought he might get the appointment, but the president went with Hummels, possibly to woo the female vote in the upcoming election, and possibly because Steinkamp sometimes did silly things, such as walk to his office instead of taking the car service that showed up in front of his Park Avenue lobby every morning at 8:00 a.m. sharp.

Steinkamp was impulsive, and known up and down Wall Street for that quality. He sighed. He could only be himself; that was, in his mind, the key to life. Be yourself. Have no regrets.

He stopped at Sal's and leaned in through the open service window that faced the street. Sal, an old-timer, a Greek immigrant with a potbelly bulging under his dirty white apron, beamed at the sight of Steinkamp. "One coffee, light and sweet, for the big shot of the big shots," Sal said, filling a to-go cup and tossing two packets of sugar onto the service-window counter.

"Good morning, Sal," Steinkamp said, topping off the coffee with a tankard of cream and waving to Sal Jr., who was cooking bacon at the diner griddle inside. Steinkamp loved Sal, Sal's son, and the entire Panagakos family. He loved their hard work. He loved their spirit. "And good morning to Sal Jr. as well."

"Hey, boss." Sal's son waved. "How's my money doing?"

"I wouldn't have the slightest," Steinkamp said, and the guys in the diner all laughed. They had said some version of the same thing to him every morning he stopped by, and he'd been doing it for ten years now, answering with pretty much the same line. But they all laughed nonetheless, bless their hearts.

Sal wiped the counter clean with a white rag. "Hey. Meant to tell you, boss. A lady asked for you. Asked when you'd be coming through again."

"Oh, yeah." Steinkamp smiled. "Was she pretty?"

Sal shrugged. "Maybe a little. Maybe she doesn't make your standards." Sal still had a Greek accent, an inventive immigrant's grammar, and a singsong lilt to his English. "You can have any woman in the world, Mr. Big Shot. Why bother with some lady on Nassau Street?"

Steinkamp smiled. People asked for him all the time in lower Manhattan. Brokers, bankers, traders. They knew him by sight, or from the occasional newspaper article. The presidents of the district Fed banks were faceless bureaucrats mostly, but Steinkamp had been around long enough to be ever so slightly famous. They stopped him on the street, or at the deli on Chambers where he liked to grab a Reuben, to ask which way interest rates were going or if the Fed would taper its bond-buying activity. Or sometimes just to shake his hand.

Lately, though, they'd been asking about the president of the St. Louis Fed, Larry "Let 'Em Fail" Franklin. Franklin and Steinkamp had been at loggerheads—pretty nasty loggerheads. Franklin was a moralist and had been touring the country, speaking at college campuses and biz schools, making clear that if another Too Big to Fail bank started to totter in the United States, he would oppose any kind of bailout. "If banks get into trouble," Franklin had told the *Chicago Tribune*, "then they need to get out of it themselves. Bankers need to be held responsible for what they do."

Steinkamp thought this was ludicrous. Well, yes, bankers did need to be held responsible for their actions, but in 2008, the Federal Reserve had been the only thing left between a crapped-out world economy and financial Armageddon. The Fed had been heroic in keeping the credit markets working, and in propping up one sickened brokerage house after another. If any more banks had collapsed, there would have been riots in the streets. To Steinkamp's mind, "Let 'Em Fail" Franklin was a menace. A menace to the United States—hell, to the world. And he, Steinkamp, was the last man standing between Franklin and future financial chaos.

"Hey, speak of the devil." Sal pointed across the street. "There she is."

Steinkamp dropped a $5 bill on the counter, put a lid on his coffee, and turned to see who wanted to meet him. He didn't mind. A little bit of celebrity made up for all those hours in committee meetings. He worked his lips into a wide smile.

But one glimpse of her face, and Steinkamp suddenly thought that maybe it hadn't been such a good idea to get off the train a stop early. She was young, but looked old, with pale skin and black hair. She wore a green trench coat, which was odd, as it was June and warm and would only get warmer through the day. Yet that wasn't what sent a shiver down Steinkamp's spine. There was something about the look on her face: not exactly aggrieved, like some of the people who accosted him, but not happy. Determined. That was what she was. Determined to do something.

Something bad.

"Phillip Steinkamp?" she asked as she crossed Nassau Street and stepped onto the sidewalk. She had a trace of an accent, from some place Steinkamp couldn't quite pin down. Spanish? Portuguese? No, that wasn't right. . . .

"That's him." Sal grinned and pointed at Steinkamp. "The big boss."

"I'm afraid I'm late for work." Steinkamp's words came quickly. "If you need to contact me, you should call my office. You can look it up online. We'll be happy to schedule an appointment." He was suddenly afraid, very afraid, and annoyed at Sal for confirming his identity. He took one long stride south, down Nassau, when the woman stepped in his path and pulled something from the pocket of her trench coat.

Steinkamp knew immediately that it was a gun.

"Mother of Jesus," Sal said behind him, from the counter window. "She's got a gun!"

Steinkamp froze. His eyes locked on the weapon, a nasty, streamlined piece of gray metal. He could not look away. The woman raised the gun with one hand and aimed it at Steinkamp's chest.

"No, lady, don't. I don't know you. This is a mistake."

Someone screamed from across the street. A taxi horn blew. The woman in the trench coat pulled the trigger three times in quick succession.

The first bullet winged Steinkamp in the shoulder. The next, coming a fraction of a second later, hit him in the right arm. But the third bullet ripped open his blue Brooks Brothers shirt and plunged into Steinkamp's heart, stopping it instantly. The president of the Federal Reserve Bank of New York let out a weak gasp, then crumpled to the ground as pedestrians up and down the street dove for cover, screaming in terror. Only Sal, at the open service-counter window of his diner, didn't duck or flinch. He stared at the woman, stunned, as she prodded the lifeless body on the pavement with her scuffed high-heeled shoe.

"Is he dead?" Her voice was flat, emotionless.

"I—I think so," Sal said, not really knowing why he said it. "You killed him."

She turned to face Sal. She spoke calmly and clearly, as if to make sure that anyone listening would understand every word. "Garrett Reilly made me do this."

Then the woman in the green trench coat stuck the pistol in her mouth and pulled the trigger one last time.

The ringing phone was getting on Garrett Reilly's last nerve.

He checked the incoming number on his work phone, but didn't recognize it. Someone was calling his direct line, not the front desk, and his caller ID said it was from a pay phone without an area code attached. Nobody called him from pay phones, and certainly not clients. Garrett remembered pretty much every phone number he'd ever dialed, and the number on the caller ID wasn't one of them.

So he ignored it.

Anyway, he was busy. He'd found the thing he'd been looking for—that dark, tangled pattern—and there was no chance he was going to let it slip away now.

This particular pattern wasn't easy to pick out—in fact, it had been incredibly hard. Garrett likened finding it to how astronomers had spotted the first planets outside our solar system. The exoplanets, as they were called—he had read about this in a *Discover* magazine in the waiting room of a doctor who Garrett had heard played fast and loose with Roxicodone scrips—were too far away and too small to be seen by regular telescopes, but astronomers had been pretty sure they existed. They just had to find another way to see them. So the astronomers looked for the effect the planets had on the things that they *could* see, which in this case were bigger, brighter stars. Every planet orbiting its own sun makes that star move, or wobble; the gravitational pull of the planet tugs at the star, distorting its orbit in specific, detectable ways. So astronomers studied stars—the visible—to find proof of the invisible.

Which was what Garrett was doing as well, only in Garrett's case he was watching money, not stars. Somewhere out there in the vast swirl of international finance, Garrett believed he'd found evidence of an enormous accumulation of money—sitting in a dark pool—that someone, somewhere, wanted to remain hidden. Dark pools were common enough—private exchanges that countries or investors used to trade equities away from the gaze of journalists or regulators or governments. This particular pool of money was buying and selling stocks in coordination with real-world events, and Garrett could see the ripples of that buying and selling as they radiated out through the global economy.

Gather up enough money in one place, Avery Bernstein had once told Garrett, and it begins to create its own gravity. Words to live by, Garrett thought.

Garrett pushed back from his desk and looked across the trading bull pen of the sleek Jenkins & Altshuler offices. Young men and women were busily tapping on their keyboards, buying and selling Treasuries and corporate-debt issues, derivatives and credit default swaps, none of them paying Garrett any notice. Garrett didn't feel particularly close to any of them anymore; over the last year he'd begun to drift away from his Wall Street friends. He'd begun to drift away from everyone. And he no longer had that burning desire to make as much money as possible, to conquer the world. Where had it gone? He wasn't sure. He was no longer sure of anything.

A few traders had their faces pressed up against the windows that looked out onto lower Manhattan and the Hudson River beyond. Police sirens had begun to howl about ten minutes ago, and Garrett's coworkers were speculating on what had happened. A fire? A terror attack? Whatever it was, the NYPD was taking it seriously. Garrett didn't care. He was discerning order out of the chaos of the global information flow, hunting for a narrative in the random noise of the modern, interconnected world. What could be more important than that?

His phone rang. That same number, a pay phone, with no area code listed. Garrett thought about answering, then ignored it once again. He went back to his screens, and the pattern that was unfolding there.

On June 4, at 7:30 a.m., GMT, Sedman Logistics had moved down 5 percent on the Nordic exchange, a smaller European stock market based out of Stockholm. Within five minutes an intrusion hack was made against a corporate network in Munich. On the sixth, Hunca Cosmetics dropped 7 percent on the Borsa Istanbul. Two minutes later, an IT system went down in Lyon, France.

Two days ago, Navibulgar, a Bulgarian shipping company, tumbled 10 percent in after-hours trading on the Bulgarian Stock Exchange, and within thirty seconds twenty thousand customer passwords disappeared off a department-store server in Liverpool. Then this morning, about half an hour ago, two auto-parts manufacturers were hit hard on the Borsa Italiana, Italy's small stock exchange, each dropping more than 20 percent in minutes.

Garrett scanned the international news ticker on his Bloomberg terminal, looking for a correlated real-world event. But none came. Not yet. But he was sure that there would be one. The tug and warp of invisible money created gravitational ripples, and next would come the visible criminal strike. This was a surefire pattern; Garrett could feel it in his bones. Complicated. Dense. Dark. And coming this way.

Whoever had done this—and he was pretty certain one person, or one group, was behind it—was good at the job. They were criminals, but talented ones, able to hack and steal across a number of platforms, in a number of countries, all with relative ease. The attacks had started small, but they were growing.

Clearly, they had financial backing. You needed a lot of cash to short stocks and move markets, and you needed to be willing to lose that money if things didn't go your way. A sovereign wealth fund was probably the source, or perhaps a fabulously wealthy investor. But having that much money to back a criminal enterprise seemed extraordinary to Garrett. Why spend so much just for a few thousand passwords? You could buy them on the darknet for a fraction of the price.

They also had people on their payroll. A large number of people, who were able to move in and out of the defenses of department stores and sophisticated IT companies without being found out. In the world of hackers, those people were called social engineers. They were illusionists, performers, conjurers—people who lured the innocent, or not so innocent, into doing things they wouldn't normally consider doing. They dangled money, or sex, or sometimes they just pulled the wool over your eyes. Outside the world of hacking, social engineers were simply called con men. And these guys were exceedingly good con men.

Garrett stretched his legs and rubbed at the edges of his forehead. His head was beginning to hurt again. He'd managed a few hours of sleep after his long night with Avery Bernstein's persistent ghost, but now he wished he'd managed a few more. He fished a pair of tramadols out of his pocket and dry-swallowed them. The more medication he took, the harder it was for him to see patterns; the narcotics dulled his senses. But he'd already done the heavy lifting for the day. He felt he could coast through the afternoon.

He checked the prescription stash he kept in his work desk. He was good for another week or so. His anxiety slacked off noticeably. He knew that was a bad sign: only addicts cared how much product they had on hand. But he just needed to get through the day.

His phone rang again. The same number. Outside, the sirens kept screaming. They were not helping his head. Frustrated, he grabbed the handset.

"Garrett Reilly, bonds. Who is this, and what the fuck do you want?"

There was a moment's silence on the other end of the line. Garrett thought he could hear traffic, an engine rumbling, a car horn. A pay phone, for sure.

Then a voice cracked the silence—a muffled voice, as if the caller was trying to disguise his or her identity, maybe talking through a piece of thick fabric. "The president of the New York Fed has been shot. Assassinated on Nassau Street thirty minutes ago. The news is about to break." The voice clearly belonged to a woman. She was tense, nervous. On the edge of true fear. "It'll be everywhere."

"What?" Garrett asked, half-listening. The words didn't quite sink in. "Who is this?" He blinked rapidly to concentrate. The president of the Federal Reserve Bank of New York? Killed? Who the hell would want to . . . ?

Suddenly the thought occurred to him. The dark pool. A stock sell-off. A correlated real-world event. Could it be? A pulse of excitement—and fear—ran from his heart, out to his fingers, then back to his brain.

"Holy shit." His voice was a whisper.

"But Garrett, you have to listen carefully. The woman who did it, she mentioned you. By name. She said you told her to shoot him."

Garrett's mouth went dry. The pulse of fear became a wave of dread. He knew, immediately, who was calling him, why she was using a pay phone, and why she was trying to disguise her voice. Garrett tried to form the words for a response, but he could barely manage "I had nothing to do with—how could—" The words came out in a strangled grunt. His thoughts flashed to Avery's ghost, to his own subconscious warning. How could he have known so clearly, and yet . . . "I never told anyone to shoot anybody in my life."

"That doesn't matter now. She killed herself. At the scene. She's dead."

"Why would I want the New York Fed president killed? It makes no sense."

"It gets worse. The FBI. They're coming to your office. They're going to arrest you. They'll be arriving in a matter of minutes."

"Ale—" Garrett started to say the caller's name, but caught himself. What if the call was being recorded? What if the NSA—or the police—were listening? His head was swimming. There was a moment's silence on the line. Outside, the sirens suddenly stopped. Garrett closed his eyes to gather his thoughts. To concentrate. To think. Think hard, and push the pain and drugs from his mind.

The FBI were coming. They were coming for him.

"Garrett," the voice on the phone said. "*Run.*"

When she returned to her office, the first thing Captain Alexis Truffant saw was a message scribbled on a Post-it note and pasted square in the middle of her computer screen: *See me. Now. Kline.*

Alexis tried to calm herself, then hurried up the two flights of stairs toward her boss's office on the fourth floor of the Defense Intelligence Agency building. She stopped at a bank of windows that looked out over the shimmering Potomac and suburban Virginia beyond the river. The DIA was located on Joint Base Anacostia–Bolling, just south of downtown Washington, DC, and the Potomac bordered the base's western edge. She took in the brilliant June morning, patted down her green-and-brown US Army combat jacket, then marched into General Kline's office.

He starting talking before she had a chance to salute. "Reilly bolted from his office before the FBI got there. They're saying somebody tipped him off." General Kline was standing behind his desk, and his face was flushed and red. "You know anything about that?"

"Sir." Alexis stood at attention. "It's Washington. Information travels fast. Rumor faster."

"That is not what I asked you, Captain." Kline charged out from behind his desk in a rush of motion. Barrel-chested, he had a head of thick gray hair and a booming voice. He had been head of the DIA's Directorate of Analysis, responsible for understanding all the threads of intelligence that came into the military daily, but he'd been transferred to a bureaucratic pencil-pushing job six months ago. Now he was reorganizing how analysts disseminated reports to junior field officers—and he hated it. He vented that anger at everyone within shouting distance.

Kline stood toe-to-toe with Alexis. "Answer the question."

"Sir. Why would Garrett Reilly have anything to do with the shooting of a Federal Reserve president? He's a bond trader. He works for us—"

"Worked for us. He quit Ascendant. Or have you forgotten that bit of his history?"

"I haven't forgotten." Alexis knew that no incident in Kline's career was more painful than the collapse of the Ascendant project. Ascendant had been his brainchild, an attempt to assemble a team of out-of-the-mainstream thinkers to help America fight the next generation of wars. Cyber wars, economic wars, psychological wars—outside-of-the-box wars. Garrett Reilly had been the lynchpin of that team, a master of pattern recognition, an aggressive, no-holds-barred street brawler who would take the fight to the enemy in ways that they would never see coming. And Garrett had done exactly that to China, throwing the country into a brief turmoil—and perhaps even averting World War III.

But then Garrett had quit, a broken man, damaged emotionally as well as physically. Ascendant had fallen apart. Kline's career, as well as Alexis's, had stalled; the brief hint of her promotion up the ranks had disappeared. They'd both been reassigned, transferred, then neglected. The close bond between the two of them had frayed. And Kline still hadn't forgiven Garrett Reilly. He hadn't even come close.

"You have no idea if Reilly had anything to do with this morning's shooting. He's a subversive, willful, obnoxious son of a bitch, and I wouldn't put it past him to do absolutely anything he pleased, including having someone assassinated," Kline said.

"But why would he do it, sir? For the money? He has plenty. For notoriety? There are hundreds—maybe thousands—of people trying to track him down every day. He's desperate to avoid recognition."

"We are not in the business of guessing Garrett Reilly's motivations."

"I can guarantee you he did not have—"

"*You cannot guarantee me anything!*" Kline exploded.

The two of them fell silent as the room echoed with his words. Kline stalked back behind his desk and slumped into his chair. Alexis stood motionless in the middle of the room. She kept her eyes focused on the back wall. She was tall and lean, with an athlete's spare body. She had olive skin and blue eyes and she kept her fine, black hair tucked up in a bun. She was generally acknowledged to be beautiful, and men often reinforced this idea by lying down at her feet and promising her the world, something she had been trying to dissuade them from doing for her entire life. She was serious, hardworking, and above all, ambitious—but the last eight months had blown a ragged hole through all of that.

Still, Kline was being willfully blind, and Alexis knew it. There was no way Garrett Reilly could have had someone shot.

Kline looked up at Alexis, his voice quieter. "All we really know about Reilly is that he walked away from Ascendant, has been erratic at his job, and that he's been taking way too many painkillers. Are you still tracking his medical records?"

Alexis shot a glance at the office's open door.

"No one can hear you. No one is listening."

"I am." She'd been pulling Garrett's online prescriptions for months now— illegal as that was—and had been growing alarmed at the quantities of drugs he'd somehow persuaded doctors to order for him. She'd shared her concerns with Kline. Now she was sorry she had.

"And is he still taking them?"

"He's still getting the prescriptions, so I can only assume that he is."

"Then he is a drug addict and we both know it. Now if you have hard evidence that Garrett had nothing to do with what happened this morning, tell me."

Alexis hesitated. "I do not."

"Do you know where he is now?"

"No, sir."

Kline sucked a breath in through his teeth. "Do you still have feelings for him?" Kline hesitated for a moment, as if searching for the appropriate phrasing. "Do you love him?"

Alexis shot a look at Kline. A year ago, she'd had a brief affair with Garrett. The affair had ended almost as soon as it started, but the emotions involved had been intense. In a sense, she and Garrett had fought a war together. They'd saved the world, and that was a bond not easily broken. But still—love?

"No, sir. I do not love Garrett Reilly." She wasn't entirely sure that her answer was true, or that Kline had any right to ask, but at this point that seemed of little importance.

Kline stared up at her iridescent blue eyes. "Then I just don't get it. Here's a guy who completely screwed us over. Walked away from the program after a great triumph. Left us in the lurch when we needed him to build Ascendant and continue to protect this country. Left us with no one to fall back on. Funding cut. Made us look like fools. If he did all of these things—and you know he did—then why in God's name would you help him? He has no loyalty. *You cannot trust Garrett Reilly.*"

Alexis waited before answering, letting the heat of her boss's emotions leak out of the room. Then she spoke quietly, trying to sound as rational as the moment would permit. "Somebody shot and killed the president of the Federal Reserve Bank of New York this morning. And they went to the trouble of trying to pin the blame on a member of Ascendant—"

"A former member of Ascendant."

"They knew who he was, they must have known what he did. In China. And here. They have been tracking him. And I suspect they are trying to get him—and us—out of the way. I don't believe it's random. Something is happening, sir. Something big, right now, which would seem like the exact moment when we need Garrett Reilly the most."

When Alexis finished, the room settled back into silence. Kline nodded ever so slightly, as if to acknowledge the truth of what she had said without lending that truth too much weight. Then he reached across his desk and slid a piece of white printer paper toward Alexis. She glanced down at it.

"A transcript of an NSA recording of a call made from a phone booth on the corner of Alabama and Fifteenth, forty-five minutes ago. Ten blocks from here. My source at NSA just sent it to me."

Alexis took in a sharp breath of air.

"Interfering with an FBI investigation is a federal offense, punishable by severe jail time. If the voice on that conversation is yours"—Kline's tone was quiet, almost a whisper—"there is nothing I can do to help you."

The rumors had been circulating through the First European Bank of Malta for a week.

Matthew Leone knew them well enough, even if he wasn't involved in the banking or securities side of the business, but was just an assistant VP of human resources. They were everywhere, the rumors, discussed at the coffee machine and in the men's room, then later at bars on the waterfront that the bank employees frequented after work, and they went something like this: The bank had too many bad loans outstanding, spread throughout Europe. The bank had also put a lot of cash into risky investments, and bank insiders knew it. Some of those insiders had told Russian mobsters, who had started to pull their cash out first, before the news broke and all the regular, Maltese depositors wanted their money as well. If the other shoe dropped—if a new shock hit the bank's balance sheets—it would collapse.

Leone didn't believe the rumors, even if he had some reason to think they might be true. The bank president, a Swiss named Clement, had brought all the bank's employees together yesterday morning in the lobby of the main branch to calm their nerves. "We are solvent," Clement had said. "There is nothing to worry about. The rumors are false. They are being spread by speculators looking to short our stock. When you interact with the public, reassure them. Tell them everything is fine. And go about your business."

Rather a short meeting, Leone had thought at the time, for such an important topic. He and Abela, his Italian friend from legal, had stood in back.

Both of them wanted to ask about the darkest of the rumors, that some kind of economic hit man, a destroyer of companies, had his sights on the bank and was looking to take it down, but both Leone and Abela were junior employees, and nothing was more suicidal, careerwise, than confronting the boss at a staff meeting with less-than-upbeat questions.

Anyway, it was a crazy rumor. There was no such thing as an economic assassin, and both Leone and Abela knew it. And even if there were, why would such a person target a small, unimportant bank in Malta? But strange times made for outrageous rumors, and the entire company was on edge. Ten minutes ago the latest gossip had trickled in from accounting: bank regulators had landed on the island that very morning to give the firm a financial stress test.

"We fail the stress test, we're bloody screwed," Leone said in his thick Liverpool accent, as he poured himself his fourth coffee of the morning. "They'll shut us down."

Juliette, from the comptroller's office, shook her head. "Don't be ridiculous. The bank is fine. Just rumors. Because of the 2008 meltdown. Because of Greece. People get nervous. But it will be fine."

Juliette was pretty, and French, and both Leone and Abela had asked her out. Both had been rebuffed. Leone didn't mind so much because she was a brunette, and Leone had a thing for redheads. He'd met one the night before at a bar on the water, a startlingly pretty young woman, and things had gone quite well. He hadn't slept with her, but they had flirted until two in the morning, and they'd exchanged numbers and e-mail addresses, and Leone had secured a date for this very evening. So even if the bank did go under, Leone had a chance at sex, which, while secondary, wasn't so terrible. Part of why he'd moved from England to Malta was because the girls were prettier here. That, and the weather.

Leone watched Juliette strut off in that particular French way she had—a straight, arched back, a slight shimmy of the hips. "The French." He sighed.

Abela laughed. "Are you seeing the redhead tonight?" He had been at the bar with Leone and had appreciated that woman's feline, almost predatory beauty.

"I think so." Leone and Abela spoke in English. Everyone in Malta, especially at the bank, spoke English, which was why Leone had never bothered to learn Maltese. "She's supposed to text me a meeting place. She said she might even stop by the office."

"Okay, we like her already," Abela said with a leering smile.

Leone had been checking his phone all day, but no word had come in from the redhead, Dorina. At the bar, she had told Leone where she was from— Hungary or Romania or some place East European like that—but Leone couldn't quite remember through the fog of gin and beer. He still had a hangover.

"We'll talk later," Abela said. "If there is a later."

Leone grunted a half laugh, then shuffled off to his desk in the corner of the open bull pen of cubicles. He passed a swath of windows that looked out onto the sparkling blue waters of Valletta harbor and the Mediterranean. Leone waved to a few coworkers, some of whom waved back. Most everyone else was glued to phones or computer terminals. Leone guessed that they were checking the bank's stock price, or scouring the wire services for the latest bit of news. He thought he'd overheard someone say that a banker in New York City had been gunned down a few hours ago. An important banker—a Federal Reserve president. What the hell was going on in the world?

Strange times. Very, very strange.

Leone sat at his desk and waited. There wasn't much to do—no point in looking over the CVs of job applicants if the bank was going to go under. He checked his Facebook account, as well as his Tumblr and Instagram. He lingered on the Tumblr page. He'd posted a number of pictures of other redheads there, and he liked to gaze at them. He wasn't sure why he was so obsessed with girls with red hair, but he was. There was something about their eyes, blue usually, or sometimes green, and the fair skin, so often smattered with charmingly light freckles. The entire package drove him into paroxysms of ecstasy, and he didn't mind if anyone else knew it. He had five hundred followers for his Tumblr page, and almost all of them loved to wax rhapsodic on the virtues of gingers the world over.

And speaking of which, where was Dorina from Romania? Or Hungary, or wherever the hell she came from. He peered into the next cubicle. Edgar from operations was picking at a salad and waiting for his array of phones to ring. Edgar oversaw the bank's two hundred ATMs scattered across Malta and neighboring Sicily. Everyone inside the bank saw his department—and his phones in particular—as a canary in a coal mine: If the public got wind of the rumors, they would start withdrawing money from the bank's ATMs. If they withdrew enough money, the ATMs would run out of cash. If the ATMs ran out of cash,

Edgar's phones would ring. That would be the starting bell of a bank run, and everyone was afraid of a bank run. It was the scariest of all outcomes—when banks failed, economies went under. That's when the rioting would start. That's when the rocks would come through the windows.

Edgar waved at Leone, as if to say, *So far, so good,* then continued nibbling at his salad as a text came through on Leone's phone. Before he had a chance to check it, Maria from the front desk arrived at his cubicle with a package. He signed for the package, then checked his phone. The number came up as Dorina's, and Leone's heart quickened.

Did u get it? the message read.

Get what? he wrote back almost instantaneously.

Package.

Leone glanced at the envelope from the front desk: a DHL package, addressed to him. He had assumed it was another résumé; he got a dozen a day, easily, from all over Europe, sometimes twice that number. The return address was from a hotel on the island, and the sender's name was D. Gabris.

Was that Dorina's last name? Gabris?

He tore open the envelope. Inside was a smaller letter-size white envelope, which he quickly opened. No letter was inside, only a small, green thumb drive. Leone held it up to the light: a four-gig USB external memory stick with a smiley face drawn on the green plastic.

He texted Dorina. *A thumb drive? You sent?*

Guess what is on it? The reply was immediate.

Leone held his breath. He texted back slowly, fingers trembling. *Pictures?*

Look and find out.

Leone licked his lips and started to guide the thumb drive into the USB slot on his work computer. He stopped as the drive was halfway in. The bank had a rule: absolutely no external memory devices were to ever—*ever*—be plugged into the bank's internal network. The IT people had sent endless memos on the subject and had gathered all the departments in the cafeteria earlier in the month to lecture employees on the dangers of network penetration. "Think of the bank as a fortress," the bearded troll from IT had said. "The fortress must never be breached. If it is breached, it will crumble." The IT department was so serious about the issue that they had software set up to block any foreign devices that might download program's onto the bank's computers. But Leone had been given a two-day administrator's permission to install an approved piece of human-resources software on the network, and he still had a few hours left on his access.

The IT people had also warned everyone on the evils of browsing the Web from work, and downloading pictures and playing games, as well as going on Facebook. But everyone else did these things, so why couldn't Leone investigate a harmless thumb drive? Abela had a whole file full of pregnant-women porn mixed in with his legal briefs. He'd shown it to Leone just last week, even though Leone had asked him not to. Leone knew he was in no position to cast stones at people's fetishes, but looking at pictures of naked pregnant women was just a touch too deviant, even for him.

His phone chimed. Dorina again. *Well?*

Rule against outside devices, he wrote quickly. *Can't do it.*

2 bad they are good.

Leone grimaced. He rubbed his thumb against the ridged plastic of the drive and breathed deep. He texted her. *Clothes?*

Why bother sending pictures with clothes?

He hesitated.

She sent another text: *May not make date tonight.*

His thumbs clicked out an immediate reply: *Why not?*

Disappointed.

"Damn it, damn it, damn it," Leone muttered. She had gone to the trouble of sending him nude selfies, and he couldn't even do her the honor of looking at them. Now she was pissed, and he had lost any chance of seeing whether she was a true redhead, or just faking it.

"Bollocks." With one quick jab of his right hand, he slotted her thumb drive into the USB port of his work computer. In a breathless rush, he clicked on the drive's tab. A folder opened, but it was empty. He clicked it again, surprised, then closed it and looked for other folders on the thumb drive.

There were none.

He texted Dorina again: *Drive is empty. No pictures.*

He waited for a reply.

Hello? Dorina? A mistake? Sent me wrong drive?

Still, no reply came.

Dorina? Hello?

He waited another five minutes, hopeful that Dorina would check her phone and write back, that she would realize her mistake and send a new thumb drive. Her hair was so spectacularly red, and her face so pale and lovely.

Suddenly, it occurred to him that there might never have been any pictures on the drive.

He snatched the thumb drive from the USB slot and jammed the memory stick into his pocket. It had been sitting in his computer for ten minutes now. Leone didn't understand much about technology, but he reckoned that ten minutes was more than enough time for something horrible to be downloaded onto the network. He figured half a second was probably more than enough time, but what the hell did he know?

Then Edgar's phones began to ring.

First one. Then another. And another. Leone stood and watched as Edgar raced to answer each one, putting successive customers on hold as he grabbed the next receiver. "First European Bank of Malta, can you hold, please?" Edgar said over and over.

Oh God, Leone thought, horror-stricken. I have done something unspeakably stupid.

He started quickly across the bull pen toward the front door. He had to get the thumb drive into a trash bin as fast as possible, away from his cubicle and away from any trace of his involvement. Breaching the network was a termination offense. Why hadn't he remembered that earlier? Because he was hungover and lonely, and he had a one-track mind. God, sometimes he hated himself.

Abela called out from his office as Leone strode past, but Leone made as if he didn't hear his friend. Was it his imagination, or were all the phones in the central bank office suddenly ringing in a rising crescendo—at operations, trading, customer service. Employees answered in a cacophony of languages: Maltese, English, Italian. Out of the corner of his eye, Leone saw the older VP of banking come sprinting out of his office—running as if he'd just heard that the building was on fire—toward the IT offices.

Oh shit, Leone thought. The building is on fire. I set it on fire.

When he turned left into reception, he was stopped dead in his tracks. Four Maltese policemen, dressed head to toe in their spotless royal-blue uniforms, were marching in the door. They were trailed by a half dozen stolid-looking men in dark suits. Their faces were grim and set, and their eyes flashed to Leone as he tried to hurry to the exit. Leone knew immediately that they were bank examiners, and they were not happy.

"I just have to use the WC." He pointed desperately at the hallway.

"You cannot leave," the first Maltese policeman said, thrusting out a beefy hand.

"But I have to go." Leone clutched the thumb drive.

"This office is closed and quarantined," one of the grim-faced men in suits said.

"But why?" Leone asked, even though he knew full well the answer.

"You've been breached."

"I didn't do anything," Leone wailed, a pitiful look on his face.

The bank examiner stared at Leone, eyes full of indignant scorn. "Maybe, maybe not. But as of this moment, your bank has no assets. It has officially collapsed."

G arrett walked north and east through lower Manhattan, keeping mostly to side streets and away from avenues. He walked fast, with his head down, only glancing up when he heard sirens. Police cars and fire trucks seemed to be racing through every intersection, and at Houston and Avenue A, a cop gave him the once-over from the driver's seat of his cruiser. Garrett tried to ignore him and kept walking, but he felt as if his hair were standing on end, and that his face had reddened to the color of an overripe strawberry.

He walked to put distance between himself and the Jenkins & Altshuler offices, but also to try to collect his thoughts—to figure out what had just happened, and think his way out of it. But the meds had seeped into his bloodstream, and his mind felt fuzzy, his brain clouded. He hated himself for relying on the crutch that the pain drugs had become. He was half a person when he was medicated, and he was for certain medicated now. For a moment, on Allen Street, he thought he heard Avery Bernstein whispering something in his ear.

"Not now," he grunted to Avery, and to the air, sounding like a ranting homeless person. "Not fucking now!"

He closed his eyes and tried to concentrate. As much as he wanted to tell himself that it made no sense, that this was all some terrible misunderstanding, the truth was that it made perfect sense. And that was what was so terrifying.

Garrett had led the Ascendant program. He had guided it through a face-off with the Chinese government—and US intelligence services as well—and he had won. He had spotted a threat that no one else had seen, then responded in kind. But Garrett had done it anonymously, invisibly. People around the world had spent the last year trying to track him down, to find out who, exactly, was the brains behind Ascendant, and Garrett had felt their probing, their intrusions into his life—the amateurish attempts to hack his bank account, to hijack his cell phone, or to simply taunt him into the open on darknet bulletin boards.

Now, if an attack was coming—and he had no idea what that attack might look like—then whoever was behind it would figure that Garrett and Ascendant might be poised to intercept it. It stood to reason that they would want him out of the way. They would want to frame him and put him on the run. And they had succeeded. *He was scared. He was running.*

He considered stopping at his apartment, but ruled that out almost immediately. That would be the first place the FBI would be waiting. He walked a wide circle away from his building on Twelfth and Avenue C and continued uptown. He called his best friend, Mitty Rodriguez, a like-minded freelance computer programmer and sometimes black-hat hacker, knowing he could ask her for anything, and that he could trust her. She'd heard about the shooting, but knew nothing else, and they set up a meeting for later in the day, at five o'clock.

"Meet me at that place," she said, "where we ate last Saturday."

Garrett appreciated her paranoia. At this point, anybody could be listening. He hung up, then took the battery out of his phone. That kept the police from tracking him, but it also took him off the grid—out of the information flow—and he felt the immediate loss of that in his bones. Garrett needed data the way he needed oxygen. Without a continuous stream of data to analyze, his mind went round and round in circles and eventually crashed.

He bought a sweatshirt and jeans at a discount store, using only cash, then changed out of his business suit in the bathroom. He bought a pork sandwich and a soda at a bodega on Ninth and wolfed them both down. He was nervous, and that made him hungry; his whole body was on overdrive. He walked up to Fourteenth Street, watched the street for a few moments, then dashed into the subway and took the Q train into Queens. A few transit cops were lingering at some of the stations, so Garrett bought a *Daily News* and buried his face in it for most of the trip. That seemed to work; no one paid him any attention. He got off at Queensboro Plaza and killed time by walking the streets and then sitting in a park.

Through it all, his heart pounded like a drum machine and his skull ached. He felt as if he might jump out of his skin. The tramadols were wearing off. He'd grabbed his stash before he'd fled his office, but he didn't want to take any more pills; he needed to think, and to think clearly.

He tried to reason out who was behind what had happened, but he didn't have enough information. He was cut off, adrift. He was an information junkie in withdrawal, longing for a fix in the form of a blast of digital intelligence. But he knew that a fix, right then, would alert the police to his whereabouts and get him arrested.

Why the fuck were all his thoughts coming back to addiction?

He toyed with turning himself in. Just walk into a police precinct, blurt out his name, and let the FBI come get him. But he had no idea what they had on him—fabricated evidence, some kind of bullshit eyewitness testimony. If he did surrender, he would be at the mercy of law enforcement, a cog in the bureaucratic machine, and he might not get out of that machine again for days. Or months even. That was a nightmare scenario for Garrett. He trusted no authority, anywhere, ever. Police, military, government—they were all, to his mind, self-serving and corrupt. His paranoia about those in power verged on the pathological, born of a lifetime of being on the outside looking in.

Anyway, he couldn't afford to be locked up, for any amount of time. He saw clearly that what had happened to the Federal Reserve president was the start of something else—the dense, complicated thing of his nightmares. A thing that was unfurling immediately, in real time. He had seen it, and now he was a part of it.

At four thirty in the afternoon he wedged himself in an alley between two small apartment buildings on Thirty-Sixth Avenue in Queens and watched the comings and goings in front of a Brazilian restaurant. He scanned the street for any sign of surveillance cars, cops, or undercover agents. Anyone who might have deciphered his cell phone conversation with Mitty. But all he saw were old Brazilian men tottering into the restaurant for an afternoon beer and some *salgados*.

At five, a beat-up Ford Explorer pulled up at the fire hydrant in front of the restaurant. Garrett didn't recognize the SUV, but he could see Mitty in the driver's seat, her mop of frizzy black hair draped over her shoulders. Also, he could hear a Kesha song blasting from the radio. Mitty loved Kesha.

He ran across traffic and threw himself into the backseat.

"What the fuck is going on?" she barked as soon as he had closed the door. "Did you hit that guy in mergers, like you said you would? Is he pressing charges? You gotta cut that shit out, because—"

"Just drive." He lay flat on a bed of old beef-jerky wrappers and empty Mountain Dew cans. "I'll tell you everything. But first I need someplace to hide."

She put him in a spare bedroom above a tire-repair shop that her uncle Jose owned on Northern Boulevard. Mitty said her uncle used the room to catch up on sleep when he worked late, but also, she suspected, to meet with his mistress on Wednesday nights. The room was tiny, with a single window looking out onto an alley littered with trash, and it smelled like sweat and old cigars, but Garrett didn't care—he would take what he could get. He told Mitty to take the battery out of her phone; the FBI would start tracking his friends and family soon, and she was just about the only friend he had these days. She did as he asked, but grudgingly, and Garrett finally felt he was safe, at least for a while.

He told Mitty about what he'd found, the dark pool, the hacking attacks, and then about the anonymous phone call, and what the woman on the other end had said, and Mitty responded right away with theories. She had been a member of Ascendant; she knew the players, and their history.

"That bitch Alexis is trying to set you up. She's trying to frame your ass."

Garrett threw his hands in the air. "Why would she want to do that?"

"She's pissed at you for quitting Ascendant. And because the two of you were a thing, and now you're not."

Garrett knew Mitty was taking his side against Alexis more out of friendship and loyalty than any well-considered opinion, but still, he needed to streamline his thought process, not go off on tangents. "So she had a banker shot just to blame me? A theory has to make sense for me to consider it."

"It makes plenty of sense." Mitty frowned. "Sorta. She's always been high-and-mighty, and I don't trust her."

"Thanks, that's really helpful."

"Whatever."

Mitty had turned on a small television when they first got into the room and switched it to CNN. There'd been ten minutes of coverage of the shooting in the last hour, but a reporter on the scene—and another at a police press conference—had said the shooter was an obsessed female stalker, but they hadn't released her name. Nobody had mentioned Garrett or Ascendant or even the possibility of its being anything other than a random killing. Garrett had a flash of intense paranoia: Had he imagined the entire phone conversation? But how would that be possible? He had known nothing about the shooting until he answered his work phone.

No, he told himself. Do not think that way. Simple logic was still his friend. A to B to C. Do not deviate from known facts and hard data: categorize, test, analyze.

"Whoever called you made a mistake," Mitty said. "The shooter was some crazy bitch with a gun, and she capped this dude, and no one on TV has mentioned anything about you, or a pattern, or anything like that."

"So you're saying that I'm imagining all this?" Garrett booted up the laptop that Mitty had brought from her home. "I might take that personally."

"No, no way," Mitty said a little too quickly. "I'm just—you know—examining it from all angles."

Garrett glared at her briefly, then connected to the tire shop's Wi-Fi—Mitty said her uncle paid for high speeds to watch Venezuelan porn when business was slow. Garrett logged on to his virtual private network to search the Web for information on the shooting. His VPN let him go online without being tracked. He let the digital data wash over him and felt intense relief. He was back in the global information flow, where he belonged, moving from website to website, news feed to opinion piece. He checked the markets and interest rates, going from graph to chart to an endless scroll of numbers. The Dow had sunk on news of Steinkamp's death, and the VIX—the Volatility Index—had skyrocketed. He ran videos and read interviews and blog posts. A veil of anxiety had descended on Wall Street. The smart money was on edge. *Everyone was on edge.*

All the while, Mitty kept up a running stream of commentary at his ear, complaining about Alexis Truffant, bitching about the Dominican whore her uncle brought to the bedroom, and spending a good twenty minutes on her new diet. "Just Coke Zero and cottage cheese. It's a cleanse."

"That's not a cleanse. A cleanse is—forget it." Garrett found a news item from Agence France-Presse. "There's been a bank run in Malta." Garrett scanned the news update. "Started just after the Italian stock drop. It lines up perfectly."

"What's Malta? A coffee drink?"

Garrett ignored her. He pushed back from the laptop and massaged his temples.

Mitty watched him, concern softening her face. "Head hurting again?"

Garrett nodded imperceptibly. *Yes.*

"You got meds?"

He shrugged. Yes, but he needed to stay off them for a while—not that Mitty needed to know that.

She watched him for a moment. "I'll run to the corner, get us some beers. Maybe some snacks. That'll help, right?"

"Sure," Garrett managed to mutter. "But be careful."

She returned fifteen minutes later with a six-pack of Schlitz, a bag of potato chips, and a plastic bottle of Motrin.

Garrett drank a beer and swallowed six pills. "See anyone out there? Watching you?"

"Chill. I got it covered. I'm the Puerto Rican James Bond." She rubbed his neck and shoulders silently for a few minutes, and the pain in his head lessened. He was grateful for Mitty. She was excitable, opinionated, and bitchy, but she was also smart and intensely loyal. She would walk through fire for him.

"You should get some sleep," she said. "Make sense of this in the morning."

He nodded, but kept working, broadening his search. He researched the bank run in Malta. No one was saying exactly how the run had started; no one seemed to know. News clips showed angry depositors throwing stones in the streets. Mitty drank a second beer, then a third, then passed out on the bed, a laptop open on her stomach. Garrett must have drifted off as well, because he woke with a start at 2:00 a.m. to the sound of a window breaking. He sat bolt upright in his chair. Mitty was snoring peacefully on the bed.

Garrett went to the bedroom door, cracking it open to listen. There was movement below, in the tire-repair shop: someone, or something, padding around amid the equipment. Garrett slid into the hallway, then stepped slowly down the cramped stairway that led to the machine shop. The smell of rubber and grease was overwhelming. A bank of windows on the far side allowed a streak of orange halogen light to wash across the piles of tires and the empty car bays.

Garrett stepped into the room and listened. There was only silence. He tried to slow his heart rate—the blood was pumping in his ears. A flash of a thought occurred to him: he had quit Ascendant to get away from the exact things that were happening to him at this moment. And yet his past had caught up with him. With a vengeance. He wanted to scream, but stifled the impulse.

He moved past the car bays and machinery to the entranceway—and froze. The door to the street was open, its window smashed. Garrett crouched low, expecting a blow from behind, but none came. He turned to scout out the rest of the waiting room, but it was empty.

Garrett straightened and took a deep breath. What the hell was going on? Then he heard it—footsteps from above, up the stairs, in the bedroom. Without thinking, he raced back across the work bays, yelling as he ran. "Mitty!"

He sprinted up the stairs, fists clenched, and stumbled into the spare bedroom. The light was on; Mitty was sitting up in bed, rubbing at her eyes.

"Dude, what are you yelling about?" She winced in the light. "I was asleep."

Garrett searched the room. Other than for Mitty, it was empty. The window was open, but Mitty had opened it when they first came in. Everything else seemed untouched.

"Someone broke into the shop. Front door is open. Window is smashed."

"Nobody steals used tires. Trust me. You can't give 'em away."

"They weren't looking for tires. They came up here. To this bedroom."

Mitty shook her head. "You're high. Go back to sleep."

Garrett sat in the chair at the desk in the corner of the room. CNN was still playing, muted, in the corner. Maybe Mitty was right. Maybe he was high, the mixture of Motrin and Schlitz jumbling his brain.

He glanced at his computer. A word program had been opened. He hadn't been writing anything—and he never used Word. Someone had typed three short sentences onto the screen. Garrett read them and grunted in surprise.

One man.

A Russian.

He is en route.

HM

I n the New York field office of the FBI, Special Agent Jayanti Chaudry was considered straight talking and intensely ambitious. She was usually in the running for the best, and most high-profile, homicide cases, and if she got one, she almost always closed it. An intuitive crime fighter, meticulous, and frighteningly persistent, she saw her relentlessness as an outgrowth of her life story: daughter of immigrant shopkeepers who spent their life savings to start a business, the first one in her family to go to college, and the first female Indian special agent in the Manhattan office. Actually, now that she thought of it, since Agent Hawani had been transferred to Denver, she was the only female Indian special agent in the Manhattan office. Or the entire Northeast.

Not that it mattered. To Chaudry, there were two types of people in her world: those who helped her solve crimes, and those who got in the way. She knew she had a chip on her shoulder; she was, after all, dark skinned and female in a white man's world—but she refused to let those issues derail her. Race, gender, and birthplace were simply distractions, and distractions only slowed you down. Chaudry never slowed down.

She checked the clock above her desk—it was nearly two thirty in the morning—and considered the case before her. New York Federal Reserve president Phillip Steinkamp had been shot and killed while walking to work yesterday morning at approximately 8:25 a.m. The shooter, Anna Bachev, thirty-eight, a Bulgarian immigrant who had lived in the States for the last fifteen years, had a history of mental illness and drug abuse. She'd had multiple stints at Bellevue, in the psych lockup, as well as two arrests for possession of cocaine. She'd already been granted citizenship at the time of her arrests, so no deportation proceedings were set. Her work record was spotty, almost nonexistent, and Chaudry guessed Bachev had spent time hooking to support herself.

Two agents had searched her apartment in the Hunts Point neighborhood of the Bronx, a filthy studio in a rotting building on Bryant Avenue, and had found multiple articles about Steinkamp. Bachev had clearly been stalking the Fed president, but something—according to the agents' report—was slightly off about the evidence: "Agent in charge should consider the possibility of fabrication. Motivation of suspect unclear and unusual. Source of newspaper clippings is indeterminate, seems beyond suspect's capabilities to accumulate."

To Chaudry, Steinkamp was an odd choice for a stalking target. He was older, quiet, and did not have a high-visibility job. He was neither rich nor, outside of a small subset of finance geeks, particularly famous. Chaudry knew that stalkers were, by definition, irrational, but when they picked targets, they weren't usually bureaucrats—balding, married bureaucrats at that.

None of Bachev's neighbors knew much about her; she'd only moved into the apartment two months ago. Before that, her name didn't show up on a lease, rental agreement, or bank account in the New York City area going back four years. She'd essentially been homeless. And broke. Which raised the question of how she had obtained the murder weapon, a nine-millimeter SIG Sauer P226. SIGs were expensive weapons. This one had been bought at a gun shop in Vermont three years ago by a collector, who reported it stolen six months later. It hadn't shown up in any robberies or crimes since. That made it black market, but even black-market guns were pricey.

And then there were Bachev's reported last words before she turned the gun on herself: Garrett Reilly made me do it.

Chaudry sipped at her coffee and puzzled over this.

Garrett Reilly?

Chaudry flipped through the stack of reports on Reilly. He was a fascinating character. Born in Long Beach, California, the son of a Mexican immigrant mother and a dad who worked as a janitor for the LA Unified School District, Reilly had shown an early aptitude for numbers. A genius for them, actually. He had been recruited to Yale by a mathematics professor named Avery Bernstein and had earned nothing but As at the school before he dropped out. He'd dropped out the day after his brother, a marine lance corporal, was reported KIA in Afghanistan. Reilly appeared to have moved back in with his mother in Long Beach and spent the next six months pestering the Army Bureau of Records for information about his brother's death. He'd made more than 120 phone calls to their DC offices. Later that year, he'd gone back to school at Long Beach State, but his grades had been indifferent, and he was cited twice by the administration for disrupting class and then getting into a fistfight with a fellow student.

Bernstein, his Yale math prof, seemed to have tracked Reilly's progress and brought him back to New York to work on the bond desk at Jenkins & Altshuler, a Wall Street trading house that Bernstein had taken over. There, Reilly had thrived. Thrived until a day in late March, a year ago, when a car bomb exploded in front of the Jenkins & Altshuler offices.

Chaudry remembered the day well. It had been a sensational terror attack, but no one was killed, and then no one was charged in the bombing. The FBI hadn't worked on that case—it had gone straight to Homeland Security, which was odd in its own right—and it was still an active investigation, unsolved and very much open. Conspiracy theories still swirled around it.

To compound the strangeness, Garrett Reilly had disappeared that very day. He seemed to have enlisted in the army for a while and been under the supervision of the Defense Intelligence Agency, but he quit two months later, honorably discharged, and then went back to his old job at Jenkins & Altshuler, which he kept even when his mentor, Bernstein, died in a car accident soon thereafter.

The threads of Reilly's life were odd and disparate, and none of them quite meshed.

When Chaudry had called the DIA right after the shooting, a general named Kline had seemed reluctant to answer her questions, citing national security concerns. It had clearly been a mistake to alert him. Twenty minutes later, someone called Reilly from a phone booth in DC, and Reilly immediately fled his office. The DIA must have circled the wagons.

Now Chaudry had no idea where he was. They'd staked out his apartment, as well as his known associates and friends—although he didn't seem to have many of the latter. Chaudry suspected that it was going to take a lot more than that to find him. Reilly was smart, he'd obviously received some training from a military intelligence service, and he knew the Bureau was looking for him. All bad, from where Chaudry sat.

But had this Reilly character actually sent a mentally unstable woman to kill the president of the New York Federal Reserve Bank? How had he made her do it? Money? Drugs? Had they been lovers? Bachev's phone records showed repeated calls to Jenkins & Altshuler, but they had been short, none lasting longer than fifteen seconds, almost like hang-ups, with no calls from Reilly's office back to Bachev. Not a single one.

And even if Reilly had some hand in the shooting, it raised the larger question of why. What possible purpose did killing Steinkamp serve? Chaudry could not see a reason. Maybe Reilly, not Bachev, was the one who was mentally unstable.

Chaudry didn't know. But she would find out, because untangling complicated cases like this one was what got her to the Manhattan field office in the first place. These cases were what she lived for, and better yet, parsing out the threads of what could be a far-reaching conspiracy was the dream of every FBI agent in the country. If she solved this, she'd be fast-tracked to becoming the youngest agent to run the Bureau's New York field office. Not youngest female Indian agent. Just the youngest. Period.

But first, she had to find Garrett Reilly. She wasn't sure how, but she suspected that he was the key to all of this. Once she arrested him, all the other pieces would fall into place.

She closed his files and considered her options. Reilly was on the run, an obscure, unknown entity swimming in a sea of anonymity. But it didn't have to be that way. So far, Chaudry had kept Reilly's name and picture out of the press—the official word was that Bachev was an unhinged stalker. But perhaps Chaudry needed to change tactics. If Reilly was as smart as he appeared, then she would have to use every bit of leverage to bring him out of the shadows.

Garrett Reilly needed to become a celebrity in his own right.

Alexis Truffant filled her to-go coffee mug and headed out the door of her suburban DC condo. Mentally, she was already bracing herself for the day, which promised to be difficult. Yesterday had been a string of disasters, starting with the shooting of the New York Fed president, and ending with a grilling by a pair of humorless FBI agents. Alexis had answered the FBI as best she could, sticking to the truth mostly, and carefully talking her way around her involvement in tipping off Garrett Reilly. The agents hadn't seemed to know about the NSA recording of her phone call, and General Kline never mentioned it, so she found she could answer almost entirely truthfully. Almost.

The agents wanted background on Garrett and his involvement with the DIA. Kline parried those questions in the usual DIA way—national security this, and national security that—but Garrett was clearly in their sights. They wanted him badly.

But she'd be damned if she would help the FBI get him. Garrett could not be involved in the shooting of a federal banker. Garrett might yell and scream, be difficult and subversive, even punch someone in the face in a bar brawl, but assassination was not in his character. She knew him well enough to know that. In truth, she still had feelings for Garrett, no matter what she'd told Kline earlier. She might not love him—perhaps she never had—but the two of them were connected. Emotionally connected. And she could not ignore that. Not yet, at least.

She walked downstairs and through a hallway to the parking garage. The drive to DIA headquarters was ten minutes, and barring traffic, she'd be there at eight sharp, as she always was. Alexis liked order and predictability. She punched the unlock button on her car key fob and smiled at the reassuring chirp of her Honda Accord. She was halfway to her driver's-side door when a voice rang out.

"Alexis."

She practically jumped out of her skin.

Garrett Reilly stepped out from behind a concrete support beam. He was wearing a gray I ♥ DAYTONA BEACH sweatshirt and jeans, but he had on black wing-tip shoes, as if he'd changed out of most of his clothing from the previous business day, but not all of it. He looked strung out, exhausted, as if he'd aged years since she'd last seen him, not months. She felt a pang of guilt: Had she done that to Garrett? She had recruited him. She had seduced him. Maybe she had broken him as well.

"Jesus Christ," Alexis hissed. "You cannot be here, Garrett. It's not safe. And how the hell did you get here in the first place?"

"There's an attack coming." He moved closer to her, talking quietly, his eyes dancing back and forth, scanning the empty garage.

"I'd say the attack's already happened."

"That's just the beginning. Tip of the spear."

"*What?*"

"You heard me," Garrett said much too loudly for Alexis's comfort. "It's part of a pattern."

"Okay, okay," she said, trying to stay calm. Her eyes flashed across the garage as well. She guessed that the FBI had not put her under surveillance, but that was just a guess. "Tell me about it. But quietly. And fast."

"I've found an investment pool that's tied to illegal activity."

"Explain."

"A fund. A secret fund. Pretty big—a couple of billion dollars. It only trades in dark pools—"

"Dark pools?"

"Invisible exchanges where investors buy and sell stock out of the mainstream. So no one knows they are doing it. Thirty percent of the stocks traded in the US right now are done outside of the major exchanges."

"That's legal?"

"It's finance. Legal is a secondary concept."

"Okay," she said. "What's the name of the fund? Who runs it?"

"I don't know. I can't even prove definitively that it exists."

Alexis crossed her arms. In the distance, thunder rumbled. Or perhaps it was just a truck lumbering across the city. She studied Garrett. His skin was pale, his eyes were lined with red, as if he hadn't slept well in a long time. Alexis could feel the anxiety radiating off his body, as if his paranoia were a physical thing, a second skin that enveloped him. Some part of her wanted to wrap him up in her arms, put him to bed, let him sleep for a week.

Another part of her wanted to run screaming for safety.

"Don't worry," Garrett said, as if reading her mind. "Mitty drove me. And we stayed off the highways. We watched for cop cars. No one followed us."

If Alexis were caught with Garrett Reilly, not only would her career be over, but her life would be as well. Kline had already warned her once. She was breaking any number of federal laws, consorting with a suspect in a capital murder case, and now the proof of her complicity was standing in her garage.

"Why do you think this fund exists?" she asked, trying to keep Garrett's eyes on hers.

"I can see ripple effects. When it sells equities and derivatives. Little variations in price that don't make sense on the open exchanges. Repeated patterns—"

"Patterns."

"What you pay me to find."

"*Paid* you. You quit."

Garrett shrugged. "Repeated patterns of selling. Selling stuff that's on the margins of the financial system. Derivatives, swaps, low-volume equities. Stuff that you would buy if you wanted to make sure no one was really paying that much attention to what you owned. Or what you did."

"Okay. This fund. You know what it's doing?"

"There is a correlation coefficient of plus one."

"It moves in perfect lockstep?"

"Yes. A sale and then a real-world event."

"And the real-world event is?"

"Attacks on corporations and banks. And now the killing of a Federal Reserve president. They're ratcheting up. Getting bigger."

Alexis heard another crash, thunder for sure. A summer storm, far away, over the western suburbs, but closing in fast.

"You're saying there's a fund out there—an invisible fund—that paid for Phillip Steinkamp to be shot? That this was a planned assassination? Do you realize the implications of what you're saying? The level of conspiracy?"

"It's bigger than just killing someone. The fund is dedicated to creating a systemic volatility event."

Alexis tilted her head slightly to one side. "In English, please."

"Taking down the US economy."

Alexis checked each hallway and stairwell in her building before Garrett followed her, clearly terrified that another resident would see him with her. Garrett wanted to laugh at this, but he couldn't exactly blame her: he was a wanted man. That gave him the slightest of thrills; now he really was dangerous. Of course, he didn't feel dangerous. He felt hunted.

When Garrett stepped inside Alexis's condo apartment, he was flooded with memories. He had been here once before, a year ago, and he and Alexis had spent the night making love. That had been their only night together, but he remembered it perfectly: the sheets, her skin, the orange sunlight streaming in through the windows the next morning. He sat on the far corner of a couch in the living room, and contentment washed over him. He realized he'd wanted to get back here for the last year—not to have sex with Alexis again, but just to sit quietly, in her apartment, alone with her. To talk. To be near her.

He cursed himself silently for being a sentimental fool. Alexis Truffant had used him for his abilities, then tossed him aside when their relationship no longer mattered. He had to force himself to remember this, to imprint it on his consciousness: Alexis had screwed him over and would again if the circumstances demanded it. *He had to keep his distance.*

Garrett watched as Alexis called Kline's office and told his secretary that she was having car trouble, and that she would be in the office in an hour or so. Then she brewed more coffee and poured Garrett a cup, offering him food as well—breakfast cereal and eggs—which he declined.

"Where's Mitty now?"

"A few blocks away. She's fine. She knows to wait."

Alexis sat across from him in a padded brown chair, sipping her coffee, her eyes seeming to note everything about him. Garrett realized his fingers were twitching, so he gripped the sofa armrest hard to make them stop. His head ached, and the blood in his veins felt thick, as if it were dry and clotted, as if his heart might explode at any moment from the exertion of pumping. He knew this was withdrawal, a hallucination, but it was powerful, and growing. He had his bag of meds in his back pocket, but he needed to stay off them, at least for the moment. He breathed deep to ease his rising panic.

Alexis seemed to sense this. "Garrett, listen, I don't want you to take this wrong, but are you still taking prescription medications?"

Garrett blinked in surprise. "Fuck you for looking at my medical records." Christ, he thought to himself, is there absolutely no part of my life that's private? Am I an open book to the world?

"You had a top-level security clearance. We have to be careful with everyone who has ever worked for us. You can understand that."

"No, I cannot understand that. My personal business is my own. Not yours. What the hell is wrong with you people? What is wrong with this country?"

"I understand you're upset, but—"

"You don't." An ember of rage glowed in his chest. "You understand nothing about me. You never have."

They sat silently for half a minute. Garrett's mind raced. He replayed the conversation they'd just had in his head. Had he been too defensive? Yes. Well, no, the DIA *had* dug into his medical records. That was wrong. And illegal. On the other hand, he was taking too many drugs—even he recognized that. Maybe she was actually worried about him. No, no, and no. His thoughts were ping-ponging back and forth. He slammed shut his eyes and tried to focus on what he had told himself only moments earlier: He had to keep his distance from Alexis. He did not love her anymore. *Keep. His. Distance.*

"Did you say something?" she asked, brow creased in concern.

"What?" he asked. Had he said his thoughts out loud? He slapped his open palm against the sofa cushion, trying to jolt his mind to reality, to the present. He was a mess. His mind was a mess. "No. I was just—nothing."

She nodded slowly, as if to say, *Okay, I believe you. Sort of.* "Can you tell me a little more about this pool? And who you think is behind it?"

"If I had to guess, I'd say a nation-state. Not an ally. But maybe not a full-on enemy either. They're sending someone into this country. To destabilize things.

That's what they've been doing now for weeks. In Europe. Hacking, stealing, causing a bank run."

"If it's cybercrime, why send someone into this country? Why not do it remotely?"

"It's not just cybercrime. It's social engineering. Conning people. You need to be here in person to do that. To make the dominoes fall in the right order."

"I saw an intelligence report on the bank run in Malta. You're saying that's a part of this?"

He nodded yes.

"But Europe is not the United States."

"They're connected. Corporations in London, banks in New York, data centers in Hong Kong. Nothing is truly separate anymore."

"And who is this person they're sending?"

"An assassin. A financial assassin."

Garrett watched Alexis's reaction, how her lips tightened, how her eyes shot quickly high and to the left, looking out a window, avoiding his gaze. That was a tell. She didn't believe him. She thought he was crazy, a deranged drug addict. Maybe she thought he *did* have something to do with the Steinkamp killing.

"Garrett," she said calmly, "why don't you get Mitty to come up here. You guys can hang out in my apartment, and I'll run your theory past Kline—"

Garrett laughed. "And then he can call the FBI, and they can take their time coming down to your apartment to arrest me?"

"If I'd wanted you arrested, I wouldn't have called you at your office," she snapped.

Garrett fell silent. She had a point. Paranoia was wrapping itself around his brain like a noose, cutting off his thoughts, limiting his ability to see the world as it was.

"It's just—a billion-dollar fund? Targeting the US economy? A financial assassin? I mean, it's pretty fantastic. What other sources do you have?"

"Hans Metternich. He found me last night. Left me a note. That they were coming. Coming to this country."

"Hans Metternich? The man you said you met on a subway a year ago? A spy we could never find, no matter how hard we looked?"

Garrett stood abruptly. Anger shot up through his body, out to his limbs.

He stabbed his hands in the air and paced the room. "I'm here to give you a piece of critical information. I don't even work for your fucking program anymore. And all you think is that I'm nuts? How often have I been wrong in the past?"

"Calm down."

"I will not calm down!" he shouted, marching to the window. He stared out at the row of trees separating her apartment building from the next set of suburban condos. A swimming pool lay just below the window, the blue water sparkling in a blast of yellow sunlight. Garrett knew he was behaving erratically, his anger surging, and that Alexis was on the verge of calling the cops. But why did he even give a shit? The whole world could go down in flames for all he cared: Wall Street and DC and investors and the FBI. Everyone—Alexis included—could go to hell. Let the economy crater—it would serve America right. Rome falls, and something else takes its place. Let them all burn in . . .

No.

He had an attraction to the chaos—he knew that. Some part of him was drawn to the maelstrom of destruction, that darkest desire to see it all collapse, to watch the rich and the powerful—the very people who always seemed set against him—go down in flames. But there was also a spark of resistance in his brain, the faintest dim light of refusal. He might be angry and isolated and hunted by his own government, but under it all, he did not want everything around him to fall to pieces. He had some humanity left. He could love life more than he wanted his enemies to suffer. Chaos might call to him, but he still craved order more than anarchy.

Now he just had to convince Alexis.

He walked across her living room. His eyes tracked the photos on the walls, the books lying on the coffee table, notes on the refrigerator, the gym bag in the corner. He blocked out his rage and let the surroundings wash over him, all the hints and clues about Alexis's life, the telltale signs of where she had come from, and where she was heading. He didn't force the process; he just let it unfold, as it always did when he was at his best. A pulse started at the base of his spine, a tiny dot of understanding that began to grow, and suddenly . . . he knew.

"You need this. You need it badly."

"Excuse me?" Alexis asked.

"You've been demoted," he said, not waiting for her to respond. "No, transferred. Within the agency. Kline too. You're both doing something meaningless. Your career is stalled out." He pointed to the coffee table. "The half-read books. Fluff fiction. The magazines. *TV Guide*. The gym bag in the corner. You go every day. The errands list on your fridge is trivial make-work. You have time to kill. Your job doesn't take up all your waking hours. It doesn't even come close to filling them. That's a change."

Alexis let out a soft laugh, but Garrett ignored it. He was right. He could feel it.

"If you're trying to impress me, Garrett, it's not working. You wouldn't need to come to my apartment to guess those things."

"Not guesses, observations. And I don't give a shit about your past. It's your future that I'm trying to keep from becoming a disaster."

Garrett saw Alexis stiffen. He walked to a wall near the hallway to her bedroom and studied a framed photo. A knot of army officers were hoisting beers at a backyard barbecue.

"You called me from a pay phone, but not from a secure line at the DIA. They're not going to track calls out of the DIA, but you didn't want anyone to overhear you. You were acting without orders from Kline. You've grown apart. He doesn't trust you anymore. Ascendant crashed, and he took the fall. He thinks you're responsible for what happened. He's pissed. At me, I'm sure. But at you too. At his disciple, his wonder child. For getting too close to me. That's a body blow for Alexis Truffant."

Garrett glanced quickly at Alexis. She sat frozen in her chair. He tapped on the glass frame of the photo. "How old is Kline now? Fifty-four? Fifty-five? When is mandatory retirement in the army? Sixty-two? He's not going to make it. He'll quit in a year, maybe less. Everyone else is smiling, drinking beer. He's standing apart from the gang, staring in the other direction. Look at his face. He's worn-out. Finished."

He turned back to face Alexis. "And when he goes, you'll be left all alone. No mentor. No coattails to ride on. Just you and the old-boy bureaucracy of the intelligence services. You can work as hard as you want, but you won't get anywhere, and you know it. That's how a career fizzles out into nothing. And your career means everything to you. It's your reason for living."

He let his words sink in. "You need me to be right. So you can fix it. So you can move on. And keep moving up."

She sat there, saying nothing, just looking at Garrett, her breathing slow and steady. Garrett could almost see the gears in her head grinding; she was processing what he had just said, trying to come to a decision. And she was not happy about it.

"You have to give me something specific," she said, finally breaking the silence. "I can't just go tell DIA brass that there's an economic assassin entering the country without knowing who it is, what he or she would look like—and why they're doing it in the first place."

Garrett nodded briefly, then strode toward her front door. "Done," he said, and left the apartment.

Mitty booked them a room in a motel north of Alexandria. The Happy Inn was broken-down, with a few tourist rental cars in the parking lot, but Mitty guessed that most of the rooms were used by prostitutes and their johns. That seemed to suit Garrett fine. They didn't need to use a credit card, and they registered as husband and wife, under fake names, like everyone else in the place. Mitty had fun with that part: DeAndre and Shirlee Horowitz, she told the uninterested clerk.

The motel had Internet, but it was slow and cost $19.95 per day extra, which Garrett bitched about but paid for nonetheless. He was beginning to run out of cash.

"If we use my ATM card," he said, "the FBI will be here in minutes."

She brewed some instant coffee, then walked across the street to get sandwiches from a Subway store. When she returned to the room, Garrett already had his computer sitting on his lap.

"I want to build a profile," he said. "A profile of the guy coming to the country."

"How?" Mitty said. "You don't know shit about him. In fact, you're not even sure he really exists."

"Let's start with the assumption that he does exist. Take it as a given. Maybe that's crazy, but let's run with it."

"Okay."

"So we need to figure out what he would look like. Not physically, but his background. What country he comes from, where he worked, went to school. All that kind of stuff."

"Not possible," Mitty said. "I mean, seriously, Gare, how the fuck you going to do that?"

"Probability."

Mitty stared at him, then lay on one of the twin beds and used the remote to flick on the television. "Remind me why we're doing this again? I thought you quit Ascendant. I thought you hated those people."

"I'm doing it because someone is trying to frame me for murder. The sooner I catch them, the sooner I don't have to sit around motel rooms. With you."

"Love you too. Kisses."

"We'll start with age, gender, country of origin." Garrett typed. "Native language. Education."

"You know why I think you're doing this? Because you're still in love with her. She burned your ass, and you're going to spend the rest of your life trying to prove to her that you're worthy."

"Wait, I'm confused. Earlier, you said she's angry at me because I screwed her. Now you're saying I'm obsessed with her because she screwed me. Which is it?"

"Haven't decided yet. Maybe both. I'll know better after I eat."

Garrett ignored Mitty, and she switched the channel to a house-hunting reality show. Mitty loved reality shows. They could be about anything—she didn't care: redecorating, building motorcycles, clearing out storage lockers. She couldn't get enough of them, and if that defined her as a mouth-breathing dumbass, well, so be it. She ate her sandwich as she watched, listening as Garrett's fingers click-clacked on the keyboard next to her. After a few minutes her curiosity got the better of her. She rolled over on the bed to sneak a peek at what he was doing.

"Once you've got the questions, how you gonna define them?" she asked, despite her better judgment.

Garrett smiled. "Like I said, evidential probability. Work our way backward to an optimal personality. What would be the prime characteristic of a person coming into the country to do economic hacking? Would they be twenty years old? Twenty-five? Thirty? Forty? Assign a value to each age. Ninety percent, eighty percent, et cetera."

"Yeah, but how do we assign values? Our percentage assignments are guesses." She'd done just as much programming in her life as Garrett had, maybe more. She might not have had the statistical background that he did, but she was a quick study and loved numbers almost as much as Garrett did. That was part of why they remained friends. That, and beer. And video games.

"We do as much research as we can, right now, online. What's the average age of arrested hackers? In the US? Abroad? We can find those numbers. Anything we don't know, you and I discuss, and then guess. Guesses are assigned a lower value than researched answers. Bayesian statistical analysis."

Mitty lay back on the bed, staring up at the ceiling. "And the discussion between us—how are we gonna resolve disputes?"

"Occam's razor. Simplest answer wins. If there is no obvious simplest answer, then split the results into two questions and give them equal weight in the profile."

Mitty thought about this. She'd gone to Fordham University on a free ride, the first person in her family to graduate from college. She'd studied social work when she first got there, figuring she would go back to her old neighborhood in the South Bronx to help immigrant families looking for their version of the American dream, but then she took her first computer-programming class and never considered social work again. Coding was like writing a story, only you were doing it in this language that was both made-up and yet made perfect sense. And the coolest thing about it was that when the story was finished, it came out the other side—on a computer screen—as an entirely different beast. What started as a series of if/then propositions transformed itself into a living, breathing program. Mitty loved that.

"Could work," she said. "But you might come up with nonsense. I mean—you build a hypothetical profile, but the real person, the flesh and blood, they're totally different. Because real people never fit a profile exactly."

"Agreed." Garrett continued to enter queries into his database. "But it's better than nothing."

Mitty shrugged, then flipped through the channels on the motel TV. She skipped over Fox News, then quickly cycled back to it. She stared at the screen. "Oh shit, big guy. We got trouble."

Garrett looked up from his computer to the television and saw his own face staring back at him.

• • •

Alexis saw the news reports as well. She watched them from her office at the DIA. They were short, obviously cribbed from an FBI press release, and to the point: Garrett Reilly was now an official "person of interest" in the killing of Phillip Steinkamp. He was on the run, unknown location, possibly armed. Anyone with information leading to his capture should call the Federal Bureau of Investigation at the following number. Cable news flashed a passport photo of Garrett on-screen, then spent a few minutes speculating on what this all meant. A twisted love affair? A crazed loner? Or—speculated on with more relish—a broader conspiracy?

General Kline walked into her office in the middle of the CNN broadcast and watched it with her. He shook his head slowly, muttering, "Bad, very bad," under his breath. Then, louder: "We need to get as far away from this as possible."

"They're trying to force him out of hiding," Alexis said.

"We need to start scrubbing Reilly from our records." Kline sat opposite Alexis. "Anything you want to tell me?"

Alexis considered her options. She was considerably less certain of Garrett's innocence now than she had been before seeing him—he had been erratic, strung out, and raging, but he'd also been spot-on, as usual, and she wasn't ready to turn him over to the police. Not yet. Her instincts told her to wait.

She studied General Kline, the age lines etched into his face, the streaks of gray in his hair. Was Garrett right? Was Kline burned-out, about to retire? Would he leave her in the lurch to find her own destiny at the DIA? Possibly. *No, probably.* But she still couldn't involve him. He was her boss, and her mentor; he had helped her rise through the ranks, and she would protect him for it, no matter what the future brought. And protection for Kline, at this point, meant ignorance.

"No," she said. "Nothing."

He stared at her, as if waiting for her façade to crack, then left her office without saying anything else.

Ten minutes later an e-mail showed up in her in-box from a Gmail account. The sender's name was Profiler. She read it once, briefly, then printed it out. She considered deleting the e-mail, but she knew all e-mails, deleted or otherwise, sat on government servers for what amounted to eternity. She folded up the printout, jammed it in her pocket, then walked out of the building to a small wooded area on the south end of the base. The day was warm and lovely, as opposed to her mood, which was like a battered ship crashing against the rocks. Alone, unwatched, and in the shadow of a spreading elm tree, she unfolded the printout and read it carefully.

A profile. Of what he should look like. We made assumptions and tried to match the assumptions to what we already know. Inference from facts. Then calculated probability.

- *He will be male. 99% certainty. Professional hackers almost always are. And only a pro could do what he's done so far.*
- *Young. Again, 99% sure. 20s, early 30s.*
- *Probably from Eastern Europe. 85%. Ukraine. Russia. Most non-state criminal hackers are. Attacks in Europe have seemed random, but avoided eastern countries. Ergo, that's where he's from.*
- *Will have degree from University. Math/Science. Probably Moscow. There have been a steady stream of cyberattacks from Russian technical colleges. 75%.*
- *May have worked/lived in west/US. 75% chance. Fits pattern of hackers who work here, return to native country. Maybe software development. Check Silicon Valley employment records. Chinese techs turned hackers are classic example.*

Following items skew more random. Thought you should have them anyway.

- *On surface, no connection to organized crime. He will be clean. But higher probability that deeper in his BG will be ties to criminal activity. 60%. Friends, girlfriends, parents even. Check weak ties to mafia.*
- *Will enter country on student visa. 60%. Easiest to obtain, draws little attention.*
- *Passport should be legit. Arouse less suspicion. Again, 60% chance.*
- *Travel itinerary should match attacks in Europe. Munich, Lyon, Liverpool, Malta. All in last month. He will have overseen these personally. Correlate man to his travels. 60%.*

Following are more than two standard deviations from median on Gaussian bell curve. In other words, guesses.

Alexis stopped reading for a moment and marveled at the way Garrett's mind worked. There was nothing, no bit of human behavior, that he could not reduce to a number, or a pattern. In her mind's eye, she could see him typing the e-mail, a snarl on his face, as he used probability to bolster his argument. She couldn't help but smile—he always stayed true to form. She realized now that this was why she hadn't turned him in: he was who he was, capable of some things, but not others. Not murder.

She kept reading.

- *Once in US, he will go off radar. Disappear. Use myriad stolen identities. This is his core competency. You must catch him at the border, before he goes underground.*
- *He will have a network of people in place here to help him. US citizens, probably. More efficient, less dangerous than bringing foreign nationals into US. There are plenty of black hats for sale here. He is a social engineer, con man—this is what he does best. Will find others to work for him. Probably already has.*
- *Finally—whatever he is doing has a political aspect. It is theater. For a larger cause. Find the cause, you get closer to uncovering the act. He is a hired hand. Someone else wants this done.*

That was the end of the list, but not the end of the e-mail. Garrett had typed a few last sentences. They were abbreviated and rushed, like the list, but they were pure Garrett as well.

Am not crazy. I am right. You know it. You have to move fast.

That was it. She read the list two more times, considering the numbers involved, and what it might—or might not—tell her about someone entering the United States. US Customs could not arrest every young Russian male entering the country on a student visa. They would fill up the holding cells on the East Coast within days. And even if they did spot him, what could they charge him with? Planning economic terror? It wasn't as if he would be carrying explosives or the schematics for a skyscraper. Without Garrett in front of her, without his twisted confidence, it all seemed like a paranoid theory. Tinfoil-hat stuff. And yet . . .

He *was* rarely wrong. Perhaps that in itself was enough of a thread to go on. She grimaced, slipped the printout back into her jacket, and thought about how she could alert the country's ports of entry without seeming like a crazy person herself.

"Feel better now?" Mitty asked as she drove through the Maryland country-side, rolling farms on both sides of the car. They'd already been driving for two hours, and they had many more to go, keeping off highways and sticking to less monitored back roads. "You saw your honey again, in the flesh. The two of you didn't jump into bed, but you proved that you still got it—you still got a statis-tical swinging dick—so everything's right with the world."

"I'll feel better when you stop talking." Garrett was lying on the backseat and trying to ignore the smell of old ham-and-Swiss-cheese sandwiches. "And when they find the guy."

"If he exists."

"He exists," Garrett said. "It's just a question of when he shows up."

The young man in seat 34J opened his eyes and tried to stretch his cramped legs. They'd been flying seven and a half hours since Frankfurt, and he'd only gotten up once to use the bathroom. The scent of airplane food wafted up from the galley four rows back—boiled vegetables and dried-out rosemary chicken. The drone of the engines no longer registered in his brain—it had become white noise.

He glanced at his neighbor in 34H, an overweight American named James Delacourt, passed out in his seat, his stomach spilling over his seat belt. The young man in 34J thought to himself, I am going to kill Mr. James Delacourt. Not in the physical sense, but I will kill him nonetheless—destroy him, utterly and completely.

And that process has already begun.

Delacourt lived in Bethesda, Maryland. He was flying home by way of Miami, where he was meeting a potential client. The young man in 34J had learned this by buying Delacourt a series of drinks—beers at first, then a martini, then three vodkas poured straight from the airplane minibottles into a cup—until the flight attendant, realizing how much she'd served the two of them, cut them off. But by that time it was too late; Delacourt was plastered.

The American had boasted to the young man that he could hold his liquor, but, of course, he didn't really have any sense of what holding one's liquor meant. An average Russian could drink an average American under the table, and the young man in 34J was Russian, although he now considered himself a citizen of the world—a citizen who was well practiced at alcohol consumption. In fact, he could drink most Russians under the table. He wasn't particularly proud of this ability; it was simply an asset he employed when going about his business. So James Delacourt never stood a chance.

Over the four hours of conversation they'd had, the Russian had extracted a series of crucial pieces of information from Delacourt. The young man could be charming, if needed. He could be anything. He was a chameleon—another of his abilities—able to mold the surface of his personality to match any occasion. He could laugh at a lame joke, tell a story of his own humiliation, or spin a discourse on political corruption in third-world countries; he could flirt with women and argue sports with men; he could be loud and aggressive, or wallflower passive. He could do all of this in English, with barely an accent, in his native Russian, and in passable Chechen as well.

What always surprised people about the young man was that underneath the surface of that interesting, entertaining, and changeable personality lay a vast, gray blank slate of a psyche, a psychological wasteland. A mind that had long ago inured itself to compassion . . . or caring.

But no one ever figured that out until it was far too late.

The Airbus A340 bounced in turbulence, so the young man in 34J closed his eyes and meditated on a faraway land: a sweep of forest, interspersed with rolling hills and swaths of grassland. The place was lovely, speckled with sunshine and wooden homes, a mixture of his memories of a Caucasus of long ago and the imaginary idyll of his dreams, because the real Chechnya, he knew from sporadic trips, was a savaged war zone blended with ever-evolving construction sites. Modern Chechnya was in a constant state of being simultaneously destroyed and rebuilt. It was not the place of his dreams.

Every time he returned, he marveled at how Grozny, the capital, had changed beyond recognition, at least from when he had grown up there. But he had grown up there during the worst of the worst, the first Chechen War in 1995, and the holocaust that was the Battle of Grozny. His entire neighborhood—the Zavodskoy district—had been reduced to rubble. He had fled with his parents into the countryside, waiting out the invading Russians. The irony was that his family was not Muslim, or even Chechen. They were Slavs, ethnic Russians who'd moved to Grozny when his father got a job in an oil-tools factory.

But that was the irony of the Soviet era, and of the Russian Federation that followed: It didn't matter who you were, or what you represented; the system was going to grind you to dust one way or the other. The system did not care. The young man had learned this lesson early in life and had never forgotten it—learned it through his family's poverty, his father's alcoholism, his mother's uncured depression. That was Russia. The young man took it as a guiding principle, and lately he had extended it to the larger world as well. He felt it was written, tattooed, on the inside of his skull.

You are completely on your own.

Life, to the young man in 34J, was a continuous struggle against uncaring and implacable power. That power was sometimes the state, sometimes the police, sometimes mobsters, sometimes even the God he didn't believe in. Those forces tended to blend into one—they were all trying to keep him down, push him into submission and surrender, but he would never bend to their will. Never.

The young man pulled his tablet from his flight bag and checked his notes.

Once he'd had enough to drink, Delacourt, the fat American the young man planned to destroy, couldn't stop talking about himself. The young man now knew the name of Delacourt's wife (Nancy); the names of his two children (Thomas and Sophie); their dates of birth (5/18/03 and 12/22/01); Delacourt's own birthday (that had been a surprise; the young man thought Delacourt looked considerably older than he actually was, but perhaps that was the weight); the name of their three cats (Misty, Poops, and Butter); his favorite sports team (the Redskins); the name of his elementary school (Banneker Elementary in Milford, Delaware); his mother's maiden name (McClendon— that had been hard to extract without raising suspicion, but the young man had managed it by asking about Delacourt's ethnic heritage, which had quickly led to an exchange of parental last names); and the make of his first automobile (a brown VW Rabbit, a vehicle in which he'd lost his virginity).

All in all, a good haul. With a little time and a decrypting program, the young man had enough information to crack almost any password in any of Delacourt's accounts—bank account, brokerage account, ATM card, cell phone account, office log-in, laptop log-in, even his account at the gym, if he had one, which the young man doubted. Almost nobody in this world created completely random passwords; they were too hard to remember. Most people simply reverted back to things they would never forget—birthdays, maiden names, sports teams—and stuck them into myriad online forms, thus making it essential that a good hacker learn a few core data points about his subject before cracking open his or her life.

The young man in 34J allowed himself a faint, satisfied smile. He was handsome enough, with a sharp jawline and a narrow nose. He was about five foot ten, and slim, with thick black hair that he kept short and neat. Women thought he was good-looking, but not spectacular, and that worked just fine. The young man in 34J did not like to call attention to himself; he preferred to pass unnoticed, and that's exactly what he did most of the time. His English was excellent; he had spent two years at an American high school in Colorado, and then one year at a software company in the Bay Area. He didn't hate his time in the United States, although high school had been a grind, but he didn't love the place either. The country was, for him at least, too proud and puffed up with its own importance. To his mind, Americans hadn't suffered enough in their history; they lacked emotional depth. They lacked souls.

Russia had a soul, although he had to admit it was twisted.

The young man looked down at his tablet again. Delacourt hadn't given up his Social Security number—no one ever did—but with some luck the young man could work that out quickly. He had gone to the Moscow State Technical University, majored in mathematics, and so was adept at crunching numbers—especially large numbers—and he'd long ago worked out a path to cracking American Social Security numbers.

He ran through the necessary steps in his head: Once you knew the place and date of your target's birth, figuring out the first five digits of his or her Social Security number was straightforward. The first three digits—called the area number, or AN—told you where the person had been born. If you knew the place of birth, you knew the AN. The next two—the group number, or GN—were correlated to the place and date of birth. How the Social Security Administration assigned those numbers was publicly available knowledge and easily discovered. With a little perseverance, almost anyone could figure them out.

Unlocking the last four numbers was considerably harder, and what you needed was the SSA's Death Master File, a list of every past Social Security number ever assigned, but only the numbers of people who were already dead. Again, the Death Master File wasn't hard to obtain. Once the young man had it, he'd run the Death Master File through a predictive algorithm—he'd gotten the idea from a study by professors at Carnegie Mellon University—which spit out a series of probable last four Social Security digits given the first five that you inputted.

If the state the subject was born in was a low-population state—and Delaware qualified—then the algorithm checked the Death Master File and delivered around one hundred possible SNs, or serial numbers. Those were the potential last four digits of your target's Social Security number. They were guesses, but they were close guesses.

With a hundred sets of numbers to test, the rest was easy: feed the potential numbers into a network of computers and have the network attempt registrations at websites that demanded the user's Social Security number. A Department of Motor Vehicles website, for instance, or a state utility. When the registration worked, you knew you'd cracked it. *You had the person's Social Security number.*

The entire process took five minutes, and most of that time was taken up typing in numbers. The actual answers came back in milliseconds. The young man had done this routine a few hundred times when he had been living in the States—sometimes just for fun, to see if it could be done, and other times for darker purposes. Given the inherent value in a valid Social Security number, the young man still found it remarkable that Americans could be so casual with them. He, personally, would lock his away in a safe and never expose it to anyone, or any company or any government. But then again, the young man in 34J knew exactly what bad things a bad person could do with stray Social Security numbers. He knew those bad things intimately.

He looked over at Delacourt. The American was snoring, a thin line of spittle hanging from his lips, about to drip onto his chest. The young man bent low in his seat, as if to tie his shoelaces, but instead reached into the side pocket of Delacourt's computer bag. After two attempts, he located Delacourt's cell phone—a Samsung Galaxy—and quickly popped the SIM card out of its slot. He pocketed the SIM card and then replaced the phone in the bag. Delacourt's phone wouldn't work, but he would have no idea why, and by the time he took it to the Verizon store to have it checked out, the young man would have taken over his phone account as well.

Basically, Delacourt's entire life now belonged to someone else.

The plane slowed noticeably, beginning its descent into Miami International Airport, and as the captain's voice crackled over the public address system, Delacourt jerked back to consciousness. The young man was sitting up in his seat, smiling.

"Damn," Delacourt muttered. "I passed out."

"Yeah, me too," the young man lied with an easy grin. "I guess we drank too much, huh?"

"Yeah." Delacourt blinked woozily. "You're a devil, buying me all that vodka." He looked over at the young man. "You really Russian?"

"I was born there. But I'm not sure what I am anymore."

Delacourt nodded, still trying to rouse himself from his stupor. "Yeah, that's the modern world, right? Nobody knows where they really belong anymore." Delacourt laughed. "I like you," he said, then hesitated, as if having trouble remembering the young man's name.

The young man helped him out. "Ilya."

"Ilya, right. I like you, Ilya. You're my kind of people. I think we share a lot of the same, you know, stuff." Delacourt grinned. "You know what I mean?"

The young man—Ilya, for the time being—nodded and smiled in return. "I do. I think we share a lot of the same stuff."

Alexis Truffant's cell phone rang the moment she walked back into her apartment.

"Truffant here," she said, trying to mask the exhaustion in her voice. From the moment Kline had stepped into her office with the news of the Fed president's shooting, Alexis's mind had been on overdrive, trying to make sense of what had happened—and how it connected to Garrett. Now, her brain needed a respite. She opened her fridge to reach for an open bottle of chardonnay, phone cradled between her chin and shoulder.

"This is Mac Gunderson at TSA." The voice on the other end of the line was clipped and businesslike. "I'm regional operations director for MIA."

"MIA?" Alexis asked, confused.

"Miami International Airport."

"Okay," Alexis said warily. She had only just delivered a watch bulletin to the Transportation Security Administration that afternoon, trying to carefully distill what Garrett had given her into a document that a bureaucracy such as the TSA could act on: Russian, student visa, engineer, distant mob ties. She had done it carefully, discreetly, without alerting Kline, and she hadn't expected a response this quickly. Perhaps they were trying to make sense of her person-of-interest brief. Or perhaps . . .

"You probably should fly down here ASAP," Gunderson said.

She shoved the bottle of wine back into the fridge.

• • •

Gunderson's office at Miami International was a tiny, windowless room at the north end of terminal two. Gunderson was big, with a gleaming shaved head and a salt-and-pepper goatee. His suit jacket hung on the back of his chair and his tie was loosened around his neck. Alexis thought he was probably on the last few hours of a long shift. He pulled up a US Customs mug shot on his computer.

"Ilya Markov. Traveling under a Russian passport. Landed five fourteen p.m., Lufthansa flight 462 from Frankfurt."

Gunderson tilted the computer screen so Alexis could see the photograph, a pale face against a white background. The young man looked handsome, with dark hair and genial blue eyes. His thin lips were compressed into a neutral scowl. He seemed weary—to be expected after a long flight—but his look also had a flatness. An emotionless quality. Maybe, Alexis thought, I'm just not used to seeing passenger mug shots.

"Born 1986 in Moscow, according to his passport records."

"Does he match the profile we sent in other ways?" Alexis looked for some hint of personality in the man's face, some twinkle in the corner of his eye. A sense of humor? A bit of flirtation with the camera? There was none of that.

"No. He doesn't."

"Then why am I here?"

"Because this guy does." Another photograph appeared on-screen, time-stamped December 11, 2009. The young man in the photo bore a striking resemblance to Ilya Markov. In fact, they had to be the same person.

"Ilya Markarov. Also born 1986, Moscow. Came in on an H-1B visa. Software programmer. Went to the Bay Area, worked for a year without incident. Left the country in 2011, never came back."

Gunderson tapped at his keyboard again. A page from a database appeared on-screen. Arrival and departure dates were listed in chronological order, starting three months ago and ending last week, June 12.

"He went to Germany, France, England, then Malta. In-outs. Just like you said he would. But he traveled on the Markarov passport, not the Markov." Gunderson traced his finger along the screen to highlight the entry and exit dates.

Alexis felt a knot tighten in her stomach. "How'd you make the connection?"

"Facial-identification software."

"I thought you guys didn't use it yet."

Gunderson just shrugged.

Alexis frowned, her mind immediately reviewing everything Garrett had told her earlier in the day. "What about criminal connections? That was one of the match points."

"Nope, not this guy. However"—a new photo came up on-screen—"this guy has multiple cross hits with the Vor v Zakonye. Work associates, a cousin, a roommate, briefly, in Moscow."

Alexis looked: this photo was also of the same young man, only now his head was shaved in a buzz cut, and the neutral scowl was replaced with a wide grin. He wore a white, button-down shirt and a red tie. He looked every inch the ambitious, up-and-coming young businessman. But Vor v Zakonye were the Russian mob. *Thief-in-law.*

"Marko Ilyanovich, born 1986, Grozny, Chechnya."

"Christ," Alexis muttered, staring at the photo. "This is a Russian passport photo, right? How could the Russians not track that it's the same guy?"

"Ever been to Russia?"

Alexis shook her head no.

"Spend a week there and you'll understand. Ten thousand bucks will get you anything. A passport. A wife. A murder. Nobody really cares, as long as you're not blowing up train stations in Volgograd."

"You get this with the facial-recognition software as well?"

"No. Once we had a match on two names we ran his fingerprints. His were on file with the Russian FSB. Federal Security Service. They had no direct hits on his mob ties, only cross-references. He has been associated with criminals, distantly, but isn't one himself. At least not that anyone can prove."

Alexis sat back in her chair and let out a long breath. Garrett had been spot-on about everything: young, male, Russian, student visa, a programmer, recent European itinerary—even the mafia connections panned out. And if Garrett had been correct about the young man's entering the country, then Garrett was probably also right about what the young man had planned: a systemic volatility event. *Crash the American economy.*

Alexis shivered visibly in the air-conditioned office. She had the sudden, instinctive sense that a disaster was looming out there—a chaos, all-enveloping, coming toward her, threatening to swallow her, threatening to swallow up everything. She tried to shake the idea from her brain, but it remained at the periphery of her consciousness, lurking there, raw and terrifying, like an awful storm cloud rising up over the horizon.

"I'll need to talk to him. Where are you holding him?" Alexis stood, patted down her green army jacket, and considered how she would initiate the interrogation.

"We're not." Gunderson grimaced. "Holding him, that is."

"*What?*"

"Your watch request came in at six thirty this evening." Gunderson held up a single sheet of paper. "This guy—whatever the hell his name really is—cleared Customs at five forty-five." The edges of the big man's lips turned down, as if that were as much of an apology as he could muster. "I have no idea where he is now."

On a constitutional level, Alexis knew that an administrative subpoena was a joke. It was an obvious end run around the Fourth Amendment, the guarantee against unreasonable search and seizure, a way to get what you wanted without ever having a judge look over your request. Administrative subpoenas allowed sanctioned government organizations—the Defense Intelligence Agency was one of those organizations—to ask for wiretaps and transaction tracking without a judge's orders. The press hated administrative subpoenas. Actually, Alexis hated them as well. She had always believed she was in the army not just to protect the country, but to protect its laws as well, and the Fourth Amendment to the Constitution was a pretty important brick in the pantheon of the American legal system.

But at two thirty in the morning in Miami, Florida, expediency won out. Alexis knew that was a bullshit rationale, but it would have to do. In the light of day she would try to figure out something better.

She went to her hotel room at the Hilton just outside the Miami airport, ordered coffee from room service, and drew up the proper document: one page, brief, simple, and direct. Boiled down to its essence, the subpoena said, I need you to give me your last twelve hours of credit-card transactions for the following names (and their variants) in the Greater Miami / Fort Lauderdale area, and I need them right away.

She called the DIA's connections at the four major credit-card companies—Visa, MasterCard, American Express, and Discover—and had the front desk at the hotel fax over the subpoena. The DIA was already part of the HotWatch program, in which federal agencies could ask for real-time financial tracking information on specific suspects. News of HotWatch had leaked into the press a few years ago, but no one seemed to get that upset about it. Alexis thought that was weird. She'd always assumed that if the American public knew the level of surveillance that was going on in their lives they would flip out, and they had, to a degree, especially when it came to the NSA listening in on their phone calls, but the American public only understood half of what the government did. When they figured out the rest, it would not be pretty.

She sipped her coffee and watched the sun come up over suburban Florida, a spectacular orange dawn above the palm trees and sprawl between the airport and the ocean. She ordered a breakfast of eggs and toast and wished that she had packed a change of clothes. At 7:30 a.m., she called the Dade County offices of the FBI and told them what she was doing and requested help. They were skeptical, but said they might be able to lend her one agent, maybe two, at some point during the day.

She turned on the room TV, watched the morning news talk shows, and waited for the credit-card companies to reply. The person-of-interest APB for Garrett was still a topic of intense discussion—all four networks led with his picture and followed up with theories on why he wanted to kill a Fed president. Alexis listened intently for a while, but when one commentator mentioned a possible homosexual love triangle, she shut off the TV in disgust.

MasterCard e-mailed first, at 8:00 a.m., with nothing. Visa and Discover replied twenty minutes later. No one by any of those names—Ilya Markov, Ilya Markarov, or Marko Ilyanovich—had used his credit card in the Miami area in the last twelve hours. Then, at 9:14 a.m., American Express reported a single transaction: Markov, Ilya, June 15, 8:23 p.m., Motel 6, Marina Mile Boulevard, Fort Lauderdale, Florida.

Sixty seconds later, Captain Alexis Truffant was sprinting across the hotel parking lot, cursing herself for not bringing a weapon as well as a change of clothes.

G arrett waited until they were deep into the Walnut Hill neighborhood of west Philly before slotting the battery back into his phone. He and Mitty had slept in the back of the Ford Explorer—or at least tried to sleep—parked on a dirt road outside Lancaster, Pennsylvania. The night had been long and uncomfortable, but Garrett figured it was better than getting arrested. Or maybe not. Maybe getting arrested was better. He was exhausted from being on the run and, from his point of view, being on the run for no good reason. He'd bolted from his offices at Jenkins & Altshuler out of fear and panic, but now, forty-eight hours after doing so, he needed to reconsider.

He was innocent, and people—the FBI in particular—needed to understand that. Also, and this he kept completely to himself—because Mitty could not see or hear a word of it—his hands had begun to tremble. Garrett suspected that was a symptom of withdrawal. He was a goddamned addict, just like some scumbag meth head wandering the South Bronx. Worse still, his brain was cycling through periods of quiet, and then frenzied, chaotic explosions of pain. He'd almost blacked out yesterday in the motel room. Sticking his face under the shower was the only thing that had kept him conscious.

He had a handful of meds left in a plastic bag, and they were burning a hole in his pocket, but he tried to push that from his mind. He wanted narcotics more than he'd wanted almost anything else in his entire life, and a voice in his head was whispering that no matter how much he tried to rationalize that desire—it was his head pain, it was his grief—the truth was that Garrett liked being high and always had. Drugs separated him from the real world; they gave him distance from his troubles, and right now he was in a world of trouble.

He dialed the central switchboard at his office and asked for Maria Dunlap, the office manager, on the twenty-fourth floor. He waited as she was connected, watching the Philadelphia row houses that lined Market Street. Kids were hanging out on the corners in the early-morning heat. A cluster of young boys smoked cigarettes on the stoop of a liquor mart. A few college students, in Bermuda shorts and flip-flops, were making their way east, toward Penn.

"This is Maria," chirped the voice on the other end of the line. Garrett didn't know Dunlap particularly well, but he wasn't crazy about her nonetheless. She was middle-aged and officious, always checking his hours worked—as if the time he spent in front of his Bloomberg terminal had anything to do with how much money he made the firm.

"Maria, Garrett Reilly here." He heard a sharp intake of breath.

"Garrett, oh, hey, where have you been?" Dunlap asked with a forced casualness.

"Let's skip the bullshit. You tell the FBI guys who are listening on the line that I need to talk to them."

"Garrett, I don't know what you're—"

"I'm going to hang up in about a minute. I really can't have them tracking me."

A brief silence settled over the phone line. Garrett sank low in the backseat of the Explorer, but he could still see the street around him. They passed an old, brick public library. A mom pushed a carriage up the access ramp.

A quick beep sounded on his cell phone. "Hello, Garrett, this is Special Agent Chaudry."

"Look, I'll just tell you up front that I'm in Philadelphia, but I'm going to hang up and pull the cell battery pretty fast, so please don't bother sending a million cop cars all running around with their sirens blaring." The Explorer Mitty was driving belonged to a friend of a distant cousin in the Rodriguez family, an accountant from Tampa. Some law enforcement agency somewhere might make the connection between the SUV and Mitty, and then Garrett, but he was pretty sure they couldn't do it in real time, on the fly. Not on the streets of Walnut Hill.

"Okay, Garrett, how about this? How about you just walk into one of the police precincts there, turn yourself in, and we have this conversation face-to-face?" Her voice had a pleasing, mellifluous quality.

"Chaudry? You're Indian? And a woman? In the FBI. That's gotta be rare. You sound young too."

"A good reason for us to meet each other in person. You could see how young I really am."

Garrett laughed. He liked her already. "When I look you up online in five minutes, I'll know exactly how young or old you are. And where you were born, your grades in high school, and what you bought last weekend at the mall. I've never dated an Indian girl before. You single?"

"Is that why you called? To ask me out?"

"I had nothing to do with the shooting of Phillip Steinkamp. I have nothing against the Fed, and I've never met Steinkamp. I'm a frigging bond trader."

"If you are so innocent, why did you run from your office before our agents could question you?"

"I have a deep-seated suspicion of law enforcement, with multiple bad experiences with people in authority, and a pathological hatred of government power."

"But you worked for the Defense Department, the ultimate in government power. Something called the Ascendant program. That seems like a contradiction."

"I'm complicated."

"Tell me about Ascendant," Chaudry said.

"No. Find out for yourself. Look, here's what I know. Steinkamp's murder is part of a pattern. A pattern of economic destabilization. Someone is aiming to attack the American economy. They want me out of the way, so they're trying to blame me for the killing."

"And who is behind it, Garrett?"

"I don't know. I'm out here on my own. But you better believe I'm trying to find out. Who shoots someone and then tells the world who made them do it? Makes no sense, Agent Chaudry, and you know it as well as I do. "

"Good point. But I still need you to come in to one of our field offices and make a statement. We'll treat you right. VIP, all the way. Just answer some questions. You and I can start a relationship."

Again, Garrett laughed. Chaudry was his kind of FBI agent. "With you?

Awesome. But if we go out on a date, it'll have to be your treat, because I'll be in handcuffs, stripped of all constitutional rights."

This time Chaudry laughed. In the sudden silence on the line, Garrett could hear police sirens in the distance. Growing louder.

"Aw, you sent the cops, and I told you not to. Way to make a bad first impression. I'm going to go now, but I just want to say, for the record—I didn't know the woman who killed Steinkamp. Never met her. Never met Steinkamp, or anyone who works at the Fed. I had nothing to do with any of it. And if you're smart, you'll begin to understand that something much larger is happening. You're hunting for the wrong person. And when the shit starts flying, you'll understand why."

Garrett didn't wait for a response. He hit end on his cell phone, then quickly popped the battery out of the back. Mitty chuckled as she drove. "She really say she wanted to date you? An FBI agent?"

"I have animal magnetism."

"I bet guy FBI agents are hot," Mitty said with a wistful sigh. "With the guns and the suits. If I robbed a bank, you think they'd strip-search me?"

"Turn left here. The street's going to be swarming with cops in a minute." With that, Garrett lay down in the back of the Explorer and waited until they got out of Philadelphia.

At the FBI field office on the twenty-third floor of the Federal Building in lower Manhattan, Agent Chaudry pulled the headset from her ears and let out a long, angry breath.

"Philly PD are going to cut off the arterial streets," an older agent—Murray, a transfer from DC—said, hanging up a phone.

"He knows that. They're not going to catch him."

Murray parked himself at a desk. "So why'd he call?"

Chaudry thought about this. Why did he call? To figure out who was heading up the case on the federal side? What difference would that make? No, there had to be a reason.

"Maybe he's just an arrogant idiot," Murray said. "He kinda sounded like one."

Chaudry walked to the window and looked out over lower Manhattan. Yes, Garrett Reilly was arrogant. And he appeared to have reasons to be so. He was also careful, yet he exposed himself to call the FBI. That contradiction demanded examination. But he was no idiot.

"Paul"—she nodded to Special Agent Murray—"will you play the call back for me?" Even though Murray was considerably older than she was, Chaudry knew he had to do as she asked. She was lead on the case, and he was, at least for the moment, her junior partner. She knew it infuriated a lot of the older men in the Manhattan field office, but so be it. She had few friends in the Bureau and wasn't particularly interested in accumulating more. Omelets required cracked eggs.

Agent Murray put the recording of the call on a speaker in the communications room. Chaudry listened to it twice, then backed it up one last time, starting in the middle of the conversation. Then it hit her. She played the sentence again.

"And who is behind it, Garrett?" Chaudry asked on the recording.

"I don't know. I'm out here on my own. But you better believe I'm trying to find out."

Chaudry smiled. "That's it."

Murray looked up from his computer. "That's what?"

"He says he's out there on his own. And he's going to figure it out. He's signaling us. That the DIA's not behind him. They're leaving him out in the cold. He's making us an offer."

"An offer to what?"

"Solve the case," she said with conviction, the thought now crystallized in her mind. "He wants to work for us."

The young man whose passport read Ilya Markov was genuinely surprised when he saw the two unmarked cars pull into the parking lot of the motel he'd stayed in the night before. A young woman in an army uniform had climbed out of the first car, and two bulky men in suits had gotten out of the follow vehicle. The men were most probably FBI, the young man thought, or perhaps Homeland Security. They made no effort to conceal themselves—they just swaggered into the lobby.

The young man sipped his coffee and carefully unwrapped the wax paper covering his barbecue breakfast sandwich. The smell of freshly baked rolls and bacon fat mixed with the scent of coffee as he sat in the window seat of the restaurant across the street from his motel. L'il Red's BBQ was the name, and he had to admit that the food was delicious. Americans could do some things right, better than almost anyone else, and breakfast was one of them.

He peeked at the motel again. No need to rush. They wouldn't come over here, he thought. But still, best perhaps not to take chances. He took a few bites from the sandwich, snapped the cover back onto his coffee, grabbed the backpack at his feet, and headed out to Marina Mile Boulevard.

The young man—and most people who knew him called him Ilya, because that was, in fact, his real first name, although he often used Ilia, Elie, Elijah, Marko (because of his last name), and sometimes, when in the Islamic parts of the Caucasus, Ali—hadn't expected to be discovered quite so quickly. He had figured on a week of walking around in the open, using his Russian passport and name, before the American authorities caught on. When they did catch on, he was prepared to discard that identity and go underground. He had planned for this eventuality. But not quite so fast.

No matter. He would simply advance the timetable of his identity switch. That was easy. And would remain easy. Everyday citizens had yet to catch up with the realities of modern information theft.

Still, he thought as he hitched his backpack over his shoulder and headed north on Marina Mile, tapping out a text on his newly acquired cell phone as he walked, somebody out there was paying attention. More than paying attention—someone had figured out that he was a threat and had done so from a minimum of clues.

That was impressive.

He reviewed in his mind what information they could have gleaned from the passport he presented at US Customs. Had they linked it to another of his passports? Or visa applications? If so, they were ahead of the game, and he would have to consider what changes to make in his itinerary. From his calculations they would be able to identify him as twenty-eight; a software engineer with American high school and work experience; from Grozny, Chechnya; and a graduate of a Russian technical university.

Other than that, he couldn't think of anything particular that they knew about him. Who his parents were, perhaps, not that it mattered. His father was dead, dragged off in the middle of the night by Chechen rebels, never to be seen again, and Ilya did not grieve the loss. His father had been a drunk, abusive, and rarely at home. When he had been at home, Ilya had come to loathe him. Ilya's mother was still alive, but she was a pensioner living in a retirement home in Tolyatti, in central Russia—a truly godforsaken bit of the motherland—and knew next to nothing about her son's whereabouts or profession, and Ilya preferred it that way. He had long ago given up on any relationship with his biological family. And anyway, her last name bore no resemblance to his, and he doubted she was listed on many official documents. The war in Chechnya had made a mockery of accurate record keeping. That was one of the main reasons he had so many passports, and they were each, in their way, perfectly legitimate. Ilya was all of those people listed on his various documents: Markov, Markarov, Ilyanovich. And also none of them. Everyman and ghost at the same time.

He was nobody and he was everybody.

Ilya glanced at his watch and scanned the cars blasting down the avenue. Traffic was picking up. He shot a look over his shoulder back at the Motel 6. The army woman would be knocking on his door right about now. He hadn't checked out; he'd simply left and figured the credit card would be charged. That reminded him. He pulled the offending American Express card out of his wallet and dropped it in a garbage can. The card was useless to him now. Worse than useless—dangerous.

Once the army woman busted down the hotel room door, they would find next to nothing inside. A roller bag he'd bought in Moscow, with some pants, T-shirts, and underwear, a dog-eared copy of *Cryptonomicon*. Nothing he couldn't replace in the States, but he would miss the Stephenson novel. The book was dense, and complicated, and its plot gave Ilya's mind a place of refuge and calm.

All his technology and cash—just under $1,000—and all his documents were on his shoulder now, in his backpack. That never left his sight. They were his tools of the trade, his weapons. He supposed they could pull his fingerprints from the hotel room desk and bathroom, but what good would that do them? He'd already given his fingerprints at passport control at the airport.

So what else could they know? As far as he could tell, nothing. Ilya had made it his life's work to remain nearly invisible, keeping his name off documents, keeping his money in accounts spread across multiple countries, paying cash when possible, changing identities randomly and as the mood struck him. The ability to blend in was part and parcel of who he was, and it was integral to how he made a living. But that in itself begged the larger question—how had they spotted him so fast? And who was responsible?

He doubted very much that standard FBI alerts could have been triggered by his arrival. That had never happened before, and he had been in and out of the country four times in the last ten years. Homeland Security might have caught on, but that seemed like a stretch, given their mediocre record of identifying potential terrorist threats. They looked for ties to terror groups, and he had none. He hadn't done anything wrong. At least, he'd never been caught at it. He was completely clean.

No, the person who figured out that Ilya was a person of interest was smart. And sophisticated. The person must have guessed at the existence of someone *like* Ilya, then stood by and watched until a real Ilya showed up. They were using a forecasting algorithm, a data sweep that allowed them to guess at the statistical chances someone matching his background would show up.

But why had they been looking for someone like him in the first place? How did they know an action was planned? This troubled him. Had he been sloppy? He had put out Web feelers for potential associates; he'd offered some cash on the darknet, had made calls to people who trafficked in hacking, but he'd been careful. Perhaps they'd tied him to the cyberattacks in Europe? But how? The money that paid for those hacks came from a fund that he had absolutely nothing to do with. Instead, he had to keep himself afloat with the bits and pieces of cash that wound their way to him through painfully obscure sources: safe-deposit boxes at rural German banks, handouts at a corrupt Greek government office, falsified refund receipts at an electronics store in southern France.

Maybe they'd been alerted by the shooting in New York? But endless intermediaries were between himself and the shooter, Bachev, innumerable layers of obfuscation and misdirection. That would have been either a lucky guess or a phenomenal bit of pattern recognition.

He paused on the sidewalk and breathed deep of the humid Florida air. Being here was like living in a sauna. A sauna mixed with car fumes and barbecue sauce. Perhaps it wasn't such a bad thing to have lost his clothing; he could buy shorts and Hawaiian shirts. Maybe even a pair of flip-flops.

Patterns. A predictive algorithm would explain why a pair of suited agents and an army officer had descended on the Motel 6, and not a SWAT team. They had no reason to arrest him and had no idea if he was dangerous. Legally, they probably couldn't arrest him. They were anticipating events, trying to scare him off. Or simply letting him know they were watching.

Well, he knew that now, for certain.

Ilya suspected he knew who was behind this. Like every other hacker in the worldwide underground, Ilya had followed the exploits of the Ascendant program, how it had attacked China so cleverly, knocking the Golden Shield out of commission, poisoning the Shanghai stock exchange, inciting riots in Chinese cities. He wasn't sure how big it was, or how well funded, but he shared the view of most other hackers that Ascendant was a stroke of brilliance, a modern tool for fighting modern wars, and a dangerous arm of the American government.

Ilya had also come to believe that he had discovered, on his own, through countless hours of digging, the person at the heart of Ascendant. A young Wall

Street bond trader, a math geek with a penchant for seeing patterns with only the faintest of clues. That would match up with how quickly Ilya had been found out. Yet, Ilya had been all but certain that the young bond trader had been neutralized. The Steinkamp killing should have done the trick . . . but perhaps that had been a clumsier attempt than Ilya had originally thought. Perhaps the young Wall Street hotshot was still in the game.

"Garrett Reilly."

Ilya whispered the name quietly to himself, an echo of respect in the saying of it. He knew quite a bit about the man—his education, his work history—and Ilya had to admit to a trace of jealousy over Reilly's talents. Maybe that jealousy had colored his estimation of Reilly's abilities. Ilya had been thinking about Reilly a lot lately. Ilya knew this was strange, but he felt close to Reilly. Intellectually close. Emotionally close.

And now, perhaps Reilly had turned his sights on Ilya. If this was true, Reilly would be a formidable obstacle. Reilly would make Ilya's task that much harder.

Well, that's okay, he thought, as a white Honda—his ride, at last—slowed down on Marina Mile Boulevard to pick him up. If Garrett Reilly is going to come after me . . .

I can go after Garrett Reilly as well.

One of the benefits of working at a Wall Street brokerage house was that the company had investments, of all sorts, all across the United States. Jenkins & Altshuler was no exception. The firm had put money into shipping companies, clothing manufacturers, railroads, and real estate. Lots and lots of real estate.

Garrett knew every corner of the brokerage's real estate portfolio. He knew which investments were paying off, and which were circling the drain. One of J&A's worst performers was a still-unfinished office tower just off Raymond Boulevard in downtown Newark. The developer had filed for bankruptcy six months ago; the place was half-empty, with intermittent air-conditioning and plastic tarps over the windows of an unbuilt seventeenth floor. Most importantly for Garrett, it had an unguarded lobby.

Mitty dropped Garrett a block from the office building, then drove herself back to Queens. Garrett told her she'd probably be under surveillance the moment she showed up at her apartment, and she should act accordingly: go about her life as if nothing extraordinary had happened, wait for Garrett to contact her, and, if arrested, demand a lawyer and then shut up.

Garrett walked unnoticed into the lobby of the Newark office tower just before five, when he knew the security firm came through and locked the front doors. He took the elevator to the sixteenth floor, then walked down, floor by floor, checking each office for an unlocked door. He found three that were both unlocked and unoccupied and chose a corner suite on the seventh floor, partially because it was at the end of a hallway, but also because it shared a utility closet with an IT start-up. Garrett figured he could hack into their Internet connection, and he did. Easily.

He sat himself in a corner room of the empty, white-walled office suites, with his laptop, a can of tuna fish, and a Diet Coke. The first thing he did was pop a pair of Percocet. He hadn't been alone for two days, and this was his chance to regain equilibrium. He had half a dozen pills left, so next he hunted online for refills from local Craigslist offerings. A few people claimed to have black-market drugs for sale, but they all wanted bitcoins up front, and no way was Garrett going to risk paying digitally and alerting the police. He would have to start rationing his meds, but that might become difficult. His thoughts were growing more disordered, and that troubled him even more than the tendrils of pain that were snaking out across his brain. He tried soothing himself with a mantra: logic, facts, patterns. Keep the chaos at bay.

"A to B to C," he said quietly. "A to B to goddamned C."

He checked the news. The market was down again, another three hundred points, and rumors about teetering banks and shaky money-market funds were mushrooming. He did a Google query on his own name, and the search engine came back with more than seventeen million hits in under half a second. Garrett Reilly was all over the Web.

"Son of a fucking bitch," he said to himself.

Garrett sampled a few of the stories, even though he knew he shouldn't. They were all over the place in terms of their accuracy and the wildness of their conspiracy theories. One article said that he was planning on robbing the Federal Reserve; another posited that he was Anna Bachev's secret husband; a news blog said he'd been to Afghanistan, converted to Islam, and was now radicalized and trying to overthrow the government. The blog also mentioned his brother, Brandon Reilly, writing that he'd been a marine killed in action, and that Garrett's rage at the United States had led him to convert. Garrett had to give the blog writer credit—it was at least half-true. He quit reading after that, but not before looking up the DNS host server of the site that mentioned his brother, finding an open port on their system, and launching a denial-of-service attack against them.

"Suck on that, asshole," he said as he hit send on his Low Orbit Ion Cannon program. The Ion Cannon would send ten thousand queries to the blog's server in the next few seconds, and another fifty thousand soon after that, with more to come. The site would crash in minutes. He knew it was childish, but it made him feel better, and while he felt he had matured some over the last year, he hadn't matured that much.

Next, he logged on to his various e-mail accounts, always through an anonymous darknet router so he wouldn't be pinged. Special Agent Chaudry had sent a short note to his J&A e-mail, thanking him for the call and promising to be in touch soon. Garrett thought that was cute, but didn't respond. She seemed smart, and on the ball, but she could wait a while. Hell, she could wait forever. He needed an update from Alexis, and he got it a few minutes later, when he checked the account he reserved for Ascendant communications.

The e-mail read simply, *He's real. He's in the States. We missed him.*

She flew into Newark Airport, rented a car, and met him in Riverbank Park, a playfield and grass park that stretched along half a mile of the muddy Passaic River. The park was mostly empty when they met, at eight thirty that night. A cop patrolled the pathway that meandered along the river, but he paid them no particular attention. He seemed more interested in a half dozen teenagers horsing around on a swing set.

"Matched all your criteria," Alexis said, sliding a pair of printouts across a concrete picnic table near a softball diamond. "He landed last night."

Garrett stared at Alexis. She was in civilian clothes—jeans and a plaid shirt, her hair down around her shoulders—and even in the fading evening light Garrett still thought she was beautiful: high cheekbones, blue eyes, olive skin, and long, elegant fingers. Yet, now that he was seeing her again and had spent an hour in her apartment the day before, reliving old memories, he found his attraction to her muted. Why had he been so crazy about her? He was no longer sure. They were such opposites. Perhaps, he told himself, he just wanted a friend. He had so precious few left.

He separated the two pieces of paper, read the first, then the second. They contained two color passport photos and a few lines of information, and nothing else.

"Ilya Markov? That his real name?"

"One of many."

"And that's all we know?"

"So far," Alexis said. "That's his entire known profile."

"He went to the Moscow State Technical University. They must have records."

"I'm working on that. The provost there is not being particularly helpful."

"The Russian government told him not to be."

"Possibly."

"Friends, coworkers in the Bay Area?"

"I made a few calls. So far, very little. Unremarkable guy, smart, kept to himself."

"English skills?"

"Fluent. No one can remember an accent."

Alexis dropped a thick paperback on the table. "We found this in his room. Along with some clothes. Nothing else."

Garrett thumbed through the copy of *Cryptonomicon*. He read the blurbs on the back cover. The book seemed to be about hacking and code breaking. It was a book Garrett would have read himself, which gave him pause.

"Could you be wrong?" Alexis asked. "Could this all just be coincidence?"

"Sure. He could be another Russian student wandering the States, looking to get laid. But I don't think so. And the fact that he fled his motel room after you guys showed up doesn't put him in a particularly positive light."

"Maybe he was looking to overstay his visa. He wants to live in the States. When he saw us, he panicked."

"You don't want it to be true."

"No. I don't. I mean—" Alexis hesitated. She seemed to gather herself, watching Garrett all the while. The suspicion in her look was gone. Garrett sensed that she'd stepped over some kind of line in her head: she believed him now; she was on board. "What is he planning, Garrett? If you have some sense, you need to tell me."

Garrett considered this for a moment, then said, "I want you to meet someone."

She drove the two of them into Manhattan by way of the Holland Tunnel, hoping that the blackness of the night and a rolled-up window would make it hard for anyone to recognize Garrett's face. They found street parking on Columbus Avenue, near Ninety-Fourth Street, then walked to a small brownstone just west of Central Park. Garrett rang the doorbell, and after about a minute the door opened and a frail-looking woman in her seventies appeared. She wore a light-blue, quilted nightgown and a pair of librarian's glasses on the bridge of her nose. She was tiny, considerably less than five feet tall, but Alexis immediately had the impression that this woman had once been a force of nature and perhaps still was.

"Hello, Garrett." She smiled warmly.

"Professor Wolinski." Garrett's voice had a tone of respect and humility that Alexis wasn't sure she'd ever heard before. "I'm sorry to show up so late."

"I saw your picture on the news." The woman had a thick Eastern European accent. Polish, Alexis decided. "And all hell is breaking loose in the markets."

"I didn't do it," he said.

She looked at him long and hard with her tight, flinty eyes, then nodded, and opened the door wide. "Of course you didn't. But you'd better not stand on the street, regardless."

She ushered the two of them into a dark living room, then drew the blinds and turned on a light. The walls were lined with books, thousands of them, textbooks and novels in a scramble of languages, stacked from floor to ceiling, like what Alexis imagined a turn-of-the-century Parisian literary salon would look like.

"Professor Wolinski, this is Alexis Truffant. She's an officer in the US Army. And a member of the team I worked for."

"Ah, yes, the Ascendant project." Wolinski looked Alexis up and down. "Avery Bernstein told me all about it. Secrets and spies and the military. So, a forward question, if you don't mind my asking: Did your people kill Avery?"

Alexis blinked in surprise. "No, ma'am, we had absolutely nothing to do with that. It was a tragedy."

"It was," Wolinski said slowly. "I loved Avery very much."

Garrett stepped between them. "Alexis, this is Professor Agata Meyer-Wolinski, dean of the economics department, Columbia University. Wrote the definitive multidimensional scaling algorithm for currency-rate fluctuations. Short-listed for the Nobel in economics. Hasn't won it. *Yet.*"

Wolinski smiled wryly. "Ah, flattery. You know that you were Avery's favorite pupil"—Alexis saw Garrett smile—"and least favorite employee."

Alexis laughed. Even though Wolinski had challenged Alexis, Alexis liked her. Wolinski had opinions, but also compassion. She was sly, and not beyond pushing people's buttons, or challenging authority. Alexis could see why Wolinski and Garrett had an affinity for each other.

Wolinski folded herself into a dark-red armchair with faded upholstery. "But that is not why you are here. With a representative of the US military. And the FBI on your trail. What do you need from this old woman, Mr. Reilly?"

Garrett scanned the room, as if contemplating what it was, exactly, that he wanted from Wolinski. "We've been tracking global events. There've been connections. A little tenuous, but . . ." He stuttered for a moment, but then gathered himself and started again. "Could a determined terrorist explode the American financial system?"

Wolinski seemed unsurprised by the question. She issued a low grunt, more curious than concerned, then shook her head back and forth a few times, as if considering the issue. She turned to Garrett. "Would you get me a glass of wine? There is a bottle of red on my kitchen counter."

Garrett nodded and left the living room. Wolinski polished her glasses, put them back on the bridge of her nose, and studied Alexis. "Are you a couple?"

"No, ma'am."

"But you were once," Wolinski said without hesitation.

Alexis didn't answer. She just watched Wolinski in the darkness.

"He's a good boy." The professor bit gently at her lower lip. "But he is dangerous, certainly. He owns a cornucopia of faults. That might impede a relationship, I suppose."

Alexis wanted to say, *No shit,* but thought better of it.

Garrett returned with a glass of red wine and handed it to Wolinski.

"Thank you." She sipped the wine. "Please, take a seat."

Alexis and Garrett sat on a couch opposite the professor.

"This terrorism. It is coming now?" Wolinski asked.

"I think so," Garrett said.

"You know why?"

"No."

"It would help to know why."

"We'd be guessing."

Wolinski thought about this, nodding her head slowly. Alexis could see the old woman's eyes dancing back and forth in the darkness, as if taking on the mental challenge of the question.

"We need to know if the threat is real, Professor," Alexis said. "In your opinion, could it actually happen?"

Wolinski sat up slightly in the chair and looked at Alexis, locking in her gaze.

"In 2005 there were two billion connected devices," Wolinski started in a slow, steady tone, as if talking to a roomful of undergraduates. "In 2010 that number had tripled. Next year, there will be sixteen billion connected devices in this world. We create two point five quintillion bytes of data every day. That is information that gets sent around the world in milliseconds. This is a good thing. A blessing. It represents openness and truth. It represents an increase in global learning and education. When I was a young girl in Warsaw, if a neighbor had a library of a hundred books, he or she was considered wealthy and learned. Today my granddaughter stores a thousand books on her cell phone. For an old woman like me this is a miracle. For my granddaughter it is ordinary."

Alexis smiled, but remained quiet. Wolinski had a certainty, a clarity. She seemed to know, not guess.

"Garrett's mentor, Avery Bernstein, made his fortune through the trafficking of data. He used it to buy and sell stocks and bonds to his—and his clients'—advantage. Information came to him in moments, and he passed it on moments later. In the intervening seconds he bought low and sold high. For Avery, another blessing. But he saw what happens when that information becomes dangerous. When a small trickle of information becomes a flood of data, real or imagined, and overwhelms our ability to sort truth from fiction. This is a real phenomenon."

"Asset bubbles. Flash crashes. Panics," Alexis said.

"Exactly."

Alexis looked over to Garrett, who was staring right back at her. She realized that he'd been gauging her reaction. She guessed Garrett knew exactly what Wolinski was going to say, and that the entire interview was for Alexis's benefit.

"Because of interconnectivity, financial turmoil can spread across the globe in seconds," Wolinski continued. "And every financial institution is linked, in some way or another, to every other institution. Banks trade with banks, which trade with hedge funds, which take out insurance policies against those banks, which bet on the debt of corporations, which store their money at that first set of banks. And all of them get lines of credit from each other. The CEOs of all of these entities believe they are cleverly spreading the risks of financial meltdown among many companies, thus limiting their own exposure. If I sell a little bit of risk to many parties, then I am shrinking the overall risk to the national or global economy."

"But you think the opposite is true," Alexis said.

Wolinski nodded. "What if, by spreading little bits of risk throughout the system, you are actually *increasing* the chances of complete economic Armageddon? What if risk works not like a wildfire, where containment is key, and small amounts of fire are actually beneficial to a forest ecosystem, but more like a flu? Like a virus? Where even the smallest exposure sickens the entire host. And potentially kills it.

"The global economy is not healthy right now. Government debt is high. Bank exposure to exotic investment instruments is murky, and their capital requirements are too low. And civil unease is growing across the planet. The worldwide system is not prepared for a true shock. A small virus, a less-than-lethal flu, can kill a patient with a compromised immune system. To my mind, our system is dangerously compromised.

"So much right now in the modern economy is predicated on real-time events. 'Just in time' manufacturing at factories and plants requires no lag time between the arrival of raw materials and their assembly into finished products. But that lack of lag time requires ready cash—or in the case of large companies, credit. And credit requires healthy banks and a credit system functioning at the top of its game. Easy credit, fast credit. Supermarkets also require this, getting their produce and meats exactly when they need them, and not a moment sooner. They also require the fast flow of credit.

"When credit stops, work stops. Production stops. Food stops. And as a British member of Parliament once famously said, 'Every city on the planet is a mere nine meals away from anarchy.' We miss one meal and we become cranky. Two and we are hungry. *But nine?*"

Garrett spoke, taking up Wolinski's narrative. "If a big bank—a really big bank, goes bad, from who knows what, bad debts, exposure to bad debts, losses, or incompetence—then investors would run for the hills. But because all the big banks are so closely linked, the process of fleeing one bank would have the opposite effect."

"Garrett is right," Wolinski said. "Instead of protecting those fleeing the institution from risk, it would actually bring the risk back on themselves. We are all in a vast theater together. If someone yells fire, you cannot save yourself by fleeing. By fleeing, you bring the fire to the rest of the world."

A chill ran down Alexis's spine. She realized she'd been holding her breath. She exhaled. "And if that were to happen?"

"Supply chains would collapse. Credit freezes, companies cannot pay their workers. Food and water would not be delivered. Electricity and gas would be shut down. Transportation would stop. ATM machines would run dry. You would be limited to the cash you have on hand. A cascading chain of failure that could race around the country—or the globe—in a matter of days. In some cases, hours. Think about that, Ms. Truffant. No power, no lights, no cash, no food in stores, no water from your tap. The entire enterprise comes to a sudden, grinding halt."

Wolinski stopped for a moment. Alexis could hear a clock ticking in the hallway. Wolinski took a last sip of her wine, draining the glass.

"You may not want to hear this, Ms. Truffant, but we live in an economic house of cards. The dollars you have in your purse have value, of course, but they only retain that value as long as you believe in them. As long as everyone using those dollars believes in them. The moment you lose faith in your money, then it is simply a piece of paper, and nothing more."

Alexis's mouth went dry. She wanted a sip of the professor's red wine. No, she wanted the entire bottle.

"It would not be easy," Wolinski said. "And it would require great cunning. But the answer is, yes, an economic terrorist could destroy the global economy. They could send us all back to the barter system. Back to the Middle Ages."

Alexis sat in the front seat of the rental car, Garrett at her side, as they drove south down Columbus Avenue. She stared out the windshield at the city's somber, gloomy darkness. She tried to imagine what Professor Wolinski had described.

Supermarkets shuttered. Lights out. No water running. The city's rapid descent into chaos. People would march in the streets. Or worse, tear the streets apart. Tear each other apart. Was this government—or any government—prepared to deal with that? It would be like Hurricane Katrina, but on a massive scale. The veneer of civilization suddenly seemed like just that—a veneer, a thin layer of rules and social niceties that held our baser motives in check. But could it really be that easy to push everything over the edge?

Perhaps it was already happening. Perhaps it was too late.

"I'll get you whatever you need," she said, as the nighttime city flashed past her window.

"The Ascendant team. We'll need them."

"It can be done."

"What about Kline? How will you explain it to him?"

"I told him I was tracking down reporting errors in intelligence collating. Why I went to Miami. And here. I bought myself a day. Maybe two."

"And after that?"

Alexis drove in silence for a moment. "I may have to go around him."

Alexis could feel Garrett's gaze turn to her, in what she could only assume was amazement. Was she really going to go out on that particular limb, on what was, at least at the moment, speculative information? Deceive her boss and risk discharge, or worse?

Alexis could barely believe the words had come out of her mouth, but they had. She looked over at Garrett in the passenger seat. "So?"

"I'm in." Garrett's mouth creased into a wry smile. "Let the hunt begin."

PART 2

PART 2

Gennady Bazanov sniffed at the thick morning air. Wisps of smoke drifted over Svyardlova Street in central Minsk, the scent of burning tires mixing with the reek of old garbage. Bazanov could even detect a whiff of gunpowder. They were the smells of disobedience, and Bazanov knew them well. He knew them from Kazakhstan, Moldova, from Ossetia in north Georgia, and most recently from Ukraine—places full of restless citizens, who thought they wanted democracy, unfettered capitalism, and freedom. But they were wrong; what they wanted was an illusion, a momentary madness, and Bazanov's job was to help make sure they understood that.

Nagi Ulyanin, a young Belarusian State Security officer, jogged to Bazanov's side as he walked north toward Independence Square.

"*My ih skoro perevezem, polkovnik,*" Ulyanin said nervously in Russian, a sign of respect to Bazanov's authority. Ulyanin wouldn't dare speak the Belarusian language to his superior. *We will move them soon, Colonel.*

"*Vozmozhno,*" Bazanov answered. *Perhaps.* Or perhaps not, Bazanov thought to himself. Perhaps it will all go to shit. Because that is what usually happens.

Bazanov saw the State Security officer shudder involuntarily. He was afraid of Bazanov, and that was the way Bazanov liked it. People should fear him. They should fear the consequences of disobedience. Even at fifty years old, Bazanov cut a menacing figure: compact and muscled, like the welterweight boxer he had once been, he kept his head shaved smooth and his dark suits perfectly pressed. Bazanov was a fixer, a colonel in the S Directorate of the SVR, the Russian foreign intelligence service, successor to the dreaded KGB. He moved from country to country, always in the old Soviet sphere of influence, making sure that the people who ran those countries made the right decisions: that they stayed loyal to Mother Russia, and the SVR in turn, and that their elections—if you could call them elections—went according to plan.

And lately, he had become a busy man. *Too busy.* From Bazanov's point of view, the world had gone completely to shit. Completely. To. Shit.

Ulyanin checked his watch and looked back down the broad boulevard. The streets were empty, and the shops were all closed, many boarded up, a few with broken windows and burnt awnings. The violence in Belarus had been devastating. Minsk had shut down. The country's economy had come to a standstill and was on the verge of ruin.

How had this happened? Simple, to Bazanov's way of thinking. A portion of the Belarusian populace—dreamers and miscreants, Bazanov would say—had voted for the opposition candidate in the national elections two months ago. Forty-seven percent, enough to force a runoff election. She was a woman, the opposition candidate, young and pretty but completely unprepared for leadership, running on a platform of closer ties to the European Union, NATO, and the United States.

But did she really think Russia would allow that to happen? After Ukraine? After Crimea? Was the opposition that naïve? Belarus might be an independent nation, but it lay directly between Moscow and the historical enemy nations of Europe. Throughout time, armies had marched across this forested backwater of a nation to attack Russia with swords and bayonets, tanks and missiles. That would not happen this time. Not a chance in the universe.

And so this flat, inconsequential shithole had exploded into civil war. A civil war, nudged forward by Russia, and Bazanov in particular, that was tearing the country apart: separatist militias in the east; roving gangs of pro-Kremlin thugs in Minsk; two divisions of Russian ground forces just over the border, waiting to roll into Belarus. That was what they deserved. Reap what you sow.

"We start the operation in five minutes," Ulyanin said. "The motorized tanks should be here. The rendezvous time is now."

"And yet they are not here," Bazanov said. "How unusual."

Ulyanin caught the sarcasm and tried to force a weak smile to his lips. "You will not be displeased, Colonel Bazanov. We will redeem ourselves."

Bazanov let out a low grunt and kept walking toward Independence Square. Belarus State Security had a lot to make up for. How they had let a national election proceed uncensored was beyond Bazanov's imagination. How could they have missed the signs of voter revolt, of electoral unhappiness? That would never happen in Russia. The FSB—the portion of the reconstituted KGB that dealt with domestic politics—would not allow it. Bazanov himself would not allow it. He would have intimidated officials, arrested opposition candidates, closed TV stations, and blown up cell towers. And if that didn't work, he would have bused in pro-Russian separatists and let them have their way with the local voters. It had worked wonders in Crimea, and it would work in Belarus.

"I hear trucks," Bazanov said as he crossed Svyardlova Street. Those would be the OMON GAZ Tigrs, the Belarusian riot police's antipersonnel vehicle of choice, gray and blue and mounted with tear-gas cannons.

"Yes, yes." Ulyanin nodded eagerly. "You see, we are not late."

"You were late two months ago," Bazanov said. "And you remain late."

Bazanov flashed back to that miserable morning in April, waking to his phone ringing in his Moscow apartment, Arkady calling from the Kremlin: "Gennady, turn on the fucking TV. Do you know what happened in Belarus? Lukashenko lost the fucking election by six points. How is this possible? Is nobody minding the goddamned store?" And then the endless meetings at Yasenevo, SVR headquarters, the hand-wringing, the blame. Ultimately, the responsibility for mopping up fell to Bazanov, as it always did. Which was fine. He was a fixer, and he would get it done.

Yet the truth was, anything that happened here, today, was a holding action, rearguard nonsense meant to stop the bleeding. The entire region was collapsing, one country after another. The Kremlin could mobilize all the tanks and soldiers it had, for as long as it could afford to do so, but Bazanov knew that what was truly called for was something much larger. A piece of business that could change the world, not just Belarus.

"The runoff election is in two weeks, Colonel," Ulyanin said. Ulyanin was a toady, and an incompetent one at that: nobody called an SVR agent by his title in the field, where any passerby could hear it. "Today's operation will break the back of the opposition thugs in Minsk. The western part of the country will react to this—shake with fear. They won't know which way to vote. And the east will side with Moscow. The combination will be overwhelming. The runoff election will swing back to Lukashenko. It will be just as you wish."

"And if it is not? Then what? Will you offer me your resignation? Or better, your head on a platter? Can I march you to the woods outside Orsha and have you shot?"

Ulyanin paled, laughing uncomfortably.

"Oh, you think we don't do that anymore," Bazanov snarled. "Don't test me."

He lit a cigarette and reflected upon the state of his life: running here, there, Chisinau, Donetsk, Minsk, trying to contain all those self-involved children, all asking for their freedoms, and all at once. If you let every last person do exactly as he or she pleased, then chaos would reign; you would be stuck with a globe full of screaming schoolchildren, without discipline or law. The very thought of it turned Bazanov's stomach.

He slowed as they reached Kirava Street. Two blocks away, in front of the lobby of the now shuttered Crowne Plaza Hotel, a gnarled wall of over-turned cars and barbed wire marked the barricade of the opposition brigands. Smoke rose from behind the ragged wall of broken concrete. The barricades were manned mostly by students, mixed in with unemployed hooligans. If they couldn't make trouble at football matches, then marching in the street would suffice.

Behind Bazanov, on Svyardlova, the OMON riot trucks had appeared, their black grill ironwork making them look positively medieval. But that was the point, wasn't it? Bazanov nodded approvingly: perhaps today would turn out better than he had thought.

"Step back, Colonel," Ulyanin whimpered. "I don't want you to be run over."

"Yes, you do. You wish I would be run over. Then maybe your nightmare would end. And stop calling me colonel where anyone can hear, you idiot."

Ulyanin hung his head and backed onto the sidewalk to let the trucks pass. Bazanov watched the Belarusian soldiers perched in the gun turrets above the truck roofs. He wished them courage. Actually, what he wished for them was ferocity. A willingness to die for the cause. If they had been Russians, he would have had no concerns. Russian security police were like dogs, bred to be ferocious unto death—at least the sober ones were.

All at once, the soldiers fired their tear-gas cannons, and Bazanov watched as contrails of white smoke arced over Kirava Street toward the barricades. Ulyanin handed him a yellow bandanna, soaked with water: "For the tear gas, for your face." But Bazanov waved it off. He'd breathed in more lungfuls of tear gas in the last year than the baby-faced Ulyanin had breathed in lungfuls of oxygen in his entire life.

A line of Belarusian special forces double-stepped down the street to follow the Tigr trucks. They carried black truncheons and Milkor Stopper rubber-bullet rifles. Bazanov instantly recognized that as a mistake. In the last month, things had gotten far too out of hand for shooting rubber bullets at bands of street opposition. Lead was what was called for, and nothing less would do: lead in overwhelming volume, that pierced hearts and shattered skulls.

Then, as if to confirm that opinion, gunfire erupted from behind the barricade. Even from two blocks away, through the tendrils of tear-gas smoke, Bazanov could see the red muzzle flashes of AK-47s from behind the car-and-concrete barriers. Bullets streaked through the air around Bazanov and Ulyanin, smashing into the building behind them, blowing out windows and pockmarking concrete. Bazanov spit out his cigarette and grabbed Ulyanin by the hand, running him toward cover. No wet bandanna would save their lives now.

"They have rifles!" Ulyanin shrieked, this time in Belarusian, his panic obviously getting the better of him. Bazanov understood the Belarus language. It was a cousin of Russian, the same alphabet, the same words, slightly different pronunciation. Hell, Belarus was basically the same country as Russia, which was why this uprising was such a betrayal.

"Yes," Bazanov yelled back. "And your men better have rifles as well."

"Of course, of course." Ulyanin was on his hands and knees now, crawling behind a parked car as the bullets pounded into the pavement all around them. His tremulous voice betrayed his lack of confidence. The security men didn't have rifles, and Bazanov knew it. This was another failure.

"Call for backup," Bazanov said, crouching near Ulyanin behind a late-model, black BMW. "Tell them to bring double the troops, double the firepower. And tell them to hurry. Make the phone call. Now!"

Ulyanin fumbled with his cell phone. Bazanov scowled and then sprinted across the street to get a better look at the fighting. With bullets singing past his head, he flattened himself against the doorway of a shuttered bakery. Shots were ringing out from both sides now, and Bazanov hoped the OMON police were aiming true. But his heart sank as he saw the first of the Tigr trucks backing up, away from the barricades. A soldier who had been manning the tear-gas gun was slumped over, his lifeless body laid out on the truck roof, arms splayed out on the slate-gray steel.

"Blyad," Bazanov hissed to himself as he reached for his phone. It was time to make calls of his own, to report back to Moscow. The day had turned into another disaster, as he had predicted it might. The runoff election was a mere two weeks away. Thirteen days, with the coming of the next dawn. He knew he should be more upset about that, frustrated with the incompetence of the Belarusian security forces, but he found that he couldn't work up the anger.

The Kremlin would yell, the tanks on the border would rev their engines, but the truth was, despite all his protestations to the contrary, he understood that the citizens of Belarus were right to rise up against their iron-fisted dictator. They were right to want democracy and all the freedoms it promised. They were right because they'd been fed a steady stream of illusions from the West. Illusions about prosperity and the good life. All day and all night, on television and in pop songs, in magazines and movies, they saw dollars and Porsches and big-breasted women. They were told they could have all of these things if they emulated the West, if they were like the hypnotized fools of Paris and London and New York. Consumers, lemmings, mindless balls of greed and avariciousness. The citizens of Belarus were like moths to a flame. They could not help themselves. They wanted the things they were told to want. Who could resist?

No, Bazanov thought as the Tigr trucks hightailed it back down Svyardlova Street for safety, chased away by a hail of machine-gun fire, he would not punish the moths. What was the point of that? You had to go to the source of the problem, instead, and everything was in place to do just that. The process had already begun.

What he would do now was extinguish the flame.

What bothered Bingo Clemens the most was that he wanted to do it. No matter the protestations to the opposite, no matter how much he complained about the work, the long hours, the dark, cramped rooms and the dangers to his health, Bingo wanted back in. He wanted to be part of the Ascendant team again. And that just killed him.

The phone call had come at seven thirty in the morning, his mother yelling upstairs to his closed door, "Bingo, a man on the line for you. From New York City. Says it's important. Top secret. He won't tell me his name over the phone."

Bingo's blood froze. Only one person could be calling from New York City with a top secret message.

Garrett Reilly.

He wanted Bingo's help. He wanted Bingo to leave his room, and Bingo hadn't left his room much for the last nine months. Not since the last time he'd helped Garrett Reilly. And that had almost got him killed. And yet . . .

He took the phone call.

"Bingo, I need you in New York," Garrett said. "The team is coming back together."

Bingo mumbled a nonresponse, running his thick fingers through his out-of-control Afro. Bingo was a former analyst for the RAND Corporation, an expert on all things military, and currently a shut-in.

"There'll be a plane ticket waiting for you at SFO."

"I saw your face on the TV," Bingo whispered. "You're in trouble."

"Consider every phone call monitored. And act accordingly," Garrett said. "And believe nothing."

"What if I don't want to do it?"

There was silence on the line, as if, Bingo thought, Garrett hadn't quite understood the question.

"Maybe I should just stay here."

"No. You're coming East." Just like that—as if what Garrett thought was the last word in what Bingo should actually do. The guy had not changed. He was still an arrogant son of a—

"And I need you to stop over in Palo Alto as well," Garrett continued. "I'll send you the address via the old method." In the past, Garrett had communicated with members of the Ascendant team through instant-messaging applets in online shooter games. The avatars they used had nothing to do with their real names, and while they could be watched and read by intelligence agencies, they couldn't be traced to physical locations. "I'll send you some burner cell numbers as well. Call me from the road." Then Garrett hung up.

The dread started immediately. A ball of worry right in the center of Bingo's stomach. Yet, despite his anxiety, he packed a bag, almost as if on autopilot. Why was he doing this, stuffing two shirts—he only had a few shirts—and a couple of pairs of beige chinos into a carry-on bag? Doing exactly as he was told to do by Garrett, as if he were Garrett's zombie slave? He knew the answer. It was simple. The month and a half he had spent with the Ascendant team last year had been the most exciting time in his life. More had happened to him in those few weeks than in all the other weeks of his life combined. No matter how much he complained about it and had been frightened by what happened, those were the memories that he replayed in his head over and over before he went to bed at night.

He'd had an adventure, and deep down inside, he wanted another one.

He finished packing and told his mother he needed to go to New York for a few days. She clucked and worried and pried, but he said it was classified business for the government. That made her cluck and pry more. His mother had been a full-on hippie in her prime, marching up and down the streets of Berkeley at the drop of a hat. Civil disobedience and mistrust of government were her raisons d'être, and the idea that her little boy—although Bingo wasn't little; he was six foot two, and he was no boy now, having just turned twenty-seven—was going to work for the government sent her into paroxysms of worry and indignation.

"Do you realize what you're doing? What this means? As a political statement?" she cawed as he dragged his carry-on bag down the front steps of their South Oakland bungalow to the waiting taxi. "Do you understand the implications?"

"Yes, I do."

That seemed to shut her up. "Be careful!" she yelled as the cab pulled away from their house and headed down Martin Luther King toward the freeway and the Peninsula. "Don't let them fuck you in the ass!" His mother had always had a unique way of expressing herself.

Bingo called Garrett from the middle of the Dumbarton Bridge, and Garrett told him what he wanted Bingo to do. That only increased his unease, but he was committed now—even though he still couldn't completely wrap his mind around how that had happened—and he told the cabbie to wait as he rang the doorbell at the front door to the condo building on High Street in Palo Alto, just east of Stanford University. He was buzzed in and went up to the fourth floor. The door to the apartment was cracked open, and Bingo knocked tentatively, and when there was no answer, he went inside.

Celeste Chen was sitting on the couch, watching daytime TV—some kind of self-help show about unwed mothers—and eating popcorn from a bag. She looked bad: hair unbrushed, old shorts on, a stained sweatshirt hanging loosely around her shoulders. The condo was a mess as well. Paper plates of take-out food were scattered around the kitchen, with empty gin bottles under the sofa and piles of dirty clothes in the living room. The place stank, like cat pee maybe, although Bingo didn't notice any cats around.

Bingo knew that Celeste—a twenty-eight-year-old linguist and code breaker—had been in China until recently, living underground with a persecuted revolutionary sect. She'd been there for six months, on the run, sick and starving, until the CIA had extracted her, against her will, and brought her home. Bingo had found this out from Alexis Truffant, but she had told him just the basics of the operation, even though he'd wanted to know more. She also asked Bingo to stop in on Celeste a few months ago and see how she was doing—but he never did. He didn't want to have to face her despair, up close and personal. Also, he didn't want to leave his room.

"Garrett wants you to come with me to New York," Bingo said.

"Fuck Garrett," she said.

"Does that mean no?"

She went back to watching the television without answering. Bingo called Garrett and told her what Celeste had said.

"Put her on the phone," Garrett said.

Bingo gave her his cell phone. He could hear Garrett talking to her, but couldn't make out what he was saying. Celeste grunted her answers—"Yes" and "No," with the occasional "Fuck you" thrown in—and then she said, "Eat shit," and tossed the phone back to Bingo.

"If she doesn't come with you, then tie her up and drag her into the cab," Garrett told him.

"You know I can't do that."

"Okay, fine. Just tell her it's for her own good."

"And if that doesn't work?"

"It has to work. The shit is hitting the fan. You both need to get on that flight to New York. This is the last conversation we're going to have on this number. Don't use it again." Then Garrett hung up.

Bingo thought about this. He went downstairs and told the cabbie it might be a while. The cabbie didn't seem to care—he said the meter would have to keep running. Bingo went back upstairs and looked around. On closer inspection, the apartment really was disgusting. Along with the endless assortment of half-empty diet-soda cans, piles of unopened mail sat in stacks on chairs and on the kitchen table—a couple of the envelopes were lined in red and looked suspiciously like past-due notices. Celeste seemed to have completely given up on life.

Bingo pulled a chair into the living room and sat a few feet from Celeste. Her eyes never left the television. He liked Celeste, but he was a little afraid of her as well: she was smart and tough and had an acid tongue that she was not afraid to use.

"Alexis told me what happened in China," Bingo said carefully, unsure how to reopen the conversation. "Being on the run and all. And the CIA pulling you out of the country. That seems harsh."

"You have no idea, Bingo. None whatsoever. Go the hell away."

Bingo sighed. He leaned his elbows onto his knees and tried to look as compassionate and caring as he could manage. He was, by nature, extremely shy.

"It hasn't been easy for me either. What I mean is, when I went home, I didn't know what to do with myself. I've been staying indoors mostly. Reading. And maybe playing a little bit of Xbox. A lot of Xbox. And the conclusion I've come to is that I'm not sure sitting in my house is a good thing. It's kinda ruining my life. Maybe ruining your life too." Bingo grimaced. "No offense."

Celeste turned from the TV and took a long look at Bingo. "How I ruin my life is none of your business. And you've gained weight."

Bingo sighed. That was true. He had gained some weight, maybe ten pounds. Or twenty. Or more. He hated talking about his weight. His dad had been an all-state high school offensive lineman. He'd been huge. Sadly, Bingo had inherited his size, but not his athleticism.

"I'm working on that," he lied. "Going to the gym."

"You said you hadn't left the house."

"I said *mostly* hadn't left the house."

"Why are you doing this, Bingo?" Her eyes narrowed. "Seriously. Why the fuck are you doing what that asshole asked you to do? Re-forming Ascendant? He's a selfish jackass who will only bring you grief. Give me one good reason why you're doing this and I'll go with you. I promise. I'll pack up and go right out the door. But it's gotta be good, and it's gotta be the truth."

That took Bingo by surprise. He started to answer, then caught himself, shook his large head no, then started again and halted once more. He began to panic. He felt droplets of sweat form on his forehead and on the back of his neck. This was his best chance of getting Celeste downstairs and into the waiting cab—without force, at least—and he was blowing it. Then, in a flash, the answer came to him.

"I'm doing this because it's what I was meant to do. And it's what you were meant to do as well."

Alexis took a shuttle flight from LaGuardia to Reagan National, caught a cab to her condo, then drove herself to Marine Corps Base Quantico in northeastern

Virginia. She tried to keep an eye out for anybody following her, or tailing her car, but as far as she could see, she was clean. The FBI hadn't put her relationship with Garrett together yet. Or if they had, they were sitting on it, waiting for a better moment to pounce. At Quantico, she checked in with the duty officer at the Marine Corps Embassy Security Group, a pinched-faced sergeant named Holmes, and asked to see Private John Patmore. The last time she had spoken to Patmore he was a lance corporal, but he'd recently been demoted back to E-1 private. His file said the cause was insubordination, which didn't surprise Alexis. Patmore was a gung ho marine, but he had a fungible—some would say erratic—sense of military hierarchy. With Patmore, following orders appeared to be optional.

She found him sitting at an empty desk in the far corner of an unused file room. She entered without knocking and suspected that he'd been asleep. She cleared her throat.

"Captain Truffant," Patmore grunted, head snapping up from his chest. He bolted out from behind the desk. "What are you doing here? I mean—not that you have to explain yourself, ma'am. Captain, ma'am." He caught himself, straightened his back, and saluted her from the side of the desk, knocking over a raft of paper cups.

"Looking for you, Private." Alexis scanned the dusty office. Filing cabinets lined one wall. Folding chairs were stacked against another. Other than that, the room was empty. "What do you do here?"

"Ma'am, I file reports. In those cabinets there. And when somebody asks to see them again, I pull them out and hand the reports back to them."

Alexis could see a layer of dust on the top of the filing cabinets. "And how often does that happen?"

Patmore gestured briefly with his right hand, as if to point to an imaginary number in the air. But he stopped, mouth open, then put his hand back down at his side. "Once a week, ma'am. At most. I don't think they put me here as a reward."

"Why'd you get busted back to private?"

Patmore winced, waggling his head from side to side. "I said some stuff to the wrong people, ma'am. Probably shouldn't have. I should probably keep my mouth shut most of the time." He let out a long sigh, and his shoulders slumped slightly. "I was bored."

Alexis smiled. "Well, you won't be bored anymore. I'm having you transferred. You're coming with me. You're back in Ascendant. But we're keeping that last bit a secret."

Alexis thought she saw Patmore lift up onto his tiptoes. "Ma'am, this private is very happy to hear that news. Very much, extremely happy."

First, Garrett hacked the Jenkins & Altshuler enterprise resource-planning system. That was just a fancy name for the company's supply-ordering site, and *hacked* was a bit of an overstatement as well: Garrett already knew all the passwords for the planning system, so all he had to do was log on as an administrator and create a false account name. The guys in purchasing changed the passwords every month, but Garrett made a point of ordering a new chair or a printer every few weeks, just to keep himself in the know. He never knew when he would need to make J&A pay for something.

It helped that Garrett was a collector of passwords. He didn't care much about computer-generated ones—they were, by definition, a random jumble of numbers and letters—but he found human-generated passwords fascinating. He could recall pretty much every password he'd ever heard or read, and at night, if he couldn't sleep, he sorted them in his mind, arranging them into categories: passwords that were all numbers (rare), passwords that were mostly letters (more common), a decent mix of the two (most frequent), or ones that were numbers, letters, and symbols (most rare). He loved trying to parse the etymology of people's ciphers, although he was regularly astonished by how many of them still used 12345678, or that almost as many simply used the word *password*. People were such creatures of habit.

Next he ordered couches, desks, chairs, and computers for the Newark offices of Ascendant. Garrett knew that the J&A purchasing department checked new orders twice a month, on the first and the fifteenth, and any order under

$10,000 was rubber-stamped, especially if it was furniture going to one of the company's real estate holdings. The guys in purchasing were not the brightest bulbs; they spent an inordinate amount of time playing Magic: The Gathering and making penis jokes. Garrett also made sure to rent the furniture instead of buying it, which made it seem more like a sales staging deal than a purchase for a working office. The office supply store in Hoboken said they'd swing by in a few hours.

Garrett went downstairs to alert the guard at the front desk. He decided to swagger his way through the problem of being recognized. The guard was old, sixty-five at least, and his tiny body seemed lost in his baggy, dark blue uniform. Garrett started talking, loudly, the moment he stepped out of the elevator. He said he was from the start-up on the seventh floor—AltaTech Partners was the first name that popped into his head—and that a furniture delivery was due by the end of the day and could the guard please show them how to get to his offices. The guard said sure, taken aback and a little intimidated by Garrett's attitude, but then seemed confused when he couldn't find a record of any company called AltaTech Partners in the building.

"We just signed the lease yesterday," Garrett said. "We're going to take over the entire floor. But not this month. Next month. And the eighth floor too, but not until the fall. At least that's the plan." Garrett winked at the old guard, figuring if you were going to lie, then lie big. "We might go totally broke before then. You just never know, do you?"

"Yeah. Been there," the guard said.

Garrett stopped talking for a moment and looked at the old man's face, lined with wrinkles and age spots and a pink scar that ran from his chin to just behind his ear. Whatever he'd done before becoming a security guard, it had been a hard life, and Garrett could see the consequences on his skin.

"Thanks," Garrett said, slightly ashamed of himself for taking advantage of the old man and his crap job status, and hurried upstairs.

Back in the office, Garrett considered what facts he knew about Steinkamp's murder, and what he wished he knew. He had tried to research Anna Bachev, but she was a virtual nonentity: no digital footprint, no search references, no social media presence. She had no financial records or court documents, either. Bachev's ghostlike history was probably why they'd hired her to do the job in the first place. It occurred to him that *hired* was the wrong term. He guessed that Bachev had been blackmailed into shooting the Fed president. She had killed herself, after all—nothing else made any sense.

But who had done it? Ilya Markov? And what was the geopolitical line of connection between Markov, a Chechen-born Russian, and Bachev, a Bulgarian? The whole thing was beginning to take on a distinctly East European flavor.

Garrett researched events in Eastern Europe. He blew right through the usual assortment of corruption stories and threats of ruble devaluations, and came immediately to Belarus. While he knew that Belarus was a country, he didn't know much more than that. It had been a part of the Soviet Union and lay between Moscow and the bulk of the nations of Western Europe; it was a bleak, flat Russian vassal state—at least, it had been until a few months ago. That was when the citizens of Belarus somehow gave a plurality of their votes to a young reform candidate for president, forcing a runoff election. Most analysts assumed elections in that country were always rigged in favor of their longtime dictator, Alexander Lukashenko, but the government had grown complacent. They thought they would never be voted out of office, but they were disastrously wrong.

Of course, those in power weren't leaving without a fight. Civil war had erupted in the country—a civil war stoked by Russia and its vast security and intelligence agencies. The runoff election was scheduled for eleven days from today, and both sides—pro-Russia and pro-reform—were campaigning, and killing each other, at breakneck speed.

Garrett pondered this. Could civil war in Belarus be related to the death of Phillip Steinkamp in Manhattan? That seemed like a stretch, yet Garrett could feel trails of connection between the two. Patterns didn't always jump out at him—sometimes they needed to be coaxed gently out into the open.

He checked one last thing while he had the time: stock and bond ripples from the buying and selling in the black pool he'd found. Nothing certain jumped out at him, but he saw some unusual oscillations in the behavior of recent tech IPOs on the NASDAQ, specifically a Brooklyn-based company called Crowd Analytics. The company website said it harnessed the power of crowdsourcing to help solve corporate planning issues. Garrett found a splashy feature article about Crowd Analytics' CEO, a bearded, twentysomething Harvard grad named Kenny Levinson. The company was his brainchild and was valued at $30 billion. Garrett had to keep his revulsion—and envy—in check as he stared at the picture of Levinson on the steps of his Brooklyn brownstone, his startlingly pretty wife and perfect child at his side. Garrett didn't want what Levinson had—but he kind of hated him for having it nonetheless.

He pushed that from his mind. He couldn't quite see the pattern that surrounded the company, but one was out there, for sure, and when it became fully visible, he would spot it.

The furniture arrived at four in the afternoon. He signed the purchase order as Earl Erglittry—his favorite anagram of Garrett Reilly—and the movers didn't give him, or his signature, a second look. The old security guard came up to peek into the offices as well, and Garrett handed him a Diet Coke for his troubles. Garrett took another Percocet and stared out the window toward the Jersey sprawl and Manhattan beyond it. The summer light was hazy and thick, and white explosions of clouds drifted overhead.

Where was Ilya Markov, and what pattern was he weaving in his travels? Garrett didn't know, and the drugs were beginning to take hold. The instincts that he relied on to discern order out of the white noise of everyday life faded from his mind. He sat on one of the new black couches and stared out at the vast country that was the United States. There were so many places to hide: so many apartments to hole up in, so many parks to disappear into, so many back roads to use for escape.

The pain in his head lessened, Garrett lay down on the couch, and for a blissful few moments, he let the world's troubles slip away and caught up on some sleep.

Ilya Markov's driver took him from Fort Lauderdale to Orlando. Ilya had found the guy on Craigslist, a student at UF named Jim who needed extra cash. The cost was $25, plus gas. Ilya had Jim drop him at a motel just south of Orlando, where Ilya spent the night sending encrypted e-mails and texting his American contacts on burner phones he'd picked up in Miami.

Ilya needed more money wired to him in the States. He had carried $1,000 through customs, just to have cash on hand, and had been planning on using his own ID to collect more at Western Union offices in Florida and Atlanta, but the raid on his motel room had rendered that impractical. A blanket digital sweep would be on his name; anywhere he went with his current identification would trigger alarms, so he needed a new identity. He could have used James Delacourt's name, but he wanted to save that for later. He had already sent Delacourt's vitals to a colleague in Moscow. That colleague would do the rest and send the results back to the States when Ilya asked for it.

He took a cab to a Starbucks in downtown Orlando, amid the cookie-cutter office towers and generic parks, bought a coffee, and sat near a young man with a goatee, who was working on his laptop. Ilya waited ten minutes, then asked the young man if he would watch Ilya's own laptop while he went to the bathroom. The young man agreed, and Ilya took his time in the men's room. He wanted the young man with the goatee to see how much Ilya trusted him; how willing Ilya was to put a valuable possession in this young man's hands. Compassionate reciprocity was a key weapon in the social engineer's tool kit.

Ilya sat down five minutes later and thanked the young man, then opened the computer and surfed the Web for a while.

Sure enough, ten minutes later, the young man with the goatee got up and asked Ilya if he'd return the favor. Ilya said sure and even offered to keep the young man's backpack under his chair for safekeeping. The young man hurried off to the bathroom. Ilya made sure no one was watching, then rifled through the man's backpack. He found a Florida driver's license, a Bank of America debit card, a loyalty card from Winn-Dixie, a community college ID, and an overdue utility bill. From those, he had everything he needed: a name, date of birth, address, college ID number, and even the beginnings of a bank account number. He didn't steal any of those cards—that would alert the young man and defeat Ilya's purpose. Instead, he took cell phone pictures of each piece of ID, then put everything back in the wallet exactly as he had found it.

When the young man returned—his name was Robert Jacob Mullins—he thanked Ilya, retrieved his backpack, and went back to working on his laptop. Ilya sent all of Mullins's information to a storage folder on the darknet. His associate in Moscow would download the information from the folder, then overnight the finished product to an agreed-upon address in Atlanta. Ilya packed up and left without saying another word.

Plenty of IDs were to be had on the black market, but Ilya didn't trust them. Every city in the United States had backroom counterfeiters ready to print out driver's licenses and passports by the dozen, with varying degrees of quality, for the right amount of money, and Ilya knew that in the next ten days he might need to avail himself of the services of one of those back-alley print shops. But for the time being, he preferred to capture the necessary information himself, and to have known craftsmen transform that information into high-quality, usable pieces of identification.

He had $700 cash left in his wallet, which was plenty for the next twenty-four hours. He paid $20 for a cab that took him to Valencia College, a sprawling campus west of downtown that looked more like a business park than a school; then he sauntered into the student union, logged on to the online bulletin board, and hunted for anyone needing passengers to Atlanta.

Within five minutes he'd found a pair of women leaving in half an hour. Eliza and Sarah agreed to carry him if he paid for half of the gas, probably around twenty bucks, and if they retained veto power over the music choices. No rap, no Phish. He agreed instantly. For the first part of the trip north, Eliza and Sarah chatted happily in the front of the car, and Ilya sat mutely in back. By the Florida-Georgia border, however, Ilya sensed that his silence was making the women nervous—Eliza kept flashing him looks in the rearview mirror—so he started a conversation about college football, then fast food, then dating, all things he cared not a whit about.

By Macon, Georgia, they were best friends. By nine that evening, he was lying on a bed in a dim motel room in East Point, Georgia, just south of Atlanta. Two hours later, she knocked on the door.

She was a true believer, or at least she claimed to be, but that was not enough for Ilya. She had to come recommended by people he trusted, and she did: three separate sources, one in Europe, two in California. They said she was smart, discreet, and good at her job. She stood about five foot five, with shoulder-length brown hair that curled in tight ringlets.

"Can you make it blond?" Ilya asked, pointing to her hair.

"I can make it any color you want."

She had a thin face, more sexy than pretty. You looked at her lips before you looked at anything else; they were rounded and full, and she highlighted them with bright red lipstick.

"The lipstick is too red," Ilya said. "Too obvious. You're not looking for attention."

"The lipstick is too red," she repeated, as if taking notes.

She was curvy, and she wore a gauzy white top, with denim shorts and sandals. The clothes clung to her body in the heat, accentuating her breasts and hips. She seemed to glide more than walk, and slink more than move. While they talked, her eyes never left Ilya's.

"You're good in bed?"

She started to undo the buttons on her blouse. "Pull down your pants and I'll show you."

"I don't want to have sex with you."

"Why not? Are you gay?" she asked, seemingly without an opinion on the matter.

"What difference would it make? No sex."

"Okay." She buttoned her blouse back up. "But the answer is, I've never had anyone complain afterward."

Ilya guessed her age at about twenty-five. "You will be reluctant at first. You're not accustomed to casual encounters. But once things get under way, you become a tiger. You lose yourself in the moment."

She nodded. "I can do that."

"Rachel Brown? You're Jewish?"

"I can be Jewish. Or half. Or not at all."

Ilya realized he could ask about Rachel Brown's ethnicity and her real name all he wanted, but he would never get an answer that he believed. Or at least fully believed. She lived—as he did—in that gray netherworld where the truth was what you made it. Whatever they decided was real, was real, just for tonight, in a motel room in an Atlanta suburb.

"You are Christian," he said. "Born-again. There's a Bible in the bedside drawer. Memorize a few useful verses. We'll find you a suitable church. We'll drive by it tomorrow, so you know what it looks like. The clothes will have to change too. More modest. But not too modest. We'll go to the mall and buy you some new things."

"I should have a crucifix. Born-agains wear them. And they draw the eye here." She ran her index finger down her cleavage. "That always works."

Ilya watched her finger plunge slowly down her neckline and then back up again, and he had to agree—that would work well.

"You've been to college?"

"Two years," Rachel Brown said. "Didn't love it."

"What did you study?"

"Communications. A little business. Mostly English lit. Chaucer and Melville and is *Moby-Dick* a metaphor for the discontents of capitalism. I didn't think it was. I just thought it was about a big fish. My professor disagreed."

Ilya blinked and took another look at Rachel Brown, or the woman who called herself that. Perhaps he had underestimated her. Perhaps she was considerably brighter than he had imagined. She had a sense of humor, and that spoke to psychological flexibility, and psychological flexibility was key for Ilya's plans.

"You've done this before?" Ilya asked.

"Well, you haven't told me what this is yet, so I can't be entirely sure." She spread herself out on the twin bed that was closest to the motel window. She kicked off her sandals and stretched her arms over her head like a cat about to curl up into a ball and sleep. "But if you're asking me if I've ever made someone believe something that wasn't true, I'd say, every single day of my life."

Ilya watched her and felt an involuntary stirring. She was extraordinarily sexy, so at ease in her body, so comfortable with its secret places. To Ilya's thinking, she could hook a man and reel him in before he even knew he was on the line.

Yes, Ilya thought, but did not say, Rachel Brown will work out quite well.

As her plane hurtled eastward across the country and into the night, Celeste Chen felt a deep sense of foreboding. Foreboding mixed with a toxic whiff of fury. To make matters worse, Bingo, sitting next to her in the back of the plane, let his own anxiety out in sporadic, disjointed comments about Garrett or Ascendant or his mother. Celeste had managed to keep things mostly in check, by drinking white wine and watching reruns of *Parks and Rec* on the seat-back televisions, but as they descended into Newark's Liberty Airport, floating over black countryside spotted with highways and factories, she could feel her rage overtaking her.

Why the hell had she agreed to come? She was not ready to be back in the game. Nowhere near ready. She wanted out. *Immediately.*

She'd never been to Newark before, but once on the ground, she didn't like what she saw: limo drivers hustling for fares at the airport, bus drivers smoking cigarettes while their passengers waited on the sidewalk. From the SuperShuttle window, the city looked dark, gloomy, broken-down, and it smelled bad as well, like a muddy low tide mixed with old garbage. They took the shuttle to a Hilton downtown, then caught a cab back out to the Valley Mall Plaza, which was pretty much empty. From the mall they hired an Uber driver back toward downtown—all on Garrett's instructions.

"Make sure no one is following you," he had said. "Travel until you are completely alone. You cannot be too safe."

Safe? She laughed at that idea. As if Garrett had any idea of what it was like to be hunted—truly hunted.

She obsessed over what she would say to him when they met. Her anger at him lay just below the surface, blistering and ragged. She had lived six months on the run in China, on his say-so, surviving by crawling from one hiding place to another, begging rotting bowls of rice, terrified every hour of every day that the Chinese government would find her, jail her, and have her executed. The memory of her experience haunted her, flashing into her thoughts again and again: in cries of surprise when a Palo Alto police siren blared or a neighbor's dog barked; in crying jags that came on her while she stood alone, naked, in her own bathroom; in sleepless nights, when visions of Hu Mei, the woman she had gone to China to help, tormented her if she dared close her eyes. An army VA psychiatrist had told her it was PTSD, and that she needed to treat it, but Celeste had told him to go to hell. She would deal with her psychic pain the way she dealt with all her setbacks: gin, death metal, and online porn.

When the Uber driver dropped them at the half-finished office tower in downtown Newark, she and Bingo scanned the empty plaza, then dragged their carry-on bags around back to the loading dock, where Alexis Truffant rolled open a steel door and met them. Amid all Celeste's gloom, she was glad to see Alexis. She liked Alexis; Alexis wouldn't lie or lead her down the garden path, and she was pretty sure Alexis was the person who coordinated her extraction from southern China, so she guessed she owed the woman her life—as much as she owed it to anyone associated with Ascendant.

But Alexis was efficient and all business, hugging Celeste and Bingo briefly, then hustling them inside and to the elevators with hardly a word. Bingo ambled along behind them, eyes wide with suspicion and with what Celeste suspected was plain old fear. She knew Bingo was not the world's most courageous human, and that coming here, to rejoin the Ascendant team, was stretching the heroic part of his personality almost to the breaking point. As the service elevator shot upward, she took Bingo by the hand and squeezed hard, as much to reassure herself as to put him at ease.

"Is this a working office building?" Celeste asked Alexis. She hadn't seen a soul in the place yet. But then again, it was almost eleven at night.

"Half-occupied. The owners are in bankruptcy. If security stops you or asks what you are doing, just say you're part of the tech start-up on seven. Our name is AltaTech Partners. That should give us cover for a while."

Celeste thought that sounded makeshift, at best, but makeshift seemed to be part of Ascendant's DNA, so she said nothing more. But it didn't fill her with confidence. None of this filled her with confidence.

She shut her eyes and pictured the Chinese countryside: the lush, tropical hills outside Guangzhou, the squalls that blew in off the South China Sea, the children splashing in the muddy Xi River. She didn't hate China, as hard as her time there had been, and visions of its green forests still calmed her nerves. In moments she would be facing Garrett Reilly again, and she needed all the composure she could muster.

The elevator stopped, Alexis checked the hallway, then hurried Bingo and Celeste to the last office before the stairs. She knocked twice, and the door opened.

"Hey." A young woman with thick black hair smiled briefly at Celeste. "Mitty. Nice to meet you."

"Yeah." Celeste shook Mitty's hand. "Sure." Celeste had never actually met Mitty in person, but she'd heard a lot about her from the rest of the team.

Mitty turned from Celeste and stared long and hard at Bingo. "Hey, Bingo. Long time. Really long time."

Bingo hung his head determinedly toward the floor. Celeste figured the two of them must have had some kind of relationship in the past, although if that was true, then they would go down in the odd-couple hall of fame. From Mitty's glare, Celeste guessed that Mitty held a grudge against Bingo, and he seemed terrified of her. Not that Celeste blamed him: from what she'd gathered, Mitty was a piece of work. Still, Celeste was glad to see her; she seemed eccentric and full of life. Celeste needed people who were full of life.

Alexis showed them into the offices. They were large—five separate executive offices, a meeting area, a kitchen, and a conference room—and mostly barren, with the walls freshly painted white and Sheetrock showing in one section of the reception area. A few pieces of random furniture were strewn around the large central room—some chairs, couches, desks, and a few computers—and little else. A bank of windows looked out onto what Celeste assumed was the New Jersey Turnpike; the glittering towers of Manhattan lay far in the distance, thick blocks of yellow light in the night air. Celeste let out a short, mirthless laugh; she had traveled across the country, and instead of settling in Manhattan, and hopping from fabulous restaurants to exclusive nightclubs, she was stuck in Newark, New Jersey, in a half-empty office tower, surrounded by a cohort of semiautistic geeks.

Story of her life.

Her thoughts were interrupted by a marine, tall and handsome, but with a hint of wildness in his eyes. He was wearing green-and-brown fatigues, and his hair was buzz-cut short. He grinned broadly at Celeste and saluted her. "Private John Patmore, ma'am. We met briefly in DC last year. You might not remember me."

"Sure." Celeste nodded. But she didn't remember him. All military guys looked the same to her, and Patmore certainly fit the mold: he looked more like a G.I. Joe doll than a human being. But a slightly crazy G.I. Joe doll—one you wouldn't let your kids play with. Not by themselves, at least. "Good to see you again."

"Hey, Celeste."

She turned to the sound of that voice, her pulse quickening. Garrett Reilly stood in the doorway of the main room. He looked different: older, for sure, and a little beat-up, as if life had not been kind to him in the intervening twelve months. He was thinner than he had been when they'd been together in DC, and not as swaggering either; that sheen of arrogance was missing. He didn't seem like a shark hunting for his next meal anymore. No, Celeste got the distinct impression that sharks were out there hunting for him. Still, she was furious at him. She balled up her hands into fists and felt herself, involuntarily, start across the room toward him, to beat him on his head and chest, to make him feel her pain. But Garrett stepped forward as well, meeting her halfway.

"So glad you came," Garrett said quickly, putting his hands gently on her shoulders. "I really need you here."

That set Celeste back a step. She started to respond, to tell him not to count on her staying for long, that he was a sorry-ass son of a bitch.

But he wrapped his arms around her in a firm hug, pulling her close, and whispered in her ear, "I'm so sorry about China. What happened. How hard it must have been for you. I thought about you every day. I tried to track you down. I was so worried." He released her and stared into her eyes. "I was heartsick with guilt. I'm just glad you're okay."

Celeste stood there, stunned. That had not gone according to plan. She grunted a nonresponse, her head swimming, then staggered to a dusty desk in the corner of the room and planted herself on its edge. Rage rushed from her body like infected pus leaving a wound. She wanted to gag from the power of it.

Was that really all it took to heal her? A few words of contrition? The knowledge that Garrett cared and felt guilty about what had transpired? *Am I that fucking fragile?* No. She was still pissed—it would take more than a hug and some sweet nothings to make up for six months underground in mainland China—but she had to admit that those few sentences hadn't hurt.

Maybe Bingo was right. Maybe she did need to get back in the game.

Garrett had planned an entire speech, rehearsed it over and over, but when he saw Celeste standing in the office, looking exhausted and scared, his brain went blank and he told her how he really felt: he was happy she was there, plain and simple. If she was still angry at him, so be it; if she wanted to berate him for his past transgressions, that was fine as well. He had sent her to China, where she had almost lost her life. He would keep his mouth shut, take any abuse she wanted to spew at him, and not lose his temper. That was the new Garrett Reilly, or at least the Garrett Reilly to which he aspired.

He moved to the middle of the large central room and told the reassembled team everything he knew about Ilya Markov, which he admitted from the start wasn't much. He told them about Markov's multiple passports and aliases, his background in tech, his employment in the United States, his fluency in English. He projected a picture of Markov on a white wall, and the young Russian stared at the team with flat-faced indifference.

"Kinda cute. But my standards aren't very high." Mitty looked directly at Bingo when she said this, and Bingo turned away quickly to look out the window.

Garrett made a mental note to himself: tell Mitty to cut the lovesick bullshit. Enough is enough.

He filled them in on Markov's latest movements, his arrival at the Miami airport, his trip to Fort Lauderdale, and his disappearance from his motel room. Garrett told them whom he thought Markov might hire—social engineers, hackers, and garden-variety criminals—and about the money he suspected Markov had at his disposal.

Then he told them what he believed Markov was trying to accomplish: sow chaos. Reap anarchy. Blow up the US financial system. Bring down the economy.

"Is that even possible?" Celeste asked.

"I don't know," Garrett said. "But he's going to try."

"Why's he doing it?" Bingo asked.

"That's part of what we have to figure out," Garrett said. "A large part."

He told them about his suspicions about Russia, and the events in Belarus. As the room fell into a collective silence, Garrett surveyed the reassembled Ascendant team. Both Bingo and Celeste looked tired and travel-worn. Celeste still appeared angry, but she seemed to have set her rage to a low boil; if Garrett could keep her focused on the task at hand, maybe the rage would leak out of her system. And Bingo—well, Bingo just seemed lost and a bit scared. But as Garrett remembered him, Bingo always seemed lost and a bit scared.

Mitty, sitting next to the two of them, was calm, a Diet Coke clutched in one hand. Garrett took that as proof that she was still working on her half-baked diet cleanse; he'd already found two containers of fat-free cottage cheese in the minifridge in the kitchen. She'd spent the day winding her way to Newark, trying to make sure no one followed her: subway, bus, taxi, on foot. Garrett knew he'd have to put up with her endless eccentricities, but he was thankful she was there nonetheless. She'd put up with plenty of his, after all.

Standing in a corner, Private Patmore was smiling, bright eyed and broad shouldered. Garrett could see the grip of a sidearm protruding from his belt. As much as Garrett didn't like guns—he thought they might just be the root of all evil—he was glad to know Patmore had one. And that he could use it. Garrett also had a specific plan in store for Patmore, and it had nothing to do with catching Ilya Markov.

He turned finally to Alexis. She seemed tense. Garrett knew she was deeply out of her element; she had gone far off the DIA reservation, and the sad thing, for her at least, was that she probably wasn't done breaking the rules. She didn't know it yet, but Garrett did. She would have to go even deeper into uncharted waters before this whole thing was over, and she would be doing it on Garrett's say-so. This operation was no longer some government-sponsored project that he'd been sucked into—this time he was in charge. If it was crazy, it was his crazy.

"Any criminal record?" Celeste asked from the corner of the room.

"None," Alexis said. "And if he had, he'd have been deported immediately. But Customs did run a check on him two days ago, and there were faint points of intersection between Markov and the Russian mob. But he's never been arrested for anything, or charged."

"Why don't we just pass this whole thing on to the FBI? Let them find him," Patmore asked.

Garrett shot a look to Alexis, who put her hands up in front of her, as if to ask for patience. "Interagency cooperation will be limited on this one. I have a small discretionary fund, but the truth is, even DIA doesn't know about this mission."

"Okay, that," Mitty said, "is seriously fucked-up."

The room fell silent. Celeste stood, walked to the wall where Markov's picture was projected, studied it for a moment, then turned to face the team. "Can we talk about the white elephant in the room here? When I turned on my TV two nights ago, your face was on it." She pointed to Garrett. "Wanted in connection with the murder of the president of the New York Fed. You want to enlighten us?"

"Someone is trying to frame me."

Celeste cocked her head slightly to the left, a bemused smile on her face. "That's it? That's all you're going to say? You're wanted for fucking murder."

"The shooting is linked to Markov, and what he's planning," Garrett said. "They want me—they want us—out of the way. Having me hunted by the FBI is the best way to achieve that."

"Well, before you called, they had *me* out of the way," Celeste said. "I was sitting on my couch drinking Boodles and eating fried pork rinds. So I'd say that the person they want out of the way is *you*. From my way of thinking, you hauled all of us out here to help you clear your name. Am I wrong?"

"No. You're not wrong. I need to clear my name, and I need your help doing it. But finding Markov is part of a larger problem. Way bigger than whether I go to jail or not."

"Whoa, whoa, whoa. You're asking us to believe that you are thinking about the welfare of the country? Before your own safety?" Celeste asked. "Because my memory of Garrett Reilly is of a guy who didn't give a shit about anybody else. Who wanted to make a killing on the market, get rich and get laid, and that was it. Everyone else could go to hell. You telling me that you're different now? That you've changed?"

Garrett started to defend himself, but then lapsed into silence. He tried to frame the argument in his mind—that while he wasn't a different person, per se, his values had changed. Maybe not wholesale, but they had inched slightly toward a broader worldview. He wasn't trying to fool anybody; he hadn't turned into Mother Teresa overnight, but he did feel a need to become more involved in the world. And anyway, keeping the American financial system safe made it possible for him to make more money in the long term, so what was good for the country was good for Garrett as well. He was about to make that exact argument when Mitty broke in.

"He has changed. He doesn't party anywhere near as much. I don't think he's slept with even one *chica* since you last saw him. At least he hasn't told me about it. I don't know if he's interested in saving the world or anything, but I'd say he's more concerned about other people." She hesitated for a moment. "A little more."

"Thank you, Mitty," Garrett said, unsure if what she'd said was a compliment.

"He still takes a lot of drugs, though," Mitty added.

"Let's move on," Garrett said.

"Lotta people have addiction issues," she said. "But he's got serious ones."

"They get it," Garrett said forcefully.

Patmore broke into a laugh. Garrett glared at him.

"Kind of ironic, right?" Celeste began to pace the room. "I mean, last time, Ascendant sucked you in against your will, and all you wanted to do was get out. This time, you're bringing us in, we're hesitant, and you're the white knight, gonna save the country."

"If that's how you want to define irony, then sure, I guess it's ironic," Garrett said. Celeste was still clearly looking to pick a fight with him; she stopped by the door and put her hand on the doorknob. She looked, to Garrett, as if she was about to bolt. "Listen, this will not be easy, and yes, there are risks involved. I am wanted in connection with a murder. I'm a fugitive, and you being here makes all of you accomplices in hiding me. But I am entirely innocent, and that will come clear to the police eventually." Garrett gazed squarely at Celeste. "That's scary—I get it. And dangerous. So if anyone wants out, okay—no problem. Tell me now and we'll get you a ticket home."

Celeste's hand played with the doorknob. Open, closed, open, closed; the door seemed to mimic her state of mind.

"But just know, I want you here." Garrett still stared at her. "Every one of you. What we're trying to do is important. Not just to me."

Everyone in the room turned to watch Celeste. She fiddled with the doorknob some more, then let go of it and sat back down on a desk. "Whatever. Fuck it. Fuck him. Fuck all of you." She folded her feet up underneath her and stared angrily down at the carpet. "Let's just catch the guy and go home."

Bingo raised his hand like a shy student at the back of class. Garrett nodded in his direction. "You don't have to raise your hand, Bingo."

"So how *do* we catch him?"

"Simple," Garrett said with all the confidence he could bring to his voice. "We catch him with data."

They spent the night sleeping on couches, covering themselves in cheap fleece blankets Alexis had bought at a dollar store, and when Garrett woke them at six so they could call Europe during business hours, they seemed more like cranky middle schoolers than a crack intelligence team. He made them cups of instant coffee, sent Patmore out to buy breakfast rolls, then assigned them each a task.

He gave Celeste the hardest job: figure out how Markov had pulled off the Malta bank collapse. Garrett had her use voice-over IP software, so the phone calls were harder to trace, and she started by calling Interpol headquarters in Lyon, France. She told the Interpol agent that she was from the Ascendant project, an offshoot of the Defense Intelligence Agency, but the agent immediately transferred her to a different department, where a keenly interested American wanted to know her location before anything else, so Garrett told her to hang up. Immediately.

"We're on a watch list," Garrett said, cursing under his breath. "Ascendant has been tagged. We can't mention it again."

"Okay. I guess we're done then, huh?" Celeste said. "We can all go home now, get back to watching *Wheel of Fortune*?"

Garrett tried to stay patient, then had her call the IT department at the now-defunct bank in Malta. He watched over her shoulder as she tracked down ten different names and numbers, most of them on the island of Malta, with a few in Italy and one in France. She called each one and told them that she was from an

American cybersecurity firm—Reilly Pattern Insight, she called it, which made Garrett smile—looking to patch vulnerabilities in their operating systems. Garrett gave her a word-by-word script to use, because the truth was, Celeste knew next to nothing about computers. A pair of employees hung up on her right away, two said their lawyers had told them not to speak to anyone, one claimed not to speak English, and no one answered at the other four numbers. But with the last call, she hit pay dirt. The IT employee—now ex-employee—was angry at the firm, and at regulators, and basically at the world at large. He said the IT department hadn't had anything to do with the penetration, but they all suspected that the British moron Leone in HR had infected the system by putting a thumb drive into a network computer, which then emptied bank accounts, companywide.

Celeste thanked him, and then she and Garrett spent the next two hours trying to hunt down Matthew Leone, assistant VP of human resources at the First European Bank of Malta. Celeste finally found him on his cell, in a hotel room in Bern, Switzerland, and he'd clearly been drinking. She put him on speakerphone so Garrett could listen, because he was slurring his words and repeating himself, but as soon as she asked him about the bank in Malta, he hung up on her. She called back three times, but he never answered again.

"Dead end; we're done," Celeste said with just a hint of satisfaction in her voice.

Garrett took a deep breath and asked her to start researching Leone. "He was the entryway into the bank. Markov used him. Think like a con man. That's how we crack this."

She stared at Garrett without saying a word.

"Is there a problem?" Garrett asked.

"I still hate you."

"Then I guess the marriage is off." Garrett moved on to find Bingo.

Bingo had spent the morning calling tech firms in Silicon Valley, even though it was three hours earlier there. He knew a couple of employees at Planetary Software, the company that Markov had worked for in 2010. Some had moved on, but one still worked in the engineering department and remembered Markov.

The engineer described him as quiet, hardworking, a bit of a drinker in his off hours. Not a ladies' man, but not gay either. At least he didn't think he was gay. Kind of hard to pin down.

Garrett pushed Bingo to ask for more details. Religious beliefs? Coding quirks? Sexual fetishes? Was he political?

The engineer seemed baffled by the questions. "Well, no, not political, exactly. But kind of like, maybe, I don't know—a nihilist. I think his family was pretty fucked-up. The system is gonna screw you over, so you'd better get over on the system first. He only said that once, when he was drunk, but I definitely got the feeling that he'd be happy to see it all come apart. Watch everything go down the toilet. Like maybe that's what happened to him when he was a kid."

Garrett thought about his own feelings about "the system," and how, on many occasions, he too would have been happy to see the whole thing come crashing to the ground: the government, the military, the banks, and the bankers. Was there overlap between Markov's vision of the world and his own? Or was *overlap* too mild—was there *synchronicity*? He walled that idea off from the rest of his thoughts. It was not a possibility he wanted to investigate now. Or ever.

"No blogs, no websites?" Garrett asked.

"None," Bingo answered. "No digital trail."

"Hobbies? Perversions? What'd he do with his spare time?"

"The guy said Markov liked to play games. Chess mostly. But other games too. Board games, word games, number games. He won the company chess tournament. But everyone said he was a ringer because he was Russian."

Garrett told Bingo to keep widening the web of Markov's acquaintances: anyone who knew anyone who might have known him or had contact with him or even seen him on the bus one day.

"No piece of information is too small," Garrett said. "It all matters."

"Got it." Garrett thought he detected a trace of boyish excitement in Bingo's voice, as if he was having the time of his life.

Weary, and in pain, Garrett took his last two meperidine and moved on to Mitty, who was building a nonrelational database. The database was a digital bucket into which they could load seemingly unrelated bits of information, then test whether those bits were actually connected to each other. What Garrett wanted to know was how Ilya Markov conned people. When he did it. How he did it. Whom he used to help him.

Mitty had the database give all its answers as histograms and clustered dendrograms—graphical representations of data—and this made Garrett woozy with joy. For Garrett, data visualization was numbers porn. It activated some primitive pleasure center in his brain; he fell into the data, no longer an observer of it. *He became the numbers.*

Mitty chuckled as Garrett pored over the data. His pupils dilated, his breathing slowed. She didn't even have enough intel on Markov to make a genuine chart—most of what the computer was giving them was simply coding noise, but it didn't matter to Garrett; noise was one step below facts, and many steps *above* real life.

"You can be a little creepy—you know that, right?" Mitty said.

Garrett gave her the finger and moved on to another part of their large, empty offices. He found Patmore in a far room with a view to downtown Newark, monitoring an Internet feed of four different cable news networks.

Patmore stood and snapped to attention when Garrett walked into the room. "Low boil out there, sir."

"How so?"

"A mountain of chatter about Steinkamp, sir. Who killed him? Was that a terror attack on the US economy? And why would a Wall Streeter like you have anything to do with it? A lot of conspiracy theories. Also about Russia. Like maybe they're going to invade Belarus. And what a shitstorm that would turn out to be."

Every mention of Russia sent a pulse of electricity down Garrett's spine. "Anyone say the two are connected? Steinkamp and Russia?"

Patmore scratched at his chin. "No, I don't think so."

"Well, I think they are. So keep an eye out for any intersections."

"Will do, sir."

"Don't call me sir." Garrett nodded to Patmore and then to the chair. "And you can be at ease—or whatever people say."

Patmore sat back down.

Garrett closed the door to the office and dug a $100 bill out of his wallet. "Listen, I have a different job for you. If you could just . . . well, look on Craigslist." Garrett circled the topic. "And maybe find something. My head. You know, I had this fracture. And it hurts like . . ."

"On it." Patmore snatched the bill from Garrett's hand. "Painkillers. A black-market seller. No digital trace."

Garrett nodded in surprise, then relief. He'd figured the request would take a certain amount of explaining. "I probably won't take them. I just need them around in case—"

"I got blown out of a Humvee in Kandahar. Went over an IED, Humvee flipped, next thing I knew I was in a field hospital. Not a day goes by my back doesn't feel like it's gonna split in two. Consider it taken care of."

A wave of gratitude washed over Garrett, and he felt as if he were about to burst into tears, and then Celeste walked into the room.

"I found something." She glanced at Patmore, then studied the odd look on Garrett's face. "Am I interrupting? Were you two about to kiss?"

Garrett shook his head in wonder. "You're such an asshole. You've become more like me than me."

"I thought you'd enjoy that," Celeste said.

"It gets old."

"Imagine how the rest of us feel."

Garrett turned to Patmore. "Thank you, Private."

Garrett and Celeste left the room and moved to the empty reception area. Celeste's laptop was open on a desk.

"I checked up on Leone's background. Nothing extraordinary. Grew up outside of London, midlevel colleges. Did some HR work in the city. Then he landed the job in Malta. Been there three years, rented an apartment, medium salary. Ordinary guy. Ordinary life."

"Okay."

"Then I thought about what you said—think like a con man—so I looked up his social media. Tumblr, Instagram, Facebook. Check this out."

She tapped on the mouse pad and a browser appeared on the computer screen. She clicked through each of the three tabs. All three social media sites were filled with pictures of women—pretty and young—with one thing in common.

"He's got a thing for redheads," Garrett said.

"A pretty obvious thing. A shout-it-from-the-rooftops thing."

"Do we know if he—"

"I checked back with the IT guy, asked if Leone had any fetishes, but the IT guy didn't know him that well. He said Leone had one friend at the company, an Italian guy named Luigi Abela from the legal department. He still lives on Malta. I talked to him. He said Leone liked redheads a lot and, in fact, had met one at the bar the night before the collapse."

"Son of a bitch."

"I'm guessing that Markov scouted this Leone guy, figured out that he had a ginger fetish, then brought one to Malta and had her seduce him. In espionage they call it a honey trap."

Garrett scrolled through the pictures on Leone's Instagram account. Leone's obsession was right there, out in the open; all Markov had to do was look for it. "He finds people's weaknesses, and then he exploits them."

"So I hope to God you don't have too many of them." Celeste smiled darkly at Garrett. "Because if you do, he'll find them and screw you to the wall." She snapped shut her laptop and walked to the front door. "I'm going to lie down in a corner and nap." With that she left the office.

Garrett considered this new information. The picture that was forming of Markov was crude, but helpful: he was careful, obsessive, smart, and so far a moral blank slate. Garrett thought about Celeste's parting blast at him as well. He did have weaknesses, although he was doing his best to cover them up, and he wasn't in any hurry to let anyone else see them. He shook those thoughts from his brain and went to find Alexis. He'd given her the oddest of the team's tasks—a speculative long shot that might help move things along.

"Done," she said the moment he walked into her room. She swiveled her chair so Garrett could see the screen in front of her. On it was a carefully worded document, with a mug shot and a logo from the New York State Department of Justice.

Garrett read it twice. "I like it. I mean, I've never read an AMBER Alert before, but it seems real to me." He tapped the screen at a paragraph of text just below Ilya Markov's picture. "I especially like the part about him abducting a five-year-old boy. You don't come right out and say he's a child molester, but it's pretty obvious that he is."

Garrett knew that a fake AMBER Alert was a nasty piece of media manipulation, but he wanted to force Markov to the surface in the same way that the FBI had tried to make Garrett show his own face, and he didn't care if he broke the rules doing it. The more rules broken, the better, as far as he was concerned.

"The right person hears that, they'll tear Markov to pieces," Garrett said.

Disapproval flashed across Alexis's face.

"What? It'll save us the trouble." Garrett knew Alexis wasn't always crazy about his morals, but then—he wasn't crazy about hers either. They were a pair that way.

"How are we going to get outlets to broadcast it? AMBER Alerts have to be verified by the police."

"It's news. Sensational news," Garrett said. "We send it to every TV station from here to Miami. And every newspaper and news website. If only a quarter of them go live with it, it might force Markov to change his plans. That's what we want. We want him feeling hunted. We want him off-balance, changing his mind on the fly."

"Okay." She turned back to her computer. "You're the boss."

Garrett watched her for a moment.

"Something else?" Alexis said, not looking up from the chair.

"They need you back in DC?"

"I'll have to go in the next day or so. There are only so many excuses I can make for not showing up in the office."

"We're going to need more help. Institutional help."

Alexis swiveled in her chair back toward Garrett. "Given that the FBI would like to see you in handcuffs, I'm not really sure who we could ask."

"The DIA could get us what we need. Passenger manifests, credit-card tracking, a secure data sweep."

Alexis narrowed her eyes. "Kline wants nothing to do with you."

"You can convince him I'm right. That we're right. You have the proof."

"I have conjecture. I have probability. And I have a lone Russian student wandering around the US. But I don't have proof. Not proof that Kline will accept. He's stubborn, and he doesn't like to be wrong. Ever."

"You could use other methods. To get him to do what we need."

The air seemed to go out of the room. Alexis cocked her head, her face a sudden blank. She examined Garrett's eyes, his mouth. It looked, to Garrett, as if she were sizing up his character for the first time, as if they'd just met—as if he were a stranger to her.

"What are you suggesting?"

"My name is linked with Ascendant. Ascendant is linked with him. And linked with you. If you threatened—"

"Blackmail? If I threatened to drag him down with me? Is that what you're saying?"

Garrett hunched up his shoulders, as if to say, *Well, now that you mention it, I suppose that is a possibility.*

"You're asking for a lot. A fuck of a lot."

Garrett was, and he knew it. But she was already in deep, so why not go all the way?

Her eyes burned into his, cold and searching, and he had to steady himself to match her gaze. He couldn't read her, but he rarely could—she had been a mystery to him and continued to be one. Was she furious with him? Had she finally had enough? Had she caught a glimpse of his true nature and found it woefully lacking? Did it even matter?

Alexis blinked once, slowly, then swiveled to her computer and went back to work. Garrett watched her back, her black hair splaying out across her shoulders, but she didn't turn around and didn't say another word, and Garrett got the distinct impression that their relationship had just entered a new—and perhaps not as benevolent—phase.

A hum of financial anxiety was in the air. Leonard Harris (R-Marietta, GA) could hear it in the hushed whispers of his aides in Washington, DC, yesterday, when Congress closed up session, and he could see it in the vacant stares of the businessmen at the airport when he got off the plane in Atlanta this morning. It was as if the entire country had gone off its antianxiety meds, and every crank rumor that you could think of was beginning to seep out of the swamp of public opinion: the end was near; buy gold. There was no more oil; ditch your car. The dollar would be worthless tomorrow; get a shotgun and run for the hills.

Good Lord, Harris thought to himself as he maneuvered his gray Lincoln MKZ through the hideous Atlanta traffic, people do love to work themselves into a state.

He checked his watch and decided he had just enough time to stuff some food in his face. He pulled off the freeway and made his way east to Atlanta's Old Fourth Ward toward a vacant lot behind a Piggly Wiggly. Because there, he knew, lay a culinary gold mine, a collection of food trucks from all over Atlanta—barbecue food trucks, Vietnamese food trucks, burger trucks, fish-and-chips trucks, even a vegan truck.

Harris loved to eat: Chinese, Italian, French, Thai chicken *satay*, Korean kimchi, Ethiopian flatbread slathered in *doro wot*. All good, to his mind. He'd eat in restaurants seven days a week if his doctor hadn't told him it would kill him; so he kept it to four lunches and three dinners. He was fifty-seven, after all, an eight-term incumbent who could probably see his way to fourteen or fifteen terms, if he kept his health up.

Harris parked his car a block from the Piggly Wiggly and walked to the caravan of food trucks. The Georgia sun was beating down, and the air was thick and damp. He'd kept an extra white shirt hung in the back of his car for the interview, which was a damn good thing, because the blue one he was wearing was already soaked through.

Harris was handsome, and telegenic. He had most of his hair and didn't need glasses, which was part of why he had landed the chairmanship of the House Banking Subcommittee, one of the most powerful committees in all of Washington, DC. He had fought long and hard to get the post—put up with the myriad slights of his party bosses, done all the dirty work of a good political foot soldier—and now he was the boss. A great victory. But the job was not without duties, and interviews were top of the list: he was headed downtown to the CNN tower to a one-thirty Q&A with Wolf Blitzer. After that he had a PBS segment at four from a live remote, then a recorded talker with a radio station in San Antonio, Texas, at four thirty. And they were all going to want to discuss one thing, and one thing alone: the murder of Phillip Steinkamp.

Harris knew Steinkamp—had met him a couple of times, even had lunch with him once—and thought he was a nice guy. Terrible shame what happened. But Harris didn't have any new theories on why he'd been shot, or who had done it. The FBI had given him a briefing two days ago, but from there on it had been silence. Not that it mattered: the cable news outlets were relentless in their search for gossip—any whiff of drama was reason for a new interview, more breathless analysis, another round of inane predictions.

Harris entered the food-truck lot and thought about what to eat. He came there so often that all the drivers and cooks knew him. Today, Harris decided on Jose's Bandito Wagon. Jose was old and stooped, and he sat in the back of the truck while his wife—Sofia—cooked most of the food. And sweet Jesus, Sofia was a genius. Her chicken mole burrito was to die for, and her steak *carnitas* sprinkled with fresh cilantro made Harris's heart skip a beat.

Harris ordered two shrimp tacos, a side of guacamole with homemade pepper chips, and a Diet Pepsi to wash it all down. He chatted briefly with Jose, waiting patiently for his order, but even Jose wanted to talk about the state of the country.

"Yesterday, I take my money, send it to Mexico," he told Harris. "Safer there. I was in Mexico when the peso went poof. Disappear just like that. One day you got lots of money, the next day you got nothing. Maybe that happens here."

Harris started to tell Jose that the US dollar was perfectly stable, and a heck of a lot safer than the Mexican peso, but found that he just didn't have the energy, and anyway, his order came up in all its aroma-laden splendor, so he grabbed some napkins and a small container of *pico de gallo* and sat himself on a wooden picnic bench in the middle of the parking lot. Eating those tacos was like sex. Better than sex, in truth, because, well, he rarely had sex anymore. He rarely saw his wife, as she lived in Marietta, working as a doctor, and he was mostly in the capital, sharing a crappy little apartment with three other congressmen. Even when Congress was on recess, he and his wife didn't sleep together. They just couldn't seem to find the time. Or the passion. Which perhaps explained why he loved to eat so much. He was no amateur psychologist, but even he suspected he was filling unmet erotic desires with food.

He looked out across the half dozen other diners eating at separate tables in the parking lot. The sun slipped behind a cloud, and Harris dabbed at his sweating face. Thirty minutes until the CNN interview. What would he say? Was there really some sort of conspiracy afoot? Harris was having trouble wrapping his head around that, but he had to admit that things were looking squirrelly all over the place: the shooting of a Fed president, a bank run in southern Europe, targeted cyberattacks, the burgeoning civil war in Belarus, with the Russians moving their tanks up and down the borders of former Eastern Bloc countries as if it were the Cold War all over again.

A wall of worry. That's what they called it on Wall Street. And the worry was spreading. The market had taken a major dump yesterday. The Dow had dropped 500 points and was down another 350 this morning. Rumors were flying. Were American banks in trouble? Had brokerage houses made bad bets again? Harris had seen some blowhard on Fox yesterday saying a derivative was out there that was going to take down a major trading house. What kind of irresponsible idiot would go on the air and say that? The entire edifice that was the American economy rested on the public's believing that the structure was sound. If people didn't buy into that idea, everything would go up in flames. Even Harris knew that.

Now he had to get on TV and tell the nation that everything was fine, the world markets were fine, the banks were fine, and that Steinkamp's murder was just one of those hinky coincidences. Nothing to see here, people; move on, move on.

But even he didn't quite believe that. *Something was up.* Something strange.

Harris pushed the world of finance from his thoughts and glanced down the table. A young woman sat at the other end of the bench and laid a paper napkin on her lap. She was young, pretty, with dirty-blond hair and full lips. Harris loved full lips. Or had loved them, when he was single. A good Christian, moral to a fault, now Harris just admired those lips from afar.

The young woman looked up from her plate of food—she'd chosen the fish and chips from the Seafood Trucker, a wise choice, but not in the same league as the tacos—and quickly looked away. He'd been staring at her. She gathered up her purse and her plate of food and moved to another open table.

Moron, Harris thought to himself. Staring like a lecherous old man at a pretty young girl. Of course she moved away. I have to watch that. Harris felt sin came in all shapes and sizes, and sometimes just letting your eyes stray was all it took. That was a high standard to hold himself to, but it was nice to have high standards in something, after all. Wading through the stench of American politics took a lot out of him, and he needed his morality intact.

He finished his tacos, downed his Diet Pepsi, then wiped any traces of hot sauce from his lips. He stood, checked his watch, then walked past the young, blond-haired woman, careful not to stare again, and waved good-bye to Jose as he handed out another plate of enchiladas smothered in cheese. Then Harris stopped, let out a long breath, and shook his head.

If you sin, he thought to himself, even a little, then make up for it right away with a good deed. He walked back to the young woman. "Allow me to apologize."

The young woman looked up at him in surprise.

"For staring at you. I was lost in thought, but I'm sure it was intimidating. An intrusion. Please forgive me." He bowed slightly in apology, then started off again.

"Do I know you from someplace?"

Harris paused. That was one of the perks—or drawbacks—of being a US congressman. You were a celebrity, if only a minor one. "I'm Len Harris. I'm a congressman. From the Eleventh District."

"Oh," the young woman said, a hint of disappointment in her voice. "I thought..."

"You thought I was really important?" Harris smiled. "Not just a politician?"

The young woman laughed. "No. You reminded me of someone else. From a while ago. But you're not him." She reddened slightly, her checks flushing, as if the thought of that person, that memory, was dear to her, and just ever so slightly sensual. A lover, perhaps? An ex-flame?

An erotic pulse ran the length of Harris's body, from his head to his toes. I wish I were him, Harris thought to himself. He must have been a lucky man. "Sorry to let you down."

"You didn't." The young woman smiled—an open, trusting smile, compassionate and yet just ever so slightly inviting. "You were a gentleman. That was very nice of you. You don't see that every day."

Harris beamed. Always try to do the right thing, he reminded himself. Always. "Thank you." He noticed, for the first time, what she was reading, a paperback laid out on the table beside her food. A science fiction novel, *Ender's Game* by Orson Scott Card. Harris smiled. *Ender's Game* was by far his favorite sci-fi novel of all time, and Harris liked sci-fi almost as much as he liked food. He was a bit of a geek, and not afraid to admit it. In fact, he'd gone on and on about *Ender's Game* on the Twitter account he ran for his constituents. Well, actually, that his congressional aides ran. Harris didn't have the time to be posting tweets about anything, and definitely not about science-fiction novels.

"Great book." Harris nodded to the paperback. "I've read it, cover to cover, ten times at the very least."

The young woman looked at Harris's face, as if trying to discern something from it. His veracity? Sincerity? Was he trying to pick her up? "Number three for me."

"Then you are an incredibly well-rounded human being. You know the best places to eat, and the best things to read."

"This is a great spot. The food is to die for."

"I spend far too much time here myself." Harris patted his stomach. "Far too much time."

She laughed. "Nice meeting you, Mr. Congressman. Maybe I'll see you around."

"Yes, maybe."

He nodded good-bye to her one more time, then hurried back to his car with a mile-wide smile on his face. Those words—*Maybe I'll see you around*—stayed with him all through his interview on CNN. And PBS. And the radio-station talker from San Antonio. He couldn't figure out why exactly—something about her tone of voice, the look on her face. She seemed lodged in his brain. As he went to bed that night, his wife, Barbara, fast asleep at his side, his mind flashed back, over and over, not to finance or Phillip Steinkamp or conspiracies and the money supply, but to that pretty blonde at the food-truck parking lot.

He decided he would go back to the food trucks the very next day. Not for anything special. Just to look at her face. That's all. Not a sin. Just to have a friend.

With that thought, one of the most powerful politicians in the US Congress— the man who almost single-handedly regulated the financial industry—fell asleep, peaceful and happy.

S ir, Charlotte offices calling again."

Robert Andrew Wells Jr., CEO of Vanderbilt Frink Trust and Guaranty—known to most people around the country as Vanderbilt, and everyone on Wall Street as Vandy—grunted his displeasure as he marched down the hallway of the thirtieth floor of the bank's headquarters, heading to the stairway. His assistant, Thomason, held a cell phone in the air, trailing after Wells. "They want to know—"

"I know what they fucking want." Wells banged the stairway door open and sprinted upstairs, two steps at a time. "They want permission. Everybody always wants permission."

Wells believed in entrepreneurship: you went out and did things. You didn't ask for handouts. He believed in bootstrapping: no matter where you started in this life, in a backwoods shack or a rat-infested tenement, if you worked hard—dedicated yourself to whatever your heart's deepest desire was—you would eventually get it. Call it force of will, the cult of personality, or just plain old American self-help, Wells bought the concept of the self-made man, hook, line, and sinker.

He had no time or patience for people who sat around waiting for someone else to help them up the ladder—welfare recipients or bureaucrats addicted to the mother's milk of the state or sniveling branch directors who wanted to cover their asses before trying something new. They would never achieve greatness, those people, because they didn't understand that greatness came from within. It was never given to you. You had to fight for it. You had to earn it.

Striding down the hall of the thirty-first floor, Wells basked in that notion. He had risen from the bottom floor up, fought his way through the company, and was now top dog, leader of the nation's biggest bank. He was a master of the universe, a man with fabulous wealth and almost unlimited power—he was the 1 percent of the 1 percent, and all the world knew it.

That Wells's father—Robert Andrew Wells Sr.—had also been a banker did not put a dent in Wells's philosophical bearings. Wells Sr. had not run an institution like Vandy. He had been a midlevel player at a small Midwestern savings and loan, hardly a stepping-stone to running an international conglomerate. To Wells's mind, the distance between his father's position and his own was equivalent to the distance a homeless person needed to travel to make something of his or her life—to get a job, for instance, as a teller in one of their fifteen hundred branches across the country.

Yes, the government *had* helped bail Vandy out in 2008, backstopping their capital requirements with a massive loan from the Treasury Department, but Wells had seen to it that that loan was paid back swiftly, and with full interest. Vandy owed the US government nothing. At least, not right now. And never again.

Anyway, those arguments were quibbles, and Wells had heard them all before. The press did not like Wells, nor did the political Left. They were envious, to his mind, and had no conception of what Wells and his bank did for America—the lengths to which they went to make sure the wheels of capitalism kept grinding along. That was no small task. The press and the Left hated capitalism, hated banks, and they hated Vandy. The last three days had proven that point beyond any doubt. All that Wells had read for the last seventy-two hours was how perilous the state of his bank was—how their capital reserves were low, their loans were bad, their investments were shit. And, of course, how their CEO was making things worse with his arrogance and spite.

Wells let out a long hiss of breath and pushed open the door to the bank's stock-trading floor. Thomason kept pace behind him, as did Stephens, the young woman from Boston. Those two assistants kept his schedule, manned his phones, and made sure he was up-to-date on everything that was happening in the world. Wells could not survive without his assistants, although one was probably enough to handle the job—but a second was nice. He was giving more people jobs, and that could hardly be called a bad thing.

"Don't bug me about Charlotte again today," Wells barked.

"Yes, sir," Thomason said meekly.

Wells took in the trading floor with a satisfied stare. The room was massive, stretching out almost the entire length of the building, jammed full of busy employees buying and selling shares in the nation's—and the world's—biggest and best companies. Phones rang, conversations were shouted, buy and sell orders blinked across myriad computer screens. The room buzzed with activity, roared with commerce, and oozed prosperity—even if the naysayers argued otherwise. The place gave him strength; the room proved to him that the American economy still had legs to stand on. The future was bright. He needed that feeling because, no matter how much he believed in himself, the last few days had given him a dark sense of foreboding.

Wells marched across the room and caught, out of the corner of his eye, all the traders and analysts sneaking a peek at him. He was hard to miss, with his broad shoulders, head full of white hair, and his posse scrambling behind him like a pack of dogs. He liked that feeling—that people knew who he was and wanted to catch a glimpse of him. It wasn't just that it made him feel important—it also proved that the bank still had a hierarchy, that even the lowest stock seller could aspire to be CEO one day. Could aspire to be the next Robert Andrew Wells Jr.

Wells rapped on the metal doorframe of an office that fronted the trading floor. Aldous Mackenzie, the bank's chief investment officer, looked up from his computer screen. Behind him, through the plate-glass window, midtown Manhattan and the East River were visible in the afternoon sun.

"What's the latest?" Wells asked, stepping into the room and motioning for his assistants to wait outside.

Mackenzie shrugged. "More anxiety. Rumors about a toxic derivative coming out of our trading floor."

"That possible? Could we have missed it?"

"Anything's possible. But Christ Almighty, we paid twenty million dollars for that risk-analytics software. Thing is supposed to catch any bad bet, anywhere in the company. So . . . I'm saying no. We couldn't miss it."

Wells closed the door behind him, then noticed a young man sitting on the couch opposite Mackenzie—Mackenzie's assistant. Wells couldn't remember his name, Benny something, but he stayed close to the CIO the way Wells's assistants stayed close to him. "Could you give us a second?"

The young man jumped to his feet and practically fled the room.

"Our stock is getting hammered, Mac. Down another five points today. That's fifty billion in market cap."

"I'm well aware." Mackenzie, a large man, had a florid face and not a lot of hair left on his head. "It hasn't traded over thirty in two years. Another five-point drop isn't going to kill anyone."

"It might kill me. Or the press might kill me. Or some crazy woman with a pistol might walk up to me and blow my fucking head off."

Mackenzie didn't laugh. He pushed away from his desk. "That's why you have a bodyguard. And Steinkamp should have been using his."

"Who shoots a Fed president? What the fuck is wrong with the world?"

"Is that why you're here, Robert? To talk about Steinkamp?"

"I'm here because volatility is through the roof, stocks are crashing, banks are dropping dead in Europe, and I want my chief investment officer to tell me that Vanderbilt Frink is too fucking big to fail."

"Come on. You know it. I know it." Mackenzie put a hand on Wells's shoulder and squeezed. "We're fine, Robert. All our bets are in the black. We are a fortress, impenetrable."

"Too big to fail?" An ironic smile cracked Wells's face.

"Too smart to fail," Mackenzie said, this time without the irony.

Wells nodded a thanks, then stopped again at the door before leaving. "The Hamptons this weekend. Sally is cooking a roast. Should be good. We'll drink bourbon on the beach."

"Deal," Mackenzie said. "Bourbon on the beach."

Patmore returned with a bag full of new pills that evening. He gave them to Garrett without a word, and with no trace of condemnation in his face, for which Garrett was extremely thankful. He also gave Garrett $19 in change. Garrett considered tipping Patmore, but wasn't sure how do to it without insulting him. Plus, he needed the cash.

Later, around midnight, when some of the team had drifted off to sleep in the corners of the office, Garrett decided to sample the new meds. The pills looked like Percodans, but with black-market stuff you could never be certain. He took one and waited twenty minutes, but felt nothing, so he took another, and then, half an hour after that, two more. By two in the morning, he could no longer remember how many he'd taken, but he knew that his head didn't hurt, and the walls of the office space no longer felt as if they were slowly, incrementally, closing in on him.

He felt good again.

At 2:30 a.m., Avery Bernstein strolled into the office suites, unbidden, with a yapping white bichon frise at his side. He motioned for Garrett to follow him and walked into an empty corner room. Garrett checked to see if anyone else was awake—no one was—and padded after Avery, closing the door behind him. He turned on a single desk lamp and faced his former boss, who was staring out the window, hands clasped behind his back like a general surveying a distant battlefield.

"Something's not right," Avery said.

"Yeah, no pets allowed in the building." Garrett chuckled at his own joke.

"Glib won't get it done, Garrett. Sarcasm is a personality defect. You're missing something. You're not considering all the possibilities. I'm disappointed in you."

Garrett sighed. He hated to admit it, but he was happy to see his hallucination of Avery reappear. He considered, for a moment, that perhaps he had taken all that Percodan for that express purpose—to see Avery again. Or maybe not . . .

"Don't start that shit again." Garrett ran his fingers through his hair. "It's so tiresome."

Avery turned from the window to face Garrett. His white dog sat panting at his feet. "You are wasting your life, Garrett. Your God-given talents."

"I'm gonna have to call bullshit here—the real Avery would never say that."

"I'm pushing you. To be your most effective self. As I did when I was alive."

Garrett had to press his lips together hard to keep from crying. That was exactly what Avery had done when he was alive, and Garrett missed Avery's fatherly advice. Avery believed in Garrett, more than almost anyone else on the planet, and had guided Garrett's chaotic energy into places where it could be constructive, instead of disastrous. Day after day they had talked, first at Yale, where Avery tried to keep Garrett's frenetic brilliance on target, and then a few years later in Avery's corner office at Jenkins & Altshuler, where Avery would try to keep Garrett from ruining his career in spectacular fashion.

"I am trying to find a man who is going to attack the American economy. How is that wasting anything?"

"You're having a conversation with a hallucination. Which means you are very high. Ergo, you are wasting your life."

"Fuck you. Seriously. Fuck your judgments, your money, your privilege—and your dog. I always hated that dog."

"My parents ran a pharmacy in East Flatbush. I'd hardly call that privilege. And my dog never hurt anyone."

Garrett stared at the dog. It sat in the corner, looking up at Garrett, tiny red tongue hanging out of its tiny white face. "What do you want from me?"

"I want you to think hard about the big picture. The big picture of your own life. I want you to straighten up, work harder. Apply your genius to the chaos and give it order. That's why you were put on this earth. That's what you do."

"I'm trying." Garrett's words came out almost as a plea.

"No, you are not. Not really. You are going through the motions. You are not yourself."

Avery moved across the room toward Garrett, and Garrett's heart thumped loudly. He pointed a finger at Avery. "You are not yourself. You're a ghost, *ergo*, not yourself." Avery was so close that Garrett could smell him—smell the cologne he wore, and the faint hint of old-man sweat around his collar.

"Is that stoner logic? Because it's idiotic."

"Chinese food," Garrett said, ignoring Avery's riposte. "That place on Tenth Avenue. We went every Sunday. You remember that? That was a nice ritual."

"Grief will not get it done. Move past it."

"I can't."

"Why not?"

"Because I have nobody." Garrett's voice cracked slightly. "You left me."

"Don't be a drama queen. I didn't leave anyone. I was murdered."

Garrett winced. Avery had been murdered—murdered, most probably, because he'd been connected to Garrett, and Garrett was connected to Ascendant. A direct line of guilt went from Garrett Reilly to Avery Bernstein's death, a line that led right to Garrett's broken heart. All his problems—all his pain and his confusion and his addiction—they could all be traced back to the day Avery died, to the gaping hole that his absence left in Garrett's psyche.

"Because of me," Garrett said. "You were murdered because of what I was doing."

"Now the self-pity? Come on. I was murdered because there are evil people out there who don't care about human costs or consequences. Those people need your full attention, and they need your attention now."

"There's no such thing as evil. There's just people doing what works best for them."

"You don't really believe that."

"Maybe I do." Garrett raised his voice. "Maybe I believe self-interest trumps morality every time. Maybe I just want to be left alone."

"Grow up. Grow up and do what is required of you to make the world better."

"Of all the places I expect some sympathy, my own fucking unconscious would be top of the list!" Garrett yelled.

"Garrett?"

Garrett snapped his head around. The door was cracked open. Bingo peeked into the office. His eyes scanned the room. "You okay?"

Words failed Garrett. He stood there, silent.

"Who you talking to?" Bingo's eyes landed back on Garrett, arms still raised over his head, midgesture.

He dropped his hands to his side. "No one."

"I thought I heard yelling." Bingo checked his phone. "It's three in the morning."

Garrett glanced to where Avery Bernstein had been standing. He was gone, no trace of him left, nothing but empty space in the office. Garrett's heart sank. "Kind of hard to explain."

"Okay. Maybe you should get some sleep. Or at least keep your voice down."

Bingo left the room, closed the door, and Garrett sank to his knees in a corner. He cursed himself, his addiction, and his neediness, and hoped he could keep it together long enough to extract himself from the hole into which he seemed to be sinking. He closed his eyes and began sorting passwords in his head, hoping he'd find one that led to Ilya Markov.

B ingo woke the team at 5:00 a.m. They gathered groggily in the conference room, sitting on the floor, backs up against the white walls. Bingo closed the door and they kept their voices down. Garrett was still asleep two rooms over, and Bingo wanted him to stay asleep.

"I heard him at three in the morning. He was having a conversation with himself. I think he was hallucinating."

"I talk to myself all the time," Mitty said. "Don't mean I'm hallucinating."

"He was talking to someone. And that someone was not talking back. I listened for like five minutes."

"When you went into the room, did he seem strange to you, Bingo?" Alexis asked.

"He seemed . . ." Bingo considered his words for a moment. "He seemed scared. He seemed high."

"Do you know what kind of drugs he might have been taking?" Alexis asked.

Bingo shook his head no, but then Patmore snapped out the answer: "Percodan."

Everyone in the conference room stared at the marine private, their faces suddenly alive with surprise and simmering anger.

"He said his head hurt," Patmore said. "He gave me money. So I went and bought them for him."

"When?" Celeste asked angrily. "When did you do this?"

"Yesterday. I checked on Craigslist. There were a bunch of sellers. I walked. Not far. A guy at a corner market. Nice dude. Hindu. Or a Sikh or something. He sold me a bagful."

"How could you? You enabled a drug addict to get his fix," Celeste said. "You're as bad as the guy selling the drugs."

Patmore shrugged. "I don't believe drugs should be illegal. Just my opinion. People are gonna do what they do. Who am I to stop them?"

"Did I miss the sign on the door? Is this a fucking Ayn Rand convention?" Celeste said.

"I just don't see what the big deal is," Patmore said. "And I have no idea who you are talking about."

"The big deal is that Garrett is high, and he may not be thinking straight," Alexis said. "Especially if he's hallucinating. We can't have that. It's too dangerous a situation."

"Look, Garrett's always taken drugs," Mitty said. "The whole time I've known him. He used to smoke more pot than anyone I know. Like every day, three, four times a day. Now he's switched to scrips, which I admit isn't like ideal or anything, but he's still doing his job. I just think we should let it go."

"That's nuts, Mitty," Celeste said. "If you're so high that you're hallucinating, you're not doing your job, and I don't want to have anything to do with you. And I certainly don't want you making life-or-death decisions for me or anyone I'm close to."

"Don't be an uptight bitch," Mitty said.

"Fuck you. Don't be a knee-jerk enabler of your drug-addict friend," Celeste shot back.

"Okay, okay." Alexis put her hands out for calm. "Let's take it down a notch."

The team sat quietly, then Alexis nodded to Mitty. "We get that you're loyal to Garrett, and that's fine, but we can't have someone leading us who is completely wasted. I mean, he needs to be able to differentiate between imagination and reality—"

"You really think he can't tell the difference between—" Mitty started to say.

"I'm just saying that we need to be able to trust him," Alexis said. "This is a murder case. And a possible terror attack. Garrett needs to be clear about what is going on in the world around him. Without that, he's useless to us."

"So what are you suggesting?" Mitty asked. "We abandon him? Walk away?

Because listen, Garrett is wanted by the FBI, and I don't think he did it. And neither do you, right, or you wouldn't be here. We leave, then he's on his own, he probably gets nabbed. And whatever we are trying to stop definitely happens."

"Valid point," Alexis said.

"Fuck yeah, valid," Mitty said.

"We should vote on it," Bingo said just above a whisper. "We stick around or we go."

"No. That's bullshit," Mitty said. "This ain't a democracy."

"I think it's a good idea," Celeste said. "We make a decision as a team. It's binding. Stay or go. We all abide by the vote."

"I'm good with voting," Patmore said.

"Same," said Alexis.

Everyone looked to Mitty, who grimaced, then said, "Fine," but she did not look happy about it. "If you bitches vote to leave, and then that Russian asshole does some nasty shit, well, it's gonna be on your heads. I'm just saying."

Alexis looked at each member briefly. "Show of hands. Who thinks we should close up shop, quit Ascendant?"

Celeste's hand shot up. A moment later, Bingo raised his hand as well.

Mitty stared at him, eyes narrowed to slits. "Really? *Really?*"

"If you'd seen him yelling at nobody in that room," Bingo said, "you'd do the same."

Mitty made a hissing sound between her teeth and looked away.

"Okay, who wants to stick around?" Alexis asked.

Mitty raised her hand, as did Patmore. They held them up as Celeste turned to Alexis. "Two to two. It's up to you, Captain."

Alexis frowned. The dawn outside the window was beginning to turn the sky light blue. She could see the silhouettes of the towers of Manhattan in the distance, tiny against the immense sky overhead.

"The decision is yours," Mitty said.

Alexis let out a long breath, as if she had truly not made up her mind until this point. The sun shone a sliver of yellow over New York City. She nodded briefly to Mitty, raising her hand. "One more chance. He gets one more chance." Then Alexis stood up and walked out of the conference room.

Ilya Markov read his latest text message, then deleted it, pleased, as he ducked into a liquor mart on Wilkinson Boulevard, west of downtown Charlotte. The text had been from Rachel Brown, an update on her encounter in Atlanta, and so far, so good, at least as far as Ilya could tell. Rachel was enigmatic, saying she and Harris had made contact, and that the congressman had seemed intrigued, but she didn't elaborate.

Ilya was okay with that. He trusted Rachel, even if he couldn't say why, exactly—something to do with the flat, almost detached quality of her personality. When you gave people like that a task, they just did it and didn't ask too many questions. She was a bit of a sociopath, and that was fine with him. In his line of work, sociopaths made excellent coworkers.

Inside the decrepit liquor mart—EDDIE'S JUNIOR MARKET, the broken plastic sign read—Ilya pulled an iced tea from the cooler and lingered over the newspaper rack, perusing the headlines of the *Charlotte Observer* and *USA Today*. The Steinkamp murder was all over the front page, but so were smaller articles on the state of the economy. The Dow had lost another three hundred points yesterday, making it a thousand for the week, and rumors were flying about phantom bank runs and looming credit shocks. Ilya took a moment to relish the news; he'd set a rock in motion down the side of a mountain, and that rock would soon gather company—and become an avalanche.

Ilya passed on the papers—he got all his news online—and approached the register. He had the iced tea in one hand, and with the other he held a blue work shirt and a pair of blue work pants, both hung on metal coat hangers and slung over his shoulder. He'd bought them twenty minutes ago from a Goodwill down the block, and together they made a spot-on service uniform, which was exactly what Ilya needed. With a needle and thread, and an hour to do the work, he would have a new persona ready for tomorrow morning.

He laid the iced tea on the counter and looked up at the large, unshaven clerk behind the register. He had muttonchop sideburns, his long hair pulled back in a ponytail, and he smelled of coffee and cigarettes. A small television played at his elbow, a morning news-talk show, and Ilya could hear the male and female hosts chatting in solemn voices about something heinous, or what they wanted their audience to believe was heinous, although he couldn't see the picture on the screen, as it was turned away from the counter.

"And a pack of Camel unfiltered," Ilya said, pulling out his wallet. He laid a $20 bill on the counter.

The clerk grabbed a pack of cigarettes from the rack, dropped them on the counter, looked up into Ilya's face, and stared. And kept staring.

His eyes shot back to the TV, and then to Ilya again.

Ilya smiled, surprised at the intensity of the man's gaze, then tapped the counter. "What do I owe you?"

The clerk rang up the sale, slowly, methodically, then said, "Eight fifty."

Ilya nodded to the twenty on the counter, and as the man took the money, Ilya felt a hollowness in his stomach, an instinctive dropping-out in his gut that was telling him something was very wrong here. Ilya relied on his instincts to steer him clear of danger; they had saved his life—or at least kept him out of jail—on any number of occasions, and they were howling at him at the moment.

"Passing through?" the man behind the counter said.

Ilya shook his head. "No. I live down the block. Just moved in." He smiled as he said the lie, trying to keep his voice affable. Friendliness got you what you wanted a lot faster than confrontation, Ilya had learned in his years in the game, and now he just wanted his change and to get the hell out of the store.

"Really? Down the block? Not a lot of people live around here. Like, maybe no one." The clerk shot a curious glance at Ilya, then pulled cash from the register and laid it on the counter. As Ilya reached for his money, the man slapped a beefy hand on top of Ilya's, fingers wrapping around Ilya's wrist, pinning his hand to the Formica.

"AMBER Alert, asshole," the clerk barked, all friendliness gone from his voice.

Ilya tried to pull back his hand, but the man was remarkably strong. Ilya racked his brain, panic growing, trying to remember where he'd heard the term *AMBER Alert* before. Was that some sort of police warning? Ilya was not particularly powerful, and when brute force needed to be applied to a situation, he always found himself at a disadvantage. His left hand still held the uniform draped over his shoulder.

"Where's the kid?" the clerk growled.

"What kid? What are you talking about?"

"You know what the fuck I'm talking about. The boy you snatched. You're not moving from this store until the police get here. Fucking child molester."

Ilya grimaced. He dropped the hangers with the pants and shirt and tried with his free hand to pry the clerk's meaty paw off his wrist. But the clerk's grip was like a vise. The clerk grabbed a phone and was about to dial with his left hand when Ilya decided: he had only seconds to fix the situation.

He grunted hard and held his breath, forcing the blood to his head, then began to shake—all over his body. He went into spasms. Spit sprayed from his lips. He knew, from practice, that he looked terrifying, like a man having an epileptic seizure, face dark red, head bobbing back and forth. Sure enough, the clerk stared at Ilya, mouth sagging open. He released the pressure on Ilya's hand for just a moment, gasping, "What the fuck"—and that was his last mistake. Ilya wasn't about to give him another chance.

With one fluid motion Ilya yanked his hand back from the clerk's grip, grabbed the bottle of iced tea from the counter, and smashed it into the clerk's temple, just above his eyes. The bottle shattered, sending glass and iced tea raining to the ground, and the jagged, broken end of the bottle that remained in Ilya's hand raked across the clerk's eyes and forehead. The clerk screamed, dropping the phone and bringing his hand to his bloodied face. Ilya reared back with that same jagged bottle end and rammed it into the clerk's throat, twisting once, and slicing into his Adam's apple and windpipe.

The sound was gruesome, the snap of tearing flesh, and the clerk gurgled another cry of pain and terror, then fell back onto the floor behind the register, gasping for breath and trying to keep the blood from spouting from his neck. Ilya watched him, trying to determine if the man would die, and decided, without much data, that he would not. Not yet, at least.

Ilya reached over the counter and hung up the phone, then grabbed the small TV and turned it toward him. On-screen, two anchors, a young woman and an older man, were sitting on stools and chatting in a carefully manicured broadcast studio, with the name *Charlotte Today* projected onto the lower third of the screen. Ilya didn't pay attention to what they were talking about because behind them, on a screen in the back of the studio, was his own passport photo, enlarged halfway from the floor to the ceiling, his eyes staring into the camera. The name Ilya Markov was written below the photo in a faux Most Wanted typeface. The words *AMBER Alert* accompanied his name.

"*Sukin syn.*" Ilya pressed his lips together and quickly wiped his fingerprints from the plastic of the television and the phone. *Son of a bitch.* Rage shot through his body, a blinding-hot fury. He knew immediately who had done this, and he could even guess how it had been pulled off, and his first thought was of bloody retribution. But now was not the time to contemplate revenge. His situation was too perilous. Everything needed to be put right, and quickly, before payback could be planned.

He looked back down at the clerk—rolling on the floor and struggling to get air into his lungs—and made a snap decision. He vaulted over the countertop, found a large, jagged piece of glass from the iced-tea bottle, and sawed powerfully at the clerk's throat, finishing the job he had started a minute earlier.

The clerk tried to howl, but the noise wouldn't come, drowned out by the blood and the air rushing from his cut throat. Ilya watched him die, eyes glancing back at the liquor mart's front door every few seconds. He remembered the first time he had watched someone die, as a child during the Chechen war. He and a band of friends had found a wounded Russian soldier hiding in a bombed-out basement, unarmed and begging for help. Instead of aiding him, Ilya had convinced his friends to cover the soldier in chunks of broken cement, piece by piece, the soldier pleading for his life, until the weight of it forced the air from his lungs. The Russian soldier had invaded Ilya's homeland, killed innocent people, and so Ilya had in turn killed him for his crimes.

He hadn't enjoyed it, just as he wasn't enjoying killing the clerk, but he found that he could turn off a part of his brain when he did horrible things, so that the nature of what he had done didn't cause him consternation—or slow him down. That on/off switch in his thinking was a useful tool, and the switch was currently in the off position. He suspected it might have to stay that way for a while.

When the clerk stopped breathing, Ilya leapt the counter again, locked the front door, and wiped any surfaces he thought he might have touched. That done, he spotted a closed-circuit video camera in a ceiling corner, found the camera's DVR in the back room, and erased every image on it from the last hour. When he discovered that the machine wasn't Net connected—and that no other images were stored anywhere in the liquor mart—he went a step further and opened the machine with a screwdriver he'd found beneath the cash register, removed the hard drive, and slipped it into his pocket for later destruction.

When he was finished, he carefully grabbed a replacement iced tea and two packs of unfiltered Camels, draped the uniform shirt and pants back over his shoulder, and slipped out the store's back door to head north, to get as far away as he could from Charlotte, North Carolina, as fast as he could, and to repay the favor that Garrett Reilly had just done him.

Celeste Chen cursed her arrogance as she checked the addresses on the buildings on Lafayette Avenue in the Bronx. She had been sure everyone in Ascendant would agree with her—that Garrett was a drug addict and that they needed to abandon this insane mission immediately. She was even the one who suggested that the vote be binding. There was no way she could lose. But she did. And now she was fucked, because what she really thought she should do was climb back on a plane and head to the West Coast.

Instead, she was in the Bronx, looking for Anna Bachev's apartment.

"The FBI has been all over this," she had told Garrett that morning. "There's nothing we're gonna find out about Anna Bachev that they don't know."

Garrett had nodded calmly, as if he were some elder statesman, which drove Celeste nuts. "True, but the FBI aren't sharing data with us, so we need to find out on our own."

So off she went to the Bronx. She'd never been there before, and she'd been expecting towering projects and gang members fighting in the streets. But Hunts Point, while poor and mostly black, was nothing like that. There were markets and offices, tidy apartment buildings, and seemingly happy women pushing baby strollers. It seemed like any other working-class neighborhood in a big city.

"Look for details," Garrett had said back in Newark. "Remember—he exploits people's weaknesses."

Celeste found Bachev's building—764 Bryant Avenue—and knocked on the manager's door. The manager, a dour-looking Hispanic woman in her fifties, listened to Celeste claim to be from a legal aid foundation that was working for Anna Bachev's family, then slammed the door in Celeste's face. Celeste could hear her cursing in Spanish as she bolted locks and turned up the television.

Celeste stepped outside and called Garrett on the burner cell phone he had given her. They had agreed to not use names when they spoke, and to avoid all specifics of place or time.

"Manager told me to get lost," she said. "And some other stuff, but it was in Spanish."

"Expected. Check local stores, markets, whatever. See if they know her, know anything about her."

Celeste sighed. She couldn't imagine a task she could hate more than starting conversations with strangers and trying to extract information from them. Garrett seemed to sense that over the phone. "You did it once, brilliantly. You can do it again." He was referring to China, and the detective work she had done there. He was right; she had been good at it, Celeste thought, but that still didn't make it any easier.

She found a Starbucks down the block on Lafayette Avenue, bought herself a latte, and tried to make conversation with a pair of baristas, but neither of them had even heard of Anna Bachev.

"Don't follow the news much?" Celeste asked, even though she knew she shouldn't. It amazed her how badly informed Americans were at times.

The baristas, a young girl with purple hair and a boy with dreadlocks, stared at Celeste with blank faces, and she backed quickly out of the coffee shop. She stopped in a market, but the Korean owner barely spoke English; then she peeked her head into a dry cleaner's and a pawnshop, but those also seemed like dead ends.

She called Garrett again. "Nothing."

"All right; come back," he said, disappointment in his voice, and hung up.

Celeste immediately hated herself for caring what he thought. She stood on the corner of Hunts Point Avenue and tried to think of any other angles she could exploit. Beater cars cruised past her, and a young man whistled at her from a gold-painted Camry. A Chinese restaurant was on the corner, and at the side entrance an old Chinese woman sat on an overturned plastic pail, peeling the leaves off a pile of bok choy.

Celeste walked up to the old woman. *"Nín hǎo."* Hello.

"Nín hǎo." The old woman didn't look up.

"Wǒ shi jǐngchá," Celeste said. *I work for the police.*

The old woman stared up at Celeste, then studied her from head to toe without saying a word. From the look on her face, Celeste could tell that the old woman didn't believe a word of it. But she shrugged nonetheless and continued in Mandarin, "What do you want?"

"I am trying to find out about the woman who lived here, the woman who shot the banker in Manhattan. Her name was Anna Bachev."

The old woman went back to peeling the leaves off the bok choy.

"Did you know her?"

The old woman shrugged.

Celeste took that as a yes. Her pulse quickened. "She came here sometimes? To the restaurant?"

Again, the woman shrugged.

"How often did she come to eat here?"

The old woman stopped peeling and took in the sky for a moment. "Not so much lately."

Celeste smiled. The old woman was talking. That was good. "Why not lately? Do you know?"

"Very sad."

"Depressed?"

"Yes." The old woman nodded. "Very depressed. This country makes people depressed."

Celeste nodded. There was truth in that. Especially if you were peeling vegetables on the sidewalk in the middle of the Bronx on a hot summer's day. But there was something else the old woman wasn't telling her. "Yes, it does. Makes me depressed sometimes too." Celeste waited a moment. "Was there anything else?"

The old woman squinted slightly in the midday sun. "Lose her baby."

"She had a miscarriage?"

The old woman shook her head. "No, she had a baby. But they took it away. Because she was a drug addict. They took it out of the country."

Celeste blinked in surprise. "Who did? Who took it away?" She realized immediately that she had raised her voice too quickly and spoken too fast. The old woman ducked her head and dove back into peeling bok choy.

Celeste took a long breath, then tried again, slowly, respectfully. "Could you tell me, maybe, where the baby went? Please."

The old woman said nothing. Celeste waited. The sun beat down on her. She measured her breaths. If she had learned anything from her time in China, it was patience, always patience. Finally, after a full two minutes of silent peeling, the old woman made the slightest of head gestures, nodding back across Hunts Point Avenue. If Celeste hadn't been watching closely, she would have missed it, but she didn't. She turned and looked. The old woman had nodded to a Medicaid clinic a block away. Celeste hadn't thought to look in there.

"Xièxiè, xièxiè." Thank you, thank you. Celeste hurried back across Hunts Point Avenue and walked to the front door of the clinic. The place looked like a thousand other storefront medical offices across the country. A laminated placard in the window said WE ACCEPT MEDICARE AND MEDICAID and SE HABLA ESPAÑOL. She opened the front door, walked inside, and knew immediately that she had hit the jackpot.

Half a dozen black and Latino patients were spread out across chairs in the front room. One woman rocked a crying baby. Another man cradled his bandaged elbow in his hand. But that wasn't the revelation. The revelation was that everyone behind the counter in the clinic—the two nurses, the clerk working the phone, and the doctor who poked his head in from the hallway—was speaking Russian.

Ten minutes later, walking toward the subway stop at Longwood Avenue, Celeste called Garrett one last time. "I know how they got her to do it."

"Yeah?"

"She had a baby. They took it back to Russia. My guess is, held it ransom."

"No shit." There was a long silence. "I guess that would do it."

Celeste agreed, then got on the subway, and all the way back to Manhattan, then out to New Jersey on the PATH train, she felt the barest hint of inner satisfaction. There had been a puzzle, and she had solved it. Done and done.

She was back.

Alexis watched as General Kline stepped out from a stand of trees at the edge of the park, a hundred yards from the lot off Military Road, and into the glare of the noon sun. The wash of sunlight allowed her to make out her boss's face, and he was not happy. But then, neither was Alexis; she was tired, having just driven all the way from Newark to DC in four straight hours, and hungry and scared.

"Have you lost your mind?" Kline roared. "After everything we talked about?"

Over the phone, at six in the morning—after the Ascendant team had had their makeshift staff meeting—she'd hinted to Kline in the most oblique language possible as to whom she'd been with during the last few days, and what they'd been doing. Kline had clearly gotten the point. He told her where to meet him and hung up without another word. She'd driven the rest of the morning near tears. Now, in the park, standing face-to-face with him, Alexis felt even worse, like a wayward child who'd just disappointed her loving parent.

She told him, in a low, rapid whisper, about Markov, the passports, and his background, about how Garrett had predicted it, and what Garrett thought might be about to happen, but Kline cut her off before she could finish.

"This is not our fight. He is not a member of the program. Anyway, it doesn't matter—he's wanted on a murder charge. You cannot protect him from that."

"He's being set up for that exact reason. So that he won't help track down Markov."

"You are aiding and abetting a fugitive from justice."

"Sir, it's more complicated than that. I believe time is of the essence, and the FBI doesn't understand that yet—"

Kline waved his hand in the air, as if swatting away her arguments. "You want my help? You want the DIA back in on this?"

"I don't think we'll be able to stop Markov without more sophisticated technology. We need real-time tracking, access to corporate networks. Things that you and I know DIA can get."

"For a paranoid fantasy?"

Alexis had to take a moment after Kline said that. Bingo's words, his description of Garrett talking to himself in the empty office, echoed in her head. She pushed on. "The man is a terrorist. He is set on taking down the American financial system."

"And which man are we talking about? This Russian? Or Garrett Reilly?"

Down a trail, she heard a pair of joggers chatting to each other as they ran, but she couldn't see them. She hoped they couldn't see her as well.

"How do you know Reilly's not playing you? Using you to achieve his own ends? It would certainly make sense, given that he paid someone to kill a federal banker."

"I know you are angry with Reilly for what he did to Ascendant, but—"

"Do not psychoanalyze me, Truffant."

"He's been spot-on about everything having to do with Markov so far. I see no reason to stop believing him now." That was a lie. She did see reasons to stop believing Garrett. But she would ignore those reasons for the time being.

Kline shook his head in a blur of motion. "No, no, and no. I don't buy it. Not for a second. And anyway, it's way past our authority now." He pulled his cell phone out of his pocket and held it out to Alexis. "Call the FBI. Tell them everything. Your involvement, Reilly's whereabouts. The whole nine yards. If Reilly's telling the truth, then the FBI will discover that and go after this Russian. If he's lying, then at least you turned him in."

Alexis took a long breath. "No," she managed to say.

Kline's face flashed disappointment. He gave a quick nod, as if he expected her response, then turned the phone around and started to dial. "Then you leave me no choice but to call them myself and report you all."

"I'll take you down with me," Alexis said.

Kline froze. Alexis could feel her entire life rushing at her; everything she'd worked for, all the orders she'd followed, all the rules she'd upheld—she was about to explode it all. She could barely make her mouth function or her voice come out of her throat. She had lived within the guidelines of the military, or within a family that was deeply enmeshed in the military, for almost all of her twenty-eight years. The Truffants were American patriots and did what they were told, when they were told to do it. And now she was blackmailing her superior officer.

Alexis wanted to climb out of her skin. She wanted to run away as fast as she could, anything not to see the hurt and betrayal on her mentor's face.

"You wouldn't dare," Kline managed to say.

Alexis simply nodded. She would. She would absolutely dare.

"You realize this ends our relationship. Everything we've ever done together."

Again, she nodded. Yes, she realized; she knew only too well. She was fully in Garrett Reilly's boat, and that boat would either float her to success or sink her into unfathomable failure and disgrace.

They stood in silence in the growing heat of the day, the birds singing, distant traffic echoing through the trees. Alexis waited for some sign from her boss, some inkling of emotion, or a clue as to what he would do or say.

Finally, Kline pocketed his phone. "So be it," he said, and walked away.

Sitting on the couch in Garrett Reilly's apartment, Special Agent Jayanti Chaudry tried to let the frustration and exhaustion of the case run off her shoulders. She tried to meditate, as her father had once taught her to do in her childhood home back in Elizabeth, New Jersey, but it didn't help. Meditation, as far as she could tell, was a whole lot of Indian-themed bullshit.

So much of the story of Phillip Steinkamp's murder was escaping her grasp, and the pressure to find his killer was skyrocketing. They were calling from the Hoover Building in DC every few hours, mostly executive assistant directors, but the last call had come from the deputy director himself, and it had not been fun. He had been terse, and expectant, and not particularly supportive of the job she was doing. Add in the constant media speculation and the energy drain of daily press conferences, and Chaudry was wiped out. Plus, she had barely slept.

Her brief attempt at transcendence ruined by the onrushing thoughts in her head, Chaudry picked herself up and took one more spin around Reilly's apartment. She had gone through the place once, five days ago, when the FBI had first battered down his door, but at the time she had let the forensics team do most of the investigating. They had written up their findings in four different reports, and Chaudry had read them, every single word, but she still felt she was missing something. The place was telling her something about Reilly, but what?

Walking from room to room, the space was much as Chaudry remembered it: a Spartan bachelor pad with a few pieces of furniture, some nice suits, and stacks of books on statistics and finance. Beyond Reilly's security obsession— the FBI techs had found six online cameras, two motion detectors, and bolt locks on every window—a couple of things stood out for her.

One was the inordinate number of prescription drugs secreted about the place. There were bottles in his bathroom cabinet, three by his bed, and half a dozen more in the kitchen. Reilly seemed to have pain issues, and if he wasn't already an addict, he certainly was well on his way to becoming one. Some of the prescriptions were obviously black-market fakes, but others were legit. An agent at the field office had already started an investigation into which local doctors had so casually prescribed him meds.

Two, Reilly had money, but he didn't seem interested in spending it. Agents had found multiple account statements in his desk, from brokerage houses all over the world. Reilly was nearly a millionaire, and the guy was still three years shy of thirty. He had more money than Chaudry's entire family, yet his apartment was sparsely furnished, and the furniture was a level below IKEA quality: a beater La-Z-Boy, a couch that looked as if it had been found on a street corner, and a TV that was five years old at a minimum. Only his computer technology seemed current, and even that was limited to a pair of sleek laptops, three LED monitors, and a laser printer. If he was proving himself by becoming rich, it wasn't to the world at large—no conspicuous consumption was involved. Chaudry thought that perhaps he was proving himself . . . *to himself.* As if to say, *I can do this. I really can.* That was odd, but she also kind of liked it.

And finally, Reilly was a man obsessed, but he wasn't obsessed with Phillip Steinkamp. Of his two laptops, the first was password protected and basically uncrackable. They'd sent it to DC, to the tech lab, but the hard drive had erased itself once they got close to decrypting it. But his second laptop, which he seemed to use exclusively for e-mail and was unprotected, was full of references to the many people who were stalking him on the Web. He had links to endless chat rooms and bulletin boards dedicated to discovering who made up the Ascendant team. Possible members were listed—brokers, mathematicians, programmers, and finance professors—and Reilly's name was on a few of them. In one file he saved hate mail—easily five hundred pieces of it, most of them laced with death threats. None of them had been sent exclusively to him—they were group hate blasts—but they were alarming nonetheless.

Ascendant r Nazis. Find them, kill them. Slit their throats, read one. *Die fuck-*

heads die was another popular e-mail header. A handheld video, blurry and taken at night from Reilly's living-room window, showed a group of young men standing on the street corner and pointing up at the camera, laughing and shouting obscenities. Chaudry couldn't make out if the harassment was aimed at Reilly or was just drunken revelry, but either way, the cameras and the window locks suddenly made a lot of sense. No one seemed to have zeroed in on Reilly as a leader of Ascendant, but people were certainly getting close.

However, there were no references, anywhere in Reilly's apartment, to Steinkamp or Anna Bachev or the New York Fed. Not a link, not a newspaper clipping, not a Web-browser history reference. Nothing. The FBI tech said Reilly might have erased them all, but Chaudry somehow doubted it. You could scrub your life of most evidence of your crime, but eventually, somewhere, somehow, the FBI would find a trace of it: a fingerprint, an e-mail, a thrice-removed connection to a handgun, a killer, or a payment to that killer.

Chaudry walked into the kitchen and tapped her fingernails on the cheap, faux-Formica counter. She poured herself a glass of water from the kitchen faucet and surveyed the living space. It was like any other New York living room, and yet—what was it? It was different. *Reilly was different.* She still believed that he wanted to reach out to her and would continue to want to, but maybe she had missed his overtures. They could be right in front of her face, and she was simply blind to them. She moved to the window and admired the gradations in the colors of the sign of the nail salon—Pinkie's—across the street: glowing red melted into a deep orange, which tapered into the softest pink.

Then it hit her. *Patterns.*

The nail-salon sign was patterned. Reilly's apartment was a series of patterns. Why hadn't she seen it before? She snapped away from the window and reexamined the room. Nothing was haphazard. The furniture, beat-up as it was, started black in one corner, and tall, and then the pieces got lighter in color and shorter as you crossed the room. The books that looked scattered along the wall were actually perfectly alphabetized by author, *A* to *Z*. She rushed into the kitchen to inspect the glasses: they were each stacked according to height and width, high and skinny to low and fat. She jumped back to the living room: the brokerage accounts were arranged according to the amount of money they contained, lowest to highest. The closer she looked, the more the patterns jumped out at her. The locks on the front door: one bolt to five, top to bottom; the suits:

by country of origin, US to Europe to Asia; the drugs: strongest dosage by his bed, midlevel in the kitchen, weakest by the door.

The apartment wasn't orderly—it was a mess—but everywhere you looked, if you tried, you could discern a pattern. Reilly was compelled to arrange his life so that it made sense, but the only thing that made sense to him were patterns. They were how he saw absolutely everything.

Chaudry dropped back onto the couch, bathed in waves of satisfaction. She'd cracked him, not completely, but some, and every piece helped. But now, how to apply that knowledge? She was about to start in on that task when her phone rang. It was the Manhattan field office.

"Agent Chaudry here."

"We got a hit on the Rodriguez woman." Agent Murray's gruff voice crackled on the line. "PATH cameras got her entering the train at World Trade Center. Film is from two days ago."

"Any exit video?"

"Not yet. Still checking."

"Send someone to check all the exit stations."

"On it." Murray hung up.

So Mitty Rodriguez took the PATH train? Chaudry knew the train well—she'd grown up south of Newark—and there weren't a lot of stops, just a handful in Hoboken, Jersey City, and Newark. Was Garrett Reilly near one of them, somewhere in New Jersey? And if so, why there? Her eyes tracked across the mostly empty room, and she smiled because she already knew the answer.

Wherever he was, however he reached out to her, she would use the patterns that he created to find him. Because Reilly seemed incapable of leading his life in any other way.

His burner cell phone rang, and Garrett checked the caller ID. It was a pay phone, 202 area code, Washington, DC.

He answered immediately. "Tell me."

"We're in," Alexis said quickly, and hung up.

Garrett gathered the team—three of them, at least; Celeste hadn't returned from the Bronx yet—and told them the plan. They would be pulling the passenger manifest for Lufthansa flight number 462 on June 15. They were to pose as airline-employed telemarketers, phoning to ask recent passengers about their experience on Lufthansa's transatlantic coach service.

"It's a customer-satisfaction survey," Garrett said. "If they don't want to talk to you, tell them we're offering flight vouchers for their time."

Patmore looked up warily. "We have flight vouchers to give them?"

"We're lying, Patmore," Garrett said. "We're not telemarketers either."

Patmore nodded, as if that thought hadn't yet occurred to him.

"Ask about the flight, the service, then ask about their seating companions. Did they like them? Talk to them? Explain that we're thinking of instituting a new protocol—you can choose your seatmate from a master list. Would you chose that person again? Get them to open up, describe their seatmate— what was he or she like?"

The manifest came in ten minutes later, and Garrett broke the passenger list into sections, with each Ascendant team member getting a handful of names.

No one had any luck. None of the passengers who'd been seated around Ilya Markov's seat—27H in coach—had any recollection of a young man seated near them, Russian or otherwise. Patmore and Bingo carefully modulated their voices to sound like poorly paid call-center employees, and people were cooperative, for the most part—one man cursed them and hung up, but he was the exception. Garrett felt a twinge of guilt promising them flight vouchers that would never materialize, but he wasn't robbing them of anything more than a few minutes. Anyway, it was for a good cause. That's what he kept telling himself: everything in his life was for a good cause now. That was a load of shit, but it kept him going.

Celeste showed up a few minutes later, looking hot and tired; she gave him the rundown on the old woman at the Chinese restaurant and the clinic in Hunts Point. She had asked the nurse behind the desk about Anna Bachev, but the nurse said she'd never heard the name before. From the look of surprise on her face and the way she fled to the back of the offices, Celeste didn't believe her, but Celeste didn't have any way of forcing the truth out of her either.

"We'll probe their computer systems later," Garrett said. "At the very least, this is another link between Steinkamp, Markov, and Russia. Good work and thanks."

Celeste stared at him blankly, but she didn't swear or take a swing at his jaw, and Garrett decided that this was progress in their relationship. Quite a bit of progress, actually.

At nine that night, Garrett shut down the effort; he figured no customer-satisfaction survey would call people past then, and the team seemed beat. Patmore brought in take-out Mexican food and beer, and Garrett got the distinct sense that Mitty was counting how many he drank. He tried to break into the servers of the Hunts Point Medicaid Clinic, but he couldn't find any worth hacking. He suspected they were mostly a pen-and-paper business—easier to defraud people that way. He checked trades in the black pool that he had noticed a week ago and thought he saw another ripple of buying movement around Crowd Analytics. The name had come up twice now—that was a foundation for a pattern, and he knew it.

At midnight he slipped into the bathroom and took a few more Percodans, then staggered into a corner and fell asleep on a pile of old towels. He tossed and turned all night.

At six the next morning, Mitty woke him by kicking him in the ankle. The sun was streaming in the window, and it took Garrett fifteen minutes just to get his eyes accustomed to the light. They ate a breakfast of stale bagels and got back to work. After about a dozen calls, Celeste got a hit: a woman from Fort Lauderdale remembered seeing a young man start to set his backpack down on seat 27H, but then he changed his mind and kept walking. As if he'd read his boarding pass wrong.

"He switched seats," Garrett said when Celeste told him the news. "He knew the manifest would tell us who he sat next to but that if he switched seats, it would be harder to figure out who he scammed. And he must have scammed someone."

"He could have gone anywhere. It would take days to contact everyone on the entire flight," Celeste said.

"No. We don't have to." Garrett closed his eyes to imagine the inside of the plane five days ago: crowded, grumpy passengers, patient flight attendants. Noise, crying children, people trying to jam roll-on bags into the overhead bins. He searched his imagination for some hint of a trail that Markov might have left.

"He went to his assigned seat. There were women on both sides of him. That doesn't help him with identity theft," Garrett said, eyes still closed. "He can't use a woman's name. So he moved. But it was boarding time. Chaos. People shoving bags in the overhead compartments. He wouldn't have fought traffic to go toward the front of the plane—too hard. And he probably wouldn't have switched aisles. It was an Airbus A340."

Bingo pulled up seatguru.com, a plane-seating website, for the layout of the Lufthansa flights to Florida. Bingo ran his fingers in a line down the map of the plane. "We could call people in rows twenty-eight through forty-five, seats D, E, H, and F. That's a lot of people, but not impossible."

"No, not necessary," Garrett said. "Just the passengers with empty seats next to them."

Ten minutes later, Bingo called out from a corner of the office, "Got him!"

The team gathered around Bingo's desk.

"Thirty-four H and J," Bingo said. "James Delacourt, from Bethesda, Maryland, was in H, and he sat next to a young guy named Ilya."

Garrett broke into a wide grin.

"Delacourt didn't come right out and admit it, but I think they got drunk together. They talked for a long time, and then he fell asleep. He said he 'passed out.' He woke up just before they landed. He said he thought Ilya had mentioned that he was from Russia."

"Markov liquored him up," Celeste said, "and then took advantage of him. Identity date rape."

"Ten to one Delacourt has a drinking problem. Markov found the weakness and targeted it." Garrett turned to Bingo. "Anything else?"

"Yeah, his cell phone wouldn't work once he left the plane. He took it to the Verizon store a few days later and they said his SIM card was missing. They gave him a new one, but charged him, and he was pissed."

"Good," Garrett said. "We can track that number."

"There's more," Bingo said. "Delacourt said he's been having a weird time with his credit card. That's what he thought I was calling about. There were a few minor charges—to political campaigns—that he didn't make. He couldn't figure out how they got there."

"What's that about?" Patmore asked. "Why political campaigns?"

"It's a credit-card-fraud trick," Garrett said. "You test the waters. Markov's seeing if Delacourt is paying attention. Make a small purchase, see if the card gets canceled. Then make a bigger one. If the card stays clean, then you buy the thing you're really interested in."

"So we should call Delacourt, tell him to cancel the card," Celeste said.

"No. We do the opposite. We encourage him to keep the card active, and we track where Markov uses it," Garrett said. "We want to see what he's up to."

Celeste shook her head vigorously. "Delacourt's just some schlep on a business trip. We're hanging him out to dry. All he could afford was coach, and he sat next to the wrong guy. Markov is going to screw him. We can stop that."

Garrett shrugged. "He's doing it for the good of the country."

"That's a rationalization," Celeste said.

"So what?"

"I had almost forgotten your true nature."

Garrett smiled. He told Mitty to run a credit-card watch under DIA auspices. Half an hour later they got a forwarded e-mail alert from the government's HotWatch program: James Delacourt had bought $10,000 worth of computer equipment at a Best Buy in Arlington, Virginia.

The purchase had occurred seventeen minutes ago.

• • •

Alexis arrived at the Best Buy at 11:10 a.m., twenty-seven minutes after Markov's purchase. The sprint from her office to her car had taken two minutes, and the drive from DIA headquarters, across the river, to Pentagon City had taken another eight. She slid her Honda into a parking spot in the mall lot and scanned the cars and shoppers. A mother and her three kids squabbled outside a parked Volvo. A middle-aged man tossed a plastic bag into the trunk of his Hyundai and drove off. A pair of women in fatigues strolled across the street to the mall. There was no sign of Markov.

Alexis found it hard to believe Markov would buy his computer equipment so close to the home of the US military—the Pentagon was a ten-minute walk away, five if you hurried—but then she wasn't entirely sure the Delacourt credit-card hit was actually Markov's. Maybe Delacourt himself had gone into the store. Perhaps he had been the middle-aged man with the Hyundai. Something was wrong with the whole setup. A faint alarm bell began to sound in her head.

The two salesmen in the computer department told her the only people buying laptops in the last hour had been a young couple, a man and a woman—clearly an attractive young woman, from the sly smiles on both the salesmen's faces—and they had bought a cartload of stuff: four laptops, two printers, a dozen memory cards, ten cell phones, extra cable, Wi-Fi routers, and a host of smaller items that they couldn't remember. Chris, the older of the salesmen, seemed to have focused most of his attention on the woman, because when Alexis showed him a printout of Markov's passport photo, he admitted that he hadn't looked too closely at the man.

Alexis sighed silently. Men were such idiots when it came to members of the opposite sex, and so easily distracted. The pretty-girl ruse seemed to be standard in Markov's arsenal of scams, and Alexis could understand why: *it worked*.

"Anything else you can remember about him? Or her?"

Chris nodded quickly, as if eager to make up for the blank he'd drawn on the man's face. "He was carrying a metal lunch box. Like, you know, the kind that construction guys use. Red, about that big."

The blood drained from Alexis's face. She pointed. "Like that one?" The alarm bell in her head was now shrieking.

Chris glanced over his shoulder. Sitting on the floor, tucked under the laptop display rack, was a red metal lunch box. Chris nodded and started for it. "Yeah. He must have forgotten it—"

Alexis grabbed the salesman by the arm and yanked him backward. "Leave it."

"It's a lunch box."

"You have no idea what it is." Just as Alexis said it, one of the display computers began to beep at her side. An incoming Skype call on the screen was asking to be answered. Alexis stared at it. Everything was happening at once. "Do you install Skype on your display models?"

"Not really." Chris looked confused. "Never."

The Skype call was from HappyToSeeYou. "The man who bought the computers—did he touch this machine?"

"Now that you mention it, yeah, he did. He played with it for a few minutes." Chris stared warily at the beeping machine. "But that's kinda weird. I'm not even sure how that's actually happening."

Alexis clicked the connect button on the Skype app. The image was grainy for a moment; then a face appeared on-screen.

Ilya Markov's face.

Alexis didn't hesitate. Three years in Iraq, surrounded by IEDs and hounded by sniper fire, had conditioned her: when there was a threat, you protected yourself and those around you, and you did it without thinking. Every millisecond of reaction time mattered. Those who hesitated, died.

She raced at Chris, the salesman, lowering her shoulder into his chest, and driving him ten yards backward, away from the red metal lunch box. He stumbled, trying to keep his balance, grunting in surprise as he did, and Alexis kept her feet churning, left, right, left, right, pushing him as far from the lunch box as possible.

"What the fu—" he yelled.

She gave him a last shove, throwing her full weight into him, and she could feel his legs go out from under him. Together, they hit the floor with a thud, and just before they did, white light filled her field of vision, and she felt herself carried away by a wall of pure explosive force.

Ilya sat quietly in the corner of the motel room while Thad had sex with the young woman Ilya had procured for him. Ilya guessed, from Thad's energy and enthusiasm, that he hadn't slept with a woman in quite a while. Ilya also guessed this because Thad was pale, with long, stringy, unwashed hair, bad skin, and a nasty case of body odor. But Thad, while unattractive, had three qualities that Ilya found useful.

First, he was readily available; Ilya had contacted him only last night, and Thad had agreed to help right away. Ilya had met Thad on a previous trip to the States, at a gaming convention, and had kept his name and number on file as a person to call in a pinch. Yesterday had been that pinch.

Second, he was easily manipulated. Thad wanted desperately to be part of a group, what he considered the in-crowd, and was willing to do almost anything to get there. Alienated people who were anxious to be socially accepted were perfect targets for Ilya, and he had long ago learned to read that part of their characters at a glance: the too-eager response, the submissive posture, the obsession with other people's opinions. In Thad's case, Ilya had dangled participation in a circle of underground hackers—a coterie of hip, anarchic troublemakers, whose Internet mischief was a form of performance art. Thad considered himself a budding revolutionary, but a lonely one, and the romance of marching arm in arm with comrades seemed to loom large in his fantasies.

Thad's third quality was by far the most important: a love of explosives. Not just explosives, but armaments of any kind. He was a classic weapons geek;

two years ago he'd bragged to Ilya that he kept an arsenal in his basement in Baltimore, and when Ilya had called yesterday and said he'd pay for two pipe bombs, Thad had come through for him. Thad had balked at delivering one of the bombs to the Best Buy in Arlington, so Ilya had had to throw in the offer of sex with an escort as a sweetener, and that closed the deal.

Ilya slipped quietly from his chair, watching as Thad grunted and snorted under the sheets. The young explosives enthusiast didn't seem to have any qualms about performing the act with a third party in the room; once Ilya had told Thad that he should behave as if Ilya weren't there, he seemed to lose all inhibitions. To Ilya, that meant Thad was suggestible as well as easily manipulated, which were closely linked personality traits.

Ilya ran his hands through the pockets of Thad's crumpled blue jeans—they were lying by the bed—and extracted his keys. Ilya cleared his throat by the door. "Just getting some air." Neither Thad nor the escort—she said her name was Natasha—looked up from the bed, so Ilya left without another word.

He found Thad's rusted Nissan Sentra parked across the street from the motel by clicking the unlock button on the car fob a few times, then searched the trunk. It was empty, so he rummaged through the front and back seats, but found nothing except a few old blankets.

He considered where Thad might have hidden his guns—guns Thad had admitted earlier he'd brought with him—then popped the trunk once again and peeled back a piece of black rubber that concealed the car's spare tire. There was no spare tire, but in a blue canvas gym bag were a stack of pistols, maybe half a dozen in all. He took the smallest gun from the pile, pulled back the chamber to see if it was loaded—it was—then stuffed the gun into his belt at the small of his back.

From the brief glimpse he'd seen, he figured the gun was a .22. Ilya knew how to use a pistol. He had friends in Moscow who carried semiautomatics wherever they went, and often, after they'd been drinking for days without pause, they'd drive out to the forests near Losiny Ostrov Park and fire them into trees or garbage cans or whatever else they could find to shoot at. It wasn't much of a firearms education, but Ilya didn't need to be an expert. He just needed to be good enough.

When Ilya returned to the second-floor motel room, Natasha was gone—

he could hear the shower running—and Thad was sitting on the bed, shirtless and in his underwear, drinking a beer.

"Hey." Thad looked slightly dazed. "Forgot you were here."

"Enjoy yourself?"

Thad ducked his head as if embarrassed. "She's awesome."

"Multitalented." Ilya would have to remember to give her a big tip.

Thad reached for the TV remote control, but Ilya waved a finger in the air. "Not now."

"I want to see if there's news. On, you know, the thing."

"There's news. Trust me. But you don't need to see it. Not yet."

Thad put the remote back down. "Okay. So what's next?"

"There's a lot to be done."

Thad bit his lip, as if gathering his courage. Then he spit it out. "I want to meet the others. I have guns for you. But I want to meet other people first."

Ilya smiled broadly at the young man, sitting there on the bed in his underwear. Amazing what a little sex could do for a man's confidence. The worm had turned.

"And I'm all in with you. You know that," Thad said.

"Of course I do."

"I don't mean to be busting your balls or anything; it's just—I went out on a limb for you. I want to know what I'm getting into. I'm real excited."

Ilya sat on the opposite twin bed from Thad and said nothing, deciding that silence was the best play. Thad hung his head after a bit, as if uneasy about his own neediness, and ashamed of vocalizing his wants. Ilya had observed that when people were naked about their needs, shame usually accompanied desire in equal measure. Those emotions made a lethal cocktail when mixed, and that lethality was another tool for Ilya.

Natasha exited the bathroom, dressed now in a tight T-shirt and skinny blue jeans. She had platinum-blond hair and hooded, sleepy eyelids. She was quite beautiful, and most definitely a pro: her body was clearly her place of business, and her patchy clothing did a nice job of displaying the merchandise.

Ilya motioned to her, and she bent near him, ear to his mouth. "Take a few days off. I'll send you another thousand dollars to pay for it. Have fun, go to the beach. But stay out of sight."

She smiled, pleased. Natasha—or whatever her name really was—had no idea what had transpired back at the Best Buy. Ilya had hired her to be Thad's escort. He'd told her to meet Thad at the Arlington mall and then to bring him back to this motel room and fuck him. She hadn't seen Thad plant the pipe bomb, had no idea anything had happened, and wouldn't, probably, until the police caught up with her. Or when she bothered to turn on the TV news. Either way, that would not be a fun moment in her life.

She grabbed an Orioles cap from the dresser, slipped wide sunglasses onto her face, blew a kiss to Thad, then sauntered out the door. The moment she was gone, Thad seemed to deflate.

Ilya stood and put a hand on his shoulder. "You've acquitted yourself well, and people have noticed."

"They have?"

"Absolutely." Ilya patted Thad's shoulder gently. "They're very pleased, and they want to meet you. But first let's do a thought experiment together."

"A thought experiment? What kind?"

"Close your eyes with me." Ilya kept his hand on Thad's shoulder and watched as Thad took a deep breath, then closed his eyes obediently. Thad was a submissive, a beta. Ilya closed his eyes as well. "Picture a city," he said, lowering his voice. "A modern city full of buildings and cars and traffic lights. There are men in suits hurrying down the streets. There are policemen. Crowds. Women on their phones. Can you see that place?"

"Sort of." Thad's voice was uncertain. "Yes, now I can."

"This city has rules. Things you can and can't do. Forbidden things. Some people are allowed to do them. Rich people, powerful people. But not you. You have to do as you're told, be subservient to the rulers of this city."

"Okay," Thad said quickly. "I see that."

"How do you feel about those people? About that city and its rules?"

"I don't like it. Don't like the rules."

"What would you do to those men in suits? To those policemen?"

"Nothing. I'm afraid of them."

"Don't be. They can't hurt you now. You're safe. I'm with you in the city. What would you do to them if you weren't afraid of them?"

"Kick them. Hit them. Maybe . . . shoot them."

"Good. That's good. And if I told you that's what I wanted as well, would that make you happy?"

"Yes."

"So we are in this together, you and I. We are part of a team. Destroying their city, making ourselves happy. Are you with me?"

Thad hesitated, and Ilya opened his eyes and looked down at the young man sitting on the bed. Ilya could see Thad pressing his eyelids together tightly, concentrating hard, fighting to come up with a response.

"Yes," Thad said. "I'm with you."

"Good. Now I want you to do something for me."

Ilya took his hand off Thad's shoulder and reached behind his own back, pulling the handgun from his belt. He tugged a blue bandanna from his pocket and wiped the grip with it, making sure to rub all the gun's surfaces with the cotton. He kept talking as he did this. "This is an important thing, Thad, and it will unite the two of us in the destruction of that city. It's a powerful thing I want you to do, Thad. The people who have been watching us will be very pleased when you do it. Very pleased." Ilya lowered his voice, talking slowly, falling into an easy, hypnotic rhythm. "You'll make the grade. Be part of everything. You'll be accepted."

"Okay." Confidence rose in Thad's voice.

"Raise your right hand, Thad, up in the air, but keep your eyes closed."

Thad raised his right hand.

"Keep your eyes closed and then grab this thing that I'm going to put in your hand. Grab it and hold it tight and know that what you are doing is the most important thing you could possibly do, and that I will be so proud of you, forever and ever."

Thad opened his hand and Ilya quickly slapped the gun into it, grip in his palm, forcing Thad's index finger around the trigger. Thad's eyes popped open in surprise, but it was too late. Ilya pushed the gun against Thad's temple and, with his finger over Thad's, pulled the trigger.

The sound of the gunshot was clean and loud, but not quite as loud as Ilya had expected it to be. The bullet was small caliber and came out the other side of Thad's head in a spray of skull, hair, and blood. Ilya let go of Thad's hand, and the young man slumped over onto the bed, blood soaking into the sheets. The gun was still clutched in his fingers.

Ilya looked at the body and considered that this was the second human he had killed in two days, and what did it say about him that rather than feeling guilt or even pleasure at the killing, he instead felt a sense of momentum? Both deaths, he decided, could be laid at the feet of Garrett Reilly. The clerk had died because of Reilly's interference, and Thad because of the need for Reilly's punishment. Garrett Reilly and Ilya Markov were becoming linked, their destinies intertwined.

There would be more deaths, and they would come faster and faster now, one after the other, until everything was settled and perfect. This was fine with Ilya. It was, ultimately, exactly what he wanted.

The midtown traffic was putting Robert Andrew Wells Jr. in a bad mood. Or maybe it wasn't the traffic; maybe it was the sun and the heat. Or perhaps it had been the hour he'd spent tiptoeing around Phillip Steinkamp's stifling apartment, paying his respects to Steinkamp's widow, eating the homemade canapés and finger food. Sitting shivah was such an odd way to commemorate the dead—couldn't the Jews just have a service and put people in the ground?

He winced at his own irrational prejudices and looked out the window as Park Avenue sped past his limo. Thomason, his assistant, was in the seat next to him; Dov, his Israeli bodyguard, was in the front next to the driver. Thomason was fielding calls and Dov was giving the world at large his usual do-not-fuck-with-me scowl.

Wells hadn't known Steinkamp that well. He'd had dinner with him a few times and met him at a few conferences, but Steinkamp lived in a different social milieu from Wells. Steinkamp was a government functionary, albeit a high-level one—and his slightly dingy apartment reflected that. Wells was a corporate titan. His $40 million, two-story apartment on Madison Avenue reflected that as well.

"Sir, Peters again, Operations." Thomason's voice snapped Wells out of his reverie. His young assistant was holding up one of his many cell phones.

"What does he want? And can you not use that tone of voice?" What was it about Thomason's subservient demeanor that so set Wells off? Did it have something to do with a status mismatch, and the uneven vicissitudes of class? Or was it just that Wells didn't like people who sniveled?

"Sorry, sir." Thomason waited a moment before continuing. "Peters wants to talk about the ATM changeover."

"Right." Wells took the phone. The Operations team wanted his permission to take half the automated teller machines in Manhattan off-line to switch out their operating systems—the ATMs ran on old Microsoft XP platforms, and the programming was beginning to show its age. The Operations people wanted to rejigger all the machines with some fancy, new system that would let them control everything from a central location, cutting the bank-branch labor in half. That would save money and allow better real-time monitoring, which, according to the Operations people, anyway, was a good thing.

Wells wasn't so sure. Now did not seem like the time. Hadn't the bank run in Malta been caused in part by a hack of the bank's ATMs?

Wells fingered the ribbed casing of the cell phone. "Run it by me one more time."

"Sir, we will close down half the ATMs in Manhattan at midnight," Peters said quickly. "And upgrade all software remotely with immediate on-site follow-ups. We have fifty-three separate teams to do this."

"Our people?"

"Mostly. With some independent contractors."

Wells frowned. Contractors had to be vetted and verified. His security people told him that every day. Trust no one. "Those contractors are cleared?"

"Every single one. And after the switchover, we'll have a much more robust reporting algorithm across the entire city."

Wells sighed. *Robust.* He hated that term. This was a *robust* system, that was a *robust* response. Fuck *robust*, he thought. Did *robust* help those idiots in Malta when depositors came rushing for their money?

"If we're going to start tonight, sir, I'll need to let our teams know by six this evening."

Wells checked his Piaget. It was 2:58 p.m. "What could go wrong?"

"Nothing," Peters said without hesitation.

There was silence on the line. Wells waited out his VP of operations, watching the city pass by, taxicabs and livery trucks, knots of students and gaggles of tourists, the glare of the sun washing out the glass façade of a skyscraper.

"Some customers could be inconvenienced," Peters finally broke in, admitting that there was no such thing as foolproof. "But people who get money from

ATMs at three in the morning are not our top-line demographic. And word is, JPMorgan Chase has already instituted all of these changes at their ATMs. No offense, but with that kind of head start on us, they may eat our lunch in terms of efficiencies."

Wells shook his head. *Ah, that was his play.* The competition will eat our lunch. Appeal to your boss's desire to win, to keep the stock price high, and to not get ousted by a disgruntled board of directors.

"Sir?" Peters said.

Wells touched the smooth glass of the backseat window. The glass was hot from the sun. New York had been intolerably hot, and it was only late June. What would August be like?

"Can I tell everyone we're good to go?"

Do what is right for you, for your company, for your stockholders, Wells thought. Ignore the naysayers and the snivelers like Thomason. Be strong, be bold, trust your instincts.

"Yes," he said. "Good to go."

The moment Garrett heard the news about the pipe bomb, he grabbed his wallet and ran for the elevator, figuring he would take his chances on a shuttle flight to DC. But Patmore wrapped Garrett up in his arms and dragged him back down the hall. Garrett ordered Patmore to let him go, threatening to break his nose with the back of his skull.

Celeste rushed out into the hallway and begged Garrett to calm down. "You'll never make it onto the plane. They'll be waiting for you at the TSA line." A woman from the real estate company down the hall was peeking out from her door. "Please come back into the office. Please."

He knew Celeste was right. He might not even make it to the airport. Surveillance could pick him up at a myriad of places: the tunnel, the PATH train, Penn Station. Driving was a possibility, but the team had no car, and no way to rent one unmonitored. There was always Greyhound, but surveillance would be just as much of an issue there. He'd be arrested long before he set foot in Washington, DC.

He shook loose from Patmore and stalked angrily back into the offices.

"No one died," Mitty said, coming in from the other room. She'd been the first to find the AP report online: a bombing at a suburban-DC Best Buy. Four injured. No reported fatalities. Now she was tracking every new bit of information. "That's what the news is saying. That means she's alive. She's okay."

Garrett let out a long breath. He nodded, relieved but not satisfied. "Did you try her phone?"

Mitty shook her head no. "It's a bombing, Gare. She'll be surrounded by FBI agents. They'll be all over her. We call, they'll answer."

Celeste took Garrett by the hand. "She's in the hospital. With doctors. They'll take care of her. There's nothing we can do for her right now. You know that."

He did know that, but it didn't make it any easier.

"He knew we'd be right behind him," Garrett said, pacing the offices while the rest of the team watched, Patmore standing at the front door just in case Garrett tried to bolt again. "He knew we'd track that credit card, and he wanted us to follow him." Garrett stopped by the window and stared out at downtown Newark. "He's smarter than I gave him credit for."

"And scarier," Bingo added.

"But he doesn't know where we are now. Where you are. So we're safe here, at least for the moment," Celeste said. "He's not all-knowing."

Garrett stared down at the plaza below. His head had begun to throb—the pain flared when the stress increased. He massaged his scalp, trying to relieve the ache. Then he saw it: a pair of black Newark Police SUVs pulling up to the building plaza, followed by half a dozen police cars. SWAT officers, clad in black tactical gear, assault rifles slung over their shoulders, piled out of the SUVs and ran toward the building lobby. The rest of the police officers, two dozen in all, brought up the rear, with more cars pulling up to the sidewalk as he watched.

"Yes, he is," Garrett said.

"Is what?" Celeste.

"All-knowing."

They had sixty seconds to get ready. Sixty seconds to delete e-mails, wipe hard drives, shred anything that looked remotely suspicious. Mitty led the charge, being the most tech savvy, and also having the most illegal programs on her laptop. Patmore stashed his Glock in a closet, Celeste sat at a desk, gripping the laminated wood with her fingernails.

Bingo put his hands over his head, just to make sure there were no accidental shootings. "Where I come from, sometimes they just shoot you. For the hell of it."

Celeste thought that was tragic, but her heart was beating too hard for her to say anything. She was scared—terrified, actually—but was trying to keep it together. She had no idea if they would be arrested, beat up, shot. All she knew was that a SWAT team was on its way into the building, and everyone in the office was guessing they were coming to the seventh floor.

Sixty seconds elapsed, and nothing happened. Celeste strained to listen for anything out of the ordinary. The ding of the elevator. A muffled shout. Footsteps. But there was nothing, and then, all of sudden, there was everything. A wall of noise.

Celeste wasn't sure how they had done it—managed to get to their floor and gather outside the office door without making any noise whatsoever—but they had. The door flew open with the pop of a boot on shattered wood, and in moments the offices were filled with SWAT officers, barking orders, waving their rifles around, racing from the central meeting area into each of the side offices.

"Newark Tactical! Down! Down!" the first officers yelled. A pair of them grabbed Patmore and put him onto the floor with a twist of his arm. Celeste, Mitty, and Bingo got an officer apiece, and they also were laid on the ground with astounding rapidity. The room was alive with the thumping of boots and the screams of the officers.

"Where's the shooter? *Where's the shooter?*"

"What shooter?" Celeste managed to squeak out as her face was pressed to the floor by a leather glove. "What shooter?" she said again, but she wasn't sure anyone was listening. She craned her head to watch, but all she could see were black boots and the business end of a few rifles. She heard the thud of shoes on wood, and more cracking of hollow-core doors.

"Room one, clear!"

"Room two, clear!"

"Kitchen, clear!"

An officer slammed his foot next to Celeste's head and barked at her, "Where the hell is the shooter? Where is he?"

"What shooter are you talking about?" Celeste said. "I don't know what you're talking about."

"We got a call from this office," the SWAT officer yelled, his face leering down into Celeste's field of vision. "White male shooter, armed, holding hostages, threatening to kill them. *Where is the shooter?*"

Celeste blinked, trying to clear her head. Hostages? Threatening to kill them? She let out a short laugh and said, almost quietly, "There is no shooter." And then loudly, laughing harder: "The only shooter here is you."

The SWAT team took forty-five minutes to clear out of Ascendant's seventh-floor offices. They spent most of the time talking with each other, complaining, as far as Celeste could hear, about their commanding officer and something about new protocols that they all hated. They didn't seem overly concerned about Mitty, Patmore, Bingo, or Celeste, although they did do a cursory pat-down of each of them, and one officer checked the desk drawers for anything out of the ordinary. No one looked at the top shelf of the back closet, where Patmore had shoved his pistol, and none of the officers seemed particularly surprised by the whole thing.

"You've been spoofed," an officer told Celeste. "Happens a lot lately." He was older, with a sun-weathered face, and with all his battle gear and his helmet he seemed even bigger than he actually was, and he was no small man. He towered over Celeste. "Two separate phone calls. One male, one female; both said there was a man with a gun in your offices, and he was going to kill people."

Celeste tried to make light of the idea. "Well, I guess we survived." But her mind was racing. Whoever had spoofed them knew exactly which office to target, in which building, in which city. They knew where Ascendant was hiding. *They knew everything.*

"We get about one a month. There's a robbery, there's a rape, an assault. We show up, but there's nothing going on. Teenagers. Stoners. People with a gripe. One day, someone's going to get shot by accident, and then the shit will really hit the fan," the officer said. "Excuse my French."

Celeste shrugged, as if it were all a big joke, but her hands were shaking.

"Can you think of someone who would want to play a trick like that on you? Someone with an ax to grind with your company?"

Celeste looked across the room to Bingo and Mitty, who were listening carefully to the conversation. Mitty shook her head ever so slightly.

"No, not really," Celeste said. "We're a big, happy family."

The officer peered around the offices. "Technology firm?"

"Start-up," Celeste said. "Brand-new."

The officer pointed to a couch in the corner with a blanket draped over it. "You sleep here?"

"Tech is brutal business. We can't get behind."

He seemed to accept that as a reasonable answer, and the officers packed up to go. He gave Celeste his card as the SWAT team tromped out the door. "I just want to thank you for bringing your business to Newark. The city needs it."

"Sure." Celeste tried to close the door after him. It was hanging on one hinge, and the lock and doorknob were completely shattered. She stood there a moment, to catch her breath, when there was another knock. She opened the door. "Yeah?"

It was the older SWAT officer again. "One of my guys noticed that you have five desks, five machines, but there's only four of you here. Is anyone missing?"

"No. Just an extra desk. We're hoping to start hiring soon." Celeste smiled broadly at the officer. "If you know anyone with programming skills, send them our way."

"Okay, sure." He gave the place one last look. "Will do."

G arrett ran.

He ran down the back stairs as the SWAT team came up the elevators. He ran out the loading-dock door as they came in through the front lobby.
He ran east on Raymond Boulevard until, when he stopped, he could no longer
see the top of the office building they'd been hiding in.

He hadn't wanted to run, but the team told him he had to. They had only
seconds to decide, and Celeste had been adamant: if the police were coming
for anyone, they were coming for him. They had no grounds to arrest anyone
else—so the rest of them would be safe. They literally pushed him out the door.

He didn't think about any of this as he ran. He simply ran until he was too
exhausted to run anymore. Then he walked, turning right on Chapel, a street
full of brick warehouses and empty storefronts. He was sweating and thirsty,
and the pounding of his heart matched the pounding in his head. He stopped
at a corner store and bought a bottle of water, downed it in a few gulps, then
walked until he came to another corner store. There he bought a pint of cheap,
blended whiskey—just to calm his nerves, he told himself—and kept walking,
the bottle of booze in a brown paper bag in his back pocket. He took another
right and came to the trestles of an elevated railway. No one else was around;
only a few rusting cars kept him company. He sat underneath the railway bridge
and tried to collect his thoughts.

But first he swallowed a handful of the black-market Percodan that Patmore had bought him. He hadn't planned on taking them with him, but as he'd

been rushing out the door, he remembered that he'd stashed them in a desk drawer and swiped them as he left. Now he was glad, because they were the only thing standing between himself and paralyzing head pain. He didn't count how many he took; he just gobbled them down and chased them with a mouthful of whiskey.

A homeless man appeared from the shadows, pushing an old shopping cart piled high with bags and clothing. The man looked emaciated, a greasy jacket slung over his thin shoulders. He stared at Garrett, but Garrett ignored him and tried to think.

Who had alerted the cops? Had it been Ilya Markov? And if so, how the hell did he know where Garrett was hiding? It didn't seem possible, yet the timing lined up with the AMBER Alert and then the bombing in DC. Somehow, Ilya had discovered Garrett's hiding place, discovered the makeshift headquarters for the entire Ascendant team, and attacked it. When Garrett thought about it, he realized that Markov had attacked two separate branches of Ascendant— DC and Newark—at the same time. And he hadn't exposed himself while doing it. Markov was hitting at Garrett, and Garrett wasn't anywhere nearer catching the man.

Markov was a master at spreading fear, yet he remained a shadow.

That struck a line of panic directly into Garrett's chest. He tried to reason back as to why he had taken on this task in the first place, banging down another mouthful of whiskey. The booze tasted horrible, rough and cheap, and settled uneasily in his stomach. He had seen a problem on the horizon—a pattern building that spoke of economic terror—and he had alerted Alexis to that problem. When she had scoffed at the idea, that seemed to push Garrett harder to take action. But why had he done it?

Mitty had accused him of wanting to impress Alexis, and there was truth in that, but something deeper was going on. Yes, he was trying to save the country, in his own twisted way, but Garrett didn't believe in altruism; everybody had a motive for their selfless acts, even if they didn't understand it. Garrett had a motive for what he was doing as well—but he was a long way from grasping what the hell it was.

A voice interrupted his reverie. "Can you help a brother get something to eat?" The homeless man had shuffled over to Garrett, hand open and outstretched.

Garrett's first reaction was to tell him to fuck off. But then he stared up at the man's face, his smashed-in nose, missing teeth, the scabs that dotted his cheeks and neck, and revulsion and sympathy flooded his mind in equal measure. Life had devastated this old bastard so badly that Garrett could no longer tell his age, or even his race. He reminded Garrett of the old security guard at the Raymond Boulevard building, only more hollowed out, more tragic. Garrett pulled out his wallet and tossed him a $20 bill.

"God bless you."

"Whatever," Garrett said quickly, turning away from the man's ravaged face. He drank again from the whiskey and found that it was almost all gone. Had he really drunk that much, that fast? And what about the painkillers—how many had he taken? Mixing the two probably hadn't been such a great idea.

He pushed all of this from his mind and tried to focus on Ilya Markov. Garrett had struck first. He had identified Markov as a threat, had tracked him through his credit cards, then flushed him out of hiding with an AMBER Alert. He had provoked Markov, and Markov had struck back, and struck back hard.

But how had he done it? How? How? *How?* And why was he spending his time and energy going at Garrett instead of focusing on what Garrett assumed was Markov's larger purpose—attacking the US economy?

Garrett closed his eyes, and when he opened them, rays of sunlight were streaking through the girders of the train trestle, illuminating heaps of black dirt littered with bottles and boxes and discarded clothing. It was, in its own decaying way, a beautiful sight, and Garrett marveled at it—the lushness of the ruin, the craggy shapes laid out by the old shirts and pants. He realized then that the drugs had taken hold.

Suddenly, Garrett couldn't quite remember what he'd been so anxious about. Yes, Ilya Markov was mysterious and smart, but was he really a threat to Garrett's existence? Maybe. Or maybe he was somebody else's problem. Garrett grinned. That was the beauty of Percodan and whiskey: after you mixed the two, everything was somebody else's problem.

He drained the last of the alcohol from the bottle, then stood up, his head spinning slightly, brushed the dirt from his pants, and realized that his phone was chiming. He'd stuck a disposable cell in his pocket, and now a text was waiting for him. He glanced at it.

Police gone. We were spoofed. All clear.

Garrett read the text again and laughed. Spoofed? So those weren't FBI agents raiding his offices? They were regular old Newark cops?

He typed out a quick response: *Not looking for me?*

The answer was immediate: *No. Crazed shooter.*

"Holy fucking shit," Garrett muttered under his breath. Markov had sent the police to his office—had known exactly where to send them—but hadn't wanted Garrett arrested. The edges of his vision had suddenly become blurry. He blinked twice to clear his sight, but that didn't help. He turned to his phone again.

They arrest anyone? Garrett wrote. Had he spelled that right? Arrest with two *r*'s or one? He was having trouble remembering things, which was odd, because Garrett remembered pretty much everything.

No. And then: *Where are you?*

Garrett looked around the neighborhood. A vacant lot was to his left, and farther under the train trestle lay a rail yard, idle now, with lines of boxcars and flatbeds stretching off into the distance. But he wasn't sure where he actually was. Somewhere in Newark. And not a nice part of town either. He hadn't paid attention when he ran. His cell phone had no maps app, and while a street sign was down the block, Garrett found that he was having trouble focusing on the letters.

Better explore, then text back, he thought. He took a tentative step forward, but his foot couldn't find solid ground, and all of a sudden he realized he was falling, toward the soft, lovely dirt, and falling fast. The world around him was twisting, up suddenly becoming down, and down, up. He tried to put his hands out to break the fall, but the earth was rising toward his face too quickly, and the next thing he knew, he was awash in blackness.

No matter how much he argued, the FBI—with the help of two DC Metro policemen—would not let General Kline into Alexis Truffant's hospital room. He'd managed to get to the third-floor trauma unit of George Washington University Hospital by showing his DIA ID and blustering to the nurses, but getting through that final locked door was, for now at least, an impossibility: no family allowed, no coworkers, no media.

After his third attempt at talking his way into her room, one of the Metro cops asked him to leave the floor and, when he wouldn't, escorted him politely, but firmly, to the elevator, then down to the cafeteria in the basement.

"Please wait here, sir," the cop said. "Someone will come talk to you. Eventually."

Kline paced among the weary residents and anxious visitors, muttering to himself, then bought a cup of coffee and an apple and sat in the corner. He didn't touch the apple, or the coffee. Instead, he cursed his own stupidity.

How could he have let Alexis steer events, acceding to her using DIA resources to help Reilly in his insane quest? He should have said, right at the start, that domestic terror was always to be handled by domestic police, that this entire concept—an economic terrorist entering the United States to sow anarchy—fell squarely in the provenance of the FBI, not the DIA.

"We're a frigging analysis group," he whispered to the air. "We analyze. That's what we do." He noticed an elderly couple staring at him from another table. He scowled at them, and they looked away hurriedly.

"Damn it, damn it, damn it," he said, and got up to pace some more.

"General Kline?"

Kline spun and found himself face-to-face with a pair of FBI agents. The first was a man, older, with gray hair and a paunch that protruded from his unbuttoned suit jacket. His face was fleshy, and he looked slightly distracted—maybe not too happy to be here. The other was a woman, younger, dark skinned—Indian or Pakistani, Kline guessed—and sharp looking, as if she had already sized up the situation and knew all the answers.

She extended a hand. "Special Agent Jayanti Chaudry. This is Special Agent Murray. We'd like to ask you a few questions if you don't mind, General."

"Yeah, sure, of course." Kline pointed to the table where his coffee, now cold, and his apple sat.

Chaudry and Kline sat down, while Murray went to grab a pair of coffees.

"We just flew in from New York," the female agent said.

"New York?"

"We're on the Steinkamp case."

Kline gave her a sharp look, then nodded vigorously. "I already spoke to two sets of your agents about it last week. And about Garrett Reilly."

"I know you did. And thank you for that. But now I'm wondering, in the light of what happened to your captain—"

"Is she okay?"

Chaudry stared at Kline, examining his eyes. "She's fine, sir. They're going to release her in an hour or so. Some cuts, some bruises. They're monitoring for concussion symptoms."

"Good. Okay. Good."

Agent Murray sat down next to Chaudry, slid her a coffee, and sipped at his own.

"Sorry I interrupted," Kline said, and immediately he was angry at himself for apologizing. These assholes had kept him waiting for hours; he had every right to know about Alexis's condition. But he was nervous. Nervous because he had a secret now, and the FBI would undoubtedly want to pick at that secret. But how much had Alexis told them?

"General, do you know why Captain Truffant was at that Best Buy this morning?" Chaudry asked.

"No idea."

"She doesn't report to you?"

"She does. But not her hour-to-hour movements. Not even day-to-day, sometimes. What did she tell you?"

"Let's not worry about that quite yet. What projects was she working on?"

"That's classified," Kline said with as much finality as he could muster.

"So you won't tell us?" the older agent said, surprise in his voice.

"I can't tell you."

"We could bring you down to FBI headquarters and keep you there for a couple of days. Ask the DA to file obstruction-of-justice charges, and then ask you the same question," Chaudry said. "Would that make it easier for you to answer?"

Kline said nothing, thinking about this threat. He was pretty sure national security would trump an obstruction-of-justice charge if they faced off in front of a judge, but he was also pretty sure that a court battle over this would mean the end of his career—not that he had much of a career left.

"An internal reporting project," Kline said. "How information gets disseminated throughout the organization."

"That's it?"

"She was working on something else. But I don't know the details."

"Something having to do with Garrett Reilly?"

Kline stared down at the coffee sitting in front of him, at the ripples on the surface shimmying back and forth in the cup. He thought of the prisoner's dilemma, the problem in game theory where criminals are pitted against each other by the police, prompted to rat each other out and get the best deal for themselves. If both prisoners squealed, they would get equally bad, but not terrible, sentences. If both prisoners kept their mouths shut, then the day would be saved. But if only one prisoner ratted out the other, then he or she would get a light sentence, and the other prisoner would spend the rest of his life in jail.

Had Alexis told them everything she knew? Had she turned Kline in, offered him up as the ringleader of this disaster?

It was possible, but Kline didn't think it was probable. Alexis was stubborn—stubborn and loyal—which was why her attempt at blackmailing Kline had been so heartrending for him. No, he thought, maybe this is the moment for something else entirely.

"General Kline?" the female agent said. "Was she working with Garrett Reilly?"

Maybe this was the moment to start acting like a general again, not some sulky child who had had his favorite toy taken away.

"She was." Kline watched as Chaudry's eyes widened. "But she was doing it on my say-so. Everything that happened is my responsibility."

When they let him see Alexis, she was sitting on the edge of her bed, sipping a glass of water, dressed in a white hospital gown, closed up in back, and she had a series of purple bruises and jagged cuts on her cheeks and forehead. She looked awful, but Kline tried not to let that show on his face. She brightened at the sight of him, and he nodded to the space on the bed beside her, silently asking if he could sit there. She nodded yes, and he sat on the edge of the hospital bed, his left leg grazing her right. She put her glass of water down on a steel tray at the side of the bed and turned to him, her face full of emotion.

"What did you tell the FBI?" Kline asked.

"Nothing." Alexis swallowed. "You?"

"Everything. The truth." Kline thought about this. "Well, I told them it was all my idea."

Alexis winced. She let out a long breath. "I'm sorry. I'm so sorry."

"Yeah, I am too." Kline reached for her hand and held it tightly in his. "But we are in this together now. We are in it deep. And somebody out there is trying to bring us all to our knees."

AmeriCool Environmental Services prided itself on being a computer-savvy company. They had their own in-house IT team, and when they installed HVAC systems—giant air-conditioning units that could cool entire buildings in the middle of a Virginia summer, or heat pumps that could keep South Boston warehouses warm during a brutal New England January—they guaranteed their clients that 90 percent of the problems they encountered could be fixed remotely, through online monitoring systems in the company's Maryland headquarters. This promise of modern technological solutions had allowed AmeriCool to nab new customers up and down the East Coast at an astonishing rate. AmeriCool was poised to be the number one HVAC company in the United States. They were growing by leaps and bounds.

Except for when their Internet went down.

When the Internet failed, groans went up from IT, curses from scheduling, and window-rattling rage from the executive suite on the second floor of their ever-expanding offices in a business park in suburban Silver Spring. AmeriCool had its own warranty contract with the local cable company, for immediate technical response and ASAP repair service, but in reality, no matter how much attentiveness their Internet provider promised, most days it took hours for service to come back online. And hours meant lost revenue and pissed-off customers.

But not today.

Today, a miracle happened. At 9:05 a.m., AmeriCool's Internet service went dark. Completely, absolutely dark: no e-mail, no websites, no Skype, no cloud connection, no backup, no IMs with clients, no remote monitoring of HVAC units in New York or Philadelphia. At 9:06, the IT department scrambled to check the source of the problem. At 9:11, IT told Todd Michaels, the VP in charge of technology, that the problem was most probably outside their offices. At 9:12, Michaels called down to the receptionist and told her to get their cable-company service rep on the line to start getting service back. At 9:13 a.m., eight minutes after the initial disruption, Jenny, the receptionist, looked up the direct line to Infinity Cable Service and was even dialing their number when the repairman walked into the lobby.

She'd never seen him before, and she knew most of the Infinity repairmen. But he was wearing the usual blue work uniform, with the plastic laminated company badge, and he was carrying a banged-up toolbox in his right hand and a laptop bag in his left. The name on the badge was Robert Jacob Mullins, and the repairman introduced himself as Bobby. He was young, and Jenny thought he looked handsome—kind of shy, with a wide grin and thick black hair. He asked about her necklace—her dad had given it to her as a college-graduation present—and she blushed. She wasn't sure why.

"We didn't even call," Jenny said. "How'd you know our service went out?"

"The office beeped me five minutes ago, and I was in the neighborhood. They got an emergency alert from our system. They said you guys had a service guarantee. That puts you top of the list."

"Wow. Cool."

"I'm new, though. Can you show me where the uplink box is?"

Jenny called the IT department, and Luke—company wags called him the Great Bearded One—waddled up from in back to show Mullins the small server farm and Internet connection box. Luke brought Mullins to a glorified maintenance closet that was stuffed with racks of computer servers and had coaxial cables running every which way out of a large, black junction box. Cool air blew down from a ceiling vent in a steady gust, and LED lights blanketed the room in a crystal-white glare.

"I shouldn't have to log into the system," Robert Jacob Mullins said. "Everything should be outside of your firewall. But if it isn't, and I need to log in, could you just give me a temporary admin password?"

Luke stared at the Infinity repairman. "How come I've never met you before?"

"I just started last week."

"And you might need to get inside our firewall? I've never done that before."

"Temp password is all. To make sure your speeds are maxing. You can lock me back out again five minutes later."

Luke stroked his red, unkempt beard.

Mullins shrugged. "You know what, I don't blame you. Security first. No problem. I can do it back at the office—it'll just take me a little longer. I'll be back in forty-five minutes." Mullins grabbed his work box and started for the door, but bearded Luke put his fleshy hand in the air.

"I'll get you a temp password. Just get us back online. Everyone's going batshit crazy right now."

"Okay, will do," Mullins said with a generous smile. "Much appreciated."

Luke went off to create a temporary password, and the man who claimed to be Robert Jacob Mullins popped open the uplink box for the company's Internet connection. Instead of working on the cables, he simply switched on the timer on his wristwatch and stared off into space. He thought about how soul killing it would be to work in an office such as AmeriCool's, surrounded by dull careerists and striving executives. These people were beneath his regard. His mind wandered to Garrett Reilly and the events of yesterday. The bomb hadn't killed the young army officer in Arlington, that much the TV had told him, but it, along with the Newark police raid, had sent a powerful message: I know you, know all about you, and can find you anywhere.

He wondered how Garrett Reilly was feeling right at this moment, as events encircled him and began to choke off his options; he hoped that Reilly was thinking of him as well. He hoped that Reilly was obsessed with him, spending all his waking hours figuring out how to stop him. And while Reilly struggled to stay free, to stay alive even, the main purpose of the plan would gain speed and would soon become unstoppable. There would be a pleasing symmetry to that. With that happy thought, and the passing of 180 seconds, he stepped out of the maintenance room and hunted down Luke.

"Actually, I am gonna need to get into your system. I gotta restart our download-speed monitoring program."

Luke handed the repairman a printout with a username and log-in password. Luke pointed to an unused port on the back of a server computer. "Use that port on the network switch."

"Five minutes, tops," Mullins said.

Luke grunted something unintelligible and disappeared back into the IT offices. Mullins removed his laptop from its carrying case, plugged an Ethernet cable into the server, and logged on to the AmeriCool computer network. He didn't bother pretending to do any cable repair work; now he just needed passwords and access codes. He ran a search for a specific client company—Advanced Worldwide Credit Processors—that used AmeriCool to regulate the climate of their server farm in Hoboken, New Jersey. AWCP—as industry insiders called it—was responsible for 27 percent of all credit-card transactions on the East Coast of the United States. Anyone who could hack into AWCP's servers could potentially bring all those transactions to a halt—every single one of them.

Mullins found everything he needed in a file named "AWCP—PSSWDS+USRNMS" and copied the information onto his laptop. The whole process took three minutes. Then he unplugged his computer from the network and waved good-bye to Luke.

"All good," he said as he walked toward reception. "You'll be back online in two minutes. Just gotta go outside and flip a switch."

He stopped briefly at the receptionist desk and asked Jenny if she was single. She said she had a boyfriend, sadly, and she seemed to blush again, ever so slightly. Mullins shrugged, said, "Okay, maybe next time," and ambled out of the lobby.

Ilya Markov walked out of the AmeriCool offices, took the elevator to the first floor, then walked across the parking lot to the cable switch box, a six-foot-tall, green steel rectangle plopped onto a base of beige concrete. He opened the box—he'd cut the padlock half an hour earlier with a bolt cutter—and simply reconnected a single coaxial cable to the line that fed AmeriCool. That was why their Internet had gone down, and that was all it took for it to start working again. They would be up and running immediately.

Ilya preferred that nobody at the cable company know that their systems had been compromised, so he yanked out a handful of copper wiring that appeared to connect phone service to a separate building in the business park. Copper wire was still big with thieves, and stealing some would help explain why the junction-box padlock had been snipped, diverting attention from what he had actually done.

He stuffed the copper wire in his pocket, closed the junction-box door, and walked casually back across the parking lot, lighting a cigarette as he went. The smoke was fine and slightly gritty on his throat. He felt calm and satisfied. Now he needed to get to a separate Internet connection and log on to those servers in Hoboken.

The plan was coming together, and it would soon unfold in locations up and down the Eastern Seaboard, all at the same time, in a finely tuned choreography. He paused for a moment and hoped that Garrett Reilly would appreciate that choreography as much as he did.

Inside the offices of AmeriCool, cheers went up from IT and scheduling, and sighs of relief were breathed in the executive suites. Vice President Michaels told everyone to get on the phone to clients and make sure all their systems were running smoothly, and he even stopped by Luke's office to pat him on the back and congratulate him for getting them up and running so quickly.

"Not a problem," Luke said. "Easy as pie."

Congressman Leonard Harris felt as if he were on autopilot: he was no longer in control of his arms or legs. He was walking down the street, one foot in front of the other, the hot Georgia sun beating down on his shoulders, yet he was simultaneously floating above the sidewalk, propelled by a force he didn't understand. It was the strangest feeling. Of course he did understand the force behind it, but his brain refused to acknowledge it. What his brain said was he was going to see her science-fiction collection. That's all. Just look at the books. Nothing wrong with that.

They had met yesterday, at the food trucks, just like the day before, and the day before that. At first, Harris had looked for the girl with the wonderful lips out of the corner of his eye, pretending to be looking for an open seat, a place to eat his lunch undisturbed. He had sighted her across the tables, then made a show of surprise when he happened to sit nearby and looked up from his food, staring into her smiling face. They talked about books mostly, politics a bit, where she'd gone to school—Emory University—and even the Braves and their pitiful pitching staff.

He felt that he'd been charming at that second meeting because she laughed at every joke he made. He'd walked away from the encounter feeling as good about himself as he'd felt in the last ten years. Of course he went back the next day, and made no pretense of surprise when he sat next to her with a tray laden with barbecue ribs. They talked and talked—he couldn't even remember about what—and they agreed to meet again today, same place, same time.

Rachel Brown said she was twenty-nine, had grown up in Florida in a broken home, with a father who left and a mother who was too busy raising three other children to pay much attention to what Rachel did. Harris had been moved by her story—she was exactly the kind of person who could pull herself up from poverty and make something of her life. She was a model constituent, even though he noted that she did not live in his district. That was a shame.

He'd showered that morning with special attention to his underarms, and he'd shaved carefully, slowly scraping away the night's growth of facial hair. He'd dressed more casually as well, in a short-sleeved shirt that hugged his waistline. He was proud that he had not grown paunchy with age. He'd spent the morning thinking about what they would talk about, laying out possible topics, trying to see if they could branch out into something new—her past, his family background, places they both had visited.

He didn't feel that anything was wrong with the relationship. She was a single woman, and he was a married man, and that was how it would stay. He was faithful to his wife, a good husband and father, and she would undoubtedly soon find a young man to spend her life with. She had let drop yesterday that she was on the rebound, relationship-wise, and was disenchanted with all the boys who wanted to date her.

"So frigging immature," Rachel Brown had said. "Like children."

He had shaken his head knowingly at that. "Around you they probably lose their sense of propriety."

She murmured quietly when he said that, and that sound had stirred his loins with a powerful jolt of sexual energy. He fought mightily to push that notion from his brain, but once the conversation had gone there, everything she said seemed to have a double meaning. Was he imagining it, or was sex the idea behind each sentence?

"I get bored in the afternoons, just lying around my apartment," she said.

"You should get out more, see some people."

"I'm seeing you." She smiled that amazing smile. "Does that count?"

More was stirring where there definitely should not have been any.

"When it's hot like this, I just can't sleep. I toss and turn," she said.

He pictured her naked in bed. "Me too." That was a lie. He turned the air conditioner on, full blast, all summer long.

"In the middle of the night, I read my sci-fi novels. I feel like I'm escaping to another world."

"Sure."

"Where are you headed this afternoon?"

"I have a staff meeting at four. Nothing until then."

"You want to take a walk? My apartment is five blocks from here. I could show you my collection."

At that exact moment his autopilot kicked in. Some part of his brain, some grown-up, married, middle-aged part of his frontal cortex, said no, do not take a walk with Rachel Brown, do not see her science-fiction collection at her apartment five blocks from the food trucks. That is a mistake. A huge mistake.

But some other part of his brain—some primitive, hungry, aggressive region that he didn't even know the name of—disengaged his frontal cortex, turned it off completely. No matter how obvious the consequences of what he was doing, he did it anyway. He walked out of the food-truck parking lot, following behind this young woman, talking to her about the weather, how the Grant Park neighborhood had changed, how he hated neckties. It was as if she had thrown an invisible lasso around his neck and were dragging him, like a steer to slaughter—only the slaughterhouse was her apartment.

He knew what was coming next, and he wanted it, possibly more than he had wanted anything else in his entire life. It reminded him of the old joke he'd once heard from a fellow sci-fi geek—vagina was the fifth fundamental force of the universe. You could not fight it.

She lived on the second floor, in a one-bedroom apartment with hardly anything on the walls. Harris thought that was odd, but he was too preoccupied to say anything, and plus, he didn't want to offend her. There was some furniture, a cheap couch and a dining-room table, and a bookcase for sure, packed end to end with paperback science-fiction novels. She showed him her favorite titles—a few Asimovs, a classic Bradbury, two Zelaznys, more Orson Scott Card books, and a whole shelf full of Neil Gaiman. And then, as she was showing him a dog-eared copy of Frank Herbert's *Dune*, their hands touched. It was electric. He stared at her, a deer in headlights, and she dropped the book and held his fingers in hers.

Without another word, she led him into her bedroom. There was a futon in the corner, jammed right under a window and covered with a single sheet. She kissed him once, briefly, then again, and he kissed her back, passionately. Before he knew it, she'd taken his clothes off and was on her knees, and he was in her mouth. The sensation was exquisite. They fell onto the bed and made love for an hour, and every minute of it was ecstasy for Harris.

When they were done, he lay there on the futon in the tiny, empty bedroom, stroking her young skin, like a puppy dog licking the hand of its master. That was a bit how he felt—like he was a dog and Rachel Brown was his master. How else could he explain his behavior?

She didn't say much, just looked at him with adoring eyes, and then his cell phone rang, his office calling, but he didn't answer, and the reality of the world came crashing back on him. It was three in the afternoon, and he'd just had extramarital sex with a girl almost half his age. He popped off the bed, breathing hard. He had a staff meeting in an hour and couldn't show up sweaty and reeking of sex. He excused himself, almost tripping over his feet, and asked if he could use her shower.

"Of course," she said, and he rushed into the bathroom, but found no soap and no towels either. He rinsed himself quickly, shook himself dry, and threw on his clothes. Rachel Brown was still lying on the bed, curled up in a sexy ball, naked, watching his every move. She seemed oddly amused.

"I have to run," he said. "People are waiting for me."

"Okay."

"I'm sorry."

"Don't be." She got up from the bed, still naked from head to toe, and wrapped her arms around him, breasts pressing up against his chest. She kissed him long and slow, and he could feel himself getting hard again, his brain seizing up with passion. She let out a low groan of pleasure, and he thought that he might have another orgasm right there, just from the sound of it, but he pushed himself away from her, finally regaining control of his body, and staggered to the door.

She followed, catlike, and watched as he unlatched the locks and started for the hallway.

He stopped, midway, and looked back at her. "That was—"

"Amazing. I thought so too."

He smiled, again involuntarily, and rushed out the door. As he was hurrying down the steps, running as fast as he could back to his old life, he thought he heard a woman's laughter behind him, and a sudden chill cooled all the sweat on his wildly overheated body.

G arrett woke on a bed he didn't know, in a room he didn't recognize. He wasn't even entirely sure he was awake. The room was dark mostly, but a Mickey Mouse night-light in a far corner threw yellowish light on the walls. The room didn't seem to be a child's room, despite the night-light—there were no toys or blankets or posters of boy bands. The room was depressingly brown, and the striped wallpaper was peeling near the door.

Garrett's head hurt, severely, as did his shoulder and chin. He felt as if he'd been punched in the mouth, and that somebody had wrenched his arm backward, which maybe they had—he wasn't sure. He was also thirsty and disoriented and sick to his stomach. His throat was raw, as if he had thrown up numerous times, but he didn't remember doing that either. He didn't remember much. Just a dark space under some train tracks, and an old homeless man. Garrett tried to feel for his wallet—maybe the homeless guy had tried to take it—but found that he couldn't move his right hand to reach down to his pants.

He squinted into the darkness. His hand was somehow fixed to a radiator grill that stood next to the bed, just under a closed window.

"What the fuck?" he muttered. He tried to pull his hand away, but couldn't. When he turned over on his side to get a better look, he could see that his wrist was pinned to a pipe with a length of red flexi-tie. He tugged hard on the flexi-tie, but it wouldn't budge, and the plastic dug deeper into his flesh. He wanted to yell more loudly, but a weariness washed over him instead.

His brain was still fogged in, and that dreamlike feeling began to race through his thoughts.

Perhaps he wasn't in a strange room, tied to a bed. Perhaps he was someplace else entirely. But where? He wasn't sure. He didn't have the strength to reason it out. His eyes slipped shut and he fell back to sleep.

He woke again, and time had definitely passed. The makings of dawn glowed outside the window: a wash of pink light, a hint of blue in the sky. He was on the second floor, that much he could discern, with a long stretch of grass and fencing beyond the window. More than that, he couldn't see.

Garrett's head still hurt, but in a different way—a less generalized hurt now, and more a sharp pain in his skull. He recognized that pain—it was the pain of drugs leaving his system. It was the pain of real life settling back on his shoulders. He tried to move his hand again, but found that it was still attached to the radiator, and it occurred to him that it had been attached that way for a purpose. To immobilize him. But why? Had he been captured? Had Ilya Markov tracked him down? Was he a prisoner?

"Hey!" he shouted. "What the fuck is going on?"

He listened and could hear someone walking up a flight of stairs, not particularly fast, then waiting just outside the door to the room.

"Hello?" he said. "Someone there?"

The doorknob turned, the door opened, and Mitty walked into the room. Garrett stared in surprise. She squinted at him in the dim light, then shook her head. "You wanna shut the fuck up, please? People are sleeping."

"Who's sleeping? Where am I? And why is my hand tied to the fucking radiator?"

"You're in a house in New Jersey, doesn't matter where. The people who are asleep are the rest of the team, although by now they're probably awake. And you know why you're tied to the radiator. You know exactly why."

"What are you talking about?" Garrett yanked hard at the flexi-tie, but his wrist wouldn't move. The radiator didn't budge either—it was planted solidly into the floor.

"How's your head?"

"It hurts like a bitch."

"You want some water?"

"What I want is for you to cut this twist tie off my fucking wrist."

Mitty bent over Garrett, putting her face just above his. "No." Then she walked out of the room, closing the door and locking it from the outside.

"Hey! What the . . . ? Mitty! Get back in here! Mitty! You hear me? Get back in here and tell me what the fuck is going on!" He shouted like that for a few more minutes, then his throat felt raw again, and his stomach started to do flips as if he might throw up, so he fell silent. He breathed steadily through his nose, sorry that he hadn't taken Mitty up on the offer of a glass of water.

He craned his head again and looked up at the red plastic that was keeping his hand to the radiator. He reached over with his left hand and tried to unlock it, but he knew from experience that was impossible. The only way that thing was coming off was with a pair of pliers or a very sharp knife.

He mumbled curses under his breath because he knew, the moment Mitty had said it, why he was tied to a bed in a house that seemed to be a million miles from any signs of human habitation. He knew and he hated it. Hated them for doing it and hated himself for being trapped like this.

He yelled again at the locked door. "If this is your idea of some half-assed intervention, it's not going to work! You're not going to change me. I'm not going to become a different person just because you're draining the drugs from my bloodstream. You can go fuck yourself! All of you can go fuck yourselves, you hear me? I'll do whatever the hell I want!"

His stomach roiled. He groaned once, turned on his side, and threw up off the bed onto the floor. The vomit burned his throat on the way up, and the burn lingered as he lay there, gasping for breath.

That done, he turned back onto the bed, closed his eyes, and immediately fell asleep again.

He woke to full daylight. The sun shone through the room's only window, illuminating a bare, depressing wall and a beat-to-crap dresser. Garrett felt chills run up and down his body. He was sick and exhausted, and he could still smell the puke in his nostrils, although when he looked down to the floor, he could see that someone had been in the room as he slept and cleaned up his vomit. He had no idea how long he had been out.

Without warning, a sadness washed over him and made him want to weep. He was alone. All alone in this godforsaken room, miles from anywhere he knew or cared about. The sadness was one of grief. Of missing. He missed Alexis and he missed his mother, but they were alive, and he had some hope that he could see them again. More painfully, he missed his father, whom he had never known; he missed his bright shining marine of a brother; but most of all he missed Avery Bernstein, who would never laugh with him again or tease him about his obnoxious personality or comfort him when the world turned sour. Avery had been Garrett's surrogate father—and now Avery was gone, and that was life's most horrific trick. How could it even be? Gone, gone, gone.

Garrett howled in pain, howled with loss, howled with the black reality of another day without the men in his life whom he had loved. How could he go on without them? And now he was tied to a fucking bed in some shithole without any drugs to make that pain better. Who would do that to him? *How could they do that to him?*

He howled for as long as his body would let him, then passed out once again.

He woke, and it was afternoon, and Celeste Chen was sitting on the edge of the bed.

"Hey," she said.

He grimaced and sat up and realized, after a moment, that his hand was free. He felt at it—a red line went all around his wrist, with peeled skin and dried blood.

He looked at Celeste. "Yeah. Hey."

"Get you anything?"

His brain was sludgy and slow, but the drugs were gone, and his stomach, while raw, didn't feel quite so horrible. "Coffee?" He continued to feel at his wrist.

"I can do that." She got up, went to the door, and paused there. "You can jump out the window if you really want to, but we took your wallet, and I don't think you'll get very far. Plus, it's a long drop. You'd probably break your ankle."

"Thanks for the warning. Really nice of you."

She shrugged and left the room. He got up shakily. He was still wearing his blue jeans, but he didn't recognize the T-shirt he had on, a gray New Jersey Devils shirt. He looked out the window and had to agree with Celeste: there wasn't much around to run to. He could see a warehouse in the distance, and some kind of smoke-belching factory on the other side of a weedy field, but that was about it.

Celeste came back in with a cup of coffee and a plate with a piece of un-toasted bread on it. "No toaster. So you'll have to eat it like this."

She gave him the bread and coffee, then went back to the door. "We're downstairs, when you're ready to talk." She left again, this time leaving the door unlocked.

Rage flared inside Garrett's brain. *Talk?*

They wanted to fucking talk? As if he were some misbehaving teen and they were his collective parents? As if he had stayed out past curfew or had had a kegger in their living room, and now they had to talk about what kind of adult he would grow up to become? They could all go to hell, with their holier-than-thou bullshit. They had no idea what it was to be Garrett Reilly, and how he handled the ups and downs of his existence was his own damned business.

And yet . . .

He knew they were right. And that killed him, just frigging killed him. He drained the coffee, then staggered downstairs. Mitty, Bingo, Celeste, and Patmore were sitting in a dusty living room, on a ripped couch and a pair of teetering chairs. The windows were curtained, and the room was mostly dark, except for a floor lamp in a corner. A reproduction of Washington crossing the Delaware hung on the wall.

Garrett pulled up a chair and sat in it. "Where I am?"

"Irvington, New Jersey," Mitty said. "Crossroads of the world."

Where was that? He had no idea, but then again, he didn't really care. "How did you find me?"

"Homeless guy," Mitty said. "After you passed out, he took your phone and texted us."

Garrett remembered giving the old man money. Had that been a smart move? Maybe he owed the guy his life.

"Alexis is fine, by the way," Celeste said. "She's back at the DIA. We haven't spoken to her, but we got e-mails from Kline. The FBI is all over them, but she's not in jail, and she's not in the hospital."

"There've been no more sightings of Ilya Markov," Bingo said. "TV news is all over the bombing. National terror attack. There was surveillance videotape of the bomber coming into the store. The guy had a girl with him. But the guy wasn't Markov."

Garrett blinked in surprise. He started to object, to ask if they were absolutely positive it wasn't Markov, but then realized that this made sense. Markov had gathered a team, and he wouldn't endanger his own safety by planting a bomb himself. He had gotten someone else to plant the bomb—but who would do that? Who would risk their own freedom for Ilya Markov?

"Have they identified the man in the video?" he asked.

"Yep," Bingo said. "Thad White, twenty-four years old, from Baltimore, Maryland. Wannabe terrorist and explosives enthusiast."

"That's great. He can lead us to Markov," Garrett said quickly.

"They found him in a motel in DC," Celeste said. "Self-inflicted gunshot wound to the head."

"Son of a bitch," Garrett muttered. Another killer, another suicide. What hold did Markov have on these people? Garrett stared at the faces of the Ascendant team. They weren't looking at him with anything resembling compassion. They seemed angry, their faces set and hard, as if they were about to tear him to pieces. He tried not to take it personally, to look away from their stares, but it wasn't easy.

"He's smart, don't you think?" Patmore asked.

"Markov?" Garrett said.

"He knows what's going on. He has a plan. He's one or two steps ahead of us at every turn. That's what I think," Patmore said.

Garrett nodded. That seemed reasonable. "Yeah, sure."

"Smarter than you," Celeste said.

Garrett shrugged, tilting his head to one side. "Maybe."

"A lot smarter than you when you're high," she said.

Garrett exhaled. Right. Okay. "If this is where you tell me to straighten up and fly right, be a good little boy, you can just save it, because I don't take to lectures well—"

"You made a mistake," Celeste said.

Garrett stopped talking, the words catching in his throat.

"You made a mistake with the AMBER Alert. You showed him your hand too early. You tried to outclever Ilya Markov, but that was a mistake, and it almost cost Alexis her life," Celeste said.

"Bullshit," Garrett said.

"You provoked him. You did it because you weren't thinking clearly. You had a false sense of security. You thought he couldn't find us, couldn't find you. But you didn't think long and hard enough. Because Alexis wasn't safe, was she? She wasn't in hiding," Celeste said. "You made a mistake and you put her life at risk."

Celeste stopped talking and the room fell silent. Garrett started to answer, then stopped. He thought about this. Had he made a mistake? Setting out an AMBER Alert had seemed like a good way to smoke out Markov, just as the FBI's telling the media that Garrett was a person of interest seemed like a good way to get Garrett as well. They were equally good strategies, Garrett thought, but then he realized that neither of them had worked.

"You need to stop taking pills," Celeste said.

Garrett felt another surge of anger shoot up through his blood. He started to respond, but Celeste cut him off.

"You stop or we walk. All of us. We'll just get up and take the train home, fly back to the West Coast, whatever. We go home. If the FBI comes to question us, we'll tell them the truth. Because you endanger people's lives. Our lives."

Garrett said nothing. He couldn't believe that they were pulling this. It was juvenile. Who the hell cared if he took drugs? He took them for his own reasons, and those reasons were private and none of their business. He looked to Mitty. "You too?"

She nodded. "Sorry, Gare. I love you and all, and I want to help. But I want to live too."

He scowled at her. Mitty avoided his gaze.

"That's the deal. Take it or leave it," Celeste said. "So what's it going to be?"

He grunted wordlessly and sank lower in his ratty chair. He could smell the mold wafting up from the floorboards. His mind was raging, the anger and the hurt swirling around in an electric storm. Celeste got up off the couch and exchanged looks with the other three members of the team. They all rose with her. She shot a last look at Garrett, then opened the front door. Garrett caught a brief glimpse of a yard cluttered with garbage bags and old clothing. One by one, the Ascendant team left the house.

Garrett's stomach suddenly clenched in pain. Was this really happening? He had brought them together. They were a team. They weren't perfect, but they meshed, each complementing the other; they couldn't leave. Why not? Because they were ... He searched for the word. They were ...

... a family.

And suddenly he realized why he was doing everything he'd done over the past two weeks: why he had notified Alexis, asked for the team to be brought back together, worked to keep them involved and motivated. He realized why he was trying so hard to save the country. He was doing it because he wanted a family around him. And Ascendant was the only family he had left.

"Okay," he yelled.

Bingo, the last to leave, stopped in the doorway. Mitty, Patmore, and Celeste looked back in.

Garrett felt all the pride leave his body—all the defenses, all the ego, all the arrogance. He was, at that moment, a child, desperate not to be left alone.

"I'll do whatever you want," Garrett said. "Just don't leave."

G ennady Bazanov hurried through the stand of birch trees, trying to listen to the morning breeze rustling the leaves. Summer sunlight cut through the tree branches and dappled the ground around his feet. Bazanov could even hear the call of songbirds above him; that is, he could hear them when the grind and roar of tank engines less than half a kilometer away died down.

The tanks were supposed to belong to Belarusian separatists, fighting against the fascists in Minsk who were bringing tyranny to their country, although Bazanov knew full well that they were Russian-owned T-90s, from the Twenty-Fifth Motorized Rifle Brigade stationed just west of Moscow. The separatist ploy was a convenient fiction, a smoke screen that the Kremlin could hide behind as it tried to undo what was left of the Belarusian democracy movement, and the tanks were an efficient way to batter the Belarusian Army—or what was left of that as well.

Bazanov checked his watch and lit a cigarette. He had parked a few hundred meters to the south, in Lyady, a miserable junction town in eastern Belarus, whose geographic curse it was to lie on the border with Russia. He had parked near an abandoned school—no one dared live in Lyady since the separatists had arrived—and walked through the empty town north into the birch trees, just as he'd been told.

The man from the SVR had called late last night, identifying himself only as Luka. He wasn't Bazanov's normal handler, which meant that whatever he had to say was important. Extremely important. He sounded young, and completely without a sense of humor—or compassion. "Eight thirty, two hundred meters north from the old church." His voice was cold and precise—the voice of exactly the type of vicious functionary that the SVR seemed to favor these days. Bazanov shivered with the memory, even though the June day was hot, and getting hotter. The smoke from the intermittent shelling and the fires that it caused didn't help blot out the sunshine or the heat—it only seemed to make matters worse.

Bazanov drew hard on his cigarette and kept walking. He was nervous, and he hated himself for that. He was a colonel in the glorious Russian intelligence service after all, a decorated officer in the Russian Army, and a longtime patriot. He had nothing to worry about. But when they called from Yasenevo, you worried, even if you felt there was no cause; they were getting their orders from the Kremlin, and the Kremlin could bury anybody.

"*Polkovnik* Bazanov." *Colonel Bazanov.* The voice seemed to come from nowhere, and Bazanov jumped in surprise. He spun around, and a black-haired man in a shiny suit appeared from behind a tree. He had sucked-in cheeks and black eyes that matched his suit. He was tall, and thin, like some sort of badly drawn cartoon character that was all arms and legs. Bazanov blinked in surprise: How the hell had he missed him standing there? Bazanov had walked right past him.

The thin man in the suit stepped forward and nodded without offering his hand. "Good morning." The briefest of smiles appeared on his lips.

"Luka?" Bazanov figured the name was some form of greeting code. Bazanov had little chance of ever knowing Luka's real name.

The thin man shrugged, half yes, half no. Bazanov took a deep breath. Luka was a classic SVR message boy: say no more than absolutely necessary, spread fear through ambiguity. He was young, no more than thirty, and he had the presumption to try to intimidate Gennady Bazanov? Bazanov scowled, trying to mask his fury.

"We have been following events in the United States," Luka said. "And you as well? You are in contact with your man?"

Bazanov took a deep draw from his cigarette and pondered how to deal with this errand boy. Of course he was following events in the United States. He had coordinated the entire thing. How could he not be following events there? It was his fucking job. Yet, truth be told, he was not in constant contact with Ilya Markov. Markov had broken off with him a few days ago and had not resurfaced, nor would he. This was not unexpected; he had put Markov on the job because of Markov's reputation as a man who could appear anywhere, at any time, without warning—even if you spotted him in one place, a week later he'd have you so turned around that you would be convinced you'd seen him somewhere else entirely. He was *that* good.

But Bazanov could not necessarily say this. The Kremlin wanted control above all else—and they were sending this SVR boy to regain it. If Bazanov admitted he'd lost control—well, it might be a quick end to Gennady Bazanov, and he knew it.

Bazanov tossed his cigarette to the ground and rubbed the burning ember into the dirt. "Yes, I am following events," he said, opting for feigned omniscience. "And in contact."

"When was the last time you spoke to him?"

This time Bazanov decided to be the one to play it coy and ambiguous. "Why is this important?"

The thin man from the SVR grew still. In the distance, the rattle of automatic-weapons fire crackled through the silence. Bazanov listened carefully, trying to calculate what direction the firing was, and how far away. He wasn't worried about his own safety, but rather about the road he would need to drive back to Minsk. If the separatists and the government forces were skirmishing too far to the south of the M30, then he would have to drive considerably out of his way to get back, and that would add hours to his day.

"It is important because it is important."

"Don't play with me," Bazanov snorted, his temper getting the better of him. "You don't scare me, and you won't intimidate me into doing whatever you say. The best way to get me to do my job is to just tell me whatever the fuck it is that you want me to do and get it over with."

The thin man stared at Bazanov without betraying a trace of emotion. Not a flicker of anger—or concern or compassion—crossed his face. He pulled a cell phone out of his pocket, then typed out a text with his thumbs. Bazanov watched him, curious, suddenly thinking that maybe he had played his hand wrong. Perhaps this errand boy was not an errand boy at all, but an inhabitant of the inner circle, a dreaded crony of the Great Dark Lord himself. If so, Bazanov had made a crucial, and potentially fatal, error.

Text sent, the young, thin man turned his attention back to Bazanov, but still didn't say anything. The silence was powerful, and frightening, and Bazanov worked hard to control his fear. Then, over the thin man's shoulder, walking out of a field and into the stand of white birch trees, Bazanov could see a trio of soldiers. At first glance, Bazanov would have said that they were separatists, wearing jeans and sneakers, with T-shirts covered in green flak jackets. But their haircuts were buzz short, and recently cut, and they moved across the forest floor with practiced, catlike steps. They moved like Russian special forces commandos—Spetsnaz men—slowly and with caution, and they held their AN-94 assault rifles as if they'd been born with the guns in their hands. The leader of the three dropped to his knee, in a shooting position, while the other two turned to protect him, their eyes scanning the trees and the fields beyond the forest. The first soldier brought the AN-94 to his shoulder, then cocked his head to peer through the sight.

He aimed the gun directly at Bazanov's chest.

"*Derr'mo,*" Bazanov grunted. *Shit.*

"You are in contact with your agent in the States?" Luka said again, in exactly the same bloodless tone he had used the first time.

Bazanov looked up at the sky, and the brown artillery smoke that was clouding it, then nodded to the SVR man. "I was. A while ago."

"Did you know there had been an AMBER Alert? On the East Coast? Four days ago?"

"An AMBER Alert?" Bazanov repeated, surprised. What the hell was an AMBER Alert? It had something to do with law enforcement in the United States, but what exactly he could not remember. His eyes snapped from the man named Luka to the special-forces goon aiming the gun at Bazanov's heart. If they shot him, he would have no warning. One second he would be alive, the next he would be dead; he wouldn't hear the shot or even see the puff of gunpowder smoke that would signal that the bullet was on its way into his body. He decided to lie.

"Yes, I did, of course," Bazanov said.

"Did it not worry you that perhaps American intelligence has located him?"

"Yes, yes, I was worried," Bazanov said quickly, trying to keep up with the conversation. "But I have faith in him. He is close to the target, so now he will be completely invisible."

The Kremlin man took a long, steady breath.

"We are almost there," Bazanov said, hope in his voice. "The whole thing is almost done."

"If he has been discovered, then there is real trouble," Luka began slowly. "If there were links to Russia—to the Kremlin—then it could become an international incident. And with the state of relations between world powers, events could spiral out of control."

Control, Bazanov thought, always control. "No, no, no, it won't happen."

"If your man in America were to be caught, he would be traced back to us."

"Absolutely not. I have thought of this, and there is no connection, no proof. A lone wolf, a rogue who follows his own instincts. As was discussed at the Krem—"

"There were no discussions. Ever."

Bazanov winced. Right, right, nothing had been spoken of, ever, in any way, shape, or form. "Of course. Apologies." Bazanov glanced at the Spetsnaz man, who continued to kneel, unflinchingly, with his rifle aimed at Bazanov. In the distance a howitzer fired, causing the leaves on the birch trees to shiver as the ground rumbled. "What is it that you would like me to do?"

"There cannot be loose ends."

"There will be no loo—"

"You are personally responsible."

"I am, of course. I will make sure of this." Bazanov searched for a more appropriate way to grovel. To save his own skin. "I am a patriot. Now. Forever."

Luka pulled out his phone and tapped out another text. Bazanov held his breath. Fifty meters away, Bazanov could see the second special operations soldier reach into his pocket and pull out a phone of his own. He read the text—Bazanov assumed it was the one Luka had just sent—and then whispered something to the soldier whose rifle was aimed at Bazanov's heart. The soldier continued to aim at Bazanov, and Bazanov tightened the muscles in his chest, as if that would somehow protect him from the high-caliber bullet that threatened to rip apart his body.

Then, without warning, the solider stood, pointed his rifle at the ground, turned, and walked out of the forest. The other two soldiers followed him.

"We are all proud of you, *Polkovnik* Bazanov," Luka said. "Of your service to your country. It is our sincerest wish that our pride only increases with time." Then Luka turned and walked away as well.

Bazanov watched him go, sure for the first time in fifteen minutes that he would live to see the afternoon. A great weight lifted from his shoulders. But then he realized that he had much more to do. He had to make sure Ilya Markov could never be traced back to Bazanov, to the SVR, the Kremlin, or to anyone else in Mother Russia. But that was not so simple a task, certainly not from godforsaken Belarus. He walked slowly back to his car, parked by the abandoned school in Lyady, and made up his mind: he would not drive west to Minsk. No, he would drive the opposite direction, east to Moscow, get a plane ticket to the United States, and see to it himself that all went according to plan, because it was clear from his morning in the birches of a Belarusian forest that his life depended on it.

The house was big and perfect for the number of guests he had in mind: six bedrooms, four bathrooms, two entertainment rooms with a pool table and an air-hockey game, a vast kitchen and dining room, and a deck that wrapped around the ground floor and fronted the beach. Ilya booked the house through a vacation-rental website, and it was expensive—six grand a week—but he knew that a bunch of miscreant hackers liked nothing better than lounging around a beach house while they wreaked havoc on the rest of the population. Plus, no one would bat an eye when a gang of grubby twentysomethings invaded a house on the Jersey Shore for a week. Wasn't that why the Jersey Shore had been invented in the first place?

The last of them rolled into the house around one in the afternoon. He gathered them in the basement billiards room, which was painted sherbet orange and smelled faintly of beer and bong water. A seventy-two-inch flatscreen TV hung on one wall, a framed oil painting of the Piazza San Marco on the adjoining one, and a signed poster of Snooki on the third. That seemed an appropriate troika to Ilya.

There were fifteen of them in all; Ilya knew six of them by reputation, four because they'd spent time in jail, two from the hacker's collective Anonymous, and the last three he knew personally because they were Eastern European immigrants. Eleven were men, four women; none was older than thirty-five. Most wore T-shirts and shorts, two were in bathing suits and flip-flops, and one wore a stained white linen suit that had obviously been purchased at a thrift store.

They all claimed to be true believers, but Ilya suspected they believed in money more than anything else. He didn't care: betrayal, if it happened, would come too late to change anything.

He pulled a thick-tipped black Sharpie out of his shirt pocket and wrote, in large block letters, directly on the only wall without a painting, a poster, or a TV.

"First order of business: CR Logistics," Ilya said as he wrote. "Based in Louisville, Kentucky. The fourth-largest trucking company in the United States, and the number one provider of food delivery into New York City. They move trucks full of beef, soda, vegetables, pasta, ice cream. They fill up supermarkets all over the city."

Ilya continued to write on the wall. "This is their website. And this is the name of their back-end IT subcontractor." He wrote an acronym on the wall. The hackers all had their laptops perched on their knees or laps, and Ilya could hear the click-clack of their fingers as they busily copied down what he was writing. He hoped that the best of them were already probing at the company's websites.

"You want us to hack it?" said a young man with bleach-blond hair who went by the name ClarKent.

"I do," Ilya replied.

"Take it down? Denial of service?" a woman named Uni asked. She wore thick makeup, as much, Ilya thought, to hide the circles under her eyes as to make a fashion statement. Hackers tended not to sleep much.

"No. Do not take it down."

"Steal industrial secrets? Drain their accounts?" a long-limbed teenager from Pittsburgh shouted out. He had sleeves of green and red tattoos up and down both arms. Ilya thought he could make out unicorns on them. And snakes.

"No." Ilya hauled a large FedEx box onto the billiards table and cut it open with a kitchen knife. Inside was a small suitcase, dark green and about the size of an airplane carry-on bag. He unzipped the bag and pulled a layer of T-shirts, socks, and underwear off the top. He waited a moment before emptying the rest of the contents. The room went quiet.

"What I want is more complicated than any of those things. I want you to track down every connection to CR Logistics on the Web. Every account, every warehouse, every client and customer, every bank or credit union. I want you to find all their employees, executives, directors, drivers. I want the details, from top to bottom, of how they run their business. And then"—Ilya smiled—"I want you to destroy their credit rating."

A few of the hackers laughed. A few blinked in surprise. A young man with Jesus hair and matching beard said in a thick Ukrainian accent, "That is it? Just hack credit?"

"Yes, that's it." Ilya flipped the small suitcase over, and onto the billiards table fell a pile of $100 bills. They were balled up and wrapped with rubber bands, and they landed on the green felt with a satisfying thud.

"One hundred and fifty thousand dollars," Ilya said after letting the wide-eyed hackers stare hungrily at the money for a moment. "Whoever does it first, gets it all."

Ilya left the money on the table and went upstairs, knowing that if anyone tried to steal a bundle of cash, the other hackers would tear him apart. Greed was the best security system he could ask for. He poured himself a glass of vodka, lit a cigarette, then went out to the porch and sat in the shade. The heat was intense, thick and wet, and Ilya watched as sunbathers and swimmers waded into the waves of the Atlantic Ocean, splashing and floating on boogie boards.

He drank a second glass of vodka, then a third, smoking cigarette after cigarette. An hour passed, then another, and Ilya only moved to refill his glass. The crowd on the beach thinned slightly as the sun dipped lower in the sky, but the temperature didn't change, staying hot and humid. Ilya's T-shirt was rimmed with sweat, but he didn't mind. The moisture cooled him.

At two minutes before six, Uni appeared on the porch with her laptop under her arm. "Done," she said.

Ilya was surprised: that had been accomplished faster than he would have thought possible. She sat next to him on a deck chair, opened her laptop, and showed him her work. They scrolled through hacked databases, emptied bank accounts, altered tax returns, a series of forged letters—including half a dozen demanding immediate repayment of outstanding loans—and a press release stating that the company was filing for Chapter 11 bankruptcy.

"And the result?"

She showed Ilya a memo released by a corporate-credit-rating agency. The time stamp on the memo was 5:52 p.m. CR Logistics had been downgraded to an extreme credit risk.

Ilya smiled. He looked at the girl who called herself Uni. She was prettier than he originally thought—or perhaps that was just her competency.

"Wait here." He went back down to the billiards room, scooped all the money back into the suitcase, and pulled it off the billiards table. "You all lose," he said to the remaining hackers. They spit out curses and grunts of disappointment. Ilya wrote the name of another company on the wall, and underneath it a series of usernames and passwords.

"Here is the next target. A credit-card-processing company. Here are usernames and passwords to their servers. A backdoor portal. Attack the company. Disable all its servers. That is your next chance to win. I will be back with more money in a few hours. Again, winner takes all."

With that, he hauled the suitcase back upstairs and gave it to Uni. She beamed with pleasure.

"Do you have a car?" he asked.

She nodded yes.

"I want you to drive me someplace."

She agreed, and they went out to her beat-up green Hyundai, which sat parked by a cyclone fence. She put the suitcase in the trunk, then drove him north on the Garden State Parkway. They said little as they drove, and they made good time, as traffic was light. Ilya watched the scenery and wondered briefly where Garrett Reilly was; he could have been in any of the towns they passed, in any number of buildings or houses. It didn't really matter; wherever he had run since Ilya had unleashed Newark's finest on him, Ilya would find him.

He had Uni drive away from the Jersey Shore and onto the Jersey Turnpike. When they got close to New York City and the sun had set, he had her take surface streets into Hoboken. She parked near the water, on Frank Sinatra Drive, and they got out to look at the Manhattan skyline across the river. The Battery, to the south, gleamed with enormous towers, as did midtown to the north. The Hudson River was slow moving, and black, as tugs and Circle Line ferries fought against its endless current.

"Can it be done?" Ilya asked, gesturing to the city across the water.

"The entire city?" Uni asked.

He nodded yes.

"Why all of it?"

"Why not?"

"There are innocent people."

He let out a short hiss of disgust. "Doesn't it bother you?"

"What?"

"The money, the power, the waste. All those people protecting their own interests. Hoarding and then forcing the rest of us to beg for scraps. To serve them. And you and me, we are on the outside looking in. Always on the outside."

"I suppose it bothers me."

"So we send a message. I exist. Outside of your kingdom. I am important. Outside of your view. And I do not consent to your rules. I do not consent to being fingerprinted, photographed, tracked, my conversations monitored. I won't support a system that feeds the wealthy, not the poor. That only looks after its own. Where most people on the planet live in shacks, on pennies, and a few live in penthouses with maids and butlers and views of the ocean. We send a message: We can bring it down. See how easily we can bring it down."

She looked at him. "Is that what we're saying?"

"Yes. That is what we are saying."

Uni seemed to think about this. "I thought you were from Russia."

"In Russia it is even worse. There are people with power, and then there is everybody else. The problem is across the planet. But it starts right here. In this city. In this country." Ilya looked at her. "So, again—can it be done?"

"Maybe. With help."

"The help is all around you. I've made sure of that."

She smiled. "Then, yeah, why not? It can be done."

He looked over at her and reached out and stroked her face with his hand. He could see, in the soft dusk, that the makeup she was wearing hid pockmarks and acne scars as well as exhaustion. He didn't mind; it made her even more attractive. To Ilya, the ruin of her face was alluring and hinted at a life of struggle and isolation. Struggle gave life meaning.

He kissed her, and she kissed him back. Then they climbed into the backseat of her Hyundai and had sex under an old blanket, with the lights of Manhattan shimmering in the background, and Ilya felt, as his body was intertwined with hers, that he was a medieval crusader having a last night of pleasure just outside the gates of the castle that he would storm in the morning.

Sobriety did not feel good. Not to Garrett, at least. Sobriety felt hot and constricting; it felt like a thin layer of normalcy encasing his body, but underneath that normalcy was a jittery, crackling pulse of need. Desire threatened to break through the skin of normal, to smash everything, to go wild. He tried to shake it off and focus on the task at hand.

"If he knew where we were," Garrett said, wiping the sweat from his face with the bottom of his T-shirt, "why did he send the Newark PD to raid our offices instead of the FBI?"

They sat on the front porch of the abandoned house, as rays of sunlight streaked across the grass and onto the oil depot in the distance. The day had been hot, and the evening wasn't any cooler. Thick, humid air had settled over the East Coast, blanketing it in a layer of summer misery. "The FBI would have arrested all of you. They would have found me. But he spoofed us instead."

Garrett looked at the team, sitting on the porch with him, Patmore standing in the grass a few feet away. None of them seemed to be fully back on board yet; none of them seemed to trust Garrett. But he couldn't do much about that. He simply had to keep trying.

"Why?" he asked the team. "It doesn't make sense."

"He was fucking with us," Mitty said. "Yanking our chain."

"But he doesn't do that," Garrett said. "He doesn't joke around."

"How do you know he doesn't joke around? You know him so well now?" Mitty asked.

"He tried to kill Alexis. That's not yanking anybody's chain," Garrett said. "And, yes, I do know him so well."

"You wanna explain how?" Mitty said.

"I know him because we're alike."

They stared at him, surprise in their eyes. Garrett shrugged. While he would be the first to admit that he wasn't particularly self-aware—that much had been proven over the last twenty-four hours while he was tied to a fucking radiator—he still thought that he and Markov were remarkably similar. Similar life stories, similar talents, maybe even similar goals. That was the beginning of a worrisome pattern, and Garrett was reluctant to follow that pattern to its logical conclusion. But at some point he knew he would have to do exactly that: he would have to explore their likenesses and explain it to himself.

Patmore turned away from the lowering sun. "He wasn't sure it was you in the offices. He had some information, but not all the information, so he hedged his bets. A shot in the dark."

Garrett swigged a mouthful of water from a plastic bottle. His head was alive with pain, but he wasn't going to tell anybody, and he wasn't going to let anybody know how he felt, either. He'd made up his mind to bear his burden without complaint. He would sacrifice everything to keep Ascendant together and at his side. He was ashamed of that need—of that vulnerability—but his need outweighed his shame, and he had made peace with that.

"How did he know where we were?" Garrett said out loud. "How could he have possibly known?"

"Maybe one of us told him." Celeste scanned the faces of the team. "Maybe one of us is a traitor."

Mitty let out a laugh, but no one else did. "A double agent? Cool."

"Does that pass the plausibility test?" Garrett asked. "Why wait until that moment to turn us in? And anyway, how would he have gotten to any of us to make us traitors? When would he have done that?"

"Maybe one of us contacted him instead," Celeste said. "That's plausible."

Garrett paced. The floorboards of the abandoned house were rotted and streaked with black. They groaned under his weight. "Which of us would do that, and why?"

"Money," Bingo said. "He offered money. You said he had a lot. Maybe one of us wanted in on it."

Garrett looked from face to face—Mitty, Bingo, Patmore, Celeste—and considered the possibility. Mitty was out; she wouldn't betray Garrett, no matter how much money was involved. Anyway, she didn't give a shit about money and never had.

Bingo was a possibility, but a remote one. Betraying people took a level of willpower and courage that Bingo just didn't possess.

Patmore was inscrutable, but he'd also had any number of chances to walk out of the offices, hail a cop car, and turn them all in. And if he were caught, he'd be court-martialed, and he knew it. Which left . . .

Garrett studied Celeste's face. She wasn't crazy about Garrett—he knew that. She blamed him for her time in China. She had nothing particularly to lose by being arrested, and Bingo had told Garrett that he'd seen overdue notices littering her Palo Alto apartment, so she conceivably needed the money.

"Don't go there," Celeste said dismissively. "If I'd wanted to screw you over, Garrett, I would have done it a long time ago. And the truth is, I don't want to screw you over anymore. I don't hold grudges—I just sink into despair."

Garrett smiled at the self-deprecating joke. He felt, instinctively, that she was telling the truth.

"I know it was me who brought up the possibility, but I don't think one of us contacted him," Celeste said. "I think he found out some other way."

It gave Garrett no small amount of relief to know that the family he had chosen had not betrayed him. "Probably right. But we'll need to know what that other way is, or he'll keep finding us, and keep coming after us. And eventually, he'll get us."

Bingo raised his hand, as he always did when asking a question. "But that brings us back to—why didn't he tell the FBI where we were? If the FBI arrests us, then we're out of the way, and Markov doesn't have to bother with us anymore."

A silence settled on the team. The sun had slipped into a pink haze in the west, and the darkness began to grow behind the house, east over New York City and the Atlantic.

"There's a reason," Garrett said. "We're just not seeing it. But it's right there. In front of our faces."

"We're missing it because it's not about him," Celeste said, walking down the steps and kicking at the brown weeds in front of the house. "It's about us."

"How so?" Garrett asked.

"You called him a social engineer."

"Yeah?"

"A con man. And what do con men do?"

"Trick people," Bingo said.

"And how do they do it?" Celeste asked.

"Sleight of hand, misdirection," Garrett said.

"Right, but to misdirect you, they have to get your attention in the first place. They have to talk to you. Engage you in a relationship."

Garrett blinked in the gathering gloom. Celeste was driving at a point, and it was becoming clearer. "You're saying he's talking to us."

"No. I'm saying he's talking to *you*," Celeste said. "He's engaging you in a relationship. Because he's a con man—*and you're part of the con*."

Garrett retreated into the house after that revelation. The truth of it startled him so badly that he needed time to process the idea. *He was part of the con.* Seen through the lens of that idea, what had happened over the last few days began to make sense. He flicked on a light—a bare bulb on the living-room ceiling—and padded back and forth on the dirty floor. The rest of the team loitered on the porch and the grass. The sun had gone down. Night was thickening all around them.

Garrett went back to his first principles. A to B to C. Logic was his friend. What did he know?

Markov was highly intelligent.

Markov had a plan, but it was unknown to Garrett.

Markov had stayed a step ahead of Garrett this entire time.

Markov was establishing a relationship with Garrett, long distance, through proxies. It was a dangerous, scary relationship, but it was one nonetheless.

Ilya Markov did not want him arrested. A jailed Garrett Reilly was somehow at odds with his plan.

Garrett paused in the middle of the room and closed his eyes, trying to find the pattern in all of this. He waited, hoping he had not killed so many brain cells that his one true talent—his ability to cut through the white noise of everyday life—had deserted him. He tried to still the incessant buzz in his mind, the rattle of thoughts and opinions, banging this way and that, from neuron to sparking neuron.

Markov was playing with Garrett. That's what Markov did. He thought one step ahead of his opponent. If Alexis and the DIA could track Garrett's prescriptions online, then why couldn't a talented hacker such as Markov do the same? He had found Garrett's vulnerability—addiction—and used it to make Garrett run. Which meant that . . .

Garrett knew in a flash what to do. He walked from the living room to the porch. The team, in the middle of conversation, fell silent.

"He's playing a game. He's guessing our next move by forcing our hand. He expects us to do one thing"—Garrett shook his head, amazed that he hadn't come to this conclusion sooner—"so we have to do the opposite."

Hans Metternich considered himself a war theorist. Admittedly, he was an amateur theorist, certainly no PhD on the subject, but most of his adult life had been spent in the trenches of modern warfare, so he felt this gave him insight that most academics did not have. And while Metternich had never been in a firefight, parachuted behind enemy lines, or seen a laser-guided missile explode, he did not believe that the future of warfare depended on any of those things.

The future of modern warfare, Metternich mused as he picked his way through the crowd of tourists walking Fifth Avenue, would hinge on information: who had it, who lacked it, how you acquired it, and what you did with it once you possessed it. Information was not just power; it was a weapon—a razor-sharp weapon that could be used to disarm, confuse, and terrorize your enemies. Information, or the lack thereof, could bring down an army. It could, he thought—maybe a bit melodramatically, he had to admit—even bring down a country.

All of which was why Garrett Reilly and his ongoing combat with Ilya Markov were so fascinating to Metternich. Both men were information soldiers. They were the warriors of the future, fighting invisible battles while the rest of the world watched sports on television or drank itself to death. Metternich wasn't particularly rooting for either man, Reilly or Markov—although he felt more emotional connection to Reilly—but he understood that their battle was a harbinger of things to come. Also, it was a good way to make money.

Metternich was not an information soldier—he was more of an information merchant. He bought data cheap and sold it dear, which was why he stopped on the corner of Thirty-Sixth Street and Fifth Avenue and stared in the window of NYC Gifts, a small trinket shop squeezed between a lingerie store and a Burger King. Brightly colored luggage was stacked in one window, and T-shirts, baseball caps, and disposable cell phones were scattered across the other.

He stepped inside and felt the blast of air-conditioning cool the sweat on his neck and forehead. An Italian family crowded around a counter, pointing at digital cameras and jabbering in broken English. A middle-aged couple browsed T-shirts toward the back. Separate clerks were helping them, while a third clerk—a woman, young, with short, platinum-blond hair and a skull earring—smiled at Metternich. "Welcome to New York City Gifts. Would you like to see some of our watches? They're all authentic, straight from the factory. Starting at twenty-five dollars."

Metternich glanced at the watches in the counter and tapped his finger over one. "Yes. That one perhaps. The gold. It's a Rolex?"

The young woman opened the counter and pulled out the gold watch, speaking quickly the whole time. "Absolutely, a Rolex, straight from Switzerland, fifty dollars. We have the box as well, waterproof, with a lifetime guarantee . . ."

As she spoke, Metternich scanned the store. His eyes landed on the young clerk helping the Italian family. She was also a platinum blonde, also with her hair cut short and a skull earring in her left ear. She was, as far as Metternich could tell, the first clerk's identical twin.

The first clerk handed him the watch, and he put it carefully around his wrist. He noted that she had a long, thin tattoo running along her forearm, a string of 1s and 0s. Binary code. Now he was certain: this was the person for whom he was looking. "Twins?"

The first clerk nodded cheerfully. "I'm Jan. She's Jen."

Metternich nodded. The names were another hit. "Actually, I was hoping you could help me. I'm looking for someone. Maybe you know him." ·

Jan stared at Metternich, the wide smile disappearing from her face. "This is a gift store. Maybe you need to go someplace else."

"I like this watch very much." Metternich pulled out his wallet and slid five

$100 bills across the counter, making sure that the clerk saw them and that they were secured with the palm of his hand. He had seen a man who looked like the store's owner standing in the back, talking loudly on the phone, in what Metternich thought was Armenian. The man was distracted, deep in conversation.

Jan stared at the money.

"I'd be willing to pay top price for the watch."

"What makes you think I know who you're looking for?" the clerk asked.

"You were recruited online. For a job. You and your sister. But you didn't get it. You weren't happy about this. There was a darknet bulletin board. You should be more studied in what you post online. Anyone can read those things."

Jan frowned. She shot a look across the store to her sister—a look of fear—but Metternich could see that her twin was busy pulling camera bags off a shelf. "I don't think I can help you."

"His name is Markov."

"Don't recognize it."

"But you were in contact with someone offering the job. I would pay more for the watch, by the way. If it were a good watch. Verifiably authentic." He slipped two more $100 bills under his palm.

Jan shrugged. "I guess I was in contact with him."

"How did you communicate?"

"E-mail."

"No phone numbers?"

Jan shook her head no. At the back of the store, the Armenian hung up the phone and looked out over his business. His eyes landed—and locked—on Metternich.

"That's what I know. You taking the watch or not?" Jan said. "My boss sees you."

"Yes, please." Metternich pushed the $700 across the glass to Jan.

She pocketed the money in a flash. "Enjoy."

"One more question. Did anyone you know actually get the job?"

Jan's boss was still staring at them and was clearly about to cross the store to them.

"Would you like to look at some of our cell phones?" Jan asked.

Metternich let out a low laugh. This was turning into an expensive conversation. But if it worked for him, it would be worth it.

"Same price?" Metternich pointed to a flip phone under the glass.

"Same."

"I'll need more than a name. I'll need a phone number." He palmed another $500 and placed his hand—and the money—on the glass counter.

The Armenian was striding toward them. He looked suspicious—and tense. Jan pulled a plastic flip phone from under the counter, opened it, and punched a number into its tiny keyboard. She handed Metternich the phone.

"Name?"

Jan hesitated. The owner was fifteen feet away. "Uni. Better coder than me. But I'm cuter." She yanked the bills from under Metternich's hand and stashed them in her pocket, just as her boss walked up.

"Everything good?" The owner of the store stared at Metternich. "We can be helpful?"

"You have a lovely store. And your employees are extremely helpful." Metternich held up the watch and the phone. "I've just bought two items. And at a fair price." He smiled at the owner, then nodded appreciatively to the young clerk. "I will recommend you on Yelp."

Metternich walked quickly out of the store, took a hard right on Fifth Avenue, and ducked down Thirty-Sixth Street. He checked the number Jan had punched into the cell phone, then entered it into his own phone with deep pleasure. The information had cost him $1,200, but that was cheap. Once he spoke to his contact at the phone company—and paid him as well—and then tracked the location of the owner of that phone number, those ten digits would earn him fifty times that amount of money.

Satisfaction welled up inside of him. He might not have ever experienced bullets whizzing past his head or seen young men die in the trenches, but to his mind he had just engaged in a skirmish in a war of the future.

And he had won.

Deep disappointment washed over Agent Chaudry as she stood in the dark of the concrete plaza in downtown Newark. She had failed to grab Garrett Reilly, yet again, and this time she had been so certain she would find him. Everything had lined up for her—she'd had the DIA on her side, links from Captain Truffant's phone and from her e-mail, as well as receipts for plane tickets and rental cars over the last week. General Kline had ordered his subordinate to open all her books and records to the FBI, and the information had led them to the seventh floor of the half-finished office tower on Raymond and Market.

Only they were gone.

Garrett Reilly and Ascendant had fled before Chaudry and the Bureau got there. Another missed chance. And the pressure was mounting. The Bureau was on war footing: from the murder of a federal official to a domestic terror bombing, the case was now on the front page of every newspaper in the country. The director of the FBI himself had called her that morning, his voice brimming with impatience, explaining that the president's chief of staff had called *him* only ten minutes earlier, wanting to know what the hell was going on. They had put three separate teams on the bombing in DC, with a liaison to coordinate their efforts with hers. They had given her two dozen extra agents in Manhattan, as well as a new forensics team from the NYPD.

And still she wasn't getting the job done. Standing at the base of the building where Reilly had recently hidden himself, she could only scrape her heels against the cement and wonder where he had gone. She was trying so god-damned hard.

In order to think like Reilly, Chaudry had immersed herself in the world of patterns: for the last twenty-four hours, anywhere she could possibly find a pattern, she sought it out, wrote it down, studied and analyzed it.

For instance, seventeen field agents worked in the Manhattan FBI office; thirteen were men, and four were women. But the men were, on average, seven years older than the women, and of the last four hires, two were female, and two male. When she looked up the average retirement age of an FBI agent—fifty-eight—she realized that at the current distribution of hiring, women would outnumber men in the Manhattan office in nine years.

That revelation made her exceedingly happy. Score one for patterns.

She categorized the last four digits of phone numbers in her contact list, but found nothing there, so she turned to spending data from the receipts she found at the bottom of her purse. A nice pattern emerged from those pieces of paper: she spent around seven bucks in the morning—on coffee and snacks—then averaged twenty-three in the afternoon, before dropping back down to eight-fifty when she stopped at the Korean deli near her house. She liked that information as well and made a note to be more careful with her credit card in the middle of the day.

All in all, she enjoyed seeing the world through numbers; she'd always been good at math, and it felt right to her, even if that put her squarely in the cliché of the Indian girl who was a numbers geek. So be it.

Yet it hadn't paid off. Reilly's friendship with Michaela Rodriguez had no pattern. His relationship to Ascendant had no pattern. His running to New Jersey had no pattern. And the part that killed her was that the Newark PD had raided that very same office three days earlier. They had been spoofed, had kicked down the door, guns at the ready, had seen every member of Ascendant—and had walked away. How could they have been so blind?

She knew how. If you weren't actively looking for a suspect, that person could be right in front of your face and you wouldn't notice him or her. The Newark PD was not in the Garrett Reilly business, so he had escaped their grasp. And truth be told, when she read the report of the spoofing, nobody mentioned an office worker who bore any resemblance to Reilly. Perhaps he had fled the premises before they got there.

But all of this raised another question: Who had spoofed those offices in the first place? Was it this Ilya Markov that Captain Truffant had gone on about? There was no evidence that he had anything to do with the bombing at the Arlington Best Buy, or the shooting of the Fed president. Yet Truffant seemed convinced he was behind all of it. Was Truffant paranoid? She didn't seem like the type, but she was an intelligence officer, and they were, by nature, afraid of their own shadows.

It was all maddeningly complex, an opaque mystery, the veil of which Chaudry was not penetrating. How could this possibly be? She was a master criminal hunter. She did not fail. *Ever.*

Agent Murray walked out of the lobby of the building shaking his head, followed by a phalanx of other agents. "Nothing in any of the other offices. We checked every one." He stopped a few feet from Chaudry and eyed her expectantly. She was still the boss, but her position was becoming tenuous. The director of the Manhattan field office might decide to replace her at any moment; and if that happened, Murray might well step into her shoes. "So, what next?"

Chaudry clenched her jaw, her eyes sweeping over the landscape of Newark and New Jersey beyond. A soccer stadium was lit up in the distance.

"Head back to Manhattan. We'll review what we've got."

Murray nodded faithfully, following orders, but Chaudry could see the beginning of a gleam in his eye. She was giving up for the day, stifled, and that meant he was one step closer to taking over the case. She didn't blame him for his eagerness; he had every right to be as ambitious as she was.

They got in the white Chevy Malibu and drove east, onto Route 9 toward New York, along the elevated highway, past the smokestacks and rotting swamp piers. Chaudry watched the passing scenery with disgust: she hated New Jersey, hated being there, hated being *from* there.

"We'll get 'em tomorrow," Murray said, as they entered the Holland Tunnel. "Never give up, right?"

She looked over at her partner, his hands gripping the wheel of the car, eyes forward. Would he do a better job than she would? Perhaps she had gotten too mired in the weeds of the case—maybe it needed a fresh set of eyes.

"Yeah, tomorrow," she said halfheartedly.

They came out of the tunnel into the artificial night of Manhattan and inched through traffic on Canal Street. Murray turned right on Broadway and headed south toward the Federal Building and the FBI field offices.

Chaudry's phone chimed, a text coming in. She checked it.

Where are you?

She tapped out a reply. *Who is this?*

Your bud Garrett.

She glanced over at Murray to see if he was watching her, but his eyes were glued to the street. She typed, *How did you get this number?*

You gave it to me. In an e-mail. Remember?

Yes, she did remember. Of course. But why the hell was he texting her now?

Where are you? he wrote again. *I thought we had a thing.*

Chaudry tensed. Was he playing with her? Or actually reaching out to her, as she had predicted he would? She couldn't let him slip away, not this time. Her heart raced as she tried to figure out how to play the situation. She needed to keep him on the line.

Driving back to the office. Where are you?

The response was immediate. *What kind of car?*

White Chevy Malibu, she wrote. She paused, then typed, *In the market for a new ride?*

She pressed her lips together, her body tense with expectation. Was that the right tone to take? She should tell Murray to call the office and dispatch agents to triangulate Reilly's cell phone, but Reilly would be expecting that; he was smarter than that. She needed to move their relationship to the next level. She needed to—

"Holy shit," Murray screamed suddenly, slamming on the brakes. Chaudry's head snapped forward, her seat belt locking, her chest and shoulders pressing hard against the strap.

Thump. Someone had slammed their hands onto the hood of the car. Chaudry looked up in surprise, her hand instinctively going for the grip of the Glock in her holster.

But there, staring through the front windshield of the Malibu, a trace of a smile on his lips, hands on the hood, was Garrett Reilly. The look on his face was one of utter casualness, as if this were all going according to plan, and he had a fun little bit of mischief in mind. Mischief that he couldn't wait to share with Chaudry.

"I surrender," Garrett Reilly said. "Arrest me."

PART 3

Anthony Marsh had been manager of the D'Agostino's supermarket on Third Avenue and Twenty-Sixth Street for three years. Before that, he had been an assistant manager at the same store, and before that, produce manager for the D'Ag in Greenwich Village—the one all the way over on the West Side. Marsh, thirty-seven years old, with a closely cropped mustache and a taste for bow ties, liked the work. It was challenging, but not overly so, and required his organizational as well as his people skills. He liked the hours, his coworkers, even his bosses—the D'Agostino family—who dropped in to see how the store was being run every other week or so. But mostly he loved his customers: neighborhood types who came in to grab a six-pack of beer, a box of cinnamon-raisin cereal, or a package of trimmed pork chops.

Shoppers loved coming to his store, and Marsh loved them for being happy. It was a mutually beneficial relationship.

But today . . . today made him question everything. Today was a disaster, and rather than getting better, it was getting considerably worse by the minute.

His shift started badly with the news that the store's credit-card processing was off-line. That had happened, briefly, in the past, but this outage seemed to be more serious—and was taking longer to fix. Normally, the store's backup plan was to shift all credit processing to another company, but that backup company seemed to have been knocked off-line as well.

"Not a problem," Marsh had told his cashiers. "We'll do it the old-fashioned way. By hand. Write down the credit-card numbers for processing later in the day."

The cashiers weren't happy about that, but they didn't have a lot of choice, and pens and notebooks were brought to each checkout line. But it slowed checkout times considerably, and customers got cranky when they had to wait in line to pay and get their groceries. But as Marsh tried to calm nerves at the checkout counters, he learned that his customers had another reason to be cranky that morning.

"Goddamned ATMs aren't working," a young man grumbled as he paid for his milk and ground coffee with his last $20 bill. "All over Manhattan. Nobody's getting cash."

An older man on the same checkout line said he'd heard on the radio that ATMs in Brooklyn were spitting out other people's money, and that some bank customers' accounts had been zeroed out.

Marsh had to scratch his head at that one. Credit-card processing was down at the same moment that ATMs were on the blink? What were the chances of that happening? That had to be like a meteor strike in its rarity. He told his cashiers to let some customers—ones the cashiers recognized—pay on credit, writing down their names, addresses, and phone numbers. He figured most of them would be good for the money, and at this moment of crisis the idea would probably buy the supermarket some goodwill. But he hadn't planned on other customers, ones the cashiers didn't know, demanding the same treatment, and getting testy when they were denied the opportunity to pay later as well.

"You let white people pay later," an elderly African-American woman hissed at him in the bread aisle. "But black folk gotta pay cash."

"No, no, no," Marsh tried to explain. "That's not it at all. It's just that we know those people. They're from the neighborhood. And a lot of them happen to be Anglo. No, what I mean is . . ." He stuttered to a stop, sensing that his words weren't helping matters, and the elderly woman shoved past him with her grocery cart.

He shelved the whole concept thirty minutes after he'd okayed it, but the damage had been done, and he heard a number of people in the aisles griping about the store's discriminatory management. Then Marsh realized the bread shelves were only half-stocked, and he hurried to the cramped storeroom at the back of the store to find out why. Marsh found his three stock boys drinking coffee and talking about the dates they'd been on last night.

"Guys? What the hell? Why is the bread aisle half-empty?" Marsh grabbed the stock list and scanned the room for delivery pallets.

Juan, the oldest of the three, shook his head sadly. "No deliveries, boss. Nothing since yesterday."

"Not possible." Marsh checked the delivery schedule. "We've got five different setups for this morning. Did you call?"

"Nah, man," Juan said. "Figured you would."

Marsh grunted in exasperation: the stockroom boys were the yawning abyss of his job. "You gotta tell me if we're short so I can call. Otherwise, how am I supposed to know?"

"It's just—you been kinda busy this morning, boss." Alberto and Michael, the other two stock boys, nodded rapidly in agreement. "What with the bank riots and all."

"Bank riots?"

"That's what I heard," Juan said. "Maybe just a rumor. But—crazy out there."

Marsh suddenly felt as if he was having trouble breathing. "Just—clean up or something."

The stock boys scattered to opposite ends of the storage room.

Marsh grabbed the landline and looked up the numbers for the delivery companies that were on today's schedule. He tried the first, CR Logistics, but got a busy signal, which was strange. Their line was never busy. That was the whole point of being a shipping company—your customers could reach you 24-7. He tried the next shipper, but their line was busy as well, and the third, Brown & Franklin Freight Lines, was completely out of order. Baffled, he tried going online to contact the supply-chain management offices of each of the companies, but the D'Agostino Internet server was down.

"What is going on?" Marsh said to himself, his heart now beginning to pound. Before he had time to investigate, a female voice, edged with hysteria, crackled over the store's PA system.

"Manager to dairy! Manager to dairy!"

That was probably Rosario at the front. If there was a true emergency—a fire or a bomb threat—they had codes, red and blue, to yell over the PA, and

Marsh had drummed those codes into the employees for years. Just saying *Manager to dairy* didn't mean much, but the tone of her voice, the cracking of her vocal cords, made Marsh jump from his seat and scramble back into the store.

He jogged past the produce section, breaking into a run by the time he passed the potatoes, and noticed that they were short on bananas and berries. He wanted to stop to check the rest of the produce, but a crowd of people had gathered around the apples and the peaches, blocking his path back into the area. The aisles at the D'Agostino were narrow, and the store, like all Manhattan groceries, was cramped. Why were there crowds in produce? Were they short on everything?

"Manager to dairy!" Rosario's voice rang out again, and Marsh forgot produce and ran, full tilt, for the dairy section. He skidded around the shelves stocked with tortillas—also low, he noticed—to find half a dozen customers and three D'Agostino employees gathered in a scrum around the milk section. A middle-aged woman in jeans and a sweatshirt was clutching four half gallons of milk in her arms, and a second shopper—a young woman in shorts and a tank top—was trying to pry them loose. An older man and a teenaged boy were on either side of the wrestling women, reaching into the center of the battle and either trying to dislodge the milk or break up the fight—Marsh couldn't tell which. Two other shoppers, both women, were being restrained by two of Marsh's employees, Jerome from the deli section and Suzie, a part-time bagger. The third D'Ag employee, Alicia from the back office, was dancing around the scrum, desperately trying to push people apart, but having little luck with that.

They were all talking over each other, not loudly—Marsh guessed because they were putting their energies into grappling with each other—but fast enough that Marsh couldn't make out what they were arguing about. He hesitated for a moment, then grabbed the woman in a tank top by the shoulder and started to haul her backward.

"Hey! Hey! People! Come on, let go. Let go." Marsh pulled hard at the woman in the tank top, but she had a lock grip on the milk-carrying woman's forearm, and she wasn't about to release her.

"She's taking all the milk," the woman in the tank top grunted. She turned toward Marsh and snapped her teeth at his hand, barely missing him.

"Jesus Christ," Marsh yelled, pulling his hand away. "There's no reason to fight over the milk. We'll have more milk brought in this afternoon."

"No, you won't," the woman clutching the half gallons said. "No one's got any milk left in the whole city. I've got three kids!"

"I've got kids too," the tank-top woman shrieked back. "You fucking bitch! Give us some of that goddamned milk!"

"Hey, there's no need for that." Marsh stood slightly back from the scrum now and clutched at the hand that had almost been bitten. The whole thing reminded him of separating fighting dogs, which he'd tried once, when a German shepherd and a pit bull were scrapping in a dog run in Riverside Park, and he'd almost lost a finger. "There's no need to use that language."

"Fuck you!" the woman in the tank top said, much louder now, so that people in other aisles could hear her. Marsh noticed that shoppers were gathering at both ends of the dairy section, craning their heads to watch the scuffle.

"We're good," Marsh said to the knots of shoppers. "We're fine. Please clear the area."

But nobody moved. A pair of teenaged boys got closer, and an older man grabbed an armful of cottage-cheese containers. "There's no food anywhere on Third Avenue," the old man said. "I've been to three stores. The whole city is out of food."

"That's not true," Marsh said. "The Gristedes is open. And I'm sure the Whole Foods has plenty of milk."

But the old man's words seemed to energize the crowd, and before Marsh could turn around, a dozen more shoppers were charging into the dairy section. Men and women of all ages grabbed at containers of whatever they could reach: cream cheese, Greek yogurt, tubs of margarine, and plastic bags of shredded mozzarella. The first thing that came to Marsh's mind was that none of these shoppers would be able to pay for the food they were grabbing. What they were doing was as good as looting.

"Stop it! Everybody, calm down!" Marsh yelled. He shoved at a man in a Mets jersey, but the man hissed at him, yelling, "Don't touch me, douche bag," then threw a punch at Marsh's face.

Marsh's head snapped back, and the room tilted on its axis. Marsh actually saw stars—flashes of gold and white in front of his eyes—but only for a moment; then he grabbed at Jerome's shoulder to steady himself. He felt that he was about to collapse.

"I got you, boss," Jerome said, holding Marsh under his arm and trying to pull him away from the fight.

"Gotta stop them," Marsh said, but the room was still spinning, and the side of his head was beginning to ache.

"We can't," Jerome said. "They've gone crazy."

Marsh threw his arm around Jerome's neck. Jerome was a teenager, not more than seventeen, tall and scrawny, and Marsh pulled him close, half because he wanted to make Jerome understand, and half because he didn't seem to be completely in control of his own arms and legs. "Jerome. We have to call the police. Call them right away."

"Already did," Jerome yelled. He tugged Marsh farther down the aisle, away from the fight, but more and more shoppers were pouring into the dairy section, clogging the escape route.

"When are they coming?"

"Ain't coming," Jerome said.

"Why not?" Marsh shoved away from Jerome, his balance returning. But he knew immediately why the police weren't coming: if this was happening in his D'Agostino, it was probably happening in supermarkets all across the city. As if to confirm that thought, a large woman pushing an empty shopping cart bore down on him, not seeming to care that he was directly in her path, and he screamed in fright as she crashed into his knees, sending him sprawling to the floor.

Then, the customers that he had loved so much began to run right over him, kicking at his arms and midsection, and Marsh thought to himself, Why are you doing this to me? But he knew the answer to this question as well.

His customers were scared. And they were hungry.

Agent Chaudry let Garrett Reilly sit in a holding cell on the twenty-third floor of the Federal Building all night long. She had taken away his belt as a precaution—even though the risk of his committing suicide seemed small—and confiscated his wallet and three cell phones as well. She had an agent bring him a plastic bottle of water and a pair of coconut-almond KIND bars, then let him sit there, by himself, without contact with the outside world, until morning.

She wanted him to worry. She wanted him to sweat.

But she wasn't sure she got that result. She had watched through a two-way mirror as Reilly drank the water, ate one of the two KIND bars, then laid his head against a concrete wall and fell asleep. He woke a few times, paced the cell briefly, then slept some more.

At eight thirty in the morning, she'd had enough. She had Agent Murray roust Reilly and bring him to an interrogation room. Murray sat Reilly behind a desk, in the crosshairs of two separate hidden cameras, handcuffed him to a metal loop on the table, then joined Chaudry in an observation room next door.

"Ready as he'll ever be, I guess," Murray said.

Chaudry wasn't so sure, but time was not her friend—the director of the Bureau would be rolling into the Hoover Building in an hour. His first call would be to the New York field office. *To her.* She called DC and linked them into the video feed; then she went to the bathroom, splashed water on her face, reapplied a bit of lipstick, and walked into the interrogation room.

"Good morning, Agent Chaudry," Reilly said with a smile as she took a seat opposite him. He looked around the small, windowless room. "At least I'm assuming it's morning. You look tired. No sleep?"

Chaudry arranged a yellow legal pad and a file folder on the desk in front of her and picked up her pen. "Why did you choose the building in Newark?"

Reilly seemed surprised by the question. He tapped the desk a few times. "I knew it from the J-and-A real estate portfolio. Newark is kind of broken-down, but on the upswing. A bunch of geeks wouldn't stand out."

"But why that building?"

"Unfinished and in bankruptcy, so there wouldn't be a lot of guards or security. And I knew we'd leased some offices to a few tech start-ups, so I could use their Internet."

"You knew that how?"

"I'd seen the J-and-A reports a few months ago. It said who leased space."

"And you remembered that specific building, with those specific tenants? Even though you were on the run?"

"I remember everything. For instance, your quote in your high school yearbook. 'Injustice anywhere is a threat to justice everywhere.' Martin Luther King Jr. It's nice. Maybe a little clichéd. But you were in high school, so you get a pass."

Chaudry took a deep breath. She knew that at least half a dozen FBI agents were watching the interrogation in the New York offices, and probably half a dozen more were watching the feed in DC. She would go slowly and not let Reilly throw her.

"Where were you when the Newark PD raided the office?"

"I ran down the back stairs."

"Where'd you go after that? Did you have a plan?"

He narrowed his eyes and smiled. "Are you trying to figure out how I make decisions? What patterns I might follow?"

"How about I ask the questions."

"Okay, sure. But shouldn't we banter? So I'm relaxed and comfortable?"

"I'm interested in how you see the world. We plug things like that into our database of perps. The information comes in handy in future cases."

"I like how you drop the word *perp* in there. Am I a perp? *Perp. Perp. Perp.* Weird word. But I like the way it sounds."

"You're in handcuffs; therefore, you're a possible perp."

Garrett tugged at his chain. "I keep forgetting."

"Does being handcuffed bother you?"

"It would be better if I were naked, with a girl. But it's okay. For now."

Chaudry noted that on her pad. "Where did you end up? After you ran."

"I overdid it with some alcohol. Maybe some Percodan as well. I passed out."

"You do that often? Drink too much? Take prescription medication?"

Reilly shrugged. "I used to really like pot. That was my mood-altering substance of choice. I gave that up for prescription meds—as you know, from when you searched my apartment."

"How did you know that? You were watching?"

"I was sent video alerts when you broke into my house. I thought you were cute, wandering around, trying to figure out who I was. Although at a certain point I did want to kill you for digging through my stuff. That was a violation of my privacy. People still have rights in this country. Or maybe they don't. It gets confusing."

"Do you often want to kill people?"

"That's a little on the nose, isn't it? I mean, if you want to trip me up, get me to confess, you could be a little more subtle."

"Confess to what, Garrett?"

He smiled broadly. "That's much better."

"Is there something you want to tell me?"

"I think you have a beautiful smile."

Chaudry exhaled. "Let's talk about Steinkamp."

Garrett leaned forward in his chair. "Maybe you'll find this offensive, but would your parents be pissed if you married, you know, outside the faith? You're Hindu, right? If you brought home a half-Mexican guy like me? Would that be trouble?"

"My father holds no prejudices. He'd be fine if I brought you home. Except that you're a little young. And you're a criminal."

Garrett laughed. "My dad, he was raised Catholic, but I'm guessing he wouldn't have cared if I married outside the Church. My mom said he hated the whole thing—the pope, Rome, priests. Said they were a bunch of sexless creeps. She worried a lot, after he died, that he was in hell, you know, an apostate, because of his beliefs. Of course that didn't stop her from totally screwing up her own life. I'm not sure where she thinks she'll be headed." Garrett looked at Chaudry again. "I never met my dad. Died when I was a baby. But my mom's still around. You probably know that as well. Is it in my file? I have a file, don't I? I hope I do."

Chaudry watched him carefully. She had prepared for Reilly to be combative or possibly mute, but not like this—so at ease. She had figured that he would be cagey with her—that he would skirt subjects, try to deflect attention. But this was different. This felt—she struggled to find the word—*casual*.

"Garrett, you surrendered to me. You must have had a reason for that. You wanted to talk about what you'd done. . . ."

"I was tired of being on the run."

"Not because you committed a crime?"

"Because a man named Ilya Markov wants me hunted, and your pursuit of me was eating up my bandwidth. I figured it was more productive for me to turn myself in and start fresh."

"People turn themselves in because they are guilty of crimes."

"Look, if you want me to confess, I will; all you have to do is ask."

That caught Chaudry short.

He smiled at her, a wide, disarming smile, the corners of his eyes creasing as he did. "Just ask, and I'll tell you whatever you want."

Chaudry made a quick mental calculation. If she asked him to admit his guilt, was that coercion in the eyes of the law? Was that his plan? Perhaps it was a legal ploy for later, for the trial, or for some smart lawyer to twist into a wrongful-arrest suit. She racked her brain for an answer, but none came. She could feel all the eyes on her, all those older, white male FBI agents in both New York and Washington, second-guessing her, wanting her to fail.

"Okay, Garrett Reilly, how about you confess to the murder of Phillip Steinkamp?"

"Sure." He looked up at the camera hidden behind a mirror in a corner of the room. "I killed Phillip Steinkamp."

She noted the time on her sheet of paper: 8:52 a.m. "How did you orchestrate it?"

"I don't really know, but I can make something up if you'd like."

Chaudry looked up, frustration leaking from the downturned corners of her mouth. "Then you're not really confessing, are you?"

"I'm trying to move the process along, Agent Chaudry. I've been here a while, and you're wasting my time. If I tell you I did it, then you can investigate that, see that it's not true, and we can move on."

"You realize your confession will hold up in a court of law."

"You'll never bring me to a court of law because you'll figure out—eventually—who the real killer is, and you'll release me, and I'm actually hoping that you'll apologize to me when you do, because this whole thing has been a giant pain in my ass. And when you do release me, it will allow me to finish the more important job at hand."

Chaudry stopped leaning on the table, sat up straight, and folded her arms. "And what important job is that?"

"Tracking down Ilya Markov and stopping him from destroying the American economy."

"Tell me about this Markov."

Reilly did. Speaking quickly and precisely, he described the man and his exploits, as well as his own attempts to track Markov down and predict what he would do next. Chaudry studied Reilly's face and eyes as he wove the story, more than she listened to the actual words. If she hadn't known better, she would have sworn that Reilly believed every word of it, down to the last detail of the Lufthansa flight he claimed Markov had taken and the seat he sat in.

About five minutes into his story, the door to the interrogation room opened, and Murray poked his head in. Chaudry tried to hide the annoyance on her face, and Murray winced. He looked scared.

"Can we talk?" he whispered.

Garrett was surprised to admit it, but he found that he enjoyed spending time with Agent Chaudry. More than that, he just plain liked her. He tried to reason out why that was.

She was pretty, and that always helped, as far as Garrett and his relationship to females was concerned. He knew that was immature and simpleminded, but he liked looking at her thick black hair, and the way her red lips were set against her brown skin. He'd been teasing her when he asked whether her parents would disapprove of her dating a half-Mexican like himself, but he was interested in the answer nonetheless; junior year of college he'd tried hard to sleep with a Hindu poli-sci major from Artesia, but she'd turned him down flat every time. She'd pulled the "My daddy would disapprove" card, but he suspected it was her disapproval, not her father's, that had kept them out of the sack.

However, Chaudry's looks were only part of the story for Garrett. She'd been tracking him, nonstop, for ten days now. He liked her single-mindedness. It reminded him of his own tunnel vision. She was ambitious too—he could tell by the way she held herself: tall, erect, chin up, eyes sizing you up the moment she entered the room. She was always looking for an advantage.

All in all, that was a good package for Garrett. But there was something else about Chaudry that he couldn't quite pin down, something that made her doubly attractive to him. He replayed their conversation in his mind, thought about the way that she had steered it, and the stern demeanor she presented in her look. And then he realized the answer: she was *presenting* a demeanor. That wasn't who she was; Agent Chaudry was faking it. She had another side, and she was keeping it hidden from Garrett.

Garrett considered what she was faking, what she would hide from him, and then it hit him, and he knew for certain why he liked her so much.

She didn't actually believe he was guilty.

She was pretending, trying to fit Garrett Reilly's supposed guilt into her view of the world, but she knew that the fit wasn't right.

The moment that realization came clear to him, the interrogation-room door opened, and Chaudry reentered, followed by the older agent, Murray, and a pair of younger agents, who stood by the far wall. Chaudry walked wordlessly to Garrett. Her face showed a strain that Garrett hadn't seen before.

She pulled out a small key and abruptly unlocked his handcuffs. "Your story checked out. All of it."

"It did?"

"You're surprised? After all that?"

"No, I'm . . . I'm pleased."

"How nice for you. Here's the thing, Reilly—as of about twenty minutes ago, the world started falling apart." She motioned for him to get out of his chair, and quickly. "So stand the fuck up, because you work for me now."

The call came in to Alexis's cell phone as she was walking out the door of her condo, to-go coffee cup, as usual, in hand. The person on the other end of the line requested her presence at the New York City FBI field office that day. The caller, a male secretary—Alexis couldn't remember his name—didn't leave any room for negotiation.

"You are expected by noon." He hung up.

She called Kline, and he okayed the travel. He told her to do whatever they asked of her. He said he would check to see what they wanted and try to update her before she left. She went back to her apartment, packed an overnight bag, then called a cab to take her to Reagan National. She looked at her face again in the mirror: her makeup covered most of the bruising on her left side, and the scrapes on her chin and cheek. Her body still ached from the blast; her shoulder felt as if it might just pop out of its socket at any time, and the muscles in her hip and leg were raw and painful. She took two Motrin, thought of Garrett and his prescription medications with a bit more compassion, and hoped the plane ride wouldn't be too cramped or too turbulent.

In the cab she bought a shuttle ticket from her cell phone, but it took her seven tries before the purchase was finally approved. She thought that was odd. Then, waiting for the ten-thirty departure to LaGuardia, she stopped at a gate for a flight to Phoenix and watched, along with a group of about a dozen weary-looking business travelers, the television hung above a row of seats. The lead stories were all connected, all about the panic that was beginning to grip the East Coast of the United States. The first was about a breakdown in credit-card processing across the Eastern Seaboard. Someone had hacked four financial-services processors and basically stopped all their transactions. Some stores were writing down credit-card numbers to be charged later, but others were accepting only cash. Lines had begun to form outside supermarkets.

Suddenly, her trouble buying a shuttle ticket on her cell phone made sense.

But that was just the beginning. The follow-up story was that ATMs belonging to some of the nation's biggest banks had started malfunctioning overnight. A few were spitting out cash that didn't belong to the users, thousands upon thousands of dollars in twenties and fifties. But most of the ATMs—especially the ones in Manhattan—had stopped dispensing cash at all. Some bank customers were forcing their way inside branches and demanding their money. No one at any of the affected banks had commented publicly.

Finally, three separate trucking companies that delivered food and fuel to New York City had all mysteriously gone bankrupt over the past twenty-four hours—or at least they had seemed to have gone bankrupt. Company officers were denying it, saying their books had been altered, but subcontractors had stopped working with the companies until the mess was sorted out, and drivers were refusing to get into their rigs until they were paid—in cash. The companies' bank accounts were suddenly empty, and their credit ratings had plunged. In consequence, all deliveries from the affected trucking companies had stopped cold, and given that those three companies shipped 60 percent of all the meat and produce coming into New York, little new food was arriving in the city.

Manhattan, one news anchor commented, was an island that made or grew essentially nothing for itself. If cut off from the rest of the country, it would wither and die, and it would do so quickly.

A pit formed at the bottom of Alexis's stomach. A few of the businessmen watching immediately got on their cell phones. Alexis overheard one calling his wife, telling her to get as much cash as she could out of the bank, while another called his office and told them he was canceling his trip to New York. He hung up and stalked out of the terminal. A third, a worried-looking paunchy man in a gray suit, turned to Alexis with saucer-wide eyes.

"What the fuck is this all about?" he asked, not to Alexis in particular, but to the world at large. He wandered off to make a phone call before Alexis could answer, but she felt that even with what she knew, she couldn't help him.

They called her flight, and as she was standing in line to board, Kline rang her cell phone. From what he could gather, Garrett Reilly had surrendered to the FBI in New York and was being held at their headquarters in lower Manhattan.

"Surrendered himself?" Alexis asked, not fully taking in the words. "Why?"

"Don't know. They're interrogating him."

She approached the flight attendant collecting boarding passes. Her mind raced. What had prompted Garrett to give himself up? And what about the other members of the team? Where were they?

"Whatever he's done, he did on his own," Kline said over the phone. "Just cooperate and try to make the best of it. I'll back you up."

"Okay." Her thoughts jumped from the TV news to Garrett to what the hell they could want from her at the FBI. "Have you seen the news?"

"No. I just got into the office."

"Financial hacks in New York. ATMs, credit-card processing. People are freaking out."

"Shit," he said quietly, and Alexis could hear him rise out of his squeaking desk chair, most probably to turn on his television. "Call me when you land."

She hung up, boarded the plane, and took a seat on the aisle in case she needed to stretch. The flight wasn't long, but she still got up and shook out the kinks in her muscles every few minutes. When she walked through the terminal at LaGuardia, she thought she sensed a stillness among the passengers waiting to board their flights. A quiet anxiety. Or maybe she was imagining it; she couldn't be sure. She caught thirty seconds of a live TV report from a bank branch in Columbus Circle, something about a window being broken by an angry customer, but she thought she'd better move on and get to the FBI field office.

She took a cab into Manhattan, and the thickset Slavic driver raced down FDR Drive. The cabbie barked into his cell phone nonstop as he drove, in a language she didn't recognize, until, head aching, she asked him to stop. He glared at her in the rearview mirror, but hung up, and then a few minutes later asked, "You air-force lady?"

"No. Army." She was wearing her fatigues.

"Sorry about noise. Talking to my uncle. He buys gold for me."

"Gold?"

"In case . . . you know . . ." The driver shaped his finger into an imaginary gun and pulled the trigger. "The shooting comes."

"There's not going to be any shooting," Alexis said adamantly.

"Okay, army lady. You say so."

When they got off the East River Drive, the cab passed a bank branch with a crowd milling about outside, as well as a supermarket with a line snaking out the front door. Those scenes made Alexis's heart race.

The taxi driver smiled. "You see? I tell you. Buy gold, buy gun, stay inside."

They arrived at the lower-Manhattan Federal Building just before noon, where she passed through a metal detector and submitted to a brief patdown, then took the elevator to the twenty-third floor. She presented her ID to a secretary at the front desk.

"Take a seat, please." The secretary typed Alexis's credentials into a computer. "Someone will be with you."

Alexis noticed that the secretary didn't say someone would be with Alexis *soon* and settled in for a long wait. But she was surprised when Agent Chaudry appeared a few minutes later. Alexis had met her before, in Alexis's room at George Washington University Medical Center. Chaudry had asked questions, almost all of which Alexis declined to answer, citing national-security grounds. That had seemed to make Chaudry exceedingly angry, and Alexis got the sense that the FBI agent was used to having her way—in all things.

"We meet again," Chaudry said, without offering her hand to shake.

Alexis rose painfully and stood at attention, as rigid and straight as her aching body would allow. "Ma'am, your office asked that I come."

"You know Garrett Reilly turned himself in?"

"I do." Alexis kept her eyes focused on a back wall, to the right of Chaudry.

"And he's cooperating with us?"

"I did not know that."

"As much as he cooperates with anyone, I suppose." Alexis turned slightly to look at the female FBI agent. Chaudry looked pensive, eyes half-closed. She folded her arms across her chest. "He asked for you."

"He did?" Alexis hadn't meant to sound surprised, but she did.

"Said you were crucial to the enterprise."

Alexis started to answer, then held her tongue.

"You believe him? All this stuff about Ilya Markov? Attacking the economy?"

Alexis let her shoulders slump slightly—it hurt her hips to stand at attention. "I do. That's why I backed him. Because I believe him. And events this morning . . ." She didn't quite know how to finish the sentence.

Chaudry moved a step closer to Alexis and whispered in her ear, "He's working for me now. Not you. He does what I say, or I throw him back in jail. I'll make up charges: conspiracy, murder, flight from justice. I don't give a shit. Even if they don't stick, he'll sit two years in a federal prison awaiting trial. Same goes for you. I know you called him from DC the day of the murder. There are tapes sitting at the NSA—aiding a fugitive in a capital murder case. Life in prison. So, just like him, you belong to me. You do whatever the hell I say. Understood?"

Chaudry was standing only a few inches from Alexis's face. The two women were about the same height, and Alexis could feel the agent's breath on her cheek and ear. She could smell coffee as well as a hint of perfume—not expensive, but not garish either. Alexis wasn't afraid of Chaudry, but she didn't take to being threatened either.

"What would you like me to do?" Alexis's voice was cold and hard.

"I have to solve the Steinkamp case. And keep the economy from going down in flames."

"I don't know that I can help you with either of those."

"What you can do is keep Garrett Reilly in line."

Deputy Mayor for Public Affairs John Sankey pushed open the door to Room 9 and was met with the overwhelming scent of two dozen middle-aged men and women all crammed in a room together: body odor and perfume, coffee and egg-salad sandwiches, breath mints and cheap aftershave. The smells mixed with the din of banter and telephone calls; the result was a place Sankey equated with an unnumbered circle of hell. He let out a disgusted grunt, then held a stack of press releases above his head.

"Statement from the mayor, press conference in the Blue Room in an hour," Sankey bellowed above the chatter.

A few reporters snagged copies of the press release, while most of the others ignored Sankey. They knew canned statements from the mayor were worthless as breaking news; they wanted to fire questions at him. They wanted flesh and blood. Mostly, Sankey knew from experience, they just wanted the blood.

"His Honor asks that you keep the reporting on the current situation calm and rational." Sankey was shouting slightly, but trying not to seem desperate. "That you stick to the facts, and not report rumor."

The press crew laughed derisively.

"Have you seen Twitter lately, John?" asked Stan O'Keefe from Channel 7 news.

"I have a Twitter account, yes, and I check it periodically." In truth, Sankey checked Twitter obsessively, had scanned it only three minutes ago, and knew he had a public relations nightmare on his hands. #NYCmeltdown was the fastest-trending topic, with thousands—maybe tens or hundreds of thousands—of tweets and pictures from supermarkets and banks all across the five boroughs: lines, broken windows, empty shelves.

Scarcity, unease, panic.

"His Honor can ask for all the calm he wants, but social media says otherwise. Twitter says run for your fucking life," O'Keefe said.

The room roared with laughter.

Cripes, Sankey thought. Reporters were cynical bastards. "We do not run this city on the whims of Twitter. Come on, guys, you're professionals. You report the news, not innuendo and rumor. Do me, the mayor, and the people of this city a favor and do your jobs."

DiMatteo, from the *New York Post*, tossed a Coke Zero into a garbage can. "Our job is to report what the hell is going on, and your job seems to be to deny it."

"That's unfair."

"Really? The Dow dropped two thousand points this morning. Had to stop trading. Started again and it went down another thousand. And counting."

Sankey wiped the sweat from his face on the back of his suit-jacket sleeve.

Lorraine Chu, from the *New York Times*, held up the press release and read aloud from it: " 'There is plenty of cash on hand in banks and food in the stores.' " She looked from the paper. "Has the mayor been outside lately?"

A mix of affirmative grunts and low laughter came from the room.

"He plans to tour a supermarket directly after the press conference," Sankey said.

"Tell him to bring his boxing gloves," DiMatteo shouted.

"That's exactly the type of joke that becomes a rumor, and the type of rumor that people take as fact," Sankey said, growing irritated. "It fuels the mood of chaos and fear, and it becomes self-fulfilling."

"Thanks for the lecture," O'Keefe said. "Very educational."

Sankey let out a disgusted groan and headed for the door. Leigh Anderson, from National Public Radio, one of the few reporters that Sankey both liked and trusted, was waiting for him there. She was younger than the rest of the media crew, and considerably less cynical.

"John." Her voice was just above a whisper. "A word?"

Sankey nodded, pausing by the door.

She stepped closer to him. "We're working on a story. The gist is, this is a planned attack on the economy. A form of terrorism."

"That's just rumors. And anyway, I can't comment on that."

"Because you don't know? Or because you've been told not to comment?"

"I can't comment on that."

Anderson nodded, scribbling in her reporter's notebook. "Got it. You've been told not to comment."

"That is not what I sa—"

"Here's the real thing, John. The terror attack, we're working on an angle that says this is just the beginning. That there's something bigger in the works. Like spectacularly scary and disaster-producing big. That's aimed at bringing the entire country to its knees. We have deep intelligence sources. Do you know anything about this?"

Sankey pressed his lips together in displeasure, then shook a finger angrily in Anderson's face. "That is exactly the kind of irresponsible news story that I'm talking about. That is speculative and rumormongering—"

Again, Anderson cut the deputy mayor off, with a slashing motion of her hand. "No, John. We're talking about a terror attack. The point of terror is to instill fear. That's what a terror attack is all about—it's baked into the name. *Terror.* Now, you can deny everything, but it won't stop us from going to air at four o'clock with the story. So I'll ask you again. Do you know anything about a coming terror attack against the city?"

Sankey shook out a kink in his leg, tapping his foot repeatedly against the base of a desk. He let out a hot breath. "Anonymously?"

"If that's the only way you'll talk."

"We have heard the same thing."

"Muslim extremists?"

"Don't know. Possibly."

Anderson scribbled in her book. "What is the city doing to prevent it?"

"Everything it can. No holds barred."

"And the city hall reaction?"

Sankey looked out at the mob of reporters, most of whom had gone back to talking on their phones or filing updates on their stories. The room was loud again, and frenetic. Sankey wanted out of there, fast. He turned to face the NPR reporter. "Off the record?"

Anderson nodded yes.

"We are very fucking scared."

As far as Garrett could tell, mass hysteria had been around as long as there had been people congregating in groups. In ancient Rome, mobs of citizens would spontaneously gather in the dead of night, driven by rumors or fear, convinced that Jupiter himself had been spotted on the Capitoline Hill, or that hordes of exotic, savage animals were at the gates of the city, about to overrun it. In the 1500s in France, nunneries were overwhelmed with nuns who could only meow like cats, never speaking actual words. In Milan in 1630, the entire population of that city became convinced that someone had poisoned the food and water supply. The mob dragged a pharmacist from his workshop, and he confessed—on the rack—that he was responsible for the poisoning, and that he had been in league with the devil and unnamed foreigners.

Garrett found that tidbit intriguing: foreigners were often blamed, but few of them were ever actually found.

In 1835, Londoners became deliriously happy with the news that newly invented, high-power telescopes had allowed astronomers to see zebras and monkeys on the moon. The news spread around the globe, to mass celebrations, before it was extinguished in the face of absolutely no verifiable facts. On an October night in 1938, much of the Eastern Seaboard of the United States become convinced that aliens had landed in New Jersey and would soon be taking over the planet. Orson Welles's radio broadcast became a classic example of media-fed mass panic. But it was hardly the last. There would be World

War II Japanese-citizen internments, 1950s Red scares, 1980s satanic day-care scandals, and on and on and on.

The pattern, to Garrett, was plain to see. Certain ingredients were needed. A period of true danger: war or famine or unemployment or civil unrest. A group of outsiders who had been responsible for problems in the past: foreigners, savages, criminals. A population crowded together in tight spaces where rumor and gossip could freely circulate. Big cities were often the starting point of the hysteria, but sometimes it was teens jammed together in schools, or religious devotees hidden away in monasteries. That last part seemed to be important: populations were most susceptible to panic and delusions when the surrounding culture was strict and controlling, with specific rules about what people could believe. When the society had rigid ideas of what was considered normal, and anything outside of normal was frowned upon—that bred hysteria. It was almost as if mass delusions were a form of rebellion against the existing order.

Garrett pondered that. What were the restrictive conditions in the United States that bred hysteria? Political correctness? Fear of terror attacks? Or was it the opposite, a vast shift in what was considered normal: the acceptance of gay marriage maybe, or the rapid legalization of drugs? Sitting in a small room in the back of the FBI field office in lower Manhattan, a trio of laptops open on a desk in front of him, he read article after article on the madness of crowds. Once a fire was set under a mass delusion, it took on a life of its own, resistant to facts or rationality. It spread like a virus. It some ways, Garrett thought, it was a virus—it infected a host, burned through its immune system, then moved on to the next victim.

He read one theory that said fear, and our panicked reactions to fear, was cooked into our DNA. If you were an early human, living on the plains of Africa, and you heard a mysterious rustling in the night, you were best served by reacting to that sound, quickly and decisively. Nine out of ten times, it might have been an overreaction, but overreacting to any possible danger kept you alive. The humans who didn't overreact were eventually eaten. Therefore, only the most paranoid of our species passed their genes on to the next generation.

That meant humans were genetically programmed to panic. Ilya Markov seemed to have figured this out long ago. How he had learned it, Garrett had no idea, but the man had become a student of delusion, a master of hysteria.

All around Garrett, on the streets of New York City, was evidence of Markov's genius.

It occurred to Garrett that mass hysteria was the opposite of a pattern. Popular delusions occurred when people attributed causality to events and things that didn't actually exist, whereas Garrett sought patterns—or in his case, meaning—out of that same chaos. In a way, mass hysteria was his life counterpart; it was why he sought out patterns. Hysteria created fear; patterns subdued it—they were two sides of the same coin. Suddenly he understood that mass hysteria was that dark thing he had felt coming, that he had been terrified of the night before Phillip Steinkamp was shot. He also knew that it wasn't out there, a storm he could see raging over the horizon. No, delusion and hysteria lived inside Garrett Reilly and always had. He reveled in them; they gave him power. The thought astounded him, but he knew it was true.

The dark thing was not coming. It was already here.

He was the dark thing.

Celeste and Mitty were the first to show up at the FBI field office. They had spent the night in Mitty's apartment in Queens, and Celeste, instead of complaining about it—which Garrett had fully expected—said it had been comfortable, even fun, that they'd drunk wine and talked until three in the morning, and that the shower she'd taken in Mitty's bathroom this morning was the best thing she'd experienced in days. Garrett was amused that they'd become friends, but it made sense—they were both outsiders to the core.

Alexis arrived next, having flown up from DC that morning. Garrett was surprised at how unscathed she looked, given that she'd been in a bomb attack, but when he got a closer look at her under the bright fluorescent office lights, he could see the dark bruises under her makeup, and the red scratches and cuts on her chin.

"Was it scary?" He reached out to touch her face, but stopped inches away.

"No. I didn't have time to think."

"When I heard, I . . ." He couldn't finish. What he'd felt when he thought Alexis might have been killed was a mixture of dread and rage that seemed beyond his ability to articulate to another person, particularly to Alexis. "I'm just glad you're okay."

She nodded, saying nothing, and that was all the time they had for personal conversation.

Agent Chaudry stepped between them, grabbing Garrett by the arm. "She lived. Enough small talk. We have work to do."

Garrett understood then that something was going on between the agent and Alexis, some tug-of-war involving governmental politics and police power. He guessed that Chaudry was simply asserting her alpha-dog status, and that Alexis had no choice but to be submissive, but still—their relationship would be interesting to watch.

Bingo and Patmore arrived a few minutes after Alexis. They had grabbed a motel room in downtown Newark, bunking out together in a Comfort Inn, but seemed no closer than they had before they'd spent the night together.

"So what's next?" Agent Chaudry said, once they were all gathered in the back room of the field offices. "What's the brilliant idea?"

All eyes turned to Garrett.

"He's setting fires. All over the place. You can't see the fires, but you can see the smoke, and psychologically that's worse than the actual fire." Garrett fingered a remote control, and a TV in the corner played a cable news channel. A breathless talking head was going on about shocks to the economy, and what it meant, why it was happening, and what the future held for the citizenry of the United States. "The fear is worse than the actual thing. The fear sets everyone on edge. The fear sets us up for the next shock."

"But what is that shock?" Chaudry asked. "What's he getting at?"

Garrett thumbed the remote control again, switching to a local channel, where a reporter was doing a live report from an eerily deserted Times Square. A smattering of riot police could be seen behind the reporter, cutting off access to Forty-Second Street.

"People are going nuts," Mitty said. "Everybody's going completely wacko."

"And 'everybody' is the answer," Garrett said.

"How so?" Chaudry asked.

"Large numbers. Crowds. Mobs. Viral concepts. We turn them around. Make them our allies."

"Crowdsource it." Mitty let out a noise that was halfway between a disgusted grunt and a shout of joy. "Can't believe I didn't think of that."

"Reddit?" Bingo said. "Twitter?"

"For sure," Garrett said. "Maybe start our own site."

"All three," Mitty said. "Fuck it. As many places as possible."

"I'm not sure I understand," Chaudry said.

Garrett turned to face Chaudry. "People are watching what's happening, but they're in the dark, so they're letting their imaginations run wild. The consequence is, we get hysteria. That's how Markov operates—from the shadows. That's how he fans the flames. But if we're transparent with people—if we tell them what we know—then they'll see the bigger picture. They'll come up with their own ideas about what's happening and why."

Chaudry shook her head. "But they won't be any more right than we are. Or any smarter."

"Individually, they're not any smarter. But collectively, they're brilliant. If we ask enough people a question, some of them will get the answer right. They'll predict what Markov is going to do next. And if enough of them guess one way or another, then we'll have a crowdsourced answer."

"A massive predictive algorithm, made up of millions of people," Alexis said, pleased.

Chaudry scanned the faces in the room, ending with Garrett. "Well? What the hell are you waiting for?"

The first warning came from ClarKent, the young blond hacker.

"There's something going on," he told Ilya, who was smoking a cigarette on the porch. The day had progressed even better than expected, with New York City—and even much of the northeast coast of the country—tumbling into turmoil. Ilya hadn't slept in twenty-four hours, but that was mostly because he was enjoying every moment of being awake. Awake was alive now, and the prize was out there, just out of reach, but he was closing on it.

"There are plenty of things going on," Ilya said. "Which is how it should be."

"No, your name. Us. What we're doing." ClarKent opened his laptop and set it on a small table. "Crowdsourcing."

Ilya looked at the screen. It was open to a Reddit thread titled "What would you do?"—which had more than seventy thousand comments. The thread was the number one topic on the entire site and was trending far above any other question. Ilya's picture, his passport photo, was at the top of the thread, and underneath was the bulk of the question:

"Imagine this: Ilya Markov is an economic terrorist trying to disrupt the American economy. He's killed a Federal Reserve president, hacked credit-card-processing and ATM machines, sent three trucking companies into bankruptcy, and now he is closing in on New York City. If you were Markov, and you wanted to take down the financial heart of this country, what would you do next?"

Ilya stiffened as he read the paragraph, then scrolled down to look at the huge number of answers. They diverged out into discrete subcategories, with corollary answers spreading out like the branches of an enormous tree. He clicked quickly through them, reading some, skimming some, ignoring a whole swath of others. Some answers were obvious and broad: shoot the president. Rob the Federal Reserve Bank. Bomb the New York Stock Exchange. The spelling was bad and the logic often nonexistent. Other answers were slightly more specific, but equally as implausible: Short Citibank stock. Corner the market in gold. Destroy an oil refinery. But as Ilya scrolled through the replies, targeted ideas began to pop out of the lists, and those ideas were good. Not just good: some touched on what Ilya was actually planning, and others hit the nail exactly on the head. He pushed the laptop away in a burst of angry energy.

"Are there more threads like this? On other sites?"

"A bunch," ClarKent said. "A site dedicated just to that question. As far as I can tell, it went up an hour ago. A lot of activity. Also a Facebook page. A couple of darknet threads as well. There's probably more—I just haven't found them all. But your picture is all over the place. You're fucking famous."

Ilya stepped away from the laptop and sat for a moment on a deck chair. He stared out over the beach and the ocean beyond, listening to the waves crash on the sand.

This was a setback. More than a setback; this was a full-blown counterattack. Reilly was harnessing the power of the Internet against Ilya, just as Ilya had harnessed the power of hacking against Reilly. It was a smart move, and if he went through every single response, Reilly was sure to find one that described exactly what Ilya was planning. But that didn't mean that he was boxed in. With seventy-five thousand responses on Reddit alone, and more pouring in by the second, Reilly wouldn't be able to read them all, or to sort and rank them in a reasonable amount of time—certainly not fast enough to stop what Ilya now had in mind.

But that was the issue. With enough time, Reilly would narrow down the options and figure out exactly what Ilya's goal was. Without time, all he had were unexamined hypotheses.

"We carry on," Ilya said, popping out of the deck chair. "But we double our speed. Tell everyone to keep pushing. More hacks. More companies. Faster. Much faster."

"Okay. I'll tell 'em." ClarKent hurried back inside the house.

Ilya found Uni dozing on a couch. He woke her gently, told her to get ready, then pulled aside one of the East European hackers, Yuri S. Ilya had met Yuri S., briefly, two years ago in a club in Kiev. He had a reputation for flawless programming as well as for having a borderline personality. He'd been angry when Uni had snagged the first suitcase of money, but had doubled his efforts and won the second cash prize handily, overwhelming the servers of a pair of smaller credit-card-processing companies, which seemed to have kept him from exploding in an uncontrollable rage.

"We're leaving," Ilya told him. "Now is the time."

"I thought it was tomorrow. I thought everything was set for tomorrow."

"Change of plans. The timeline has been moved forward."

Yuri S. said nothing. He stared down at his computer screen, which was full of hysterical, panicked tweets and doctored pictures of ransacked grocery-store shelves. Ilya could already guess what Yuri S. was contemplating. He and Yuri S. were on the same side, but they were only partners for this exact moment in time. Ilya knew the world of freelance hackers well enough to understand that in a few seconds Yuri S. could shift his allegiance 180 degrees, and Ilya would be staring at a hardened adversary.

"Perhaps that will cost more money," Yuri S. said. "Being in a rush. What do the shippers say? You must pay to expedite."

Ilya scanned the billiards room: a pair of hackers were working quietly in a far corner, just out of earshot; a third was smoking a cigarette in an easy chair. *"Da,"* Ilya said, switching to Russian. *"No ya ne hochu eto seichas obsujdat'."* Yes, but I don't want to discuss it now.

Yuri S. considered this deeply, and Ilya was again astonished by how brazen hackers could be about their self-interest. They were unashamed of weighing the pros and cons of an offer, right in front of you, as they tried to plot how to get the most out of any employer, legitimate or otherwise. They were little more than con men and criminals, but then again, the rest of the world thought Ilya Markov was little more than that as well. But the rest of the world was wrong: Ilya Markov had something far grander in mind than some paltry amount of cash. Markov had plans for change. Plans and ambitions. Markov could see into the future.

Yuri S. sighed, as if to signal his desire to keep negotiating. Ilya pressed his lips together in frustration.

"Trust me," Ilya said, again in Russian. "I will give you more than we discussed. You will get what you deserve for your service."

"Okay. We are good."

Ilya let out a quiet sigh of relief. He needed Yuri S., and Yuri S. knew it, so Ilya didn't have much choice. But three steps further, and Ilya was already planning how to get rid of this selfish prick. Ilya waited for Uni to pull herself together; then the three of them piled into Uni's Hyundai and headed north, toward the city.

They drove for an hour, then exited the New Jersey Turnpike near Edison, pulling up at a truck yard just off the Lincoln Highway, across the road from an Exxon chemical-processing plant. Plumes of smoke rose up from cylindrical smokestacks. A side gate to the truck yard lay unlocked, as paid for, and Ilya, Yuri S., and Uni walked through it, Ilya checking the license plates of the enormous eighteen-wheelers parked in the truck yard. He found the truck that he had arranged for and pulled the keys out from under the stanchion just behind the left rear-wheel quad.

While Yuri S. and Uni climbed into the cab, Ilya pulled out of his backpack the second pipe bomb that Thad White had made for him and slotted it carefully into a metal hinge between the cab and the cargo trailer, just above one of the truck's gas tanks. The bomb had an internal fuse attached to a cell phone, and only Ilya knew the phone's number.

Ilya got into the cab. Yuri S. sat in the driver's seat, with Uni behind him, in the sleeping area.

Ilya pulled the seat belt down across his chest. "To the George Washington Bridge, please."

Yuri S. started the truck engine, and it growled ferociously, as if in direct response.

Congressman Harris had not slept in thirty-six hours. All night he had paced his tiny bedroom in the cramped fifth-floor apartment he shared with three other congressmen, pausing occasionally to look out the window at R Street below, and trying to catch a glimpse of the sky to the east, to see whether the sun showed any signs of rising. He had prayed for the sun to appear quickly, so the day would start, so he could occupy his mind with business or politics or just phone calls. Anything to keep from thinking about her. And what they had done.

Every time the memory flooded his mind, he felt his face flush with shame. But also with excitement. Sexual excitement. God, she was lovely. And young. And willing. He could barely stand to think of it. Yet the images flashed back into his mind, over and over, on an endless, unceasing loop.

But now that he was in Washington, DC, far from Rachel Brown, he would be able to resist. He had stumbled, fallen even, but he could overcome the transgression. He would fly back to Atlanta this evening, admit all to his wife, and try to rebuild his life. But first he had to get a grip on himself; he had to shower, shave, put on some clothes. It was midafternoon, and he was still in his pajamas, for goodness' sake.

He had a 4:00 p.m. appointment at the Eccles Building on Constitution Avenue. The Federal Reserve Board of Governors had called an emergency meeting, and Harris, as the chairman of the House Banking Subcommittee, had been asked to attend the end of the session. The Fed governors rarely invited a politician into one of their meetings, but events of the last twenty-four hours had been extraordinary—and they demanded extraordinary responses. The world seemed to be going up in flames—both the larger world and Harris's personal world.

So, he would wait. He would sit through the Fed meeting, rubber-stamp any demands they made, and promise to move heaven and earth in Congress to change any laws or move any money that needed moving. He was powerful enough to make that happen—probably the only congressman powerful enough to make that happen—and he knew that it was his duty. Country and economy first, wife and marriage second.

And Rachel Brown? She was a physical manifestation of his weakness. Of his lust. And yet . . . her body, her skin, her lips. God help him. . . . He resolved, then and there, to do what had to be done. He would never see that woman again.

Rachel. Not his wife.

Then his phone chimed with an incoming text. The number was from Atlanta, but he didn't recognize it. He tapped the screen.

Hey, get together again today?

Oh Jesus, it was her. It could only be her.

He typed a response, fingers shaking. *Rachel?*

One and only!

Harris's body tensed from head to toe. He considered what to write, but his brain seemed to have seized up. He had to tell her no, he would not see her, it was entirely wrong and inappropriate, and they would never meet again.

I am not in Atlanta. Back in DC, he wrote.

I know. Me too.

Harris's blood froze. She was in DC? How was that possible? Had she followed him here? As he started to type, another text came in.

Got a treat for you.

He read the words and felt a rush of blood to his loins. More shame swamped his mind. He was one of Pavlov's dogs, salivating at the mere prospect of food. Or in this case, sex.

Check your e-mail, she wrote.

Harris booted up his computer, logged on to his public, congressional account, and immediately found the e-mail, from sender Rachel Brown, with the heading *You're going to like this.* The e-mail had a link, and Harris took a long, deep breath before clicking on it.

He was taken to a video site, one he had never heard of before, and immediately a player opened, video running, fuzzy at first. Harris squinted to make out what he was seeing. He seemed to recognize the room, but only faintly—a futon, a window, a dresser. Then it hit him in a wave of horror. He knew that room. It was in Grant Park, Atlanta. He had been there recently. Only three days ago.

On the video, Harris himself walked onto the screen. Rachel Brown followed. She took him by the hand and began to kiss him. And he kissed her back. Then she started to undress him with astonishing speed, undressing herself almost as quickly. Almost before Harris could blink, he was naked, erect, and clearly recognizable as Leonard Harris, congressman from the Eleventh District of Marietta, Georgia.

Harris watched the video, frozen to the spot, mortified. On-screen, Rachel Brown did horrible things to him: wonderful, horrible things, which he now regretted with every ounce of his being, but there they were, on video, available, he assumed, for the entire world to see.

His phone chimed again.

Nice, huh?

He didn't reply. He couldn't make his fingers move.

Meet me here. An address followed. It looked to be in central Virginia. *Two-hour drive for you. See you around ten. Gonna be super fun. XOXO. R.*

Congressman Leonard Harris put down his phone, and in that same trancelike, autopilot state that he'd found himself in when he first went to Rachel Brown's apartment, he pulled on a pair of slacks and a shirt, found his wallet and his watch, put on his shoes, and grabbed the keys to his rental car. Then, fully dressed, he Googled the address Rachel had texted him, mapped out a route on his computer, and tried to remember if he knew anyone in the DC area who might have quick and easy access to a handgun.

Everything about the Eccles Building on Constitution Avenue—its white Georgian marble, its classical façade, the grand sweep of the front stairs—spoke to its solidity, to its enduring purpose, and to its conservative nature. That was the entire point of the structure: it was the home of the Board of Governors of the Federal Reserve of the United States, the central bank that oversaw the monetary policy of the country, and the building said, to anyone who saw it, You can count on us to protect your money. We are careful, thoughtful, slow moving, and here to stay. We are not going anywhere. The same could be said of the building's boardroom, with its massive wood conference table, high ceilings, draped windows, and gold-and-white American-eagle fresco above the fireplace.

That is, on most days. But not today.

The hastily called meeting of the governors of the Federal Reserve was frenetic right from the start, before the members were even seated, or the ones who were calling in were on the line. Caroline Hummels, the newly appointed chairwoman, had barely set foot in the room before Gottfried, the director of the Atlanta bank, came at her, his finger wagging in front of her nose.

"What the hell is going on in New York?" He followed her across the room. "My people tell me we're on the verge of a liquidity event. That it's 2008 all over again. We're looking at a credit crunch. Or worse. A bank run. A collapse."

Hummels pushed past Gottfried and nodded to the seven other board members and bank directors seated around the table: Sanchez from Minneapolis, Higgins from Philadelphia, Dan Stark from Richmond, and Chen, Lattimore, and Cohen from the DC board. And of course Larry Franklin from St. Louis, who was sunk deep into his padded leather chair, a furious scowl on his face. Everyone else would be on the phone.

Lattimore shook his head vigorously in agreement with Gottfried: "I'm hearing the same thing, Caroline. The rumors have been building all week. And New York is going off its fucking rocker."

Hummels shot a look at Lattimore. "Would you like that in the minutes, Jack? That New York has gone off its fucking rocker?"

Lattimore threw his hands in the air. "At this point, I don't give a shit what goes in the minutes."

Hummels turned to Adelaide, her assistant, trailing a few steps behind her. "Is everyone on the phone?"

Her assistant nodded, then punched the conference-call buttons on the phones placed across the table. "All here," Adelaide said, sitting down to take notes. The meeting would be recorded, but the chairperson's assistant always took notes as well, as a matter of habit and tradition.

Of course, one person was missing from the meeting, and Hummels felt that absence deeply: Phillip Steinkamp of the New York Fed. He had been the old pro of the bunch, the calming influence. Just the thought of him, and what had happened on that street in Manhattan, made Hummels shiver. She couldn't help but wonder if his death was related to what was happening now, to the panic in New York City, to the meltdown in the financial sector. She brushed off the flash of memory—there was no time for that now—and leaned in toward the closest phone.

"Good afternoon, everyone. Thank you for getting on the line with me—or being here—on such short notice. I think everyone knows why we're here—recent events in New York City, both this last week and in the last twenty-four hours. And of course we are all mourning the loss of our colleague Dr. Steinkamp—Phil, to some of us—but sadly, that appears to be just the beginning of the problem."

"Have you heard from the FBI?" Lattimore interrupted.

"Jack, please allow me to finish." Hummels glared at Lattimore. She knew, instinctively, that he wouldn't have interrupted Ben Bernanke when Ben was making a presentation to the board. They didn't step all over you if you were a man; they gave you your moment, allowed you at least to speak your piece. But not a woman—a woman in finance had to claw her way to every moment of airtime, had to shout her ideas over the din of male egos.

"We don't have time for tidy speeches. You can finish, but Rome is burning," Lattimore said.

"I have not spoken to the FBI today," Hummels said. "And if Rome is bur—"

"But why not?" Sanchez blurted out. "Aren't they supposed to keep you updated?"

"Right now, we need to talk about banking," Hummels said. "About the solvency of the financial system. I've heard the rumors, just as you have. Rumors of low capital at Vandy, rumors of bad loans, of a credit crunch—"

"And what about the credit-processing slowdown?" Gottfried interjected. "That has to mean something. It was all up and down the East Coast and hasn't been fixed, as far as I can see."

"I am well aware of what's happening at AWCP," Hummels insisted. "I've spoken to their CEO, and he says they are working on the problem. He said it was controllable—"

"Controllable?" Gottfried asked with overblown, self-important incredulity. "They're almost entirely off-line. That's thirty percent of credit-card commerce in the tristate area."

"That can be cleared up." Hummels tried to keep her temper under control. The president himself had warned her before he nominated her for the job, There will be people out there who are desperately jealous that you have reached the pinnacle of your profession and that they haven't. "Are you ready for that?" he had asked her. Sitting in the Oval Office, surrounded by the trappings of American power, brilliant sunlight streaming in from the windows behind the president's desk, she had answered yes, of course. But now, on her own, with a crisis coming down around her ears and the president nowhere in sight, she was no longer so sure.

"The entirety of the situation can be cleared up. But we will need to move forward, as a board, with unanimity and purpose. We need to calm the markets. We need to open the lending window to banks if they are feeling strained. The federal government's spigot of cash must be turned on, full force—"

"No."

Hummels head snapped up and to the right, to where Larry "Let 'Em Fail" Franklin was sitting forward in his seat, his sharp chin jutting out from the collar of his white, button-down shirt, his gray eyes staring doggedly at Hummels's. His lips were curled in an angry scowl, and he seemed to be trying to press his fingers through the mahogany of the conference table. "The federal government can no longer be in the business of propping up failing institutions. It's is not in our charter, it is morally wrong, and it is bad for the economy."

"Bad for the economy?" Hummels's eyes widened. "It's the only thing standing between a decent economy and an utter and complete meltdown."

"Failure is a natural part of capitalism, and nature has to take its course. And anyway, you call this economy decent?" Franklin spat out. "The economy is in the toilet."

"It is limping along," Hummels said. "And we have to keep it limping, and not let it collapse."

"It won't collapse. Some things will be destroyed, but others will grow in their place. There's rot in the system, and we are perpetuating that rot by propping up institutions that are bound to fail—"

"Save the homilies for the book tour, Larry," Gottfried said, exasperation coloring his voice. "We have serious problems here."

Franklin pushed himself out of his chair, gripping at the table as he did. "Our problem is that we no longer have moral standing—"

"Give it a fucking rest!" Gottfried yelled. "We're doing the best we can—"

Franklin waved a crooked finger at Gottfried. "You just want a government takeover of the financial services industry! That would suit you just fine!"

"You're being paranoid!"

"We are wasting time!" Sanchez barked from the side of the table. "We are all wasting ti—"

"No. This is the crux of the matter. And if you don't see that, you are a complete idiot!" Franklin said.

Suddenly, everyone was shouting, waving their hands in the air. Someone was pounding on the table; Hummels thought it was Franklin, but he was standing and shouting and turning red in the face. Two of the other governors—and they were all male, except for Hummels—were also standing, one of them pointing at Franklin angrily and the other seeming to be talking to Hummels, but she couldn't hear him.

"What?" Hummels tried to raise her voice above the din. "What did you say?"

It was Chen from the DC board, a voice of reason, but she couldn't hear him, and Franklin was moving across the room toward Lattimore, yelling louder now. Hummels thought that perhaps she should call security, but that was insane—members of the Board of Governors of the Federal Reserve didn't need the police to break up one of their arguments, did they?

"Gentlemen!" Hummels screamed. "Gentlemen!" But no one listened. Hummels could feel the tears welling up in her eyes, but she knew, instinctively, that tears would make the men in the room only crazier—tears would be like blood in the water for hungry sharks. Instead, she grabbed the crystal water decanter on the table in front of her, raised it into the air in one swift motion, then brought it down with a crash onto the conference table. The glass shattered with a sharp boom, sending shards and water and ice cubes everywhere.

Everyone in the room froze and fell quiet. Franklin, who had bellied up to Lattimore, stepped back and stared at Hummels, amazement on his face. Lattimore reached down and brushed a sprinkling of glass from his jacket. Water ran off the table and onto the carpet below in dribbling streams.

"Holy shit," Lattimore whispered.

Hummels looked them all in the eye, one by one, her breathing coming in jagged gulps. "This is not a schoolyard, and we are not children. We are the Board of Governors of the Federal Reserve, and we will comport ourselves with the respect that the office demands. We are adults, and we serve the people of this country, at the pleasure of the president. Do not forget that."

She turned to Lattimore and Franklin. "Gentlemen, return to your seats."

Lattimore sat immediately, looking spooked, but Franklin lingered at the edge of the table, a flash of defiance still in his eyes.

"Larry"—Hummels's voice cracked—"sit the fuck down or I will call the bank police and have you removed from the room. And then I will urge the president to have you removed from the board. Permanently."

Franklin opened his mouth to reply, then seemed to think better of it and returned to his seat.

Hummels took another breath, feeling her strength and power slowly returning. "Now"—her voice leveled out—"I believe Congress needs to make available emergency funds to backstop any institutions—banks or brokerage houses or insurance companies—that are facing imminent risk of collapse. To that end I have asked Leonard Harris, chairman of the House Banking Subcommittee, to join us for the remainder of—"

"Madam Chairwoman," a voice interrupted weakly.

Hummels turned in surprise, a low fury showing on her face. Adelaide was sitting behind her and to her left, her face already reddening. "Adelaide, I am in the middle of—"

"Congressman Harris—"

"—speaking to the board and I will not be—"

"—has disappeared," Adelaide managed to squeak out.

Hummels stared at her assistant in bewilderment.

"I've checked everywhere. Nobody knows where he is. He's AWOL. Didn't leave word with anyone. Anywhere."

"I spoke to him last night," Hummels said. "He said he would be here." She felt a rising panic: Harris was the key to getting Congress to authorize money in a crisis. Without his leadership, the process would take days. Weeks, maybe. Months, even. Or it wouldn't happen at all.

Her assistant shook her head vigorously, from side to side, and as she did she held her smartphone above the table to show it to Hummels. "There's something else." Adelaide tapped the phone and a news app popped up onto the screen. "A truck just blew up on the George Washington Bridge. All traffic has been stopped going in and out of the city. It's chaos."

The room gasped collectively. Hummels could feel her knees quiver, and suddenly Lattimore was yelling again, and Franklin was back on his feet, and Chen and Cohen were both pointing at Hummels, their faces alive with anxiety. The boardroom was engulfed in noise. Adelaide looked at Hummels as the room descended back into a frenzy and said quietly, underneath the screaming, her eyes wide with fear, "What is going on?"

Caroline Hummels, newly appointed chair of the Federal Reserve Bank of the United States of America, shook her head. "I have no idea."

Garrett saw the first reports of the accident on Twitter, with follow-ups coming fast and furious from online news sites. A truck had jackknifed on the upper level of the GW Bridge, and its fuel tanks had exploded, burning the entire vehicle and its unknown cargo in the middle of the roadway. Rescue workers and firemen hadn't been able to get past the flames yet, so the body count was unknown, but the assumption was that the driver of the truck had been killed. Reports from witnesses said they thought two people had fled the vehicle and walked the span of the bridge east, into Manhattan.

The bridge was sealed off. Traffic in and out of Manhattan had come to a standstill at all tunnels and other bridges. The anxiety that had gripped the city in the morning was becoming an explosion of panic, and it was amazing to witness. To judge from the media, Armageddon was nigh. Anything might happen next—bombs, shootings, hurricanes. *Anything.* The entire island of Manhattan might sink into the Atlantic.

Garrett watched it unfold in astonishment. He noticed that he felt flashes of pleasure at the sight of all that chaos. An angry little boy was still inside his head, a boy who took great joy in throwing things and breaking things and smashing the world into tiny bits. He wondered if Ilya Markov had a similar boy inside his brain. Garrett suspected that Ilya did. The link between the two of them was growing in Garrett's mind, the pattern of their relationship twisting together like the fibrous strands of a rope, becoming more and more tangled, more and more complicated. Garrett wondered if Markov, out there somewhere, could feel it as well. He wondered how Markov felt about him. He wondered and was scared.

Chaudry monitored the proceedings by calling agents in the field, and Alexis did the same, but in her case she called Washington, DC. They both yelled out periodic updates to the room, one-upping each other in what they had gleaned from their sources. Garrett thought it was amusing that the two of them were having some kind of bureaucratic intelligence showdown—who could master the data world faster and better. Of course, Garrett had more information at his fingertips than either of them, but he wasn't going to say anything. He had another thought—maybe the two of them weren't tussling over power. Perhaps they were fighting over him.

Garrett thought that would be amusing as well, if it were true, but he suspected it was more personal fantasy than objective reality, and he didn't have time to analyze the idea deeply. He and the rest of the team were too busy sorting through the crowdsourced answers that they had asked for on the Web. The results had been informative—inspiring even—as well as occasionally idiotic. More than 160,000 responses were on Reddit alone, with another 25,000 appearing on the hastily constructed website that Mitty had launched three hours earlier.

"I'm getting a lot of 'assassinate the president' ideas," Mitty called out from her computer.

"Same," Patmore said. "And 'bomb Congress.'"

"Discard them," Garrett said. "Out of hand. As well as anything else that falls too far outside the bell curve of the probability density function. It has to be doable."

Celeste called out to the group, "There's a lot of bank-related hits. Trying to make a bank run happen."

"But how do you do that?" Garrett asked.

Celeste scrolled through her screen. "Twenty-five percent mention the ATM hack."

"Original," Garrett said. "Given that it's already happened."

"Fourteen percent say shoot the bank CEO. Seven percent say start rumors about collapse."

Bingo called out from his laptop, "I get twenty percent suggesting we devalue the American dollar."

"They give any suggestions on how to do that?" Garrett said. "Because I could make a shitload of money with that information."

It became clear right away that exploding a truck in the middle of the George Washington Bridge was not an original idea: 6,447 other people had thought enough of the idea to post it online. That was an encouraging sign; it meant they were on the right track. Garrett began to see something, a slender reed of a pattern, a line of reasoning that kept cropping up from the most technical postings, the people who seemed to understand the finance business better than any of the others. He wondered why he hadn't thought of it himself, but then realized that was the beauty of crowdsourcing: you didn't have to think of everything. Others were there to do the work for you.

For a moment, the IPO stock Crowd Analytics flashed into his thoughts. Had there been more movement on that equity? Had the money in the dark pool struck again? He checked it and found that the stock had moved in lockstep with the broader market, and that direction was down, but not independently down. But the idea spun in his head: How was Crowd Analytics involved? He went back to Reddit. People who seemed to know finance kept pointing to one institution, and one person, and it wasn't Crowd Analytics. In their minds, power and size were not a good thing: they were the opposite. They were a vulnerability, and Garrett agreed.

"I think I know what he's going to do," Garrett said.

"Okay, tell me," Chaudry said quickly. "If we're going to plan an action, I need to know now. The field office is stretched thin. Almost every agent is out in the field."

"Not you." Garrett shook his head. "You're not the one who needs to know."

"I absolutely need to know," Chaudry said, louder. She shot a look to Alexis, who started across the room toward Garrett.

"Too big to fail," Garrett said. "We tell the man who's too big to fail."

Robert Andrew Wells Jr., the president and CEO of Vanderbilt Frink, called his wife from the office, told her to pack a bag for herself, one for him, and two for the kids. He told her to pack up as much nonperishable food from the cupboards as she thought would fit in the back of their town car, and when she asked him why, he said it was "to be on the safe side."

"Is this about the truck crash on the bridge? And the food riots?"

"No. Well, maybe. Just a precaution. And there's no food riots. Just people overreacting. Either way, I just would prefer to have you guys at the country house. I've arranged for a helicopter at the Thirty-Fourth Street heliport. I'll try to make it out by the end of the day. Maybe tomorrow morning."

Wells had seven acres of land on the beach in the Hamptons, with a sprawling house and garage, tucked away from the main road and fenced for extra security. When he and his family stayed there, Wells contracted a private security firm to protect the grounds, figuring you could never be too careful when you were as rich as he was.

He hung up with his wife and made final preparations for the press conference. It was lights-on in half an hour. His staff had already drawn up a statement on the current stability of Vanderbilt Frink, and a list of talking points for any gotcha questions the journalists shouted. He would try to project confidence and calm and give off an aura of future prosperity, but he knew the media would jump all over him. They would say or write anything to take him down, would have no problem blaming him for the current state of the economy. That was what the media did to rich people.

Wells texted his driver to meet him at the building's side entrance in four minutes, then met his bodyguard, Dov, at the elevators.

Wells's executive assistant, Thomason, was already at his side, whispering a litany of updates into his ear on the current news and state of the economy. "Police haven't pinpointed the cause of the crash yet, not ruling out terrorism, the bridge is closed, all traffic into and out of Manhattan is snarled."

"You contracted the chopper for Sally and the kids?"

"Fueled and ready." Thomason barely skipped a beat. "Vandy stock is down another seven points as of ten minutes ago, two more analysts rating it a sell, and the broader market is down another thirty percent at the closing bell—"

Wells put his hand up to stop Thomason as they got into the elevator. "I need to calm down."

"Yes, sir."

They rode down to the ground level. The back elevators led to the executive entrance, an unmarked door that fronted Forty-Seventh Street. Wells used it half of the time he exited the building, figuring he didn't want to be too predictable in his comings and goings. He understood that the chances of someone's trying to kidnap or assassinate him were slim, but better safe than sorry, and anyway, the last week had not been normal times for a banking CEO.

The elevator dinged for the ground floor, and Dov got out first, as was his custom, checking the hallway for threats. He waved Wells and Thomason out, and the three of them exited the building out a safety door.

The street met Wells with a wall of noise. It was pandemonium: horns honking, people yelling, engines idling. Traffic was at a standstill on Forty-Seventh, and great waves of pedestrians seemed to be running back and forth on the sidewalks. Wells realized immediately that getting to the press conference—they'd booked a room at an NBC studio at Rockefeller Plaza—was not going to be easy.

"We might have to walk, sir," Thomason said, scanning the street, and Wells nodded in agreement.

Dov opened his mouth to say something—probably to object, to say how dangerous that was, Wells thought—when out of the corner of his eye Wells saw a trio of people approaching, walking right at him, one of them holding something in the air as if to present it to him. The person holding the thing in the air—a woman—was yelling at him, but Wells couldn't hear her over the noise. Dov noticed them too and was in front of Wells in a flash, his hand reaching inside of his blue blazer, probably already on the grip of his Glock 23.

"Freeze!" Dov said in his thick Israeli accent, but the people kept coming, undeterred, which Wells thought was a bad thing, maybe even a dangerous thing, but before he could say anything, a fourth figure flashed at them from his left side, a big guy in camouflage, and he draped himself over Dov before the Israeli could react.

"Not so fast, buddy," the guy in camo said, arms wrapped around Dov. Dov tried to buck him off, but the two of them careened onto the hood of a parked car, slamming into the steel and then bouncing to the ground like wrestlers in a staged match.

"What the fuck . . . ," Wells barked, but the woman was ten feet away now, yelling at Wells.

"Special Agent Jayanti Chaudry, FBI!" she said, and now Wells could see that the thing she was holding up to him was a Federal Bureau of Investigation badge. "Robert Andrew Wells? We need to talk."

Wells didn't believe any of it. This woman did not look like an FBI agent, and if she was, why wasn't she surrounded by other agents, instead of a goon wearing fatigues and another younger man in jeans and a T-shirt. None of it made any sense.

"I don't know who the fuck you are, but I'm calling the police—and you need to let go of my bodyguard." As Wells moved toward Dov to try kicking at the soldier who had him pinned, a young woman stepped in his path. She was frizzy haired and chubby and had a canister of pepper spray in her hand— pointed right at Wells.

"Na, na, na, no way." She sounded as if she'd just stepped off the D train from the Bronx. "Back it up, buddy. Everything's going to be fine."

Wells flinched and stepped backward, looking now for Thomason, but his executive assistant was already running down the block, moving away from the trouble as fast as his legs could carry him. Wells cursed him silently, promising to fire him the moment he got out of this jam.

"You've got serious trouble," a voice snapped at him. Wells turned to see the young man in jeans strutting up to him. He radiated an almost swaggering confidence. "And if you don't deal with it, you're screwed."

"Who the fuck are you?"

"Garrett Reilly. I work the bond desk at Jenkins and Altshuler."

Wells blinked in surprise. What the hell was this all about? Yet, the name was familiar. Somewhere in the back of his head he knew who Garrett Reilly was.

"Someone's about to take down Vandy," Reilly said. "Bring the biggest too-big-to-fail bank to its knees and kill the economy."

Wells shook his head vehemently. "That's insane. It can't be done."

"Really? Have you taken a look around today?" Reilly swept his hand out across the snarled traffic and the cacophony of honking horns. "This look normal to you?"

"It has nothing to do with Vandy."

"It has everything to do with Vandy. Don't be an idiot."

Wells, an angry scowl gashing his face, stepped toward Reilly. If these people were assassins, then fine, let them shoot him, but he was not going to be told about the finance business by anybody, especially not some asshole kid. "I don't know who the fuck you think you are, but you don't know shit about my business, so let my goddamned bodyguard go, because I have a press conference to attend. I need to actually try to calm this city down, not listen to whack-job conspiracy theories."

"You have a mole in your company. Somewhere inside the bank. And that mole is on the verge of leveraging you out of business."

Wells froze. His mind raced. If there was one thing he actually did fear, it was exactly that: an employee deep inside his company, someone with access to funds and trades and derivatives, who had an ax to grind or was just plain incompetent, and who, by making terrible, horrifically stupid bets, hollowed out the finances of Vandy and leveraged the bank into the ground. Wells had called innumerable meetings on just this topic and had had endless consultants tell him how to prevent this from occurring, but still the idea haunted him: one man, secreted away on a trading desk, slowly placing bet after bet on highly speculative investments. Investments that would all come due at once and create such a tidal wave of debt that Vandy imploded before anyone could stop it from happening.

It would be a bank run to end all bank runs.

"How do you know?"

"Crowdsourcing," the young man said.

Wells let out a snort of astonishment. Was this a joke? "You asked the idiots who troll Internet comment sections what their opinion was, and you're peddling that to me as some kind of catastrophe warning? Are you nuts?" Before Reilly could answer, Wells suddenly remembered where he'd heard the name before. He was— "Avery Bernstein's boy. You're one of his homegrown quants. A pattern geek."

Reilly made no show of acknowledging this, but there was something else about Reilly, something Wells couldn't quite put his finger on—a rumor, maybe, or a scandal. The memory of it bounced around in his brain, just beyond his reach.

"If you don't find that mole, you will come crashing down, and you will take everybody down with you," Reilly said in even tones.

"We have safeguards in place. Comptrollers, supervisors, accountants. A risk-management algorithm. Every trade is vetted, every bit of leverage is taken into consideration."

"That's bullshit, and you know it. You don't know half of what goes on in your bank."

Wells pointed a finger in Reilly's face. "I don't have time for this. New York doesn't have time for this." Wells turned to the two men still locked in each other's arms on the pavement. "Let him go, or I swear to God I will have you all arrested." He turned to the woman who claimed to be from the FBI. "And if you're really from the FBI, and I seriously doubt it, then I will have you kicked off the force so fast you won't know what hit you. You'll be lucky to get a job screening passengers in Duluth, Minnesota."

The woman from the FBI nodded to the marine private on the sidewalk. "Let him go."

The man in camouflage let go of Dov, and the big Israeli jumped to his feet, yanking his pistol from his jacket. He pointed it at the man who had pinned him and yelled, "You touch me again, I fucking kill you!"

"Hey, nothing personal," the private said with a smile. "Just a friendly tussle."

Wells started down the sidewalk. He could see Thomason standing on the corner, cell phone to his ear, talking animatedly. Probably calling the police, Wells thought, which was exactly what he should have done. Maybe he wouldn't fire Thomason—not yet at least.

"You think your bank is too big to fail," Reilly called after Wells. "You're thinking, worst-case scenario, the government steps in and bails us out. The government can just print more money."

Wells stopped walking. He did think that. He turned to look at the assemblage of Keystone Kops who had assaulted him. They were standing in a group, young and ragged looking, not at all the people whom Wells expected to give him portents of disaster.

"But what you don't understand is that the people who are doing this have already thought of that," Reilly said. "They are a step ahead of you. And they're making sure, right now, that the government won't be paying attention when you call for help."

Wells felt a sharp stab of doubt in his stomach. Around him, the city heaved and growled in panic; the June air was alive with anxiety and stress, shouts of worry and the frenetic motion of uncertainty.

Reilly stared at him. "I promise you—you will never see it coming."

After the truck blew up, Ilya and Uni walked the rest of the span of the George Washington Bridge. The task was not hard, even with the hot wind blowing across the Hudson River, because the chaos of the explosion cleared out the upper level of the bridge, and as emergency crews and police streamed out of Manhattan to the fire, they all but ignored the pedestrians fleeing the catastrophe, which was exactly as Ilya had expected.

Yuri S. was not so lucky, and his misfortune was also by design. Ilya had decided that afternoon that the young Ukrainian would have to heroically give his life for the cause, and he did, although the heroic part was open to interpretation.

Yuri S. had jackknifed the truck into afternoon traffic, as planned, just at the halfway point of the bridge, crushing a Hyundai and pinning an SUV against a far guardrail. The eighteen-wheeler had skidded across three lanes and threatened to topple over, but didn't, the job masterfully done. Yuri S., it had turned out, had briefly driven rigs between Kiev and Donetsk while at university. He was a man of many talents, and it was sad—a bit, at least—to lose him. When the truck came to its metal-twisting stop, Ilya embraced Yuri S.

"A job well done," Ilya had said, and then, without warning, stabbed Yuri S. in his abdomen with a sharpened screwdriver. Ilya had to push hard on the tool to break the skin, but once that first layer was ripped, the screwdriver dove into his body easily, and Ilya twisted and churned at the Ukrainian's soft innards. Ilya had figured that when the autopsy was done on Yuri S., a sharpened screwdriver would take the coroner a bit longer to explain than a gunshot wound. Yuri S. had shrieked in surprise, but by the time he understood what had happened to him, Ilya and Uni were out of the cab and Ilya had dialed the cell phone attached to the pipe bomb.

The bomb exploded immediately, engulfing the truck in flames. The fire burned with a savage intensity, but Uni and Ilya didn't look back. Ilya had estimated that they had fifteen minutes to clear the scene before the police started rounding up eyewitnesses. And he was right.

Fifteen minutes after the explosion, just as the two of them set foot in Manhattan, the NYPD closed off all entrances and exits to the bridge, and anyone who was left on the structure would have to pass through a police checkpoint to leave. Free and unobserved, Ilya and Uni walked to 175th Street and boarded the A train downtown. The subway was full of riders staring at their phones, gobbling down the latest tidbits of news. They looked frightened, and Ilya liked that. One man even yelled, "Oh, crap," as he read an update on his iPhone. Ilya and Uni got out at Forty-Second Street, and Ilya felt like a kid about to unwrap his Christmas presents—he could barely wait to observe the effect his efforts were having on the city.

Walking through the Port Authority Bus Terminal, Ilya was not disappointed. New Yorkers were lined up, forty and fifty deep, to board buses out of the city. Scores of police were trying to keep order, but the bus travelers—or would-be bus travelers—were having none of it, shoving against each other to get to the front of their respective lines, dragging suitcases and cardboard boxes to stuff into the cargo holds of their buses, and generally behaving like frightened animals. The PA system spewed a long litany of delayed departures, interrupted by pleas for people to keep calm.

"Sheep," Ilya said to Uni as they watched the chaos unfold. "One person runs for safety, and then they all do. As if being part of the crowd guaranteed you security. A group can be sent to the gas chamber just as easily as an individual."

Uni squeezed his hand happily, and Ilya felt a twinge of discomfort; physical closeness was difficult for him, particularly if it did not directly involve sexual satisfaction. But he held her hand anyway, knowing that from here on in, everything about the future was unknown, and that he might want to experiment with human contact for a while. He might be dead tomorrow. The same could be said for Uni.

"When I'm with you, I feel like I see the world more clearly," Uni said.

Ilya liked that. From early in his life he'd felt that he saw things as they were, not as the people in power wanted them to be seen. That had always made him an outsider. Perhaps with Uni he was becoming part of a group. Perhaps.

They walked to a small grocery store on the first floor of the bus terminal because Ilya was thirsty, and neither he nor Uni had eaten since the night before. But the shelves of the store were almost empty, and the Korean man behind the cash register was watching the crowds nervously, hands hidden under the counter. Ilya picked out a pair of candy bars and a bottle of water and laid them on the counter.

"Twenty-five dollars," the clerk said.

"For two candy bars and a water?" Ilya asked.

"Twenty-five dollars." The clerk's jumpy eyes settled on Ilya.

Ilya laughed. "That's price gouging."

The clerk said nothing, but quickly put his hands on top of the candy bars to keep Ilya from making off with them.

"No, no. Don't get me wrong. I'm all for it." Ilya peeled a twenty and a five from his wallet and laid them on the counter. "Gouge them all. And keep doing it. The end comes quicker when everyone pitches in."

When they turned to face the lobby of the Port Authority again, a bald man with a cherubic face was blocking their way, smiling broadly at them. The man seemed to recognize Ilya, nodding and grinning, but Ilya had no idea who he was.

"Can I help you?" Ilya asked, preparing to fight, or perhaps flee.

"The city is in full bloom all around us." The bald man nodded toward the chaos behind him in the Port Authority's cavernous halls. "An impressive job you've done."

He had a slight accent, German to Ilya's ear, although he could not be sure. Given that English was Ilya's third language, picking out the subtleties of foreign accents was not easy for him. Either way, Ilya wanted nothing to do with him. He grabbed Uni by the hand and started to walk around the man.

"Someone is looking for you, Mr. Markov."

Ilya froze.

"No, no, not Garrett Reilly, although he too is searching for you. But Mr. Reilly is not paying me." The friendly-faced man cocked his head slightly, as if picturing Garrett Reilly in his mind. "Although I like Mr. Reilly rather a lot. I like his spirit. I feel he will do great things someday. I would almost tell him where you were for nothing." The man smiled. "Almost."

Ilya's thoughts raced. Who was this man? Could he be the link between the SVR and the hacker underground, the liaison who had first put Ilya in touch with his handlers in Russia? The name Ilya knew was Metternich, but he doubted it was real—or if any person alive knew the man's actual name. But he was infamous—a spy and a dealer in information, a danger to any and all who met him, a man not to be trusted.

"Are you—"

"No need for names," the man hissed, albeit with a smile.

"Do you know where Reilly is now?" Ilya asked, his curiosity getting the better of him.

"I have notions, but they are expensive, and I don't think you have the cash on hand."

Ilya stared at him, baffled. How had he found Ilya now, in the middle of this chaos?

"Here is what my job is right now. To tell you that your boss has arrived in New York City and urgently desires to speak to you."

"My boss? I don't have a boss."

The man shrugged and handed Ilya a cell phone. "He will contact you soon."

Ilya stared at the phone as if it were a device from the future, strange and potentially dangerous. "How did you find me?" He needed to know. For the future; for his own safety.

"To paraphrase an old saying—you're only as invisible as the company you keep." The man laughed, and his eyes flashed quickly to Uni, then back to Ilya, and Ilya immediately realized that his relationship with the young woman had been a mistake. This man, Metternich, had traced Ilya through Uni, because she was his moment of weakness, and no one covered his or her own tracks as well as Ilya did. Well, he thought, what's done is done. He would live with the consequences of his emotional misadventure. He frowned, the cheap cell phone now snugly in the palm of his hand.

"You are thinking, if I can find you, so can Garrett Reilly," Metternich said. "Well, he can. And he will, so be prepared."

The bald man winked once—in an almost insultingly familiar way—then turned abruptly and walked off. Ilya was about to call after him when the phone in his hand chimed and vibrated at the same time. Ilya read the text on the screen.

Ya v New Yorke. Nam nado vstretit'sya. I am in New York. We need to meet.

"Son of a bitch," Ilya said out loud but to no one in particular. How had this happened? He had been discovered, and now he was being summoned, all within moments. He looked up to ask the bald man—the man who he suspected was Hans Metternich—this exact question.

But the man had disappeared.

Alexis had to read the State Department bulletin on her cell phone because the Internet at the FBI field office was working at dial-up speeds. Bingo said connection times were molasses all over the city, probably a result of massive denial-of-service attacks at Internet providers throughout Manhattan. A shiver ran down her spine. When the rest of the team had come back from uptown—from the Vandy offices—she'd looked immediately for Garrett, to show him the bulletin, but he was nowhere to be found.

"What the fuck?" Chaudry said. "He came back downtown with us in a field car. Where the hell is he?" She turned her wrath on Agent Murray, who was wiping the sheen of sweat from his neck. The night was hot and sticky, even inside the FBI offices. "You were supposed to watch him."

Alexis stepped between the two agents. "I'll find him. I'm sure he didn't go far."

She checked the bathrooms on the twenty-third floor, and the empty rooms near the front of the offices, then went downstairs to look on the street. She found him half a block away, hunched over the curb on his knees, his forehead resting on the side panel of a parked Volvo station wagon.

"Are you all right?"

He craned his head slightly to peek at her, then looked back down. "Yeah. Just—you know . . ." He let out a long, exhausted breath.

"Can I get you some—"

"It's okay." He stood shakily, using the hood of the Volvo to steady himself.

"You shouldn't go off without telling Chaudry. She's pissed."

"She can kiss my ass."

"She can put you in jail," Alexis said softly, trying to sound measured but authoritative at the same time. "For a long time. You know it. I know it. You have to behave."

He waved a hand in the air dismissively, but the motion was weak. He closed his eyes again, as if willing himself to have the strength to keep going. Alexis waited. Around them, a few cars raced down Broadway. Lower Manhattan had emptied out. Alexis figured that was because there was no way to get out of the city from this far south. All the smart passengers had already fled the sinking ship.

When Garrett opened his eyes again, she handed him her phone. The State Department bulletin was on the screen. "Gennady Bazanov entered the country at JFK about three hours ago."

"Who's that?"

"SVR agent. SVR is the foreign arm of the reconstituted Russian KGB. He's a spy." Garrett looked pale and sickly. Maybe it was just the yellow of the streetlights, but Alexis began to worry. "A spy who was stationed in Belarus for the last two months."

Garrett narrowed his eyes and read aloud from the bulletin. "'Primary responsibilities included sabotage and fomenting political instability.'" He looked up. "A trickster spy?"

"Who makes mischief. Not unlike Markov."

"And you think—"

"That the timing cannot be coincidental. I think he's here to find Markov."

Garrett stared down the street. "But why? If he wanted to contact Markov, why wouldn't he just call him from Russia?"

"Maybe he's nervous about having his phone call traced. Or maybe Markov turned off his phone, shut down his e-mail. Bazanov can't find him through normal means. So he's here to make actual contact. To see him in real life."

"Or maybe he wants to take him home. Physically bring him back to Russia," Garrett said.

"Which could mean that something went wrong."

Garrett turned to look at her, his eyes lighting up, the joy of puzzle solving flashing across his face. It made her less worried. If Garrett Reilly's brain could be kept occupied, then he would survive. If his mind idled, then God only knew what would happen next.

"You think the Russians don't like what they're seeing?" he asked quickly. "You think Markov has gone off in a direction they can't control? He's doing something they didn't tell him to do?"

"Maybe. But I'm not sure that makes things any better for us. Might make it worse. At least if the Russian government was calling the shots, then we'd know they had national interests at heart. If Markov is in it for himself, he could be planning almost anything."

Garrett looked off into the night. He shook his head warily. "A lot of speculation. We think Bazanov is a spy, but we're not positive. We don't know if he has anything to do with Markov. And if he does have something to do with Markov, we have no idea if he's here to make contact or observe or take notes or just stock up on bagels. To say all these things are true, and the Russian government is unhappy, seems like a giant leap of logic. To top it off, we still don't know why the Russian government would want to make trouble in the United States right at this very moment."

"But we might know. You mentioned it yourself a few days ago. Runoff elections in Belarus are in forty-eight hours. Between the pro-Russian dictator and the Western-leaning reformer. If the West is melting down, who would you vote for? The reformer? Or the autocrat? This whole thing might be the Russians making mischief to sway the elections. It's a leap—but it's not beyond the realm of possibility."

"On a probability curve—"

"—it's about a seventy-five percent chance." Alexis thought of his rambling statistics-laden e-mail to her, and how incredibly prescient it had been. Garrett looked at her and grinned. That kind of grin had attracted Alexis to him in the first place—wolfish and charming, full of swagger and confidence, but also full of intellectual curiosity. His grin said he was in love with all the information that the world had to offer. The more he knew, the happier he was. And she had just supplied him with an answer.

"Let's go upstairs, shall we?" he said.

"Sounds good."

The moment Chaudry saw Garrett she said, "Disappear on me again, I swear to God I'll shoot you." She pointed to Agent Murray. "Or I'll have him do it."

Garrett apologized—as Alexis had urged him to do in the elevator—and that seemed to mollify Chaudry. Then he and Alexis laid out what they thought might be happening. The rest of the Ascendant team watched as Chaudry, her anger seemingly gone, considered what she'd just been told. She shot a look to Alexis, as if to silently ask her if all of this was on the level, and Alexis nodded yes.

"Put out an APB on Gennady Bazanov," Chaudry said to Murray.

"We got nobody left. Everyone's on the street," Murray said.

"Don't care," Chaudry said as she left the room. "And I don't care what the charges are. Make something up. Let's bring him in and see what he knows."

G ennady Bazanov marveled at the fear that was crippling Manhattan. It was everywhere—in the erratic driving and blaring horns of the taxis and the cars in the streets, in the contorted faces of the pedestrians he passed in lower Manhattan, in the shuttered stores and the countless policemen he saw busily being deployed to multiple street corners. This was a city caught up in a spasm of pure panic.

Bazanov had not thought that Markov could do it. He hadn't believed anybody could do it. When his bosses at Yasenevo had first come to him, months ago, with the idea of sending a psychological shock through the Western banking system, he had dismissed the concept as ludicrous. Of course he hadn't said anything at the time; he was smarter and more political than that. But inwardly, as his SVR bosses debated the possibilities, he had roared with laughter. The KGB and its successor organizations were famous—or perhaps infamous—for their harebrained espionage schemes. They had hired psychics and would-be mind-controllers, hypnotists and con men. Under Vladimirovich Andropov, they'd even had a witch cast spells on foreign leaders before summit meetings.

But longtime SVR operatives understood that one ridiculed those enterprises at one's own risk. And who was to say that they were not successful: foreign leaders had had unexpected heart attacks after all, and diplomatic U-turns had started in the most unlikely of places. Perhaps the witches had been a stroke of genius. One could never tell.

And one could not tell in the United States, either. A country that was so highly strung, so attuned to every misstep in the market, so convinced that every false prophet with his or her own TV show could predict the future—a country such as that could twist itself in knots at the slightest provocation. Ilya Markov understood that—and had acted on that understanding.

None of it mattered now. Bazanov had a job to do, and he was halfway there. He had finally made contact with Markov—although that had cost him quite a bit of money—and he would be meeting him in an hour. But how to get to the meeting spot—underneath the Manhattan Bridge—in one hour? A cab was out of the question. The streets were gridlocked with cars and buses and trucks. The subways were a possibility, but Bazanov didn't like taking subways; they made his claustrophobia skyrocket, and given the panicked mood of the populace, the mere thought of a crowd pushing in on him in a cramped train car made his heart pound.

So he ran. He was in excellent shape and wouldn't be noticed, that was for sure; New Yorkers were running every which way already in the streets. One more balding, middle-aged man sprinting downtown wouldn't raise any alarms.

He ran south on Madison, then cut over to Park. He stopped every few blocks to catch his breath, and by Fourteenth Street he was covered in sweat, but he no longer cared. He settled into a fast walk for about half a mile, his legs rubbery from the exertion and the adrenaline that was coursing through his veins.

Bazanov had gone around and around on the long flight from Moscow on how to handle Markov when he finally saw him. He wasn't sure what he would say to him, but he knew the general information he wanted to impart to the young man. You have done your job. There is panic and chaos in the streets. The world has seen it and will react accordingly; now let us both depart this country and be done with the mission.

A normal operative would agree, and they would take the first flight home, perhaps even with Bazanov at Markov's side, sipping a cabernet in business class. But Markov was not a normal operative. Bazanov's deepest fear was that Ilya Markov had something else planned—something that had nothing to do with sowing financial chaos in America or the West. Bazanov's fear was that Ilya Markov had a goal, and that it was his own and nobody else's—not Bazanov's or the Kremlin's or even that of the Great Dark Lord himself.

Bazanov got to the end of Bowery and the beginning of the Manhattan

Bridge at 9:54 in the evening. He had made the trip in forty-five minutes. He stopped to catch his breath and consider his next move—if he was earlier than Markov, then he would need to find a place to watch the young man and perhaps surprise him.

The problem was, Markov had not specified a meeting place. He had simply written *under the bridge*. Bazanov cut down a side street north of the bridge's car on-ramp and looked for any spot that would allow him to go underneath the structure. He found it on Cherry Street, a small two-way street that led directly under the bridge in an arched tunnel. The street was sparsely trafficked, with no pedestrians. Above the tunnel, cars and trucks honked and inched out of Manhattan, trying to grind their way to Brooklyn. The city's traffic had not gotten any better with the coming of the night; it seemed to have gotten worse.

The tunnel under the bridge was dank; yellowy streetlights flickered, casting faint light into the blackness. A homeless man wrapped in blankets was asleep in a shallow alcove. Bazanov could see his face—he had a thick beard and his forehead was caked in months of grime. That was not Markov; no disguise could be so realistic.

For a moment, Bazanov considered standing in the middle of the tunnel, arms at his side, so Markov could see that he was unarmed and meant no harm, but then, as he stepped deeper into the darkness, he saw an opening across from the sleeping homeless man. An archway seemed to lead to a parking lot, and a playing field and park beyond that. A chain-link fence sealed off the entrance, locked with a small, flimsy padlock. Bazanov picked up a paving stone from the cracked sidewalk and, with one practiced swing, smashed the lock and opened the gate.

He kept the rock in his hands as a precaution, then slipped behind the gate, closed it again, and turned to face the tunnel to wait for Markov to show up. He got it in his mind that he would not even bother to negotiate with Markov when he showed up. Bazanov would simply smash Markov's head in with the rock, drag his body behind the gate, cover it with a piece of plastic tarpaulin—he'd noticed a roll of it on the edge of the parking lot—weight it down with rocks, then drop it into the East River. Mission accomplished.

He was just working up the mental fortitude necessary to carry out such a violent plan when he heard a sharp crack from behind him. The noise was loud and surprising, and it seemed to fill the entire tunnel. A fraction of a second passed as Bazanov's mind tried to reason out what the sound was, but then he felt a stabbing pain in his back, just below his shoulder, and he knew immediately what the problem was: he'd been shot.

He spun quickly to confront the shooter, but as he did, another shot rang out, louder than the first one, and Bazanov felt the second bullet hit his body, again in his chest, just to the right of his heart. The force of the bullet knocked all the wind from his lungs—or perhaps, he thought, his lung had collapsed from the impact. He staggered backward, hands lashing out to grab at anything he could to stabilize his body before he fell. He blinked in the darkness and made out a figure barely ten feet away: a man, gun held chest high, a wisp of smoke still floating up from the barrel, staring at Bazanov with searching, interested eyes. It was Markov; Bazanov knew this immediately and would have known without even looking.

Markov took a tentative step forward and continued to stare at the older man with a look that suggested he was on the verge of asking a question. Bazanov knew what the question was as well: Are you dying? Do I need to shoot you again?

"*Sukin syn!*" Bazanov growled, hand clinging desperately to the interlocking ringlets on a section of chain-link fence. *Son of a bitch!*

"*Prosti,*" Markov whispered. *I'm sorry.* But his face showed no signs of contrition. It was hard and cold and still searching. Bazanov gathered every bit of strength in his body; he knew his only hope was to hail a passerby or a car and get to a hospital quickly. He yanked open the gate whose lock he had smashed and stumbled onto Cherry Street. The streetlights were still flickering, but no cars were passing under the bridge. Bazanov tried to break into a sprint, but he found that his legs had no power. He dropped to his knees on the damp pavement.

He slumped down, body resting on his elbow, craning his head to look back over his shoulder. Markov had followed him out onto Cherry Street, gun in hand, and was watching Bazanov with those lifeless eyes. A woman had joined Markov. Short and pixielike, she stood right behind Markov and also watched as Bazanov fought to stay alive.

"You should shoot him again," she said in English, a trace of erotic excitement in her voice. "One more time to make sure he's dead."

"*Ya ne umer, blyad!*" Bazanov hissed. *I am not dead, you whore!*

Markov squinted in the dim light. "Why did you come here?"

Bazanov gasped for breath as he felt his lungs filling up with fluid. He knew it was blood, had seen it many times before in his life—a soldier hit in the chest and slowly drowning to death in his own hemoglobin. He needed a hospital. He needed a doctor. Yet, that son of a whore Markov needed to be taught a lesson as well. . . .

"To kill you, you little cunt," Bazanov said in English, lashing out desperately with his right hand to snare Markov's foot. Bazanov had moved quickly, coiled and able, but his arm hadn't responded with the speed that his brain had demanded. His hand was weak and slow.

Markov stepped gingerly out of the way. He raised the gun again. "I guess it didn't work out." He aimed his gun at Bazanov's head. "Too bad."

Bingo had seen a dead body before—an OD'd junkie in an alley in Oakland—but never one with its brains splattered over the sidewalk in bright red stripes. When the NYPD detective told him to prepare for a gruesome crime scene, Bingo figured he'd get sick at the sight of it, but he had a completely different reaction when Gennady Bazanov's body was unsheathed in the tunnel under the Manhattan Bridge. The sight of him splayed out on the pavement gave Bingo a hidden thrill: Bazanov was dead, and Bingo was alive. That fact alone made Bingo strangely satisfied.

There were few moments in life when Bingo felt he had an advantage over anybody else, but this was one of them. He's dead; I'm not, Bingo thought. That's a net positive.

The streetlights in the tunnel under the bridge were strong enough to allow Bingo and the rest of the Ascendant team to make out the details of the crime scene, but little more. Celeste stood nearby, as did Agent Chaudry. Alexis and Garrett wandered back and forth across the street. Bazanov's suit jacket lay perfectly over his shoulders and torso; it looked as if it had been arranged for viewing by a mortician. A spray of blood painted the concrete, mixed with what looked like shards of skull and clumps of hair. Grisly as that was, Bingo couldn't turn away. He wanted to know why Bazanov was dead. And how it had happened.

Detective Samuelson—young and trim, wearing a short-sleeve shirt and beige slacks—aimed the beam of a Maglite across Bazanov's shoulders and arm.

"Did he have any ID?" Chaudry asked, standing behind Bingo, staring down at the body.

"Russian passport, diplomatic papers. They said he was a . . ." Samuelson pulled out a notepad from his suit jacket and read aloud, " 'Commercial sales consultant,' from something called the Kirov Oblast. Whatever that means."

"Oblast is like a state," Bingo said. "Kirov is north and east of Moscow."

"The sales-consultant bit is his cover," Chaudry said. "Spies won't enter the country without a diplomatic job."

"He also had a wallet, some rubles, two hundred bucks US, a couple of credit cards. And a cell phone."

"Did you check the call log on the phone?" Chaudry asked.

"It's in Russian. We'll have it translated back at the precinct."

Celeste stepped into a pool of light, eyes locked on the body. She, like Bingo, seemed unable to look away from the tragedy. Bingo suspected that the horror of it gave her the same kind of strange pleasure that it seemed to be giving him—psychic relief from their internal pain. "Could I see the cell phone? I'm a linguist. I'm not fluent, but I have a little Russian."

"It's in the backseat of the cruiser," the detective said. "Make sure you wear gloves when you touch it. Get a pair from my partner." He pointed to another suited NYPD detective, standing by a police car, chatting with a uniformed patrol officer. Celeste took a last, loving look at the body, then hurried off to investigate the phone. Bingo made a mental note to himself to talk to her about this later—he wanted to make sure he wasn't being too ghoulish. Or, if he was, that he had a partner.

"You said you thought he was shot over there. Behind the gate." Garrett pointed to an open gate in the middle of the tunnel. "Why?"

"First shot was probably to the back, entry wound just above the lung. No exit wound," Samuelson said. "The next shot entered through his chest, so I'm guessing he spun around to get a look at the shooter, who fired one more bullet to the front. We found two shell casings behind the gate. Nine mill, regular rounds. And a third on the street."

Bingo watched as the detective played the beam of his flashlight over the cyclone fence, the gate, the snapped lock, and then the parking lot and playfield beyond the tunnel. The playfield was empty and unlit, taking on a lonely, haunted appearance. The city had quieted down some, now that it was one in the morning, although Bingo had seen garbage-can fires on a number of street corners during the drive to the bridge, as well as the shattered windows of a dozen looted electronics stores. The sound of police sirens still echoed through the night air.

"Okay, so you were right," Chaudry said. "Bazanov was looking for Markov."

"And Markov killed him," Alexis said, walking back across the street.

"So your supposition about Markov going rogue makes sense as well," Chaudry said.

"You know who the shooter was?" Samuelson's voice rose in anger.

"Probably," Garrett said. "But maybe not."

The police detective glared at Garrett and Alexis. "Who the fuck are you again?"

Bingo thought he saw a sliver of a smile crease Garrett's face. Bingo had seen that look before, when Garrett knew he was pissing someone off and didn't care—or actually, when he pissed someone off and enjoyed it. Bingo had to admit that it was kind of nice to see that look reappear on Garrett's face—it meant he was healthy again. He'd regained his edge.

"What about that piece of concrete?" Garrett pointed to a chunk of sidewalk resting ten feet from the dead man's outstretched hands.

"Might have been holding it, trying to protect himself," Alexis said.

"No way to get prints off concrete," Samuelson said.

"Or it could be a weapon that Bazanov was holding to hit the shooter," Garrett said. "Only the shooter surprised him." Garrett walked a few feet down the sidewalk, then pointed to a jagged hole in the pavement. "He pulled it up from there."

Chaudry eyed the hole. "He was waiting behind the fence, watching the tunnel, thinking the shooter was going to walk past. But the shooter was already here, guessed where Bazanov was going to hide, and came up behind him."

Bingo thought about that scenario, then held up his hand to speak, as he always did. Garrett nodded to him, teacher to student.

"That story would follow Markov's pattern. The chess player. He lures his opponents in, lets them believe they're outthinking him, but they're actually two steps behind. Markov knew Bazanov's vulnerability."

"Which was?" Chaudry asked.

Bingo thought about the question. What was the pattern in Bazanov's behavior that Markov recognized? He wasn't as practiced as Garrett was in spotting patterns, but if he could discover this one, that would be an intellectual coup.

"Arrogance," Celeste Chen said, walking back into the tunnel from the squad car, a cell phone in her gloved hand.

"Explain," Chaudry said.

"Bazanov texted five numbers over the last twenty-four hours, with basically the same message. 'Contact me. We need to talk.' He sent that message twenty different times. Never got a response. Then, at six thirteen p.m., he texted a slightly different message to a new number. 'I'm in New York City. We need to meet.' He gets a response three hours later, nine oh one p.m. 'Under the bridge.' All these are in Russian, by the way."

"That doesn't explain your answer," Chaudry said.

"Yes, it does," Garrett said. "Bazanov and Ilya Markov knew each other. The first twenty texts prove that. Bazanov has a host of numbers for Markov, tries them all. He's demanding, aggressive. He's the alpha. Bazanov is a trained operative. Markov, I'm guessing, is not. He's the opposite. Quiet, lurking. The texts reveal Bazanov's mind-set: superior, the boss. Then Bazanov lands in the US and uses another number to get Markov. Somehow he found a way to contact him, and it works. Maybe through an intermediary. Bazanov feels he has the upper hand."

Celeste picked up the thread of the story. "The reply comes in at nine p.m. Not sure where either of them are, but we can probably trace cell-tower information. Bazanov rushes here. Maybe he was already close. He figures he's here before Markov, has the jump on him—"

"He grabs that rock as a weapon," Garrett continued, "and hides in that alcove area. He used the rock to break the lock. Again, aggressive, superior."

"He was arrogant because he felt taking down Markov would be easy," Bingo said. He felt a rush of pleasure run through his body as he joined the conversation. "Physically easy. The lack of precautions shows that. And it would have been easy, but Markov had been there all along. And he had a gun."

Garrett and Alexis nodded their agreement. Bingo had to hold back a snort of joy. They had teased out the answers—they knew how Bazanov had been killed.

"But the why," Garrett said, as if he had heard Bingo's thoughts. "We haven't figured out the why. And without that, things will not get better. They will get worse."

E xoplanets.

    Garrett felt that they held the key—the wobble and spin of the visible that shone light on the invisible. Somehow, that was the answer to all that was happening.

But how?

He stood on the bicycle path that ran between the strip of park and the churning blackness of the East River. Brooklyn lay across the water, its buildings and warehouses dotted with yellow and white lights, and Manhattan lay behind him, its towers looming in the faint dawn. Garrett leaned on the railing that kept errant cyclists from diving into the river, although no bikers were out at five in the morning. There was just Garrett, with the Ascendant team a hundred yards away, watching, waiting for him to come up with an answer.

Go back to first principles, he thought. A to B to C.

An astronomer.

That's what Garrett was. He was an astronomer of unnatural phenomena, staring up at the heavens trying to piece together the secrets of the universe. The money universe. The terror universe. But the secrets were not revealing themselves to him. They were staying invisible.

His head hurt. Throbbed. The crack in his skull was telling him that he needed a palliative remedy. Drugs. Prescription drugs. Any drugs would do, really. But he couldn't. Not now, maybe not ever again. He had mental clarity through his pain, and that was the one thing he had been missing all this time. He could not relinquish it. He must not.

Another thought flitted across his mind. Gravity.

Money created its own gravity—that's what Avery had told him long ago. Money warped the world around it, just as a massive star bent light as the light passed by. But what was the money bending now? Garrett tried to cut a path through the data swirling in his head. He stared up in frustration at the graying sky above Brooklyn. No stars were visible—they rarely were through the light pollution. Brooklyn sat out there, a borough orbiting Manhattan.

What about time? Or distance? Perhaps they were the keys. For instance— why lower Manhattan? Why had Bazanov and Markov met at the foot of the Manhattan Bridge, just across the river from . . . Brooklyn.

The borough was mere minutes away. Suddenly, the pattern began to make sense. Garrett felt it, that pulse of knowledge, an ember in his nervous system, beginning to heat up. He blinked rapidly in the dark, trying to concentrate while at the same time not concentrating at all—the complicated balance of knowing and not knowing that always preceded his understanding.

What if Crowd Analytics was the next company to be targeted by the money rushing out of that criminal dark pool? Kenny Levinson, the young CEO, lived across the river in Brooklyn. Garrett had seen his fabulous brownstone in the online magazine. If Garrett wanted to find Levinson, it wouldn't be hard. That meant Markov could find him as well.

Garrett turned his gaze southward. He could see Brooklyn Heights, the neighborhood where Levinson lived, low buildings and piers just above the river, an enclave of wealth and privilege at the far western tip of the borough.

But why would Markov want to find Levinson? It didn't fit the pattern. So far the pattern had been to buy and sell stock and follow it up with a crime paid for by that buying and selling. But there hadn't been any buying or selling yet. There was only panic. Where was the crime?

But perhaps, Garrett thought, he had the sequence wrong. Perhaps there was about to be a crime. Maybe that was why Bazanov had come to America— because he knew a final crime was just in the offing. The pattern was reversed. The final crime would be the piece that set the true chaos in motion. That made sense. It would also explain the wobble in the Crowd Analytics stock—it wasn't buying and selling for profit. It was the setting-up of positions in the company's stock. Short selling, maybe. Someone was getting ready to profit off a real-world event—a crime.

About to happen. Maybe even about to happen . . . *right now.*

With that thought, Garrett raced back across the bike path and the strip of grass, yelling as he went, "We need to go. We need to go *now.*"

Garrett didn't like Kenny Levinson the moment he saw him ambling jauntily down the steps of his Joralemon Street brownstone. Levinson was dressed in jeans and a faded Animal Collective T-shirt, with a pair of green Converse All Stars on his feet, the essence of Brooklyn well-heeled hip. But Garrett thought he looked like he was trying too hard. Garrett thought he looked like a putz.

Chaudry had found Levinson's address the moment Garrett realized that this time the crime would be front-loaded. The crime would spur the stock drop. And the crime, Garrett guessed, was probably murder: killing a young, handsome chief executive.

Levinson, Garrett knew, was worth $2 billion. At twenty-nine, he was one of the five wealthiest people under thirty on the planet, with Mark Zuckerberg having just aged out of the list. Levinson was handsome, ever present in the media, effusively—and famously—in love with his gorgeous wife and young daughter, and he owned a spectacular brownstone in Brooklyn Heights. He was the whole package.

Garrett didn't begrudge him his success—he just didn't want to stare it in the face.

An NYPD cruiser from the Eighty-Fourth Precinct arrived on Levinson's block just before Garrett and the FBI did. A pair of beat patrolmen ran up the steps and ushered a surprised—and slightly alarmed—Levinson back into this house, while Garrett, Alexis, and Agent Chaudry took up the rear. Garrett almost laughed out loud when the self-satisfied smile on Levinson's face gave way to a grimace of fear, but Garrett reminded himself to stay on task and not be an asshole, which was never easy for him.

Patmore stood guard out on the front stoop, watching the street, while Mitty and Celeste followed Garrett inside. Bingo had elected to stay inside the FBI sedan down the block, watching all the excitement from the backseat. He said he'd had enough for one day.

The brownstone was just as Garrett expected: bright and airy, with a picture window looking onto the street, and modern art that Garrett didn't recognize—or particularly like—on most walls. Levinson's wife—clutching their infant daughter—looked panicked and just as confused as her husband, but Garrett noted that she was beautiful even in pajamas and an old T-shirt.

"What is this about?" Levinson asked, three times in a row. The two NYPD cops ushered him away from the window. Garrett moved to the window himself, peeking out onto the street, and thought he saw, maybe just for a moment, a sliver of a shadow slip away onto Clinton Street, but he couldn't be sure.

"We believed there was going to be an attempt on your life," Chaudry said. "This morning. And we didn't want you out on the street before we could protect you."

Garrett watched as two more cop cars pulled up into the narrow street, completely blocking it. The police officers jumped out and took up positions on the sidewalk, on both sides of the brownstone. An unmarked car pulled up behind the police cruisers, and two men whom Garrett assumed were FBI began to prowl up and down the street.

"He's not going to try it now," Garrett said, motioning to the older of the two officers standing in the living room. "You could tell your guys outside that maybe they should check the neighborhood. See if there's anyone suspicious lurking about. That's an idea."

But the NYPD cops just stared at Garrett and said nothing. They didn't seem to like being told what to do by a civilian.

Garrett shrugged and turned to Levinson. "Have you gotten any death threats lately?"

"No one's trying to kill me," Levinson insisted. "No one's threatened to kill me. And could we not talk about this in front of my wife and child?"

"Ma'am, maybe we could walk you upstairs," the younger cop said. "Do you have a back bedroom, away from windows?"

Levinson's wife nodded and took herself and the baby up a staircase. The younger cop followed them.

"Cute kid," Garrett said. "You should have more. You know, bring more joy into the world. That kinda shit."

"Who are you again?" Annoyance showed on Levinson's face.

"I'm the guy who just saved your life. I'm your guardian fucking angel." Garrett winked at Levinson. Garrett hated winking, but knew it would make the young entrepreneur uncomfortable, which Garrett wanted. It was an itch he needed to scratch.

Levinson scowled at Garrett and turned away.

"How about your company's stock?" Garrett asked. "The IPO was seven months ago."

"So?"

"Anything unusual going on with it? A lot of short interest?"

"No. Nothing like that."

"You didn't notice fluctuations in the pricing? A pattern of buying or selling? Odd lots?"

"I don't watch the stock too closely. Money is not why I do this."

"You do it for the babes?" Garrett asked.

"What is your problem?" Levinson's perfect eyebrows flared angrily.

"How about threats against the company? Any of those?"

"We get complaints sometimes. From customers who aren't satisfied."

"What exactly is it that your company does again?" Agent Chaudry asked.

"We provide aggregated crowdsourcing solutions to corporate IT and strategic-planning departments," Levinson said, as if by rote. He'd clearly given that elevator pitch more than a thousand times.

"For that you get two billion dollars?" Chaudry asked. "I'm in the wrong business."

Garrett laughed.

"We're valued at thirty billion, actually," Levinson said. "Two billion is my share."

"Right." Garrett sighed. "Your share." He dropped onto a plush white couch. He knew he shouldn't be jealous of Levinson—but he just couldn't help himself. Garrett wasn't hurting in the money department, but Levinson seemed to float above Garrett—and his class—with an ease that sent ripples of rage coursing through Garrett's body. Two billion dollars was a lot of fucking money. What made Levinson more deserving of that than Garrett? Or more deserving of this house? Or that wife, and that family? Garrett wanted those things— wanted them badly, maybe the happy family most of all—but he wouldn't be admitting that anytime soon. Not out loud.

Levinson stepped into the center of the room. "Can someone please tell me who you think is planning to kill me. And why?"

Alexis walked out of the kitchen—Garrett thought he saw her inspecting the vast Viking range—and pointed out the window. "Someone is creating economic havoc. Tampering with the American economy. We saw that yesterday." She pointed next at Garrett. "He saw signs of the havoc on the stock market. Ripples of buying and selling that were correlated to real-world events. Crimes. Hackings, bank runs, and shootings. Murders."

"And you think that I'm next?" Levinson said.

"You were next. It's just not going to happen now. The moment has passed." Garrett pulled his cell phone from his pocket and checked the time. "Six thirty in the morning. The markets open in three hours."

"Wait, you're saying my murder would trigger a stock plunge?"

"In the stock of Crowd Analytics it would. You're the founder, CEO, face of the company. You die, the company is in turmoil, the stock plummets," Garrett said. "I'm still not sure what the stock plunge would have triggered, but your death would have started it. But we've protected you, so they won't come after you. It won't help them anymore. They're moving on to the next phase. What I need to know is, where?"

Levinson ran his hands through his shoulder-length hair, as if a troubling thought had just occurred to him. "There has been something." A wave of worry crossed his face. "Our underwriting company—Goldman Sachs—said there were rumors out there—"

Garrett suddenly picked himself off the couch. "Of a derivative? Linked to your stock?"

"You knew that?" Levinson leaned against a white wall, just under a bright-colored painting of garbage trucks. He looked as if he might be sick.

"Was the rumor that the derivative would pay off if your stock dropped under a certain price?" Garrett asked forcefully, any playfulness in his voice long gone.

Levinson nodded yes. "Under fifty-five. But I didn't believe it. Who would put money into a derivative like that? We've done nothing but go up. And why would they do it?"

Garrett moved to Levinson, to the wall he was leaning against, and got in the young entrepreneur's face. "Kenny. Buddy," Garrett said, with more than a hint of sarcasm in his voice. "I need to know something. The rumors. Did they say what bank the derivatives came out of?"

Kenny Levinson closed his eyes and rubbed at his temples. To Garrett, he looked immensely tired, as if the last ten minutes had aged him ten years. The glee Garrett took in that made him question his own moral bearings; he could be a nasty son of a bitch.

"Yeah," Levinson said. "Vanderbilt Frink."

The lobby of the Vanderbilt Frink Trust and Guaranty was grand, the walls tiled with modernist frescoes, the ceilings hung with elaborate steel chandeliers. Chaudry flashed her FBI badge at the security team behind the front desk, then chattered at them out of Garrett's earshot. The rest of the Ascendant team—Alexis, Mitty, Celeste, Bingo, and Patmore—hurried into the lobby moments later.

"You and you," Chaudry barked as she jogged back from the security desk, pointing at Patmore and Alexis. "Watch the side exits, on Forty-Seventh and Forty-Sixth Streets. I want military on those doors. Anyone comes outside, you stop them." She turned to Agent Murray. "Call for backup and wait in the lobby. When agents arrive, I want them at the side exits with the military folk." Chaudry turned to Mitty, Celeste, and Bingo. "You wait here as well, but call Murray if anyone runs. Don't try to stop them yourselves, got it? Agent Murray is the muscle, not you."

Mitty nodded, a bit disappointed, but Celeste and Bingo seemed fine with their instructions. Chaudry waved at Garrett, and the two of them marched past security to the elevators. They rode silently to the tenth floor, and Garrett watched the tension play out on Chaudry's face.

"Stop staring at me," she said.

"You get to tell me what to look at?"

"That's right," she grunted. "I fucking own you."

"When does that end?"

"When I say so."

Garrett let out a low laugh. "I need to renegotiate."

They got out on ten and were met by an anxious-looking assistant. The assistant put her hand out, as if to stop them. "Mr. Wells is meeting with senior management and I really can't let you—"

Chaudry stiff-armed the assistant in the shoulder, spinning her around and bouncing her off a wall. "Fuck off," Chaudry said, and strode past the secretary. Garrett followed, liking this more and more with every passing second. They walked to a wooden door, and Chaudry popped it open without hesitation. Garrett imagined that was what she must have been like on drug raids, and he was sorry he'd never seen her pull a gun, although this was a decent second best.

She entered, and he followed behind her. An enormous table, thirty feet long, took up most of the middle of the room. Seated around the table were a dozen bank executives, all men, except for a lone woman, and all white, except for an Asian man sitting on the far side. Wells sat in a black Aeron chair at the head of the table, and he looked exhausted; his hair was uncombed and there were dark circles under his eyes. As Garrett gazed at the faces of the executives, he could see that they all looked worn-out, as if none of them had slept in days, maybe weeks.

Wells popped out of his chair the moment he recognized Garrett. "You cannot come in here! Jesus fucking Christ, what is wrong with you people?" He bared his teeth like a snarling dog. "Have we not already talked?"

Garrett grinned. He liked Wells's anger. The wave of emotion made Garrett calmer; he liked the conflict of it. It gave him a purpose, made him choose sides.

"There are derivatives coming out of your bank," Garrett said, circling the table. "And they are set to make you and your shareholders incredibly poor, incredibly fast."

"You said that last time, and it didn't happen. Now get the fuck out of my offices!" Wells was striding around the table to bump chests with Garrett, but Garrett dropped into an empty chair before Wells could get to him.

"This room has a nice feel to it." Garrett threw his feet up on the conference table. "Airy. Spacious."

Wells charged at Garrett, rage on his face, and reached out to grab him, but Chaudry stepped between them, her badge still clutched in her left hand.

"You touch him and it's interfering with a Bureau investigation," she hissed. "Mandatory five years in federal prison. Is that what you want?"

Wells froze. Garrett loved that; he could get used to having an FBI agent bodyguard.

"Do you realize the current situation? The danger we face? What possible thing do you people want me to do?" Wells asked.

"Shut down your bank. From A to Z," Garrett said. "Every last employee, every terminal, every trade. Tell them to go home. Tell them to stop work. Shut it down. Close the doors until the moment passes."

Wells blinked in astonishment. "Have you lost your mind?"

"It's that or be known as the CEO who crashed the American economy."

The other executives in the room were mute, staring wide-eyed at this confrontation.

"I can't close down an entire bank. That's not feasible." Wells's voice was at a barely controlled whisper. He loomed over Garrett, the veins on his neck popping out. "Where is this derivative from? What desk? What trader?" Wells shook his head. "You're guessing. Asking me to shut down the bank because you have no idea of the answer to those questions."

Garrett watched the vicious scowl on Wells's face, the arms pumping, the fists clenched.

"You said there was a mole in my bank, but you've looked and looked, and you can't find him. You have no idea who it might be. You want me to take the fall for you. You want Vandy frozen up to help you, but you don't really give a shit about me or my bank, or all the people who work there. You're just flailing because you don't know what's going on."

Garrett pulled out his phone, checking the time. "It's nine eighteen. Markets open in twelve minutes."

Wells jabbed a finger in Garrett's face. "There's no mole in my bank because there couldn't be a mole in my bank. We're too solid, too careful, and I know everything that's going on in this building. Every last goddamned thing!" Wells said those last words with a victorious finality, as if saying them made them true and put the entire argument to rest.

Garrett took a long breath, then reached out and gently moved Wells's pointing finger away from his face. "And that is the answer," Garrett said, dragging his feet off the conference table and pulling himself out of the chair to face

Wells. The bank CEO was bigger than Garrett, with broad shoulders and thick arms, and Garrett, for just one brief second, imagined head-butting him to the floor. Then he remembered that the last time he had head-butted someone, he'd ended up fracturing his own skull. "You know everything, control it all. You are the all-powerful CEO. Master of the universe. You're the only one who could protect a mole."

Wells stood silently, and Garrett could almost see the light blinking on in the older man's brain.

"So either the mole inside Vandy is in your office, *or it's you.*"

J effrey Thomason could remember the exact moment his disgust overwhelmed his obsession with the finance industry. He was an assistant on the desk of a Vanderbilt derivatives trader—a cruel, self-centered middle-aged man whose every other word seemed to be *motherfucker*—and Thomason had been told, for the fourth time in two hours, to get the trader another coffee from the Starbucks in the building's lobby. Thomason got a call on his cell phone while waiting in line for the coffee. His mother told him that his father had had a stroke and was in the hospital, but Thomason could only stay on the phone for a minute, because late-delivered coffee would be viewed as a termination offense, just like talking on a cell phone during work hours.

But when he handed his boss the coffee, seven minutes later, the derivatives trader didn't even bother to taste it; he uncapped the cup and tossed the coffee into Thomason's face, screaming at him in front of the entire trading floor for letting his coffee go cold. But the coffee wasn't cold; it scalded, and Thomason had to sprint to the bathroom and run cold water over his chin and neck to keep his skin from blistering.

He should have quit right then. Just walked out the door. But he needed the money, needed the job, and quite honestly, he didn't have the balls to leave. Some part of him still wanted to succeed at Vandy. But the ember of rage and humiliation had been lit, and every minute of every day it grew hotter.

His father didn't die. He was released from the hospital a week later. Thomason became more compliant, more subservient, faster and smarter. He got a raise—albeit a small one—and was transferred first to a VP's desk, and then all the way to the top, to Robert Andrew Wells Jr.'s desk on the thirty-first floor. In the two years it took him to get there, Thomason plotted his revenge. He mapped out ways to attack the company, steal from Vandy, ruin the traders on the floor. He concocted schemes and plans, but he could never quite figure out how to pull them off.

Until Ilya Markov appeared in his life.

The meeting had been online, on the darknet. It hadn't been entirely ser- endipitous, because Thomason had been searching for someone like Markov for more than a year, someone who would provide Thomason with the exper- tise and the planning, but also with the courage to actually follow through on his ideas. They felt each other out, each probing the motivations of the other, until Thomason felt fairly certain that Markov was the real deal. He'd never seen Markov or talked to him on the phone; he didn't even know Markov's real name until a few weeks ago. But he picked up that Markov was smart, brilliant even, and that he was capable of doing real damage: to the traders, to Vandy, maybe even to the world at large.

Over the course of months, Markov had helped Thomason develop a plan. Markov coached him on wooing allies to the cause, helped him set up offshore bank accounts, and even taught him rudimentary social-engineering tricks: how to steal personal data, how to guess account names and numbers, and, most important, how to appear innocent when you were in truth horrifically guilty.

There was more to Thomason's plans than just simple revenge. He felt that he was saving the world. He'd come to realize that trading houses were mirror images of Mafia families. They had godfathers (or CEOs), lieutenants (or trad- ers); they both moved commodities (drugs or stocks), both extorted money (from strip-club owners or Fortune 500 companies); they were rapacious and paranoid and convinced that the government was out to get them, which in both cases was actually true.

But the real parallel was that both mob families and trading houses were parasites latched onto the flesh of the public. They fed on the trust and integ- rity of honest, hardworking Americans, and they never looked back. No one at Vanderbilt Frink had a conscience, and Thomason could only guess that the same held true in the Gambino or Trafficante families. Both entities needed to be destroyed, for the good of the nation and humanity, of this Jeffrey Thomason was absolutely certain. Thomason could do little about the mob, so he went after Vandy.

He was not without resources. Like-minded assistants worked throughout the building—a surprising number of them. They had kowtowed to traders and analysts and vice presidents, fetched coffee and dry cleaning, worked until midnight and over the holidays, provided sexual favors if they were women or if their bosses were gay—their bosses were all men—and basically rolled over and played dead whenever told that it was important to do so. For all of this, they did not receive praise or more money or career advancement.

Thomason's main allies were Benny Barnett, the assistant to Aldous Mackenzie, the chief investment officer, on the thirty-first floor, and Matt Raillot, the assistant to the biggest derivatives broker in the building, Otto Beardsley, one floor below. Together, the three assistants worked in three of the four most powerful offices at Vandy. Only the compliance desk was left out, and that was fine, because compliance could bring the whole scheme crashing down in an instant.

What they had was access. Access to trading platforms, to accounts, to monitoring software. They had links, passwords, account names and numbers. Some they came by honestly, but most they just pilfered. With them, Thomason and his cohort could see exactly what their bosses could see. And more important, once they had those passwords and account numbers, they could move money just as quickly, just as invisibly, as their bosses could. Thomason himself couldn't trade—the CEO of a place such as Vandy did little buying and selling—but he could tell other divisions how to behave, nudge them away from watching the things that were going on right under their noses.

And so he did.

Raillot, the assistant to the chief derivatives trader, had slowly, methodically built up positions on wildly risky loan derivatives over the last two months. The algorithms that ran those derivatives were so dense, and the positions so complicated, that only a few people in the company could have figured out what the liabilities were. But Thomason had made sure no one had the chance. He'd sent a quiet e-mail to the techs at the real-time risk-analytics desk six weeks ago asking them to focus exclusively on the company's stock positions; the derivatives traders, Thomason had written—from Wells's account—were switching over to cash and standing down for a while.

Barnett, the assistant to the CIO, had then shorted a basket of smaller stocks. The trigger to cover on those stock shorts was a jump in their share price. Their share prices would move up if the derivatives Raillot had placed on those very same stocks unwound. The whole thing was a financial Rube Goldberg machine—you drop a ball down a chute over here, and it flips a switch over there, which drops a cage on a rat down below. Bing, bang, kaboom.

Or maybe, Thomason thought as he watched the Bloomberg terminal at his desk outside of Wells's mammoth corner office, this was more of a time bomb than a jerry-rigged contraption. He had sent an e-mail to his allies five minutes ago. That had lit the fuse. The first explosion would hit in another five minutes, when the clock hit 9:31 a.m., one minute after the market opened, the execute time on the first set of derivatives coming due. Money would be owed. Not a lot of money, at least not in Vandy terms, but enough—$42 million.

A handful of other derivatives had been linked to that first one, each with a payout ratio of one hundred to one. Each of those other derivatives was valued in the $100 million range, and each was signed with counterparties at other large trading firms. Firms that were blood enemies of Vanderbilt Frink, that had signed on to those deals without a second's hesitation. At a hundred to one, each derivative was a liability in the $10 billion range. And there were a dozen of them.

And that was just the beginning.

The fallout from all the trades would put Vandy in a hole so deep, and put it in that hole so fast, that by 10:30 a.m. the bank would be unable to meet its obligations. Vandy would seize up. News of the potential collapse would hit the nation's TVs, and every single depositor across the country would race to withdraw their money from Vanderbilt Frink. Given how skittish Americans had become about their financial system in the last twenty-four hours, this bank run would be unlike any ever seen before.

It would be Armageddon by sunset.

Thomason closed his eyes to relish the moment, listening to the buzz of phones and the low chatter of people coming in and out of the secured hallways. He checked his watch: 9:28 a.m. Two minutes until the markets opened. All the bank's senior management were on the tenth floor, meeting with Wells in the conference room. That was good; they were out of the way. Now Thomason needed to grab all his papers, erase everything on his computer, then head to the airport and grab the flight that Ilya Markov had set up for him. Thomason, like Edward Snowden before him, was going to flee the country before the shit hit the fan. Markov had secured a place for him and his coconspirators in Caracas, with visas in place and temporary apartments in their names.

Did Thomason really want to spend the rest of his days in Venezuela? No, he did not. But a considerable amount of money would be waiting for him when he got there, and once the heat died down, he figured he could go to any number of exotic countries and lead the kind of leisurely existence that he'd been preparing for all his life. Yes, this path was a shortcut to riches and fame, but it was a path nonetheless.

He checked his terminal again, to see if anything big had hit the news wires, then started to send a final e-mail to Raillot at the derivatives desk, to make sure that all the other triggers were about to go off as well. Markov had told him that there would be a spectacular bit of business first thing this morning, something that would send a shock wave through a particular stock, but Thomason didn't know what that bit of business—or that stock—was. He didn't really care—he just wanted enough time to catch a cab to JFK.

And then, like a light going out, his computer froze. Just stopped dead. No e-mails going out, no new screens coming up if he clicked them. He checked his Bloomberg terminal, and it too had stopped. The scroll was dead, his news RSS had locked up, and the tiny video feed in the corner was stalled on a frame of Maria Bartiromo's open mouth.

Thomason stood up, surprised, and walked quickly to Jessica Bortles's desk a few feet away. Bortles was prim and upright and still very much on board with the Vandy lifestyle, but she was a tech geek through and through, and if anyone had an explanation for what was going on, it would be her.

"Hey, your computer working?" he asked, trying to sound casual. The minutes were now ticking down to his flight and escape from the country.

Bortles looked up at Thomason, and he immediately sensed hostility. There was a coldness, a distance, in her eyes, and the way she pressed her lips together had a sealed, grim quality. She forced a smile, but it was tepid at best. "You didn't get the e-mail?" She adjusted her glasses on the bridge of her nose.

"No. What e-mail?"

Bortles stood up, gathering her purse from the back of her chair. "I think there's a bit of a problem." She blocked the door from the office suite to the hallway with her tiny body. "And you're apparently part of it."

They stopped first at the IT desk. Wells led the way, cursing as he went, and Garrett followed, with Chaudry at his side. The geeks in IT had never before been blessed with the physical presence of the company's CEO in their offices. A few of them had never actually seen Wells in the flesh; one didn't even know that he was the head of the company.

"Shut down the entire system," Wells said, marching past the cubicles of computer screens to the IT director's cluttered office. "Do it now."

Gutierrez, the head of IT, a dowdy woman of maybe thirty-five, couldn't wrap her head around shutting down information systems to the entire building, but when Wells leaned over her desk and barked six inches from her glasses, his white, bubbled spit spotting her lenses, she squeaked that she would do her best.

"We could shut down electricity to the building, I guess. Maybe," Gutierrez said.

Garrett felt bad for her. "You've got to have a main Internet trunk line coming in, right?"

"We do," Gutierrez said. Garrett thought she might burst into tears.

"Pull the plug on that. Just cut it off."

"I'm not sure we can."

Garrett turned his palms upward with a grin. "Come on, be creative. It's fun." He looked out her door to the IT geeks beginning to cluster around a single desk. "Tell your team to shut down the e-mail system first. Then cut off the Bloomberg feed. I know that can be done, because it goes down in my office once a week. Then go floor by floor. Isolate all the trading desks one by one."

They marched out of her office before she could reply, with Wells again taking the lead and charging to the elevators. He had called up to Bortles on the thirty-first floor five minutes earlier—he said he trusted her with his life—and told her to keep everyone at his or her seat. No one leaves.

Garrett said he thought that was a bad idea, but Wells, once he'd decided to go through with Garrett's plan, had taken over and would not be dissuaded from leading.

"It's what I do," he yelled at Garrett. "My company."

When they arrived on the thirty-first floor, a half dozen employees were huddled around a woman lying on the floor, her nose bloodied and her glasses smashed.

"What happened?" Wells asked as he knelt beside Jessica Bortles, propping up her head.

"I tried to stop him," she said between tears. "But he twisted my arm and then punched me in the face."

"Son of a bitch," Wells said.

Garrett looked around the office. A hallway led to a bank of elevators, and beyond that another set of executive-office suites. Garrett pointed. "What's down there?"

"CFO offices. VPs and public relations," Wells said.

Garrett shook his head. Thomason wouldn't have gone that way. But where would he go? Down, to the lobby? Garrett dialed Mitty. She answered immediately.

"Anyone left the building?"

"Nobody. And some of these bitches are pissed about it."

"Keep holding them." Garrett hung up.

Chaudry moved to his shoulder. "The side exits?"

"Alexis and Patmore would have called. And nobody's getting past them."

Chaudry and Garrett stood there, trying to puzzle out Thomason's whereabouts. Chaudry frowned and looked at Garrett, and Garrett suspected she had come to the same conclusion as he had. "The roof?" she asked.

As they ran up the stairs to the thirty-fourth floor, they could hear an alarm blaring, and two flights later, they found the door to the roof banging in the breeze, open, the warning Klaxon screaming. Garrett charged out first. Thirty-five stories above the city, the wind and the sound of the Klaxon blended into a low rumble. Garrett's eyes swept across the cluttered rooftop. A pair of steel huts, cooling fans, and vents that blew air into the sky all surrounded a raised helipad in the center of the roof. Garrett clattered up a flight of stairs to the top of the helipad.

Jeffrey Thomason stood at the far end of the platform, staring off at the distant horizon. The rooftop offered an unobstructed view over the East River and into Queens. The building wasn't high enough to allow a view past the boroughs, but a large swath of low-slung apartments, factories, and elevated highways was visible leading off into the distance. An intricate dance of jets and helicopters angled across the sky, and Thomason seemed to be staring at them.

Garrett slowed as he crossed the landing area. "Hey," he shouted, as Chaudry ran up behind him. "You Jeffrey?"

Thomason turned. His face was drained of life, pale and white. His eyes looked watery, as if he'd been crying. "Who are you?"

"FBI, Special Agent Jayanti Chaudry," Chaudry yelled. "You'll need to put your hands above your head." She flashed her badge—it seemed to Garrett that she did that a lot—then pulled her gun from her shoulder holster.

"No," Thomason said without further explanation. He stepped backward toward the edge of the landing pad. "No, I don't."

"Where's Ilya Markov?" Garrett asked.

"No idea." Thomason took another step back.

"Hands above your head," Chaudry yelled, moving quickly across the tarmac. Without warning, Thomason stepped off the helipad, jumping to the roof below. Chaudry and Garrett ran to the edge of the pad and watched as Thomason, limping from the fall, stumbled to the edge of the rooftop. A steel-wire barrier, about five feet high and strung with lines of wrapped wire, guarded the edge of the roof. Without hesitation, Thomason slotted his shoes onto the wires and climbed the fence, stopping to balance on the second-to-highest wire. With one lean forward, he would go over the edge and tumble thirty-five floors down.

Garrett leaped off the landing pad and ran toward Thomason. "Don't," he said, trying not to yell. "Don't do this. Totally unnecessary."

Thomason turned his body slightly to see Garrett, then put up a single hand to signal that Garrett should stop where he was. "Why not? You have a better option?"

Garrett started to say yes, that there was a better option, but he tripped on his own words. He couldn't, at that moment, think of what to say. Was there a way forward for Thomason? Garrett didn't suppose that there was. Thomason was looking at a long stint in jail, endless poverty, national disgrace.

"I think"—Garrett tried to muster a coherent sentence—"I think there's no need to throw everything—"

Before Garrett could finish his sentence, Thomason leaned hard over the top wire, his upper body slipping over the edge. His shoes unhooked from the wires below his ankles, and he tumbled down, his head briefly banging on the top corner of the building. His feet flew out over his head, putting him into a somersault, and he dropped off into space without a sound.

The first thing Alexis heard was a shout—not a scream exactly, but more a strangled cry of horror. The sound came from a knot of people that had gathered on Forty-Sixth Street, on the south side of the Vandy building, not thirty yards from where she was standing. Alexis had been guarding the building's two exit doors, making sure no one fled down the stairs and onto the street. There'd been no activity, nothing out of the ordinary, until that cry, and the small crowd of people huddled around the thing on the ground that Alexis could not yet see.

She started toward them, abandoning her watch on the doors, a dread growing inside her with every step. A middle-aged man turned away, his hand to his mouth, gagging as he staggered down the street.

Alexis slowed. "What is it?" she called out.

No one answered. Another woman turned away and retched.

Alexis held her breath and pushed through the small crowd. Lying faceup on the pavement was a young man in a suit. His eyes were open, his mouth too, with a smattering of blood around his head. That was horrible enough, but the way in which his arms and legs were twisted in impossible angles made Alexis unsteady on her feet; his right arm was bent backward behind his torso, and his right leg was cocked back under his left, as if he were a rag doll lying discarded on a playroom floor. Looking at him, Alexis could almost feel the impact of his fall in her own bones; it was as if she herself had hit the pavement, body crushed in an instant. No human should ever look like that. She became light-headed.

Alexis had seen death before, many times, in Iraq: bodies blown to pieces, servicemen shot by snipers, civilians burned in their homes. But she had steeled herself for those sights; she had known they were coming—had known it from the moment she set foot on the tarmac at Baghdad International Airport. This was different. This was not supposed to happen. This was a bolt from the blue.

"He fell off that building," a man said. "I saw him land." Alexis thought she heard a hint of ghoulish pride in his voice.

"He didn't fall," an older woman said. "He jumped. Nobody falls off a building. Not in a suit."

Alexis knelt beside the body. She took the young man's broken arm in her hands and checked for a pulse at his wrist. She wasn't sure why she was doing it—the man was obviously dead—but she'd been trained in the army to always check for signs of life, and so she did it by rote. She counted silently to ten, but there was nothing, and then his fingers flinched slightly, a postmortem nervous-system response, and Alexis's stomach did a flip. She dropped his arm and stepped away from the crowd, moving quickly to the edge of the sidewalk, gasping for breath. She leaned against a car, afraid she might faint. Someone approached her from behind and asked if she was okay.

"Yeah, I'm fine," Alexis said. "Thank you."

A young woman took her by the hand. She was slight, with thick black hair and a tattoo on her arm. "Just take a deep breath. You'll be okay. You need some air." She led Alexis away from the crowd of gawkers and the twisted remains of what had once been a living person.

Alexis nodded, grateful for the human contact. "It's so awful."

"It is." The young woman ushered Alexis off the sidewalk and onto the black pavement of Forty-Sixth Street. "Just awful. Why would someone do that?"

Alexis shook her head. "I don't know." She blinked in the morning sun.

"Come this way."

Alexis, head still fuzzy, followed the woman down the block. But then something occurred to Alexis: Why was this woman leading her into the street? Alexis stopped walking. "What are you doing?"

"It's okay. You can trust me." Alexis stared at her. The young woman smiled. "You're Alexis, right?"

Alexis froze with a jolt of sudden fear. She started to turn away, wanting to run, but pain exploded at the back of her head. She knew immediately that it was a blow from something hard, a gun maybe, and she tried to yell, but couldn't produce any sound. The city spun around her, and the young woman and somebody else—a man, Alexis thought, with rough hands—dragged her a quick few steps to the open back door of a car. Had the man hit her, and where had he come from? How could she have missed him? They shoved her inside the car as she tried to regain the use of her arms, the pain spiraling outward from her brain, making black spots explode in the periphery of her vision, and then she heard the door close and an engine rumble and the world went dark as something was thrown over her head. It felt like an old blanket, crusted on her skin, and it stank of rotting food.

"Move and I'll shoot you," the young woman said. Alexis could feel the woman sitting next to her on the backseat of the car. "You dying is no big deal." She yanked Alexis's hands behind her back and then bound them with wire that cut into Alexis's wrists. Her phone and wallet were quickly stripped from her pockets.

Alexis lay motionless, wishing the pain in her head would subside and trying to gather her thoughts. She quickly understood that she'd been tricked, conned by Ilya Markov and whomever he had working with him, and a wave of guilt and remorse washed over her. Had he been watching her the entire time, maybe from a car parked on Forty-Sixth Street, waiting for the moment to strike? As the ache in her skull morphed into a throbbing pain that reached down into her neck and back, she decided that he had, and that while she was a good soldier, and a perceptive intelligence officer, she was no match for an experienced con man. A con man was always on the lookout for distractions, mistakes, and weakness. Markov couldn't have predicted that someone would jump from the building, but when he saw it happen, he'd made immediate use of the situation.

He had made Alexis his victim.

She lay there for what felt like hours, but was probably only minutes. She could hear traffic all around her, the honking of horns, and then a low, constant roar that made her think they were driving through a tunnel. She guessed that they were leaving Manhattan, going into New Jersey, perhaps, although her knowledge of the geography of the city was limited. Once they left the tunnel, given enough time, they could be anywhere. She supposed that was the point—nobody would figure out where they were headed.

She groaned with the realization that she no longer had any control of the situation. She was Ilya Markov's hostage, and he could do with her as he pleased—a nightmare scenario for her. A bleak despair invaded her thoughts: all she could do was hope that he wasn't going to kill her, and that if he did, he would be quick about it. She did not want to see it coming.

That seemed like a reasonable last request.

G arrett sat on the rough tar-pebble roof, legs crossed under him, and felt the morning sun on his face. One of the steel huts protected him from the wind, but he could hear it rushing along the rooftop and over the air-conditioning fans that hummed behind him. Chaudry stood on a far corner, talking on her cell phone, while a half dozen other FBI agents looked over the rooftop, eyes peeled to the ground. What they were looking for Garrett couldn't say—and he didn't care.

Garrett sat there for an hour at least, maybe longer. He lost track of time. He felt awful, hollowed out and desperate. Watching Thomason go over the edge, fall all that way to his death, the slow-motion memory of it—Garrett knew it would haunt him for a long time. Maybe forever. He felt responsible. He had hunted for the man—and found him. Thomason had been guilty of a crime—a crime that was ongoing—and would have paid for it one way or the other. And yet . . .

Something nagged at Garrett. What was it? Markov was still out there, but he had been stopped, at least for the time being. *Hadn't he?*

"We grabbed two other assistants trying to leave through the lobby," Wells said as he strode across the rooftop, passing the FBI agents without even looking at them. "Jeffrey had just sent them both e-mails. One was on the derivatives desk; the other worked for my chief investment officer. Little prick infiltrated everything."

Garrett unfolded his legs and stood up. He scratched at his face and turned away from the great urban vista that lay off the edge of the building. "What did they have in the works?"

"Not sure. It will take a while to untangle. They had passwords, account access. Probably had some investment vehicles loaded into the system, ready to blow up."

"They'll still do that. Blow up, that is. If they have derivative counterparties set up out there, those contracts will still be valid. They'll still cost you money. Huge amounts of money."

Wells shook his head. "That's where you're wrong. You punched above your weight for a while, but now you're playing in a league that even you don't really understand."

Garrett scowled at Wells. He hated the man—had hated him the moment he met him, the moment they first tried to warn Wells about his own bank. He was arrogant and vain, and the fantasy of head-butting him flashed into Garrett's mind once again.

"The chairman of the Fed is on her way to New York," Wells said. "I just spoke to her. I'll meet with the other bank CEOs tonight. Whatever Thomason set up, we'll just lay to rest. Make it go away."

Garrett's jaw slackened ever so slightly. "You can't. They won't agree."

"Sure they will. We've done it before, we'll do it again. You worked a trading desk. You know the drill. When it comes right down to it, we're all on the same team. If we don't look out for each other, the whole system goes in the crapper. Certain interests are too crucial to be crippled by rules." Wells stepped away from Garrett toward the edge of the roof. He gazed out over the landscape. "The view is good, but I'd like better. I think we're going to build a bigger building. Downtown. Get a real penthouse office suite going. You know, eighty stories up. So you can see the curvature of the earth. I want that."

A pit opened in Garrett's stomach. He let out a soft, involuntary grunt.

"Come on. Don't act so surprised. That's the way the machine works. A crisis, the news media panics, the public panics, things look like they've changed, but in the end—they don't. You work on the Street, Reilly. You know the game."

Garrett closed his eyes. A train of thoughts rushed into his mind, roaring as they came. Nothing was as it seemed. For every straightforward event of the last two weeks, there was an alternative explanation that either led Garrett in an entirely different direction, or betrayed something he believed true about the world. But if that were the case . . .

"It's a sleight of hand," Garrett said aloud, not to Wells, but to himself.

"What is?"

"This. Everything. He wants something else."

"Who does?" Wells was looking annoyed, as if a fly that he couldn't manage to swat were still circling his head and ruining his mood.

"Markov."

Wells frowned at Garrett, confused, then shrugged and walked away. Garrett stared off into the distance. He didn't care what Wells thought. He could go fuck himself. Garrett's cell phone rang. He checked the number. Alexis was calling, probably to get an update. He'd left her without word down on the street.

"Hey," he answered, distracted but trying to focus. "Sorry I didn't call you earlier."

Over the line came a male voice, calm, flatly unaccented, and seemingly coming from a quiet, remote location. "Captain Truffant is fine, but she won't be forever."

Garrett took in a sharp breath. Markov. Garrett knew it without thinking.

There was a moment's silence on the other end of the line. "So listen very carefully to what I have to tell you. And then do it."

Garrett told no one that he had received a phone call from Ilya Markov. He walked off the roof without another word to Wells or Chaudry, found Mitty and Patmore downstairs in the lobby, and said he was going back to his apartment to catch up on some sleep. He asked, as an aside, if either of them had seen Alexis in the lobby or on the street, but both said they hadn't.

"Did you try calling her?" Mitty asked.

Garrett shrugged. "No. I will."

"Maybe she booked a hotel room," Patmore said. "Gonna catch some shut-eye like you."

"Yeah, maybe."

Mitty grabbed Garrett by the arm and whispered, "Is it true a dude jumped from the—"

"It's true." Garrett cut her off, brushed her hand from his arm, and walked out of the lobby.

Over the phone, Markov had told Garrett to go into the Au Bon Pain bakery on the corner of Forty-Seventh and Madison and reach under the table closest to the back bathroom. A brand-new cell phone was taped to the bottom of the table, an iPhone 6. Garrett slipped it in his pocket, then gave his two burner cell phones to the busboy, as Ilya had instructed. The busboy took them without saying a word, and Garrett watched him toss them into a garbage can behind the cash register. Garrett's new phone rang half a minute after he walked out of Au Bon Pain.

"Walk to Forty-Second and Lex." Ilya's side of the conversation had little ambient noise. "Take the five train south to the Bowling Green station. Walk to Battery Park and I'll call you again."

"Listen, I need to know—"

"Your phone has GPS tracking turned on. If you turn it off, she dies." Markov hung up.

Garrett tried to come up with an alternate plan, but couldn't think of one. The streets of the city were still tense: pedestrians were scarce, and pairs of police men and women stood on most corners. Garrett walked to Lexington and Forty-Second Street. He thought about approaching a cop, then decided against it. On the train, sitting by himself in the last car, he let his mind run through the possibilities. Clearly, Markov had found a way to abduct Alexis, but how? She was an army officer, well trained, and on the lookout for suspicious activity. She, more than anyone else, would have been alert to a stranger coming at her. And she knew what Markov looked like.

Yet he had gotten her. Undoubtedly, Garrett decided, Markov did it with another trick, an illusion or a come-on; that was his play, over and over again.

Garrett got off at the Bowling Green station and walked into Battery Park. The air was hot and damp. His gray T-shirt clung to his body. Only a handful of people strolled through the park; tourists had abandoned the city. New York was a ghost town.

His phone rang and he answered quickly.

"Sit on the bench on the near side of the Castle Clinton Monument. Don't talk to anyone, don't make a phone call. You are being watched. If you do any of those things, she dies."

"I want to talk to Alexis."

"No." Markov hung up.

Garrett cursed the air. He could see the monument in the distance, a one-story sandstone fortress. Garrett sat on a wooden bench. He let out a long breath and waited, staring straight ahead, not using his phone or looking anyone in the eye. The summer sun beat down on him. His head had begun to ache again, and he cursed himself for throwing away all his meds. He sat for half an hour, then stood up to stretch his legs, figuring that was safe, then sat again for another thirty minutes. Why was this taking so long? He sat for another hour, his skin baking in the sun, and then his phone rang. He answered immediately.

"Walk to the ferry building, get on the three-thirty ferry to Staten Island. You'll be called when you arrive. Talk to no one. If you do, she dies. You are being watched." Markov hung up without another word.

Garrett walked into the ferry building. Was he really going to do this? Shouldn't he try to find a way to call Chaudry? He suspected he should, but he also felt, instinctively, that whatever he was traveling toward was some part of the answer to this entire mystery, and that he needed to travel to it alone. The FBI and the American financial system were only a part of the answer, not the totality of it. And anyway, if he notified the police or the FBI, he calculated a pretty high probability that Alexis would end up dead.

Garrett boarded the waiting ferry and sat inside, by a window on the middle deck, then turned his body away from the window so he could see the other passengers. There weren't many: a few commuters, some families, people coming back to the island with shopping bags. No one seemed to be paying Garrett much attention. Who was watching him? Nothing was out of the ordinary in the patterns of people moving about the deck, talking on their cell phones, eating snacks, and looking out the window.

Garrett tried to keep his mind blank and open, so that he would be receptive to whatever was coming, but a steady drumbeat of anxiety was just at the periphery of his thinking. Was Alexis okay? Was she even with Markov? This was all certainly a setup, but why?

The ferry took less than half an hour to cross the bay, and Garrett disembarked into the St. George Ferry Terminal. His phone rang and he answered quickly.

"Go to the Staten Island Railway station. Don't get on the train until I call you."

The line was dead before Garrett had a chance to speak. He was hungry now and realized that he hadn't eaten since the morning. Staten Island seemed like another planet, overgrown and unkempt, slightly run-down and in need of a makeover. The streets were empty of pedestrians. The Staten Island Railway station was easy to find, located right outside the ferry terminal. He swiped his MetroCard and stood on the platform. One train left, then another, and another. Passengers got on and off, and Garrett just stood there, waiting. He watched everyone carefully, but no one seemed to be watching him.

His phone rang. "Get on this train. You'll be getting off at the Oakwood Heights station."

Garrett got on the last car. As he waited for the train to leave, he watched the other riders as they made their way to seats. The pattern seemed much the same as on the ferry: commuters, families, shoppers. But now, Garrett felt a pulse of something else around him, a slight variation in the norm. He wasn't sure what it was. Someone Markov had sent to watch him? That would make sense. When the doors closed, Garrett settled in to wait out the ride.

He watched out the window as Staten Island rushed past the train—a parade of two-story brick buildings, storefronts, and wooden houses. At first, he could see the water on the left-hand side of the train, but then the tracks cut inland, and all Garrett saw were neighborhoods stuffed with small homes and yards cluttered with toys and lawn furniture. The conductor called out for Oakwood Heights, and Garrett got off the train. On the platform, there was only a mother pushing a stroller. He waited until she cleared the station, and then his phone rang.

"Walk east on Guyon Street. Keep walking until you hit a dead end." Markov hung up immediately.

Garrett walked out of the station and surveyed the neighborhood. The sun was setting in the west. The city was growing dark, and Garrett suddenly understood that all his waiting around was simply Markov wanting the cover of darkness for whatever was about to transpire. That realization did not comfort Garrett; it scared him.

There was a liquor store across the street, lit up in white neon, and Garrett desperately wanted to stop inside and buy some food—and a beer to wash it down—but thought better of it.

He walked past block after block of small houses with economy cars and minivans parked in their driveways. He didn't like Staten Island, not because it was so awful, but because it reminded him of Long Beach, California, where he had grown up. Both places were working-class suburbs of fabulous culture capitals. Garrett guessed that the people who lived on Staten Island made the city run, but that they never got paid what they deserved for it. Janitors, bookkeepers, teachers, cops, firemen. Garrett could see this in the living rooms and kitchens that he passed, rooms filled with threadbare couches and framed prints of museum art on the wall.

After ten minutes he came to a street with a DEAD END sign. A few houses lined the street, interspersed with a stretch of vacant lots that he could just make out in the darkness. His phone rang.

"Turn left, and then take the first right. Keep walking." Markov hung up.

Garrett took a look back down the street he had just walked. It was empty, with no movement, but something was telling him that he was not alone. The sky was black. Did Markov have people all through the neighborhood? Or was this another sleight of hand?

He turned left on a street whose name he couldn't see, then right on a street called Kissam. Vacant lots lined the road. Beyond the vacant lots were stands of marsh grass, reaching over his head, eight feet tall at least. In the distance, Garrett could hear waves breaking, and the howl of the wind off the bay, and it suddenly occurred to him that he was in a neighborhood that had been devastated by Hurricane Sandy—the vacant lots, the destroyed homes, the suburban landscape being reclaimed by nature.

But why had Markov chosen this spot? In the chess game that the two of them were playing, the only advantage this spot seemed to give Markov was that it was isolated. But, Garrett thought to himself, that was a sizable advantage, especially if you were aiming to kill someone.

He walked deeper into the darkness, past more and more marsh grass, until the little light that had shown him the way at the beginning of Kissam Avenue was all but extinguished. He felt as if he were in the thick of the wilderness, even though he knew he was mere minutes from homes, sidewalks, and a train station. A jolt of terror ran down his back, making his legs tremble uncontrollably. He stopped walking, to try to shake the fear out of his nervous system, and then a voice, soft and low, broke the silence behind him.

"Hello, Garrett."

E ven though Garrett was alone and unarmed, the moment Alexis saw him her heart leapt. A man was pointing a gun at them, they were in the middle of nowhere, surrounded by trees and marsh, and help seemed a thousand miles away, but still, the sight of Garrett Reilly gave Alexis hope. And hope had been hard to come by lately.

Her head still ached from where she'd been pistol-whipped. She was tired and hungry, the muscles in her arms and shoulders cramping because her hands were still bound behind her back. She was desperately thirsty as well, partly from the heat, but also from the fear. No one had spoken to her for hours— neither the girl nor Markov—although every once in a while she'd heard Markov answer his phone and whisper something to whoever was on the other end of the line. His voice was cold and flat and gave Alexis chills.

Then Garrett showed up. She had so much to explain to him: how she'd had a moment of inattention, and how sorry she was for that, and how happy she was to see him. But not now. Later. Now she had to help him get them out of this situation.

Markov pointed a gun at Garrett's chest. "No trouble finding the place?" He sounded amused.

Alexis could see Garrett in the faint light. He shrugged his shoulders, eyes squinting, running over the features of Markov's face, then flashing to Alexis. She guessed that he could not see her in the darkness.

"There was no one watching me, was there?" Garrett asked. "You used GPS only."

"We'll leave that a mystery," Markov said.

"What do you want?"

"You haven't guessed yet?" Alexis thought she detected genuine surprise in Markov's voice. But then again, he was a master of deceit. Nothing in him was genuine.

"You want me," Garrett said.

Alexis could just barely make out Markov's head bobbing up and down. "Exactly."

Alexis didn't understand. What were they talking about?

"You want a partner."

"Don't sell us short. More than a partner. A team. A family."

Alexis could see Garrett squinting in the darkness, dawning knowledge washing over his face.

"And why would I agree to be a team with you?"

"Because of what we share. Backgrounds. Goals. Because there are very few people like us in this world, who have traveled similar paths. And when you find someone who is like you, then you reach out to them. You join with them."

Garrett appeared to think about this for a moment, then shook his head. "I find people like me to be—I don't know—really fucking annoying."

Markov laughed under his breath.

"Anyway, what do I have to gain from siding with you?" Garrett said. "I've got a good gig where I am now."

"That's a lie and we both know it. You're not happy. With your job, you don't have relationships, you lock yourself in your apartment and take a laundry list of pharmaceuticals. I think you are angry at the world, at the injustice of it, angry at how you've been treated. How your family was treated. Losing your brother. All those powerful people, all those governments and police—all collaborating to keep you down."

"Nobody's keeping me down. I do fine."

"Robert Andrew Wells made a hundred million dollars last year. He has an apartment the size of your entire building. He flies around the world in a corporate jet, goes to Davos, shows up on television. Does he deserve his life? What about the people out here, living in these homes? Little shacks that get washed away by the sea? Do they deserve what they have? Is that right? Is that justice?"

"Are we really going to have this discussion? About fairness? Here? Now?"

"Humor me."

"It's capitalism," Garrett said. "You work hard, you get paid."

Alexis struggled to read Garrett's face. He didn't sound entirely sincere. But then again, he had a gun pointed at him. The wind picked up again, whistling over the marsh grass, rattling the stalks.

"Capitalism? That's your rationale? That explains everything? Do you think they could shoot Robert Andrew Wells's brother in some godforsaken shithole like Afghanistan and then lie about it? And get away with it? Would the government do that to his family? Do you think Wells would let that happen? Is that capitalism?"

There was silence between the four of them.

"There's corruption everywhere," Garrett said. Alexis thought he sounded sad. As if what Markov was saying had struck Garrett in some meaningful way. Her mind raced. That couldn't be, could it? Was Garrett Reilly so unhappy, so alienated, that the rank blathering of a criminal con man would move him?

Markov stepped closer to Garrett. "Agreed. The world is unfair. And no one will make it fairer except people like you and me. *No one.* We have the means. We have the skills. We can take down the rich, the powerful, force governments and armies to confess what they have done. We can damage them, embarrass them, humiliate their leaders. Change the way they treat their citizens. That's not some pipe dream, Garrett. It's a reachable goal. A real battle to join. You don't just have to lash out irrationally at anyone who looks at you wrong. Get into senseless fights, self-destruct. You can focus that rage. Focus your anger and get something done. Wouldn't that feel good? To know that you were doing something meaningful with your life?"

"I do plenty with my life," Garrett said, but Alexis heard no conviction in his words.

Markov let out a low laugh. "I've done my job—I've shocked the system. I could have done more, but you stopped me, and that's the way the game is played. Fair enough. But just think for a second, Garrett, if you and I had been on the same team. We could have brought Vanderbilt Frink to its knees. And then we could have destroyed, one by one, the entire banking system. We could have raided their accounts, started bank runs, shut down the trading markets. The two of us, working together, could have watched the entire island of Manhattan burn itself to a cinder. That would have been a sight. Don't tell me you don't have destruction in your soul."

"So we destroy everything. Then what? I don't want to live in that world."

"When the time is right, we rebuild. A system that we help create, that we have a stake in." Markov's words drifted off into the night.

"You think you're a revolutionary," Garrett said. "That's what this is about?"

"*Revolutionary* is an old-fashioned term. I am a catalyst for change. The status quo would crumble eventually, whether I was there or not. That's the nature of capitalism, as you put it. I just make things happen faster." Markov waved his gun in the air. "I'm not alone, Garrett. Snowden was just the beginning. WikiLeaks? Anonymous? A drop in the bucket. There are many more, ready to join us. All over the planet."

"Then why do you need me?"

"You know the answer. But I'll say it out loud if you are feeling the need to hear it spoken." Again, Markov moved closer to Garrett, ten feet away at most. "Because very few people can do what you do. Can see beneath the noise, through the chaos, and pick out the patterns. And then manipulate the chaos to suit your needs. You change the data flow so that it works for you, not against you. That is a special talent."

Alexis watched as Garrett didn't respond. He seemed to be looking down now, as if Markov's compliments had made him uneasy.

"You are good. But not perfect. You have your flaws, problematic moments. You make mistakes," Markov said. "I could help you with those. Share secrets, make you stronger. Lend you a helping hand when you are down. That would be useful, wouldn't it? Someone to turn to in dark times, someone who understands your frustration. Your anger . . ." Garrett kept his head down as Markov continued. "We can live anywhere. Here, Russia, a beach house in Thailand, an apartment in Caracas. I have them all. We move around, we make deals with like-minded governments, and then we betray them when it suits our purposes. We are invisible, untraceable—ghosts."

"That doesn't sound like much of a life." Garrett's words were halfway between a question and a statement of fact.

"Do you think the authorities will let you have real power? Do you think they trust you? Garrett Reilly from Long Beach, California? Son of a janitor and a Mexican immigrant?"

Markov fell silent and Alexis could hear a train in the distance and the honk of a car horn.

"Don't fool yourself." Markov's words had a sudden rush of intensity, as if he were spitting them out in a rage. "There is a wall between you and them, and that wall will never be broken down, no matter how badly you want it. The people who hold real power—Wells and his helicopter, Levinson and his billions—have no interest in giving you—or me, or anyone like us—true agency in this world. You are their pawn, and in your heart you know it."

Markov fell silent, and Alexis had to admit that even she was spellbound by his diatribe. Listening to his words she thought, He's not wrong. Not entirely. Alexis had always felt that nagging seed of class doubt in the back of her mind. She came from a long line of American patriots, but they were middle class and always had been. No Truffant had ever achieved real wealth or held true power, and she knew it. She suspected her father had known it as well, a secret limitation buried in his life expectations. He never gave voice to that doubt, but he had been an army staff sergeant until the end of his days. But what if he had given voice to it? What if he had fought against the unfairness? Would she have turned out a different person?

"The Russians won't let you play with their money forever," Garrett said.

"We've been siphoning off Vanderbilt Frink trading accounts for the last two months. Dollar by dollar. They have no idea," Markov said with apparent glee. "We've actually got quite a bit of money. And more every minute. And I have the next job already lined up. Six months of election fraud for the Myanmar ruling party. Easy money. Nice beaches."

Markov stepped away from Garrett again, then held his pistol out so everyone could see it. He aimed at Garrett. "So now, a decision. Tell me whether you want to join with me."

"That's it? I just tell you I want in and we're good?"

"No," Markov answered, and Alexis's heart shuddered. That one word had a coldness, a bottomlessness, that made her afraid to her core. She thought, for a moment, of pushing away from the young woman who was holding her, of sprinting into the marsh grass and trying to lose them in the night. She started to move, but the young woman gripped her hard, jamming the gun into her side.

"Don't," the woman hissed, barely audible. "Don't even fucking try."

"What then?" Garrett asked.

Markov nodded in the darkness, and Alexis could see the silhouette of his head tilt in her direction. "She needs to go. And you need to make it happen."

"I'm not going to kill her," Garrett said.

"Of course not. We will."

Alexis caught her breath and closed her eyes.

"But you have to give the order," Markov said.

OAKWOOD BEACH, STATEN ISLAND, JUNE 25, 8:32 P.M.

To Garrett, everything Ilya Markov said made sense. That didn't make what he said right. But then again, the concept of rightness had never held much weight with Garrett; morality was a human construct, not an unalterable law of nature. *Good* and *evil* were words imbued with meaning by culture, not God. The universe didn't give a shit about right and wrong.

Could he and Markov really be a team? Traveling the world, attacking the system, breaking down the walls that separated him from power? Garrett did not believe in the system, nor did he have any faith in the people who kept the system running. He wondered lately if subversion was his true calling—if chipping away at the power structure was what he did best. He was an outsider, a second-class citizen from birth, and no one was going to change that except Garrett himself. Markov's idea of revolution was crazy—the ranting of a sociopath—and yet . . .

Rage burned in Garrett's heart as strongly as any other emotion. Markov had been exactly right about that. They were, in their own odd way, a match for each other. They were almost brothers. Almost.

"I tell you to kill her?" Garrett said, as the hot wind coming off the bay snapped him out of his reverie and back to the present.

"That's it. You say the words. Then you and I go off together."

"Where? We're on Staten Island. There's no place to run."

"I have a boat waiting. A fishing boat, loaded with fuel, captained by a young Bahamian. Just offshore. There's a Zodiac beached on the rocks. Down the path. We can reach the Bahamas in a week. Then fly to Venezuela. Prep the Myanmar job, rig the election. I even had a passport made up, with your picture on it."

Garrett marveled at Markov's preparation. Garrett had been right, thinking to himself in Battery Park, that he was marching off to confront some strange destiny, and that he had to do it alone. Was this his destiny? Was Markov his destiny?

"You're lonely," Garrett said. "That's why you're doing this."

Markov smiled. "Yes. I am. Absolutely. Very lonely. I always have been. *And so have you.*"

Garrett felt a spontaneous ache in his heart. He *was* lonely. Terribly lonely, with few friends, distant family, and no real prospects for a lasting love relationship.

"You shoot her right here, in front of me?" Garrett tried to keep the tremor out of his voice.

"You want to see it happen?"

"No."

"Uni will take her into the grass. So no one finds the body for weeks."

"How do I know you won't shoot me as well?"

Markov laughed. "I might. But then again, I could have shot you ten minutes ago. But I don't want to particularly. I like you, Garrett. I wouldn't have gone to these lengths if I didn't want this to work."

Garrett could see Markov smiling in the dim light. "I have one more thing to tell you. Perhaps this will help you make up your mind. Your friend here, Captain Truffant, no longer works for the Defense Intelligence Agency."

Garrett looked from Markov to Alexis. "What do you mean?"

"She is no more a defense analyst for DIA than I am a bond trader. She works for Homeland Security. She didn't tell you because she wanted you to keep on my trail."

Garrett struggled with this information. It made no sense, yet it made perfect sense. It explained her interest in a case that had nothing to do with her job description. He looked to Alexis, mouth sagging slightly open. "Is that true?"

"He's lying," Alexis said.

"She has doubled up agency work for the last six months," Markov said. "I have the e-mails. I can show them to you if you'd like. It's all spelled out very clearly."

Garrett stepped toward Alexis. "It's true, isn't it?"

"What does it matter? Who cares what agency I'm working for?" Alexis spit out the words. "He's a con man and a terrorist and he's lying to you about everything else, and you can't listen to him, Garrett. He is tricking you. He has an alternative reason for everything. If you leave with him now, you won't make it twenty-four hours before he shoots you and dumps your body in the ocean."

"Why?" Garrett asked. "Why didn't you tell me?"

Garrett could see her face contort in the night, her mouth cracking at the edges. She let out a short sob, then seemed to swallow back her tears. "Why do you need to know any of it?"

"Because I used to love you."

Alexis hung her head. She whispered, "It doesn't make any difference."

"I think it does. So do you."

She had no answer, and Garrett wasn't surprised. Alexis had always been ambitious, and working for another agency dovetailed with his understanding of her career—that it was stalled out at DIA, that she needed new avenues for advancement.

"Well?" Markov asked. "Your decision?"

Garrett stood motionless and tried to ignore the pounding of his heart.

He thought he might be able to take Markov right there, grab at his gun hand and shove him to the ground, hit him hard, again and again, and take the pistol away before the girl shot Alexis, but it didn't seem likely. He wasn't a cop; he wasn't Agent Chaudry. He was a computer geek. His best chance of survival, as he calculated it, was to trust in his instincts. To trust in the thing that Markov needed from him: an ability to see the world as it was, not as you wanted to see it. *To see what was invisible to everyone else.* Because that, in the end, was the one thing that Garrett could do, the thing that made him special.

He looked out into the darkness and listened to the sounds of the night. He tried to think back on his subway ride downtown, then the ferry across the bay, and the train and his walk to this isolated marsh. He had sensed a pattern, something just beyond his seeing, waiting out there for him to grasp it. But was it real? Could he trust himself to know for sure? If he stalled just a while longer, perhaps it would all come clear to him. Or perhaps nothing in his life would ever become clearer than it was at this very moment, and that was his fate—to want certainty, and to never get it. Life was entropy and then chaos.

Garrett took a breath and nodded. "Okay. Kill her."

Alexis let out a shriek, a howl of abandonment, and Garrett had to squeeze his hands into fists to keep from jumping out of his skin. He clenched his teeth, then waved an arm in the air, pointing back toward the houses and the lights. "Over there." He put on a show of not wanting the thing done where he could see it. "Do it over there."

"Don't worry." Markov put a hand on Garrett's shoulder and ushered him down the cracked pavement of the abandoned road. Garrett shot a look back over his shoulder and caught a glimpse of the young woman shoving Alexis in the other direction, toward the city, but sideways, into the marsh grass.

Good Lord he hoped he was right—that all those drugs and all that pain hadn't permanently clouded his abilities.

"Is she coming with us? The girl?" Garrett asked Markov, trying to make conversation.

"Do you want her to? She's quite smart. And good in bed. I think you would like her."

"Seems like we'll have the pick of the litter, so why bother?"

"Then she stays here, and we go off on our own. Whatever you want, Garrett. However you want it."

Garrett looked over at Markov. He was a shadow in the night, nothing more. Garrett still could not see his face. Perhaps he wasn't real at all, Garrett thought. Perhaps he was an eternal shadow, an ethereal presence in the night, appearing and disappearing at will. A ghost, a hallucination like Avery Bernstein, a dead man who was fucking with Garrett's unsteady sense of reality. If so, then he had made a mistake, and Alexis would die. And he would want to die soon thereafter.

"You still don't trust me; I see it," Markov said.

"Why should I?"

"Exactly. Why should you? I wouldn't expect it. We need time. And shared experiences to bond us. I mean, really, isn't that the anchor of all relationships?"

Was Markov teasing him? Garrett could no longer tell. A scream pierced the stillness, followed by the sharp crack of two gunshots, one after the other. The sound echoed for a moment, then was carried away on the wind. Garrett shivered, listening for some aftermath of the violence, but there was none.

Markov slapped him on the back. "*Pozdravlyaem!* Congratulations. Welcome to the team."

Garrett swallowed hard to keep from throwing up. He listened as the wind died for a moment, and the sounds of the marsh and the city rose to his ears. He heard . . .

Nothing. No birds, no animals in the grass. Nothing.

He smiled.

He turned to Markov. "You're finished."

Markov tilted his head to one side, the way dogs do when they can't quite make out the source of a sound.

"It's over. Put the gun away. Or maybe take your own life. Quickly. Before you're arrested."

Markov stepped at Garrett, gun held high. "What are you talking about?"

"Listen." Markov stopped and listened. Again there was silence. "Where's the girl? Why isn't she coming?"

Markov craned his head to look back at the marsh. Garrett could just begin to make out his face in the glow of the city across the bay. He was plain looking, much like his passport photograph, but with a hint of emotion as well. Perhaps it was just the moment, the rush of trying to figure out exactly what Garrett was talking about. Or perhaps Garrett was projecting his own feelings.

"Your girl is dead. Think about it. Two shots. Why would she shoot twice? She wouldn't. She'd fire once to the head. Doesn't fit the pattern. The FBI got her. They shoot twice, a double tap. The silence. Doesn't fit either. The birds, the crickets—they're spooked. The police are all around us. In the weeds. Hiding. Waiting to take you down. They followed me here, right from the very beginning. They were on the train, on the ferry, behind me on the street. You never had anyone following me, but they did. Too clever on your part. You made a mistake. A blunder. A big one."

Markov let out a grunt. Just as when a chess player accepts a gambit—only to realize he's been tricked by his opponent—the full weight of the situation was dawning on Markov with ineluctable force.

"I'll kill you." Markov pointed the gun's barrel right at Garrett's face.

"Okay," Garrett said, a calm settling on him. He was ready to die. He didn't want to die, but if he had to, this was as good a time as any. Alexis was safe, the city would not burn to the ground, and his paranoid theories had been proven right. At least he wouldn't have to suffer through the headaches anymore. "Just get it over with."

And with those words, four gunshots exploded in the night.

Pain. Numbness and then weakness. And more pain.

Ilya Markov knew he'd been shot. He was probably dying.

He tried to squeeze off a shot at Garrett Reilly, but his arm felt horrifically heavy. It drooped toward the ground, and he heard another shot and felt his shoulder twist.

He fell to his knees. Shit, he thought, I am certainly dying.

He heard shouting all around him and saw the sudden glare of flashlights. Men running, women too, coming from everywhere out of the marsh grass.

God, how had he missed it? How could he not have realized? The gambit, he understood now, had been too great. The risk too large. Once the con at Vandy failed, he should simply have fled the city. But he had wanted to make contact with Reilly. He had wanted to bring the man onto his side. He honestly wanted that, and in wanting that—in wanting Reilly—he had made a mistake. A terrible mistake. Emotion was weakness. And most people—even Garrett Reilly—were just not ready to see the world as it truly was, full up with corruption and treachery and betrayal. The universe was a blank slate onto which only the most disciplined and powerful could imprint their desires. Only he could see what was real.

Someone shoved him to the ground, then kicked the gun from his hand and pinned his arms behind his back. He suspected that he was being handcuffed, but he didn't know why. He was dying, after all—didn't they see that?

A pang of loss filled his brain, as well as the panic that he, Ilya Markov, man of many names and no country—no home—was about to be no more. He would cease to exist, the horror of all horrors, and would then embrace the void. And with his passing, no legacy would be left behind. He had seen to it that he was invisible, and now in death he would remain so—a ghost passing quietly to the other side. He felt horrible sadness in that, but also a strange feeling of completion. As an end point to his life path, that made sense.

He turned his head slightly, but the effort was enormous. He felt terribly weak. His thoughts were growing confused. There were memories. Chechnya. Grozny. Palo Alto, for some reason. A moment of tenderness with Uni. A kiss. Closeness. And then words. A blanket of calm. He looked up from the ground and could see Reilly kneeling at his side, looking into his eyes. Was this the last person he would see?

He supposed it was.

"Are you okay?" Agent Chaudry jogged up to Garrett and shone a flashlight in his face.

"I'm fine." Garrett squinted in the light. He looked down at Markov's body, handcuffed, lifeless, lying in the dirt. "Is he dead?"

Chaudry knelt at Markov's body and checked the pulse at his neck. "Yes."

Garrett tried to sort through his feelings. Was he glad Markov was dead? Absolutely. But did some part of him feel remorse?

"Where's Alexis?"

"Back toward the street." Chaudry pointed down the road. "But I don't think she wants to talk to you."

Garrett stood up and rushed past Chaudry. A dozen FBI agents were combing through the marsh grass, and Garrett ran quickly past them, toward a clearing at the end of the road, where cop cars, ambulances, and unmarked vans were pulling up and unloading officers, EMTs, and crime techs. The darkened wilderness had blossomed into a melee of law enforcement activity.

Garrett stopped a beefy cop in a blue Windbreaker. "There was a woman. In an army uniform."

The cop pointed back toward the street. "In the last cruiser."

Garrett ran past the first four cop cars and stopped at the last one parked in the roadway. Alexis was sitting up front, in the passenger seat. A female cop was behind the wheel. The engine was idling.

Garrett reached out to tap on the window, but Alexis rolled it down without looking at him. Her eyes were ringed with black. Garrett guessed it was from running mascara. She was clutching a plastic water bottle to her chest as if it were a teddy bear.

"Tell me you knew," she said, still not looking at him. "Tell me you were certain there were cops all around us, listening, waiting to save me."

Garrett hesitated. Had he known? Had he known for certain? He'd asked himself these same questions before he'd given the order to Ilya Markov—the order to shoot Alexis. Can anyone ever know anything for certain?

He took a long breath, the cooler air from the bay blowing against his sweat-soaked T-shirt. "I didn't know. Not for sure. But there was a pattern. Probabilities. I felt them building. . . . But was I certain?"

She turned to look at him, hurt in her eyes. There was truth, and then there were lies. There was reality, and then there was the veil that everyone knowingly pulled down around their eyes to make life more bearable. Once upon a time, Garrett believed you could believe in all of those things simultaneously. *But not now.*

"No," he said. "I wasn't certain."

Alexis rolled up the window without another word and the police car drove off.

Belarus State Security officer Nagi Ulyanin waited patiently in line behind the two old women chattering at each other in Russian. Older people still spoke Russian; the youth of his country, they spoke their true native language—Belarusian—every day, all the time. Ulyanin was proud of that, and scornful of the babushkas in front of him. Yet, he thought to himself, he was glad they were voting. That was the point, after all—*everyone* casts his or her ballot in a democracy.

Ulyanin was filled with an almost inexpressible joy. Belarus was on the verge of becoming a Western-style country now. Election Day had come at last, the people were voting, and maybe, just maybe, new leadership would emerge from the carnage. And Ulyanin had helped in the transformation. He had worked from the inside of the state police apparatus, a subversive chipping away at the forces of oppression.

Ulyanin smiled. That old bastard Bazanov had never suspected a thing. Every time he'd called in troops, or more firepower or riot police, Ulyanin had seen to it that the worst companies, under the most incompetent officers, were brought to the scene. And if, God forbid, trained soldiers with true expertise made it to the front lines of the protests, Ulyanin and his fellow fifth columnists inside the secret police made sure they were badly equipped—the worst rifles, old ammunition, tanks with no fuel. He'd even mixed up orders and schedules, guaranteeing that the police arrived too late to make a dent in the protests or, worse, that their arrival time was well-known to the radicals on the other side of the barricades. A hail of bullets was always in store for the government forces.

Ulyanin glowed with a quiet satisfaction. The process had not been easy, or without personal danger, but it had been worth it. He wondered about Bazanov, that growling, bald Russian son of a bitch. He had chafed under Bazanov's rule, every single day, the humorless prick scolding Ulyanin for his incompetence or his lack of courage, cursing the backward Belarusian people and their miserable capital, Minsk. He had heard rumors, through the intelligence grapevine, that Bazanov had gone to New York City. That seemed too far-fetched to be believed, yet the gossip had been persistent. There was even a report that he'd been murdered, but Ulyanin discounted that as preposterous.

What in the world was Bazanov doing in New York City? Ulyanin had seen him in Independence Square, in Minsk, only a few days ago. Had he just picked up and moved his operation to the United States? And why? Spelnikov, a fellow subversive in the state police, had said he'd heard that Bazanov had something to do with the financial craziness in America. That it had been one of his dirty tricks, like hijacking a TV station or busing in gangsters to intimidate voters.

"On a slightly bigger scale," Ulyanin had told Spelnikov, laughing. "Hijacking the American economy is harder than paying a busload of thugs to vote in local elections."

"I hear what I hear," Spelnikov had said, and gone back to obsessively rolling his stinking clove cigarettes.

Maybe Bazanov had been behind that thing in America. Ulyanin wouldn't put it past him, or the SVR. The Russian president and his Kremlin mobsters were a crazy bunch. They would do anything if they thought it would make them money—or rid them of enemies. But what would the connection be between Belarus and New York City? Ulyanin didn't think there was any, although he had seen newspaper articles yesterday admonishing voters not to choose the uncertainty of Western free-market capitalism over the solidity of Mother Russia.

The two babushkas picked up their ballots, grabbed pens, and walked to the table where you marked your selections. That everyone else could see whom you voted for was disturbing to Ulyanin, but at least it was actual voting. Progress was being made.

Ulyanin gave his name to the pretty young election official. She looked it up, checked it off on her roll book, then gave him a ballot and a pen. "Please return the pen when you are done."

"Of course." Ulyanin moved to the table to fill in the ballot. He made his marks quickly, voting for Anna Shushkevich, the young reform candidate, and the other National Reform Party candidates on her slate. He peeked up when he was done, checking to see whom everyone else at his table had voted for. The two babushkas had marked down Lukashenko, their disgraced dictator of a leader. Ulyanin's stomach dropped slightly, but then he reminded himself that change rarely came from the older generation. Lukashenko would not win— Ulyanin was sure of this: the past could not hold back the future.

He dropped his ballot into the sealed ballot box, then gave his pen back to the pretty election official. "Thank you for all your hard work," he told her, and she smiled happily at him.

He stepped outside the union hall where the voting was taking place, breathing in deep of the summer's morning. Rain clouds were moving off to the east, revealing a glorious morning sun. The day was warm and clean and new. He walked down Vawpshasava Avenue, as cars and trucks rumbled past, and Ulyanin decided that he would take the rest of the day off. He would walk to the park, Aziarysca, and sit under a tree and enjoy life.

As he strolled along, he passed a strange-looking man, thin, very thin, with a hard, pinched face. He wore a slick black suit, even in the heat, a bit like the mobsters of Moscow used to favor. Ulyanin thought nothing of him, smiled, and kept walking, but the man's face stuck in his memory. Had he seen him before? Did he have something to do with Bazanov?

"Comrade Ulyanin," someone called out to him in Russian.

Ulyanin stopped, surprised, then turned to see who was hailing him. The thin man in the slick suit had changed direction and was striding quickly toward him, only now he was trailed by two enormous men in black T-shirts, their muscles bulging under their tight sleeves. A shock wave of fear ran the entire length of Ulyanin's body, and in a flash of insight he saw his future laid before him: a trip in a car to a deserted forest, a beating, a lecture, more beatings, and then a bullet to the head.

"We need to talk." The thin man waved his bony hand at Ulyanin. "Come take a ride with us."

Ulyanin jerked backward, away from this ghastly creature, but the goons following him were too quick. They surrounded Ulyanin and held him by the shoulder. Suddenly a car was pulling up at the curb, a black Mercedes, and the back door was popping open. Ulyanin grimaced. There was nothing for it now. He was doomed. *Damn it.* The day had been so glorious. He struggled to free himself from the grip of the musclemen, but they were too strong. Ulyanin wanted to cry. But, no, he would not. He craned his head toward the bone-thin Russian man in a suit.

"You cannot hold back the future!" Ulyanin shouted.

The thin man shrugged, uncaring. "Perhaps not. But we can try."

Garrett watched the city below through the wide bank of windows at Jenkins & Altshuler and marveled at how rapidly life had gone back to normal; stores were open, banks were solvent, the stock market hadn't crashed. The American dollar had stabilized. The press had taken to calling it the Midsummer Madness, and only two weeks after it had happened, people seemed to have already forgotten the entire event. The panic and chaos seemed like a distant fever dream: no one was sure it had actually taken place. Perhaps it had been imaginary—a mass hallucination.

Garrett wasn't sure himself. At times the memory of it seemed like a nightmare, a drug-fueled episode stoked by his own raging paranoia. Perhaps Ilya Markov was a figment of his imagination—a tale he told himself to feel important. To feel needed. To feel loved.

Or maybe not.

Garrett had gone back to work a few days after the incident in the marshes of Staten Island. The other traders at J&A had given him a few odd glances, but only one had had the nerve to ask him what had happened, and where he'd been. Garrett explained that he'd been wrongly accused of the murder of Phillip Steinkamp, and that everything had been sorted out with law enforcement, but more than that he couldn't really say: "Classified."

He kept buying and selling bonds, and he found that he did it with better results than before Ilya Markov had showed up in his life. He attributed this to quitting his painkiller habit, but he also suspected that the incident had given him a new perspective on his life. Maybe he didn't have it so bad after all. He was one of the lucky ones. And yet . . .

Markov's words popped into his head at odd moments: just before he fell asleep, or when he was trying to calculate the discounted present value of a corporate junk bond. Was he, Garrett Reilly, going to be happy doing this for the rest of his life, working inside the great capitalist finance machine? Would he forever be an outsider, face pressed up against the glass, no matter how much money he made? Perhaps he was supposed to live a different life—a life of rebellion, outside the rules, bringing change, forcing governments and the privileged to account for their actions and their crimes.

Perhaps he was wasting his time at J&A. Perhaps he had missed his true calling. The possibility haunted him.

No matter how hard he had looked in the past two weeks, he'd found nothing online or in the news about bad trades or highly leveraged derivatives coming from Vanderbilt Frink's trading desk. Nothing. Wells had been right that day on the roof—it would all get covered up, and no one would be the wiser.

Garrett had found a few news items that intrigued him, though. The day after Markov had been shot, a financial blogger wrote about a rumor that Robert Andrew Wells Jr. and four other banking CEOs had been seen dining together in the back room at the restaurant Daniel on Sixty-Fifth Street. They'd been joined by Caroline Hummels, the chairwoman of the Federal Reserve. No pictures were taken, and no official word had been released on any such meeting, but Garrett thought it made sense: all the counterparties to Vandy's bad bets had sat down over an '86 Château Margaux and filet mignon and agreed to let them slide. As if all those transactions, all those bets, had never happened. It was just as Wells said: the wealthy protected their own interests, and the government aided that enterprise. The wheel went round and round.

The other news item—and this one had broken big—was the suicide of Leonard Harris, congressman from suburban Georgia. Harris was the chairman of the House Banking Subcommittee, and he'd been humiliated by a sex video that had gone viral. No one could identify the woman on the video—her face had been carefully angled away from the camera—but the man was clearly Harris. And what they did was explicit. Police theorized that Harris had gone to meet the woman at a cabin in rural Virginia, potentially to have sex with her. Or maybe to kill her. But either way, the woman never showed up. Alone and broken, Harris scribbled a rambling suicide note, then turned his gun on himself.

The press posited it as an isolated case of adultery and regret, but Garrett thought otherwise. Garrett thought Harris had been taken out of the picture at the exact moment when he was most needed, when the American economy had teetered on the brink of ruin. Harris was another Ilya Markov dupe, and he had paid the price for his gullibility.

Garrett left work early, and Mitty met him at their favorite bar, McSorley's, in the East Village. The two of them drank beer and tequila shots. He told Mitty all about the night in Staten Island, and what had happened with Alexis.

Mitty, as always, was sympathetic to Garrett's side of the story. "You did what you had to do. You made the calculated decision, and it was the right one. If Alexis can't handle that, then fuck her."

"You think Markov was telling the truth about her working for Homeland Security?"

"Does it matter? She either works for military intelligence or Homeland Security. What's the difference?"

Garrett thought she had a point.

He called Oakland a few times that week and spoke to Bingo, who said he was moving out of his mother's house. He sounded excited to be looking for a new apartment. Garrett was happy for him and tried to say so without sounding patronizing.

"If you need me again," Bingo said, "you can just, you know, call."

"Will do. Stay safe." Then Garrett thought about that. "Actually, don't stay safe. Get into boatloads of trouble."

Garrett exchanged e-mails with Celeste as well. She said she was toying with leaving the Bay Area and moving to New York, maybe to get work as a translator at the United Nations. The thought of Celeste living in the same city made him exceedingly nervous, but he supposed there were enough people in New York to act as a buffer between the two of them. In a moment of weakness he offered her a place on his couch, but she declined.

Gonna stay with Mitty, she wrote. *We're sympático.*

Garrett laughed for the first time in days when he read that. Maybe running into Celeste in New York wouldn't be so terrible after all. The next evening, when he stepped out of the lobby of J&A, a black SUV pulled up to the curb. Garrett flinched when he saw it, but the passenger door popped open and Agent Chaudry climbed out.

She was smiling and looked much happier than when they had worked together. "Can I buy you dinner?"

Garrett chuckled, half at the idea that he would go to dinner with an FBI agent, and half that he had been so ready to bolt at the sight of an unmarked SUV.

Agent Murray drove, and Garrett noticed that he didn't look any happier than before. Garrett figured Chaudry must have come out of this case looking good, and Murray not so much. Murray dropped them at an Indian place on Hudson Street in Tribeca.

Agent Chaudry seemed to know the waitstaff. "Want me to order for you?"

"Always in charge." Garrett nodded.

"Life is just easier that way."

They made small talk for a few minutes, then Chaudry cut to the chase. "I want to know everything Markov offered you that night. I'd like you to try to give me the conversation you had, verbatim."

Garrett told her. He could remember every word they had said. That was one of Garrett's gifts, and he didn't hold back; he felt he had no reason to keep anything from anyone.

"Were you tempted? To go with him?" she asked when he was done, pouring Garrett another glass of wine.

"That night? No. Now? I think about it."

Chaudry looked surprised. "Go join a bunch of hacker criminals? Living in shitholes all around the world. That sounds appealing to you?"

Garrett dipped a samosa in a spicy green sauce and tasted it. The food was good, and he was hungry. "Maybe I didn't agree with how Markov did things. But his goals weren't so crazy. The power structure in this country needs a bullet to the head. You think an Indian woman from New Jersey is ever going to run the FBI?"

Chaudry gulped down a mouthful of wine and smiled. "I do, actually. And I'll give you a call when I get there."

Garrett laughed.

"Look, Markov was a con man, plain and simple," Chaudry said. "He didn't have real goals, other than money. We finally got some responses back from the Russian internal security service, and they said he'd been running computer scams for years. Just making money. He was a petty criminal. This was all part of a scheme."

"They're lying to cover up their motives. They paid him to attack the American economy and swing an election," Garrett said.

"Maybe they did. But that doesn't change the fact that Markov's goals were ambiguous at best. He was an amoral thug for hire."

Garrett considered this. "Maybe I'm amoral."

"Don't think that I haven't wondered about that."

Agent Murray picked them up and drove Garrett home, and he and Chaudry got out of the SUV at his apartment.

"One question," Garrett said, as they lingered by his front door. "Staten Island. How'd you know to follow me?"

"I didn't at first. But when both you and Alexis disappeared, that seemed strange. Not your normal pattern." She grinned at him. "You taught me well."

Garrett didn't know what to say. Why anyone would want to look at the world the way he did was a mystery.

"I put both your pictures out on the wire. Because the streets were empty, it was easy to spot you. We sent people to South Ferry. They watched you from there on in."

"Huh," Garrett grunted. That explained his uneasiness on the train, and later in the marshes. "Well, thanks."

She shook his hand, said good-bye, and drove off. Garrett went back up to his apartment and smoked a bowl of Fighting Buddha. He'd decided that he needed some kind of chemical mood enhancers to keep the demons—and the pain—away, and pot seemed harmless enough.

Still awake two hours later, he called Mitty. "Something's not right."

"Are you still obsessing about Alexis?" Mitty sounded groggy.

"Yes." He thought about this. "But more than that."

"If there's a problem, go do something about it. But stop calling me at three in the fucking morning."

G arrett caught the 11:30 a.m. shuttle to Washington, DC. At the airport, he called Alexis on her cell, but got no answer. Then he tried her office at Joint Base Anacostia–Bolling. A secretary said there was no record of Captain Alexis Truffant working for the DIA and hung up on him.

He called again, asking for General Kline, but was put on hold and the call was never answered. But he knew where Kline lived—he'd been there before—and so he rented a car and drove to a quiet neighborhood in Bethesda, Maryland, and parked in front of Kline's house and waited. Kline drove up around 6:00 p.m., saw Garrett, and walked up to his car.

"We don't speak anymore," Kline said without a hello or even an acknowledgment that Garrett was parked in front of his house. "And I can't tell you where she is. It's classified."

Garrett thought about this.

"She went out on a limb for you, Reilly. Many times. You should know that and appreciate that." A warm rain had begun to fall. Kline hiked a Windbreaker up around his collar. "I gotta get inside. Late for dinner."

"Was she working for Homeland Security the entire time?"

Kline shrugged. "We all work for Homeland Security. Whether we know it or not." He gave a half wave and disappeared into his house.

Garrett took a hotel room at a Best Western and spent half the night staring up at the mottled stucco ceiling. He sorted passwords in his head and thought about the last month of his life. He tried to replay the events of each day, the phone calls and the conversations, the drugs and the cat and mouse between himself and Markov. At four in the morning he realized what he'd been missing, and at eight he sent an e-mail to General Kline asking for a favor.

When the sun rose, Garrett drove south to Triangle, Virginia, and Marine Corps Base Quantico. He checked in with the security detail at the front entrance and was given a map of the base.

He walked into a modern, two-story brick building on the south end of the complex, found Room 207, a matériel and requisitions center, and sat down at a desk, unannounced, across from marine corporal John Patmore. Patmore was tapping on a computer, a stack of documents at his elbow. A dozen other marines, men and women, were doing much the same thing at different desks across the room.

Patmore looked up and did a double take at Garrett. "Sir. Good morning. This is a surprise."

Garrett said nothing. He just stared at Patmore. He'd thought about it for a while, but he still wasn't sure how to start the conversation.

"Is there a problem, sir?"

"You got promoted to corporal?"

"For services rendered," Patmore said, pleased. "Cool, huh?"

"I know it was you."

"I'm sorry. I'm confused. What are you talking about?"

"Markov's inside man. How he knew exactly where we were, and what we were doing. How he always stayed a step ahead of us. Our location, the credit-card name. You tipped him off. I can't believe I didn't see it earlier. I guess I was blind."

Patmore laughed quietly, then made a face somewhere between disbelief and anger. "You're barking up the wrong tree, sir. I didn't tip anybody off."

"The drugs were the tell. Only you knew I needed them. The others were just guessing. But somehow Markov knew as well. That's a coincidence, huh?"

"I don't know what you're talking about."

"Why'd you do it? Was it money? Did he transfer a chunk into some offshore account? Or did he give you a song and dance about revolution and changing the world? Look, I'm sympathetic. Honestly, I am. I considered joining him as well. I still think about it."

"Sir, I really think you're making a mistake. I didn't tip off anybody, anytime. And I need to get back to work."

Garrett watched the young marine. He was pretty good, his face sunny, his voice friendly, no matter what Garrett said. But Garrett had more. "I had General Kline pull your service record. You weren't blown up in any Humvee. You never needed prescription meds to dull the pain. You didn't even serve in Afghanistan. You told me that tale to get me to trust you. Social Engineering 101. So I'd take too many drugs. And it worked. You're a fucking con man, just like Markov, only you have a uniform."

In a flash, the genial, happy-go-lucky marine disappeared, and a dead-eyed, manipulative criminal sat in his place. Patmore's face was full of fury, tempered only by instant calculation. A second later, it was gone. But that was all Garrett needed. That was proof enough. He pushed the chair back and stood up, satisfied.

"Don't expect to go any further in the service, Corporal. Kline will put your record up for review. You're done."

"Son of a bitch."

"I wouldn't have guessed it. You, betraying us, and yet . . ." Garrett's voice softened. "You never really know people."

Garrett walked out without another word, although he half expected to have Patmore race after him and pummel him to the ground. But that didn't happen. He felt a little better as he drove north back toward Reagan National Airport. Not altogether better, but a bit. The betrayal hurt—he had put so much faith in Ascendant, in his new family, but at least he knew some truths now. At least he still had instincts left.

As the US Airways shuttle lifted off from Reagan National, and Washington, DC, receded into the distance, Garrett finally felt that he had put Ilya Markov—and that dark, dense onrushing chaos of Garrett's nightmares—in the past. He closed his eyes and slept until the plane touched the ground again in New York.

A week later, at work on a Tuesday morning, Garrett got a phone call from the office of Robert Andrew Wells Jr. at Vanderbilt Frink Trust and Guaranty. They were requesting that Mr. Reilly come to their building for a job interview. Garrett laughed and hung up on them.

Five minutes later Wells himself called. "I just want to talk. Ten minutes is all. I'll send a car for you."

A black Mercedes sedan was waiting for Garrett on the street, and he climbed in and made it to Forty-Seventh Street and Madison in twenty minutes. The guard told him to go straight to the executive offices on the thirty-first floor. Garrett rode the elevator wondering what the hell this was all about. He had to admit he was mildly intrigued. Even flattered. But he also knew that a lot of job offers were out there for him if he wanted them. He was a known commodity on the Street, and other firms had tried to poach him from J&A many times.

Wells's office was immense, with ceiling-to-floor windows that looked out onto midtown Manhattan. Wells was sitting behind a large, modern desk. No computer was on the desk, nor was any to be seen in the room. His assistant, Jessica Bortles, sat on a couch with an iPad in her hands. Garrett supposed that passed for a computer.

"Jess, give us a minute, please." Wells stood and crossed the office to greet Garrett.

Bortles gave Garrett a quick smile and left the room, closing the door behind her.

Wells reached out and offered his hand to shake. "Thanks for coming." Garrett shook his hand, even though he didn't feel like it. "Have a seat." Wells motioned to the dual leather couches.

"That's okay; I'll stand," Garrett said.

"You don't like me, do you?"

"You're an arrogant prick and you make too much money."

Wells laughed. "You're one to talk."

"I don't run the world for my own amusement."

"You think that's what I do? I don't, let me tell you. I run a bank that facilitates commerce around the globe. We grow businesses so everyday citizens can have jobs. And I work fucking hard every single day."

"So do coal miners. Get over yourself."

"You a leftist-radical bond trader now? That's a first."

Garrett moved to the window to get a better look. He loved high-altitude views of the city and took them in whenever he had the chance. Airplanes danced overhead. "What do you want?"

"To offer you a job."

"Pass."

"You don't even know what it is yet."

"Doesn't matter." Below, Garrett could see crowds moving east and west on Forty-Seventh Street. His mind began to sort the number of people moving in each direction: 38 percent going east, 60 percent going west, 2 percent idling and blocking traffic. Why did some people always have to clog the works? he thought to himself.

"Everything you said about this bank—about the people attacking it, what they wanted, and how they were going to do it—was right. Everything. I was wrong, you were right."

Garrett shrugged.

"What you did saved this bank. Saved my job. Saved my reputation, and my fortune. Probably saved the American economy, at least for a while. That's a pretty amazing thing—"

"I'm not going to be a bond trader at Vandy, so don't bother asking."

"Don't want you to. I want to set you up to do exactly what you did for the government, but in the private sector. Look for threats against this bank. Against me. Against the American economy. Look for patterns, look for enemies, then take them down. Destroy them."

Garrett turned from the window and stared at Wells. Was he joking? "You have an entire IT department set up to do just that."

"They're worthless. I want you. You get the job done," Wells said. "You can work out of your home, or I'll give you an office here. Hell, I'll give you an entire floor. Staff, pretty girls, whatever floats your boat. Work part-time, full-time, I don't care. Just do the thing you do."

"No."

"I'll pay you five million dollars a year."

Garrett blinked in surprise. Five million dollars? Jesus Christ. He shook the number out of his brain. "Fuck you."

"Six million."

"You don't understand. I hate your fucking guts."

"No, I get that. And I don't care. Ten million a year, two-million-dollar signing bonus, and I'll rent you a penthouse apartment in that building right there." Wells pointed to a shining spindle of a tower three blocks away. "That's the limit of what I can afford."

Garrett's breath caught in his throat. The numbers were extraordinary. He hated himself for even considering them, but how could he not? His thoughts went immediately to Chaudry's explanation of Ilya Markov's financial motivations. She'd called Markov an amoral thug for hire. Did that make Garrett one as well? *Or did it just make him a whore?*

"Think about it. Take as long as you'd like. But know this—I want you on the inside. Here." Wells swept his arms across his body, motioning to the vast office. "Next to me."

Garrett thought for a second that he might cry at those words. Why? Were they that meaningful to him? He said nothing, fleeing the office before his emotions got the better of him. He jogged out of the lobby and into the hot July morning. He loosened the tie on his shirt collar, walked west, into a warm wind, and then north, zigzagging along the city streets without thinking where he was going. He ended up at the southeast corner of Central Park and decided to walk into the park, going north again and ending up at the zoo. On a lark, he bought a ticket, then stood by the seal enclosure at the entrance. Seals swam in circles in the wide pool, breaking the water every few seconds to swallow fish being tossed to them by a zookeeper.

Garrett watched them intently, counting the number of seconds they spent underwater, and calculating how fast they made one revolution of the pool, and what the average speed was for each individual seal and then for the entire family of seals. Garrett looked across the way and saw, sitting on a bench, an old man who looked a little like Avery Bernstein, with rounded shoulders and a sweater vest. Garrett remembered his kind voice. Immediately, Garrett wished that he'd had a chance to say good-bye to his mentor in person, but he knew that moment was gone, long gone. He waved briefly to the old man, but the man was busy reading his newspaper and didn't see the gesture. Garrett figured that would suffice as a good-bye for the time being.

Then Garrett backed away from the seals and the old man, sat on a bench, and slowly, patiently, tried to find a pattern he could use for his own future.

ACKNOWLEDGMENTS

The following people were invaluable to me as I researched this book. My thanks to: Richard Campbell, for his expertise on technology and banking security; Suresh Kotha of the University of Washington, for his ideas on how to bring the world of finance to its knees; Ian Toner, for his primer on debt, derivatives, and bank runs; the great Robert M. Solow, for his insight into the weakness of the global economy; Kenneth Willman, for his introductions into the banking community; Daniel Goodwin, as always, for his views from inside the finance machine; Peter Loop, for his detailed explanations of cryptocurrencies and black markets; Yevgeniya Elkus, for her careful translation of English into Russian. And finally, to my sources at the Defense Intelligence Agency and the Federal Bureau of Investigation. You asked not to be named, for obvious reasons, but your insights were crucial.

My deepest gratitude to: Ragna Nervik, Dan Brecher, and Markus Hoffmann, for all the advice and support; the peerless Marysue Rucci, for shaping a mass of words and ideas into a book—you are the best; and my trusted inner circle of friends who lent a hand along the way—you know who you are. I couldn't have done it without you.

Finally, to Lisa, Augusta, and Nora: thank you for putting up with the obsessions, the long hours, and the weeks away from home. You are the reason I write anything at all.

ABOUT THE AUTHOR

D rew Chapman has written studio movies, directed an independent feature film, and created and written network and cable TV shows. Most
recently, he wrote and co–executive produced a season of the spy thriller *Leg-
ends* for TNT. Married with two children, Chapman divides his time between
Los Angeles and Seattle. *The King of Fear* is his second book.

Loved every heart-pounding minute of
KING OF FEAR?
Then make sure you read the first book
in the Garrett Reilly series.

"Warfare goes digital in movie and TV writer Drew
Chapman's fast-moving debut, a high-stakes thriller that
pits the online might of China against that of the United
States" (*Publishers Weekly*) as reluctant patriot Garrett
Reilly races around the globe to avert total war.

SIMON &
SCHUSTER
A CBS COMPANY